Waiting for the Silver Lining

The end is near. It is the mantra running through Alexa's mind each morning as she wakes. One foot in front of the other, step-by-step, she can make it to the end of this year – the last year. The last year of captivity. The last year of childhood. The last year of her painful separation from Bethany.

Just one more year.

It is not the positive outlook everyone tries to convince Alexa she should have. In just one year she will have money, freedom and autonomy. She should be racing towards her 'silver lining' with reckless abandon. However, Alexa knows what the consequences are for wishing for more than her due. All she wants is to keep her head down and attempt to duck under the chaos and trauma that are the usual markers of her life for just one more year. Until she can finally be free.

Naomi Metzl was born in Sydney in 1981. Waiting for the Silver Lining is the second book in the Marble Road series, following the life and struggles of Alexa Samson as she traverses her final year at the notorious Redgrove College.

Waiting for the Silver Lining

Naomi Metzl

Published by Midnight Sunrise Publishing

Printed by CreateSpace

ISBN 978 0 9924 3032 0

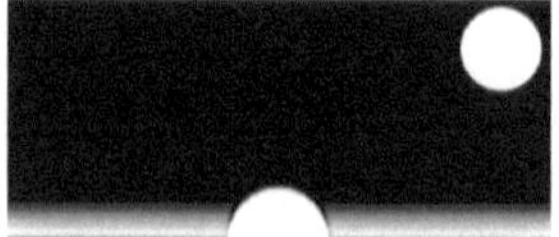

Midnight Sunrise Publishing

This book is dedicated to my beloved husband.
For all the love and support he has provided,
through the good times and the bad.

To Coldplay, for writing *Fix You*;
The musical soul of Marble Road and
Waiting for the Silver Lining.

Thou fair-hair'd angel of the evening
Now, while the sun rests on the mountains, light
Thy bright torch of love; thy radiant crown
Put on, and smile upon our evening bed!
Smile on our loves; and, while thou drawest the
Blue curtain of the sky, scatter thy silver dew
On every flower that shuts it sweet eyes
In timely sleep. Let thy west wind sleep on
The Lake; speak silence with thy glimmering eyes,
And wash the dusk with silver.

To the Evening Star
William Blake

Chapter One

THE LIGHT SLOWLY faded from the far horizon, dipping pitifully behind the densely-packed houses. It was not even an impressive sunset. One day in, and the hopeful promise of the new year was fading as quickly as the sun.

Alexa leaned her head back against the window frame, pulled her knees closer to her chest and closed her eyes, trying not to let despair overwhelm her. She wanted to believe that this year would be different – better – than the last, but there really was no point. Every year she was lulled into a false sense of hope – believing, wishing that the new year would finally deliver on its promise of better things to come. This year, she refused to hope.

Strengthening her resolve, Alexa tried to steel herself against the inevitable disasters that were waiting to attack her. She did not have to enjoy this year. No good had to come from it. All she had to do was survive it – finish school, then go and find Bethany. Whatever she had to do then, she would do. Until then, she would not let herself be sucked in to believing a better world existed, not for someone like her. She had let that happen at the end of last year, and was now paying the price.

When she had arrived back at the Whites' from boarding school at the end of last year, Alexa had believed there was reason to hope. Perhaps falling in love with her year advisor could not be described as the perfect way to end to the year, especially when she had started it dating another teacher. The difference was that that situation had never been about love.

Clinton Marsh and his promise of protection from the violence of her dormitory matron, Ms Carter, had been Alexa's reason to hope for better things at the start of last year. It proved to be a near-deadly delusion.

Clinton had taught her the consequences of putting her faith in a teacher and she had suffered them all. Even now, the thought of him made her stomach turn. It amazed Alexa that she had ever considered him so benign; a nice man who had only wanted sex in return for his assistance. The reality of that situation had made even appreciating Mr Knight a horrifying development.

That Alexa had allowed her feelings of thankfulness transition, not so slowly, to love still concerned her. She wondered if she was an idiot for trusting Mr Knight, thinking his love would make this year better, when Clinton had been the reason she had almost not survived the last. However, she refused to put Mr Knight in the same category as Clinton.

Clinton was vicious and manipulative, someone who had lured her into a relationship and tortured her when she had wanted to end things. Marcus Knight was different. Alexa knew he was the one being tortured by their feelings for each other. Mr Knight had done everything to be proper and appropriate in the face of their love. He had promised her many times that nothing would ever happen between them and his actions to date supported that claim. It was what had allowed her to feel safe in her affections for him.

Being able to love Mr Knight, knowing that he was capable of liking her in return, was one of the only remaining beacons of light Alexa had in her dark world of hopelessness, and she needed to cling on to it. She needed to hold on to anything that would allow her to make it through this year – through to her eighteenth birthday. That Marcus Knight was off-limits was almost a blessing. It freed her of so many complications, but she still could not help but wonder how much it would hurt if he was married the next time she saw him.

That fear of knowing hurt would come should have been enough to warn Alexa that the hopefulness she had felt coming back to the Whites' at the end of last year could not last. Even the Whites' warm welcome should not have allowed her to forget that every year had to round itself out with the debacle that was Christmas, but at the time it had just been so easy to believe.

Hayley's welcoming embrace had been so heartfelt that Alexa had been sure she would melt on the spot. Her arrival home had Hayley literally bouncing back towards the house. It had been impossible for Alexa not to be as happy. The Whites had now invited her back for the sixth school holidays in a row. It was a record no other foster family had come close to matching.

Alexa could still remember the warm reception Pam and Karl had given her. Where there had previously been tension, distance or outright animosity, there was openness and familiarity. They spoke about their happiness at her return, something she tried to be doubtful of, but they had appeared so genuine. There was just no justification for it, not with the trouble she had caused that last term. Then they did the unimaginable.

"You want me to stay?" asked Alexa, thoroughly confused.

"If you want to," confirmed Karl. "Yes."

"I don't understand," Alexa confessed. She had merely related her lack of true enthusiasm for returning to Redgrove College for her final year. She had not been seeking an opportunity to leave. It had never crossed her mind that she had anywhere else to go.

"You can stay here and go to school with Brett," exclaimed Hayley.

"No," replied Alexa before she could even truly comprehend the offer. "There's no way – I couldn't – it wouldn't …"

Alexa had not been able to articulate an answer. There had to be a catch. They could not honestly want her to live with them permanently. It had to be a misunderstanding, and she would not let herself suffer that kind of disappointment. The Whites had been too good to her to ever be disappointed in them.

Hayley's reaction had been instant and fierce. She crossed her arms and turned her body away from Alexa. Alexa looked between Hayley and her parents and realised that this had been Hayley's wish, not theirs. They did not look particularly surprised or disappointed by her decision. Alexa placed her arms around Hayley's shoulder, but Hayley jerked away from her, muttering something she did not understand. Then Alexa saw the tears.

It had broken Alexa's heart to think that Hayley would cry over her. It was about the sweetest thing anyone had ever done for her.

"It's not that I don't want to stay here," Alexa said softly, trying to win Hayley back with carefully constructed truths. "I just don't want to start a new school now that I have only a year to go. You know I love living here."

The answer had been acceptable enough for the conversation to move on to other topics, though Hayley remained quieter than normal for the rest of the night. Thankfully, Alexa had been excused after dinner to unpack and settle in, though it took little time to do either.

"Is that really the only reason you don't want to stay here?" asked Karl, knocking on her bedroom door later that night.

"I don't know," replied Alexa truthfully. "Maybe if the offer had been there last year, or at the start of this year, then it may've been different."

"I'm sorry it wasn't," replied Karl sincerely.

"Don't be," Alexa replied, shaking her head. Even knowing that she had not misunderstood their offer did not make her any less fearful of accepting it. "It might not have made any difference. I still keep waiting to be told that you won't have me back and that I'm being sent to yet another family. What we have now – this is good already."

"Just as long as you know that the offer is there now, and it will always be there."

Alexa had not been able to squeeze out her thanks. All she could do was nod, fearing that if she spoke or moved that she would accept their offer without a second thought. She wanted what they were offering, but being part of a proper, normal family was completely foreign to her. If she stuffed it up, she knew she would never get another chance. It would be better to learn what was expected of her first.

Pam and Karl accepted her decision without further question. Brett was disappointed, which Alexa found strangely pleasing, but he agreed with her reasoning. That left Hayley holding the grudge. It was not behaviour Alexa was used to. Hayley had never shunned her before, and it had hurt more than she knew it should have.

If Hayley had just been being petulant, Alexa could have ignored it, but Hayley's tearful pleadings the next night were as sweet as they were heartbreaking. There was no way Alexa could be mad at Hayley when all Hayley wanted was for her to be her real big sister.

"I know I can't be as good as your real sister, but I'll try," Hayley sniffed.

Alexa hugged Hayley tight, to hide her own tears as much as anything. There was no way to explain to Hayley just how much better she was than Bethany – how much better she was than both of them – and that she loved that so much that she could not dare ruin it.

"If I could stay here and go to my school every day, then I would," said Alexa, knowing they would never move for her. "I swear that's the only reason. I love it here. It's the best place I've ever lived."

"If that's true then you'll do stuff with us while you are here, not run off like you always do," retorted Hayley, her lips quivering angrily.

"I've already agreed to stay for Christmas," smiled Alexa, relieved she had something to give Hayley.

"Yeah, but you won't go Christmas shopping with me."

Hayley had crossed her arms and slumped on to her bed in a huff. Her anger was almost endearing, especially because Alexa had not refused to go shopping, she had just taken the option of not going, just like Brett had. However, she also knew that if she gave Hayley this, then it could set a precedence that would leave her at Hayley's mercy for the rest of the holidays.

With a sigh, Alexa had agreed to Hayley's demands. Being wanted was always better than being hated. Hayley had been appeased, but still far from pleased – until they started preparing for Christmas. Hayley's enthusiasm for the season was almost contagious. If Alexa could have immersed herself in Hayley's happiness it would have been, but seeing how the rest of the world lived only made Alexa more acutely aware of the fact that this was not her life.

Shopping for presents for her foster family had set Alexa's mind thinking of a present she could buy for Bethany, but there were not many present suggestions for fourteen-year-old heroin addicts living on the streets. Alexa knew that there was nothing she could buy that could possibly fix Bethany's situation, but she had needed to find something – something Bethany could hold on to and know that she would be there for her. If she didn't, she was not sure Bethany – her sole reason for existence – would make it through the year.

This ended up turning their shopping expedition into something more akin to a quest, searching for that special something that would keep Bethany alive. It took many hours, more patience than Hayley had and almost more money than Alexa had, but she eventually found what she was looking for – a simple gold locket on a long gold chain. Inside the locket was room for two pictures – one of Bethany and one of her.

Alexa prayed that it would be enough. There was always the risk that Bethany would only see its monetary value, but it was one Alexa had to take. She had to give Bethany something tangible to remind her that she was not forgotten. However, Alexa had soon found her faith in that locket ruptured. None of the few photos she had of her and Bethany would fit into the locket's small frames and she all but destroyed them in the process of trying to make them.

Weeks later, those memories still caused silent tears to fall down Alexa's cheeks. The all-encompassing fear that Bethany was somewhere dying of a drug overdose haunted every minute of

Alexa's existence, and the terror that the locket would not be enough to keep Bethany alive still gripped Alexa as tightly now as it had then.

When those fears and frustrations over her failure with the locket had erupted before Christmas, everything within Alexa's reach had gone flying across her room. Absorbed in her own pain, she had been surprised to find Karl's arms restraining her, trying to prevent further destruction.

"What the hell's going on?" Karl asked, squeezing her tighter to try and stop her struggling, but she could not have answered – even if she had wanted to. "Damn it, Alexa, you're having a damn good attempt at destroying your room, so I want to know what's going on?"

Alexa had still not been able to answer. After finally pushing out of Karl's arms, she collected the locket and tattered photos from the floor. Throwing them on the bed, she sat desolately next to them, her knees hugged into her chest as tears streamed down her face.

"What's wrong with it?" asked Karl gently, picking up the locket and photos and examining them.

"I only have two photos of us and neither of them fit," replied Alexa, measuring her voice carefully, not wanting to express the full extent of her heartbreak. "And now I've wrecked them trying to make them. I just – I just want her to survive til I can take care of her."

"Just because you can't get the photos in the locket doesn't mean that your sister's going to die," replied Karl gently.

"It's an omen. And what would I do – what would I be without Bethy?" Alexa had been barely able to squeeze out those words, her chest constricting with the thought of a world without Bethany.

"You would be … look, I'll see if I can do something with these, okay?" said Karl.

"It's no use. They won't fit."

"Trust me, okay."

Alexa had not trusted Karl. Right then she had not had the capacity to trust anyone, but Karl had returned the next night with a miracle. He had not only managed to get their photos into the locket, he even had new, less-ruined copies of the original photos.

"You need to learn to ask for help, Alexa," said Karl gently, but firmly. "There are solutions to most problems out there. Just because you don't have them doesn't mean no one else does. Trust us. We're here for you, okay."

Alexa could have jumped up and hugged Karl right then. Part of her had wanted to. She wanted Karl to know just how much she appreciated what he had done, but knew better than to allow that level of physical contact. She thought she could trust him, but it was never worth the risk.

That small miracle should have given Alexa some warning of what was to come. She had learned long ago that nothing good came without consequences, but she had chosen to ignore the past and put her faith in a brighter future. She wondered if she had expected too much, been reckless and greedy, thinking she deserved what others had. Whatever the cause, the punishment came in a familiar form.

Closing her eyes, Alexa was determined that she would never celebrate another Christmas again – no matter how much anyone begged. At least after this year she did not believe Hayley would want her near another Christmas again either.

"I'm just not sure he's the best person to call."

Karl's hesitant voice carried up the stairs and pricked Alexa's attention. He sounded agitated. If Pam and Karl were fighting then it would be over her. It was dark now and the rest of the house was quiet, making their conversation that much easier to hear.

"Who else can we call?" asked Pam. "Who else is there that knows her? That might be able to help us? We can't let her go on like this."

"I know, and I want her to snap out of this as much as you, but I'm just not sure that we should trust anyone from that place. Look at what that school has put her through. They don't care. That much was abundantly clear from our meetings. It's our fault what happened to her at Christmas and I don't want to make another mistake like that."

Alexa felt her heart begin to pound as she crept quietly out of her room and down the stairs. She did not like what she was hearing. She did not want them to be talking about the one person in the world she wanted to keep this from.

"He saved her life. He took her to the police. He stopped that mongrel from raping her again. Karl, we trust him to bring her here every school holidays."

"And to be honest, I would rather we didn't. I would prefer she just caught the train. An hour alone in the car. That thought plagues me every holidays. What could happen – what he could do to her."

"I think you're being paranoid. We can't assume that every man is going to hurt her."

"I assumed that once before and look where it got us!"

Pam did not answer immediately and Alexa slumped down on the stairs. To think she had been angry at Karl – that she had blamed him for what happened at Christmas. It was crazy, because the truth was it was her fault. If not for her, the Whites would be a happy, carefree family.

"Then what do you want to do?" asked Pam gently, but Karl did not answer.

The silence dragged on. Alexa wished she could see what they were doing. Then she heard the beep of the phone as the numbers were dialled. In the quietness of the house, she could hear the phone ringing again and again.

"Can I speak to Marcus Knight, please? Thank you."

Before Pam could say anything else – hopefully before Mr Knight could answer – Alexa grabbed the phone and threw it across the room. It hit the opposite wall, then the floor, with a frightening crack.

"What the fuck do you think you're doing?" Alexa screamed, causing Pam and Karl to recoil slightly.

"We just thought – we just wanted to …" Pam stuttered.

"You haven't been yourself since Christmas, Alexa," said Karl firmly, putting his arm around Pam. Alexa realised that no matter how much he had disagreed with his wife five minutes ago, he would support her now. "We just wanted to talk to Mr Knight – see if he had any advice."

"My life has nothing to do with him," replied Alexa, her voice quivering with the fear of Mr Knight knowing any more terrible things about her – or becoming any more entwined in her life. It was imperative that she not trust or like him any more than she already did. "It has nothing to do with the school. I don't need him or the school knowing everything that happens to me. Don't you understand? I don't want anyone to know. I don't want my life discussed in a committee."

"That's not what we were going to do," replied Pam in a strained voice that was barely above a whisper.

"Well that's what it sure fucking sounded like to me."

"Don't you dare speak to your mother like that!" yelled Karl, stepping forward and startling Alexa, with his words as much as his tone.

"She is not my mother!" screamed Alexa with such fury that

Pam cowered into Karl's arms.

Alexa hated the sight and ran back up to her room. She slammed the door and paced back and forth, guilt weighing her every step. She tried desperately to calm herself, but it was a struggle. Over twenty minutes passed before she thought that she had her temper under enough control to ease the sick, guilty burden that filled her stomach.

She could hear the whispered conversation in the lounge room and tried not to listen to the words. She knew she deserved it if they were discussing not having her back or even sending her away that day. That was only fair after what she had done, but whatever they were going to do next, she knew they deserved an apology.

Karl stood as soon as Alexa entered the room. Alexa held out her hand to stop him from speaking. She did not want her temper to prevent her from saying what had to be said.

"You have to understand. I remember my mother," said Alexa, closing her eyes and breathing deeply to remain calm. "I remember what she was like, what she did, everything. I can still see her face and hear her voice. I know who my mother was and you can't ever tell me that that is Pam. How could you say that? How could you believe – no one deserves to be called that."

Alexa was not sure whether she shook from anger or sadness as she turned away. It was not quite an apology, but she could not manage anything more. She would apologise properly when she left.

"So you didn't say that because you don't want to be a part of this family?" asked Karl, his words turning Alexa around. "Because you don't respect us as your parents?"

"I said it because it was true. Look, it's really touching that you both see me as one of your children," Alexa said softly, trying to keep her emotions, whatever they were, under control. "But you can't treat me like Hayley and Brett. They will never know the life I have. Because of you, they will never experience even a fraction of what I have. Hayley is the most amazing child I've ever met. She's so friendly and happy and innocent. The things Bethy and I had seen and done at her age.

"I want this – this whole thing – more than you could ever imagine, but it's just not possible. I can't leave her. Maybe if Bethy and me came somewhere like here from the beginning, then maybe we might've had a chance."

"We just want to help you," said Pam softly, finally speaking.

"And you do – too much. I cause you nothing but trouble and you keep having me back. You don't know how grateful I am. I just don't want to think about what happened at Christmas. I want to forget about it. And I need you both to understand that I will never think of you as my parents. I don't remember my dad, but I remember my mother and I will never, ever put you two in the same category. You – you – never. You are not her. Please don't ever say that again."

"We want you to stay, Alexa," said Karl, as if taking something back and she guessed that they had been talking about asking her to leave. "We want you to stay with us – holidays, whenever. Even when you finish school, you're welcome here. We'll be whatever you need us to be."

Alexa could not reply. She had never been so grateful to anyone in her life. All she could do was nod and look up towards the ceiling, blinking more than was necessary.

"We were thinking that we should maybe take all of you out to lunch tomorrow. It's supposed to be a nice day. It'll be good for us all to get out and have a relaxing day before the three of us have to head back to work," said Karl, changing the topic to Alexa's great relief. "You keen?"

"Sounds good," Alexa replied, looking back down, but not at either Pam or Karl.

"Good, we'll go somewhere nice."

Alexa could not help the uncomfortable look that slid over her face at Karl's comments, but before she could protest, Pam jumped in and agreed with him.

"Yes, somewhere nice. Maybe down the coast where we can have fish and chips or burgers on the beach."

"That sounds really good," agreed Alexa with relief. She could not owe Pam and Karl any more than she already did – not even an expensive lunch.

***

When Alexa returned to work, her resolution of forgetting all about Christmas was severely tested. She could not help but wonder if she somehow entered a parallel dimension over the festive season, because everyone else seemed to have a great time over Christmas and New Year. Even the worst stories of family feuds and excessive alcohol consumption would have topped her best Christmas list by a mile. However, her descriptor of 'fine, hectic and glad it's over', was generally shared by others and so further details of her Christmas experience were rarely sought.

At home, Alexa spent every minute she could with Hayley. It kept her busy and placated Hayley, who was now upset that she was leaving a week before school started. Sam had called and confirmed that everyone was still heading out to his grandparents' property for the last week of the holidays.

Despite Alexa's earlier concerns, Pam and Karl had few issues letting her go, particularly after they spoke to Gran about the situation. Gran and Pam spoke for almost half an hour, regaling many stories about Alexa and their other children. Pam was only disappointed they would not be able to take the time off to drive her out there themselves.

Alexa was looking forward to going out to Sam's, but was careful not to say so. As grateful as she was to the Whites, all she wanted was to get away – distance herself from these holidays and come back at Easter as if nothing had ever happened.

The only part Alexa was not completely satisfied with was leaving work a week early. She had to remind herself that by the end of the year, she would not need that job or that extra week of income, but she found it hard to convince herself. She found it hard to believe that she was – or would be – a multimillionaire. Such a thought was impossible to comprehend, and she could not stop herself from thinking that winning that money had just been a very realistic dream.

Money was something Alexa had always had so little of. Pam and Karl getting her holiday work this and the previous Christmas had already supplied her with more money than she had ever had, with the exception of those two weeks in the city last year. The money selling her body could earn was undeniably good and she knew it was something she would consider again if it meant saving Bethany's life. The second time around, she would be more confident demanding things happen on her terms.

It shocked Alexa just how detailed her planning for that future was in her mind, when it was a future she should never have to face. It was just so much harder to imagine having access to near unlimited funds. Ezra and Bianca never had any problems believing, and she wondered if it was because they were used to having money or because the whole situation was not tied up in so much heartache for them.

The terror of being pregnant with Clinton's child still made

Alexa anxious. The dream that had then offered so much hope now only mocked her. Ben, the round-faced policeman from her nightmares, who tried to protect her, but ultimately always died in vain, had given her the chance to save her child. It had just come too late. She had put her fate in Clinton's hands, and with one swift punch he killed their unborn child and destroyed the evidence of their affair.

That failure and Bethany's return to the streets now tainted that twenty-five million dollar miracle windfall. Alexa could not believe in it and refused to trust it. Everything else had gone pear-shaped in the most brutal and unexpected ways and she had no doubt this would too.

However, in the few moments Alexa did allow herself to believe, all she knew was that every cent necessary would go to getting Bethany clean. She wondered how much that would cost, and how much she would have left, because if there was anything else she wanted to do with her money it was repay the Whites.

"You all packed and ready?" asked Pam as they all sat down for dinner the day before Alexa was supposed to leave for Sam's.

"No," Alexa smiled in return. Every time she had tried to pack, Hayley had come in and scowled until she offered to do something with her. "But I don't really have much. It'll only take few minutes to chuck it all into my bags."

"Just as long as you pack your Christmas presents a little more gently than that," replied Karl, making Alexa's stomach churn uncomfortably.

"Err, yeah. I haven't actually opened any of them," she replied, not looking up from her food.

No one said anything and they finished their dinner in awkward silence. Alexa kept seeing herself shoving her presents under her bed, out of sight. She did not ever want to tell Pam or Karl just how hard she had thrown some of them.

"Why don't you go grab your presents, Alexa," said Pam as they cleared the table. "You can open them in the lounge room."

Alexa was not keen, but agreed. The whole family was gathered and watched as she placed the pile of presents at her feet and sat on the floor next to Hayley. She did not know what to do next. She had never received Christmas presents before.

"Here, open this one," said Hayley, grabbing a present from the top of the pile. "It's from Uncle Mathew and Aunt Linda."

Alexa cautiously unwrapped the small blue package. She

wondered what sorts of things Pam and Karl's family would have bought her considering they neither knew nor liked her.

"What did you get?" asked Hayley, doing her best to keep the proceedings going.

"A box of chocolates," replied Alexa with a smile. She was relieved it was nothing worse and could be used – or at least consumed – with very little effort or thanks required.

"Okay, this one's from Grandma Alice and Grandpa Sam," said Hayley chirpily, and Alexa thought she looked relieved as well.

Alexa unwrapped the next present and smiled more broadly as another box of chocolates fell into her lap. Hayley offered her two more presents, each containing a different breed of chocolate.

"Looks like chocolates were the in present this year," smiled Alexa.

Pam and Karl managed a strained smile, while Brett stifled his laughter with his fist. Watching Brett, Alexa could no longer contain herself and burst out laughing as well.

"Okay, next present," said Hayley, holding another package. "This one's from Uncle To–"

Brett ripped the present out of Hayley's hand before she could finish speaking. He stormed out of the lounge room and into the kitchen. The room was deathly quiet when he returned and sat down on the floor next to Hayley.

"We know these are another box of chocolates," said Brett, throwing the present from Aunt Shirley on to the pile of chocolates at Alexa's feet. "Open this one. It's from me and Hayley."

Alexa took the present from Brett with a smile. She opened it tentatively, feeling everyone's eyes on her. She hoped her reaction would be the right one.

It was a silver bracelet with a nameplate. Engraved on the topside was her name, with '♥ Brett & Hayley' engraved on the underside.

"Thank you," said Alexa, feeling her voice break, and forgetting completely the smiling reaction she had rehearsed in her head.

She took the bracelet out of the box and put it on. It surprised her that it fit perfectly.

"We measured it on Hayley first," said Pam with a slight smile.

It touched Alexa that they had considered the small size of her wrist. They had not just bought it as a token. Alexa breathed deeply and blinked a couple of times before smiling at everyone just as she had initially intended.

"Here, this is from Pam and me," said Karl, picking up a large present off the floor.

Alexa opened this present with more enthusiasm than any of the others. She felt like she was starting to understand some of the enticements of Christmas. For a second she tried to imagine a Christmas where all the activities revolved around opening presents and eating good food, without the fear or threat of anything worse than an unwanted gift or overcooked meat.

Looking down at the unwrapped present, Alexa could not say thank you this time. She could not speak at all. Pam and Karl had given her a whole pile of new clothes. There were two pairs of jeans, shorts, tops, a jacket, pyjamas, socks and even underwear. They had to be the first new clothes she had received since being given her school uniform. All the other clothes she owned were second, third or even fourth-hand, scavenged from foster homes or roommates at school.

"This is the last one. It's from Santa," said Hayley, smiling softly as she handed Alexa a rectangular present.

Alexa opened this present more slowly. She was terrified of what else they could give her. She had not received this much in her life, let alone in one day. This time, she was not able to control herself. Tears began to seep down her face as soon as she opened the photo album. Hayley had made and decorated the front title page, but it was the photos inside that tore at Alexa's heart. The Whites had given her family photos; many included her that she did not remember ever having taken. And there, mixed in with them, were the two photos of her and Bethany.

It was too much and the rare display of emotion made her feel horribly vulnerable. Before anyone could stop her, she ran from the room and up to her bedroom, collapsing on her bed in tears.

It was well into the night before Alexa ventured out of her bedroom. Hayley and Brett were already in bed and the lounge room was empty. She collected her numerous boxes of chocolates and carried them into the kitchen. Back in the lounge room she sat on the floor and examined her bracelet.

"Do you like your presents?" asked Pam as she and Karl sat down on the lounge near her.

"You can never have enough chocolates," smiled Alexa, still gazing at her bracelet.

"I am sorry about that," said Karl in a low voice.

"It's okay. I'm sorry I ran out before. I just ..."

"We understand," replied Karl, stroking Alexa's hair tenderly. Alexa could not help but shiver. It was the most paternal way she had ever been touched and it gave her a heartbreaking insight into what fathers should be like. "We're just glad you like your presents."

"Of course I do, but it's too much. I mean, this is like a lifetime of presents," Alexa replied, trying to contain her emotions as she pointed to the gifts in front of her.

"Alexa, I don't think you really understand just how bad we feel about how little we've given you. You've been coming here for over a year and we've given you nothing."

"But you've given me everything, almost," replied Alexa, looking up astounded by Karl's comment.

"You always did your own washing," smiled Pam. "I appreciated it, believe me, but I never realised just how worn out your clothes are. We'll buy you more at Easter. We just didn't want to get too much and you not like them."

"You did understand what I said before, didn't you?" said Alexa urgently, looking up at Pam. "You understood that I wasn't being disrespectful or mean when I said you weren't my mother, right? You have to know that I could never think of you the way I think of her. You have to understand that the most horrible thing I could ever do is compare you to my mother."

"I understand, Alexa. We understand," said Pam, leaning forward to take Alexa's hand. "We did need your explanation, but we do understand."

"Good," nodded Alexa, looking down as she pulled her hand out of Pam's. It took everything she had not to cry.

Alexa could not understand what was happening to her. She had liked people in the past, enjoyed their company and gotten along with them, but besides Sam and Bethany, never really loved any of them. Now, for the first time, she truly felt part of a family and back at school was Marcus Knight. Not waiting for her, she told herself, but there all the same.

"Um, tomorrow, Ezra's parents are coming by about eleven," said Alexa, moving her thoughts quickly away from Mr Knight. "Would it be okay if you guys aren't here? I just can't say – I just don't want to … not in front of people. Please."

"We'll take Brett and Hayley out early," said Karl.

"Thanks."

Walking back from the bathroom, Alexa looked in on the

peacefully sleeping Hayley. She had never expected to become attached to any of her foster families. She had had so many and very few had any fondness for her, but that had changed now and she was sure it only made things more difficult. It was so much easier not caring – lonelier, but easier.

Tiptoeing into Hayley's bedroom, Alexa climbed into the bed and under the covers next to Hayley. Hayley stirred briefly as she wrapped her arms around Alexa before going back to sleep. Alexa stroked Hayley's hair tenderly, her heart aching at the sight of Hayley's small smile. Sighing heavily, Alexa closed her eyes and willed her tears to stay at bay. Hayley would never be Bethany, but it was nice to be able to share a bed with a sister again.

Chapter Two

"SO? HOW WAS your Christmas? As bad as expected?" asked Ezra as soon as they were in the car.

Ezra was Alexa's oldest and best friend, but right then Alexa would have been happier if they were not having this reunion. She tried to give a response that did not betray just how unwelcome Ezra's question was, but by the look on Ezra's face she was sure she had not been successful. Thankfully, Ezra's parents managed to get themselves lost heading towards the motorway and Ezra was required to direct their every turn.

Christmas. Now that Ezra had mentioned it, Alexa could not stop herself from reliving the events of that dreadful day. She had promised herself that she would banish that day from her memory, but it was a promise she had not been able to keep.

The day had started innocuously enough. There had been no hint of the trouble that would engulf them, and Alexa could still not believe that she had allowed herself to be lulled into a false sense of security. Hope had a lot to answer for.

"Merry Christmas, Alexa!" Hayley had shouted as she bounced her awake. "Come on, it's almost eight. Mum didn't want me to wake you up, but it's Christmas and you have to get up. You promised you'd spend the day with us."

Alexa managed to wrangle a shower and fresh clothes before she came downstairs, but it had been a tough negotiation. Pam was dishing out pancakes when Alexa arrived in the kitchen. Alexa took her small bag of presents and immediately placed them under the Christmas tree in the lounge room.

"Merry Christmas, Alexa," said Pam, in a cheerfully tired mood when she sat down at the kitchen bench.

"Um ... thanks, you too," Alexa replied, a little unsure of Christmas greetings. She had never had the need to exchange any.

"I did try and stop Hayley, but she managed to get by me," said Pam, the apology clear in her eyes.

"That's okay. I think some kind of restraint would have been needed to stop her."

"Merry Christmas, Alexa," said Karl, walking into the kitchen.

"Yeah, you too."

"Is it present time yet, Daddy?" pleaded Hayley, abandoning the pancakes that she had grudgingly accepted from Pam.

Alexa had smiled as Karl tried to resist the pleading eyes of his daughter. It was clear that Hayley was the apple of his eye, and it made Alexa both happy and uneasy. She did not remember her father, but she knew he had hurt them. She just hoped that Karl never hurt Hayley.

Breakfast finally abandoned, Karl took the on role of Father Christmas and donned a Santa hat to distribute the presents. Hayley could hardly be contained as she unwrapped present after present, while Alexa watched on nervously. She had never participated in Christmas before, never bought anyone a present and was hoping that she had not done a terrible job at it.

"Look, Mum, look at what Alexa bought me. Isn't it great? Can I wear it today?" said Hayley, holding up the outfit Alexa had found on special.

"Oh, I thought you were going to wear the clothes we bought you last week? That's why we bought them."

"Please, Mum, can't I wear these instead?" begged Hayley.

"Of course you can. You can wear whatever you like," replied Pam.

"Thank you, thank you, thank you," squealed Hayley, as she hugged Pam and then Karl before running up to her room.

"Alexa, you didn't have to spend so much on Hayley. She didn't pressure you into buying all that, did she?" asked Pam in a low voice so Hayley would not hear if she came back.

"No, I just thought it would be good to have a whole outfit," Alexa replied, her voice shaking slightly, still not sure if she had done a good job with her present buying. "You're not angry, are you? Cos I can tell her to wear the clothes you bought."

"Alexa, if we bought her the most expensive clothes in the world and you bought her rags, Hayley would still want to wear the rags," said Karl, sitting down next to Pam. "You've made her year just by being here."

"Aren't you going to open your presents?" asked Brett as he collected all his gifts.

"I'll open them later," replied Alexa. She had no idea what they would buy her and was not sure she would react appropriately, so thought it best it was done in private. "But thank you. I really do appreciate them."

Alexa placed the presents on her bed and sat down next to them. The locket she had bought for Bethany sat on her bedside table glistening in the bright morning sunlight. It made her wish she had not agreed to stay for Christmas with the Whites. The only place she really wanted to be was with Bethany.

Sitting alone in her room, Alexa had been able to feel Christmas filling the house like a noxious gas. She was not sure what it was, but it had filled every Christmas she could remember and it made her sick. It was what had made her flee every other place she had ever been in on this day.

Hayley had come to check on her a few times that morning and Alexa had quickly offered her services to help prepare lunch, but Pam and Karl had always told her to go and relax. That was impossible. Her stomach churned harder with every second that ticked by and every doorbell that rang. Eventually, too many people had arrived for her to hide any longer.

"Alexa, this is Karl's younger brother, Todd," said Pam as Alexa came down the stairs.

"Hi," replied Alexa shyly.

Todd was much younger than Karl and quite good looking, but his smile was strained and his eyes had travelled up and down her body when Pam introduced him. Alexa had not been able to look Pam's way to see if this was how Todd normally greeted people.

"Come on, everyone's in the lounge," said Pam, smiling as she took Alexa by the hand and led her into the lounge room. "Everyone, this is Alexa."

Pam introduced Alexa to everyone in the room, but it was a fruitless exercise. There was no way she was going to remember who they were. She had barely been able to raise her eyes to look at them.

"Hi," was all Alexa had been able to manage.

Everyone had stared at her, but it was Todd's eyes Alexa felt the most. They were still running over her body. She looked over at Pam and Karl for a distraction, but that had not helped. Pam was holding Karl's hand, trying to calm him as he fumed silently. The sight had only made Alexa's heart pound harder.

When the table was set and everyone had arrived, they all filed into the dining room. Alexa sat herself next to Hayley, but to her great disappointment Todd sat down on the other side of her.

"Todd, why don't you sit over here next to Mum and Dad?"

asked Karl as everyone was taking their seats.

"I'm fine here thanks, Karl," Todd replied with a smile.

It did not matter anyway. All the spare seats were already taken. Karl gave Alexa a strange look, but said nothing more as he sat down at the head of the table.

"I just want to thank you all for coming today. This is a very special and, unfortunately, rare occasion that we have everyone here together. I'm also very glad that you all have the chance today to get to know the newest addition to our family. Pam, Brett, Hayley and I all consider Alexa to be part of this family and we hope that you'll all make her feel very welcome," said Karl, raising his glass. "Merry Christmas, everybody."

"Merry Christmas," chorused the table, as everyone raised their glass.

Alexa found the courage to look Karl's way as she lowered her glass. He smiled weakly at her as everyone tucked into the feast before them, while Hayley bounced away happily next to her.

"See, now you're part of the family, you have to stay with us," Hayley smiled, bouncing jovially into her again.

"Thanks, Hales."

Pam was also grinning at her from the other end of the table, while Brett gave her a quick smile before concentrating his efforts on filling his plate. Alexa smiled broadly in response. Now fifteen, Brett had not been around much during the holidays. It was not so much new-found popularity as new-found confidence that had increased his circle of friends and accompanying social life. He never felt the need to tell Alexa that he wanted her to be his sister the way Hayley did. She heard him talk about her to his friends. Every time he referred to her it was as his sister. He rarely even added the word foster.

Karl's speech, and the welcoming smiles from those who mattered, did a lot to reassure Alexa that Karl had not been upset by something she had done. It allowed her to eat and enjoy her first Christmas meal – for a short while. Throughout lunch, Karl eyes flicked in her direction so frequently that she could not finish even half the food on her plate. She tried to think of something she had done that morning that could have upset him, but she had not done anything, and she realised that must have been the problem. She decided that she would have to be more helpful after lunch, no matter how much they told her to relax.

However, moments later, Alexa forgot all about Karl's mood

and her attempts to placate him, when Todd's hand brushed against her leg. Giving him the benefit of the doubt and assuming it had to have been an accident, she moved to the far side of her chair, practically pressing herself against Hayley. A minute later Todd's foot brushed up along her calf. She looked over at him to try and see if he would apologise, but he was deeply engaged in conversation, a smile sitting casually on his face. She tried again to move away from him, but he could still reach her.

Alexa sat frozen, looking down at her plate, while trying to be as small as possible. She wanted to be sick. She wanted to scream, to run away, but no one was going to believe that Todd was feeling her up under the dining room table. Everyone was finishing their lunch and the conversations were becoming louder and more animated. Alexa did not know if Karl was still looking at her. She was trying desperately to ignore Todd's fondling feet in the hope it would make him stop, but he carried on, never looking her way.

Then Todd's hand slid over her thigh and between her legs. Alexa squeezed her legs together, but he was strong and his little finger managed to push through and brush up against her underpants. She opened her legs and placed her hand over his. Todd immediately moved his whole hand towards her crotch. Grabbing his index finger, Alexa pulled it back until it almost broke.

Frightened of what would happen next, Alexa quickly stood up and started collecting the plates around her. Pam rose to help, but Alexa dismissed her assistance, insisting on doing it herself while the rest of the family moved to the lounge to exchange presents. No one argued and the room quickly emptied.

It was a relief to be alone. Alexa's whole body was shaking as she carried everything to the kitchen, but she managed to calm herself by concentrating on the process of cleaning the scraps from the dishes and piling them neatly by the sink.

"Need a hand?" asked a pleasant voice from the kitchen doorway.

Alexa was surprised to see Todd walking towards her, a glass of wine in one hand and a pleasant smile sitting on his face. The friendliness of his voice and appearance made Alexa question her memories of lunch. Perhaps she had imagined it all. Hayley probably felt as though she had been on top of her all lunch too.

"No, I'm fine," Alexa replied politely.

"You sure? I know I sure could."

Alexa was confused by Todd's response – until he stepped

towards her. His smile changed, becoming slightly more menacing as he moved next to her. Before she could react, he grabbed her hand and pressed it to his groin.

"Get the fuck off me!" Alexa cried, pulling her hand back and moving to the other side of the kitchen as she tried to forget what she had felt.

"Not being very festive now, are we? What? Not working today?" asked Todd in a callously smooth voice.

It had taken Alexa a moment to understand exactly what Todd was getting at, but when she did a stab of hatred towards Pam and Karl pierced through her chest. When Bethany had asked her to leave her life, stay with her and help save her from heroin, Alexa never had a moment of hesitation complying. Those two weeks were some of the best and worst of her life, but she now realised that the way she had supported them – the services she had offered men for money – had become the one thing that defined her in most people's eyes.

"Just fuck off, okay," Alexa said, hunching her shoulders.

"Come on, we're family now," smiled Todd. "You do discounts for family and friends?"

Alexa felt sick. Her body was shaking. She had never been spoken to this way before. As much as she had hated giving herself to those men, they had mostly treated her well – and her services had always been offered to them before they had ever asked. This was something else completely.

Alexa tried to walk away, but Todd grabbed her wrist and pulled her back, putting himself between her and the exit.

"What? Your day off?" Todd asked when Alexa again pulled away from him.

"As far as you're concerned, I'm off every day!" hissed Alexa.

"That's a little unwelcoming, don't you think?" replied Todd, his voice becoming more aggressive as he moved in closer. "I know what you are."

Alexa was furious as she tried again to push past Todd, but he caught her easily around the waist. She struggled, but he pressed his body against hers and pushed her against the fridge, grinding his hips into hers and kissing her wildly.

With every bit of strength she could muster, Alexa pushed Todd off her. Todd's eyes were wide with rage. Then she felt a stinging slap across her cheek. Her reaction was swift, pushing Todd hard to the floor and rushing past him. She was already at the door when she heard the sound of breaking glass and a pained cry.

The kitchen was instantly flooded with worried faces staring at the blood pouring from Todd's hand. He had obviously broken his fall with his wine glass, and Alexa could see a few shards of glass still protruding from his palm.

"What happened?" asked Pam, looking over at Karl who appeared to be in a state of shock.

Alexa hesitated, wondering how she could possibly explain – wondering if they would believe her.

"She made a move on me," cried Todd, throwing his uninjured arm up to point at Alexa. "I knocked her back. I mean, at Christmas, in front of the kids – trying to drum up business," he added slyly. "She didn't like it, so the little slut pushed me over."

Alexa felt the air suck out of her lungs, leaving her gasping for breath as she looked desperately around the room.

"And you want us to accept her as part of the family? Look at his hand!" cried Karl's mother.

"I didn't do anything wrong!" cried Alexa, finally finding her voice, but even as she spoke she knew it would not make any difference. They were never going to believe her now.

Karl looked at her gravely. He opened his mouth to speak, but his mother beat him to it.

"For someone like you, I suppose you see nothing wrong with your actions."

"Someone like me?" gasped Alexa. There was nodding and exchanging of looks that told her that the whole family knew about her stint in prostitution, even after Pam and Karl insisted she not discuss it with anyone. "I didn't do anything –"

"Alexa, go to your room," said Karl calmly, but sternly.

"No, he made a move on me!" replied Alexa. She knew this would be her last day at the Whites, but she was not going to let them kick her out without defending herself – not after what they had done to her.

"Go to your room."

"No! I'm not being blamed when –"

"GO TO YOUR ROOM!"

Alexa was stung. She had never seen Karl so angry, but she had no intention of staying in her room. She was not going to sit around and wait to be accused of making moves on Todd.

It took Alexa less than five minutes to pack. She left her unopened presents on the bed and climbed down the drain pipe next to her window. Anger and confusion propelled her down the street and towards the train station. Memories of the previous hour rang menacingly through her head. The Whites had welcomed her into the family, but disowned her at the slightest hint of trouble. Karl had not even let her explain.

Alexa heard the train approaching and ran for the station, not bothering to try and buy a ticket. There was no time for that. She just wanted to get away, but she was too late. The train pulled away just as she reached the platform. She sat down angrily on the empty platform, knowing it would be another half an hour until the next train. She wondered where she would go. There was Sam's, but that was not where she really wanted to be. She reached into her bag and her heart stopped. She had forgotten the locket. There was just enough time to go back before the next train, but she was not sure she would be able to return to the house and leave again without anyone seeing her.

The conflict kept Alexa glued to her seat, her head constantly twitching, looking between the train tracks and the exit.

"Alexa! Thank goodness. I've been looking for you everywhere," exclaimed Karl, running down the platform. Alexa ignored him. "Where are you going? Please, come on, come home. Everyone's left."

"Get lost. Why come back? So you can throw me out?" Alexa spat angrily, though her voice shook badly.

"Why would we throw you out?"

"You believed him! You didn't even let me explain," Alexa cried.

"I believed you," replied Karl earnestly, forcing her to face him. "I didn't want you to have to stand there and cop any more abuse. I'm sorry I didn't handle it better. I should have, but it all took me by surprise. I was so angry. I heard what Todd said to you, and wanted to come in and help you, but I wanted to see what your response would be."

"What did you honestly think I would do? What kind of person do you think I am?"

Karl did not answer. He looked ashamed, but did not turn away. Silence swelled between them until Alexa's anger burst through.

"Why did you tell him? Why did you tell any of them?" she cried.

"I'm sorry. I really didn't think they would ever say anything. Pam and I were so confused when we found out about that situation. We care about you and want you as a part of our family. We didn't know how to help you, so we turned to our families. I'm sorry."

The train pulled into the platform and Alexa's hands tightened around the straps of her bag. She closed her eyes and stood up.

"We stuffed up, okay," said Karl as she walked away from him. "Do we get another chance?" he asked, when the train doors opened.

Alexa kept her eyes closed. The train held at the station while she lingered near the open doors.

"Yeah, okay," Alexa finally replied, stepping back from the closing doors.

Karl instantly stepped forward and put his arm around her shoulders, guiding her to the car. Alexa pulled away from him, trying hard to contain the rage that still boiled within her. It was a silent drive. She was welcomed back cautiously when they arrived home. Hayley gave her a teary apology for having asked her to stay, which Alexa quickly dismissed. She did not blame Hayley for what happened.

"Alexa, why don't you go get changed," said Karl, after sending Hayley and Brett to their rooms, leaving Alexa sitting on the lounge, her anger steadily building again.

"Why?" Alexa snarled distrustfully.

"We're going out."

"Where?" she demanded.

"I'll tell you in the car," said Karl, gesturing for her to go upstairs and change. "It's okay, I promise, please just trust me. I will tell you where we're going in the car."

"Why should I trust anyone?" shouted Alexa, jumping up from the lounge.

Karl looked over at Pam as if they had been expecting this reaction. He put his hand in his pocket then held it out for her.

"You'll probably need this if you're coming with me," said Karl sombrely.

Karl placed the golden locket in Alexa's hand. She looked at it for a second before realising what he meant.

"Seriously?" she asked, not quite believing.

"If you want to go, yes, I am serious," replied Karl earnestly.

"You don't want me to go, do you?" Alexa asked Pam, seeing the concern etched on Pam's face.

"I'm worried that it'll only make your Christmas worse," replied

Pam, her voice soft but strong. "I don't want more disappointment for you today."

"I just need to see her," replied Alexa, touched by Pam's sincerity. "If I can give her this then maybe I can give her a reason to live until I can help her. It's hard to sit back here and not help her, but I know there's nothing I can do for her yet. I just want to see her – just this once."

Pam nodded and turned away. Alexa thought she had seen tears in the side of her eyes and wished she could have hugged her. She had come back intent on staying angry at Pam and Karl, but it was impossible. They cared and she was determined to allow them to stuff up as much as they needed, because no one else had ever cared before.

Karl drove in silence. Alexa wanted to ask him what had happened after she left, but was worried about the answer. He eventually told her that he had confronted Todd with the truth as soon as she had left the room. Alexa wondered why he could not have defended her while she was there.

It became clear that Brett and Hayley were now aware of her time working in the city. They had wanted to know what Todd had done and why. Alexa knew that Hayley was too young to really understand, but she wondered what Brett would think of her now.

"Thank you for doing this, Karl," Alexa said eventually, compromising on what she wanted to say with what she should say.

Karl laughed mirthlessly.

"If you hadn't been with us, you would've been out here with Bethany. Before today, I was certain that we were offering you the better Christmas, but if you were here today and not with us ..."

Alexa closed her eyes. In the back of her mind she wondered if her day really would have been so much better. Disaster had a way of finding her.

As they drove along the near-deserted city streets, Alexa tried not to get her hopes up. Even knowing where Bethany was staying was no guarantee of finding her. Although she had always managed to find Bethany, it normally took days, not hours.

They pulled up out the front of the boarding house that had been Alexa's home. Alexa could feel Karl's eyes roving as they walked up the stairs and knew what he was thinking. It was what she was thinking about too – her other life, that world that, even now, she would go back to if she knew it would guarantee

Bethany's survival.

Despite there being no answer, Alexa kept knocking for five minutes before allowing herself to believe Bethany was not in her room. They hopped back in the car, but after an hour and a half of driving there was still no sign of Bethany.

"Do you mind if we walk around for a bit. She likes gardens. I think she may be in Hyde Park," said Alexa, as the sky began turning a deep orangey-red.

"Sure, I'll just find a parking spot," replied Karl, though Alexa could see he was not keen. He saw the city at night as a dark and dangerous place, but to her it was her second home and she feared nothing but not finding Bethany.

They walked the full length of the park twice without the slightest hint that Bethany had been there. Alexa was gutted. She did not know any more places to try.

"What do you want to do?" asked Karl, as they stood in the middle of the park. Alexa was close to tears.

"I don't know. It can take me days to find her. I want to keep looking, but ..." Alexa looked up at Karl, knowing how long they stayed was not up to her.

"Why don't we go back to the car and drive around a bit longer. We can come back here again before we leave," suggested Karl kindly.

Alexa nodded and slumped into the passenger seat. Karl was being more generous than he wanted to be and she knew she should be grateful, but it just felt like yet another thing that was being dangled in front of her before being ripped away just as she reached out to grab it.

As Karl pulled the car back on to the road Alexa continued to glance over at the park. Her stomach suddenly leapt into her throat as she saw a familiar shadow walking towards the war memorial.

"Wait, wait," Alexa cried, the car door already half open. Karl slammed his foot on the brake and she leapt out of the car and dashed across the road. "Bethy! Bethy, stop."

The shadowy figure slowly turned and Alexa sprinted the last twenty metres between them.

"Lex? What are you doing here?" asked Bethany, visibly shocked and even a little frightened by her sudden arrival.

"I've come to see you. I know you asked me not to, but it's Christmas and I couldn't not see you," replied Alexa, throwing her arms around Bethany's thinning body.

Bethany did not move or return Alexa's embrace. She just stared over Alexa's shoulder, her body tensing as if getting ready to flee.

"Who's that?" asked Bethany cautiously.

Alexa turned to see Karl walking slowly across the park towards them. She put her hand out. He immediately stopped, but looked on edge as he watched them.

"That's Karl," said Alexa. "He brought me here to try and find you. I have your Christmas present."

Alexa pulled the locket from her pocket and undid the chain. Bethany watched, unmoved, as Alexa fitted the chain around her neck. Bethany reached down and opened the locket, but her expression did not change as she stared down at the pictures of Alexa and herself.

"It's to remind you that I'm coming back for you," said Alexa, touching her finger to the locket. "As soon as I get out of school, I'll be here for you. I'll get you out of here and we can be together and no one will ever tear us apart again." Bethany seemed unimpressed by her words, but Alexa continued nonetheless. "I'll have the means to look after us, okay. It's all going to be fine. You just have to hold out for one more year. One more year and everything will be okay.

"But I'm warning you now, Bethy," Alexa added in a defiant tone. "If you ever sell this locket or use it in any way to buy drugs, I won't be here for you. I'll turn my back on you forever if you use this locket to score. It's the only thing I won't forgive."

Bethany's eyes flickered slightly with Alexa's warning, but otherwise remained as emotionless as before. Alexa knew Bethany had heard every word. She could see it in her eyes.

Alexa gently stroked Bethany's face before turning and walking away. She did not glance back around to see if Bethany was watching her leave. It was breaking her heart to force herself away from the only family she truly had, and she did not want to do it. She walked straight past Karl and headed for the car.

Karl did not talk as they drove. Alexa wrapped her arms around her chest to contain the heaving sobs, but nothing could stop the silent tears from falling.

Chapter Three

THE SCENERY FLASHED before Alexa's eyes, changing slowly from houses clumped right on top of each other to open land, and finally expanses of empty, dusty bushland. She blinked away the tears that were burning the sides of her eyes. Christmas was over, she told herself. Her relationship with the Whites was the best it had ever been and in one more year she would have control of her life. She would have Bethany.

The tunnel was still very long and dark, but Alexa knew there was an end to it. She could not see it yet, but understood that all she had to do was keep moving forward and the end would come, time would pass. What she tried not to think about was what was lurking in the shadows.

"So how were your holidays?" asked Alexa, re-starting conversation with Ezra to distract her mind from those dark thoughts.

"Yeah, okay. I just hung around home most of the time," replied Ezra easily. Alexa liked that Ezra was so used to her moods that she did not hold a grudge. "Did you work again?"

"Yep. Every day," replied Alexa with a slightly derisive smile, knowing how her friends viewed holiday work. "Still, it's money," she added, trying to fit in. She actually quite enjoyed her job and was sorry she could not do it on a more regular basis.

"Not that we really need it," whispered Ezra with a smile.

Alexa tried not to roll her eyes. Ezra shook her head incomprehensibly as they continued to whisper their conversation.

"Bianca's right. You really do need to get more excited about this," said Ezra seriously. "You could've chilled the whole holidays rather than stress about money. I kept thinking about what I will be doing next Christmas holidays."

"That's still a whole year away," pointed out Alexa, but she knew Ezra would never really understand.

The money she earned in the summer was the only money she had. There was no one else providing for her. She also knew that she could not explain what she foresaw for her next summer holidays. With or without the money, she would be back on the streets searching for Bethany and trying to take her somewhere safe to withdraw. It was certainly not what Bianca or Ezra had planned.

"Besides," added Alexa with a sigh. "Anything can happen between now and then and, knowing me, it probably will."

"Things can't be much worse than last year," said Ezra with a genuinely supportive smile. "That was just a shitty year. This year will be much better."

Alexa raised her eyebrows at the word shitty, making Ezra laugh. Shitty did not even come close to describing the last year – or any the years before that.

"Nup, I can't do this whole optimism thing."

Alexa tried briefly, but images of Christmas and Todd forcing himself on her flickered across her mind. The hope for better things only made her bitter about what she did not have and she knew she could not think that way. She needed to be grateful for everything she had; she had never had so much.

"Fine then, think of it this way; at worst, it can only be as shit as last year and you got through that," replied Ezra with a slight sigh. "So you just have to survive one more shit year. Does that make you feel better?"

"Yeah, heaps," smiled Alexa. "At least I won't be disappointed if I look at things that way."

With the conversation directed towards more mundane topics, it was not long before they were closing in on Sam's home. Alexa directed Ezra's dad to the property. It had been over a year since she had been there, but she was sure she would never forget the way. She had run away from more than a few foster homes to Sam's grandparents, with Bethany in tow as often as she could.

Sam's grandparents lived on a hundred acres of land, less than an hour from Sam's original home with his parents. When they pulled into the property, Sam, Chad and Bianca were all sitting outside on the porch. Alexa saw Sam grin widely as they approached. As she and Ezra stepped out of the car, he dashed into the house, returning with his grandparents. Alexa was saddened to see that they had aged in the time since her last visit.

Sam walked over to the car and hugged her. A hug from Gran and Pop quickly followed. As Pop let go, Alexa thought that he must be the only grown man she allowed to touch her in such an intimate way. It made her wonder if she would shy away if Mr Knight tried to hug her.

"How have your holidays been?" Gran asked Alexa.

"Not too bad, I guess. Oh crap," said Alexa, looking over Gran's shoulder to see Mel standing at the front door. "I thought she was staying with friends." Gran turned to look at her granddaughter, and Alexa suddenly realised she had spoken aloud. "I'm sorry."

"It's all right. Sam told us the things Mel said about you at school," replied Gran gently, rubbing her shoulder.

"And she didn't stop once she got home either, but we put a stop to it. I don't know what's gotten into her lately," said Pop, a slight scowl on his face.

"Half the things she's been saying are probably true," muttered Alexa, feeling guilty that they were defending her against their own granddaughter.

"You've had a rough year and made some very stupid choices, but that doesn't give her the right to speak so badly of you, especially when you've done nothing to her," said Pop.

That was not exactly true, but Alexa knew it was better they believed that than know the truth. Alexa still hoped that Mel would simply get over her infatuation with Clinton now he had been absent for so long.

Sam and Chad unloaded the car while Ezra's parents chatted with Gran and Pop. After a mandatory afternoon tea, Ezra's parents started their long journey home, while Ezra and Alexa settled in to begin enjoying the last week of their holidays.

The afternoon was spent showing Ezra around the property. Chad and Bianca had both arrived the day before and Alexa had seen it all many times. Everyone was eager to catch up about their holidays, but it was a conversation Alexa was equally keen to avoid. She tried bribing them with the chocolates she received at Christmas, but that only started them asking about her Christmas.

"I can't believe this is going to be our last year of school," said Ezra, changing the topic to appease Alexa for the third time. "It seems so long ago that we started at Redgrove."

"Really? School? Do we have to? We're going to be back there in a week," complained Alexa.

"Are you going to like any conversation we have today?" asked Chad with a smile.

"Not at this rate," replied Alexa, smiling in return.

"I think it'll be a good year," said Sam. "A bit stressful at the end with the finals and all, but it can't be much worse than last year."

"Try telling that to Alexa," said Ezra. "She has a wonderfully pessimistic outlook for the year."

"I have a wonderfully pessimistic outlook for every year and I don't think I've been wrong yet," replied Alexa simply as she got to her feet. "Come and get me when you've finished talking about school and Christmas."

***

"Do you guys want to go for a walk?" Bianca asked Alexa and Ezra the next morning after breakfast. Chad and Sam were off trail-biking around the property. "I need to talk to you about something."

"Sure," Alexa and Ezra responded together.

Ezra and Alexa followed Bianca, who seemed quite anxious as she walked far away from the house. They finally stopped when the house was well out of sight. When they sat down, Bianca looked around again to make sure they were alone.

"So what's going on?" asked Alexa, wondering who they were hiding from. She chuckled to herself at the thought that Bianca had already had too much of the isolation of Sam's place.

"I need to talk to you guys about something. I've kinda done something and now I don't know what to do," said Bianca anxiously, but did not continue.

Ezra and Alexa both looked at Bianca, waiting for some further explanation. Alexa tried to remember all the things she had been scared about doing wrong the first few times she had come out to Sam's place and all the things he had taught her about living in the country. She was almost excited about the prospect of bonding with Bianca over something.

"You know how I went back to Europe with my family for Christmas, right?" said Bianca, again checking that no one was nearby. Alexa looked at her, confused by the direction of the conversation. "Well, we went to Switzerland for Christmas and some skiing. Anyway, I kinda met up with an ex of mine."

"Oh, Bianca, no," moaned Alexa, immediately realising where this was going.

"I didn't mean for anything to happen. It just happened. I couldn't help it."

"Believe me, you can help it. Please, just tell me you kissed him and there was nothing else," Alexa pleaded. Bianca would not meet her eyes as she drew circles in the ground. "How many times?"

"What's that matter?" cried Bianca indignantly.

"So more than once, then?" asked Alexa, making her point. Bianca did not answer. "Bianca, no! See, I don't even think you can accidentally sleep with someone once, but more than that – you can't say that you didn't mean it to happen."

"I didn't expect you to be so critical," said Bianca harshly.

"Why?" asked Alexa, and she could see that her surprise caught Bianca off-guard.

"What, you can be a professional whore and we're not supposed to judge, but I get together with my ex and somehow I'm a slut."

Ezra gasped slightly as Alexa sat stunned. She had never told her friends about her life during those two weeks, but there had been rumours and it was clear that everyone had found out the truth. However, never once did she think that any of them would throw it back at her the way Bianca just had – the way Pam and Karl's families had.

In that moment Alexa truly hated Bianca. She got to her feet and started to walk towards the house, but stopped and turned back when her anger boiled over.

"Whatever I have done, I have never, ever cheated on anybody," hissed Alexa. "So you can think whatever you want about me, but I think what you have done is a thousand times worse."

"It's not about who's done the worst thing in their life," said Ezra, trying to calm the situation, holding her hands out to Bianca and Alexa. "Bianca, you know it's not great what you did or you wouldn't feel so bad, but we're your friends. We'll always be your friends. Doesn't matter what happened."

"They're my friends too," protested Alexa, pointing towards the house.

"What am I going to do?" cried Bianca into her hands.

"Tell Chad. That would be a good start," spat Alexa, not impressed by Bianca's expression of helplessness.

"He'll hate me."

"No shit."

"You should tell him," said Ezra in a soothing voice. "You guys have been going out for a while. I think he probably deserves to know."

"Why did you have to do it? I thought you really liked Chad," cried Alexa, imagining how heartbroken Chad would be if he ever found out. Next to Sam, he was the most genuine, loyal guy she had ever met.

"I did – I do. I just forgot how hot Victor was and it was just a bit of fun, but now I'm here with Chad I feel so guilty. Chad's really kind and sweet and I shouldn't have cheated on him, but I needed to tell someone. I don't want to tell Chad. It'll just wreck things between us. Please, promise me you guys won't say anything about this to anyone."

"I promise," replied Ezra immediately.

"You're asking me to choose between friends," said Alexa, closing her eyes to try and control her anger. It was a lie. She would never tell Chad in a hundred years. She never wanted to be responsible for hurting him. "If Chad finds out, he'll never speak to me again."

"He won't find out. Not unless one of you says something," retorted Bianca harshly. "So do you promise or not?"

"Keep your goddamned secret," replied Alexa, storming off, hating Bianca's demanding tone more than the request.

Everything, thought Alexa, everything was turning to shit. If this was how the year was starting, she could only imagine how it would end.

Walking around the property, Alexa tried hard to let go of the rage that was building within her. She put her hands in her pockets only to find them empty. Her razors must be in her bag. The thought was depressing. She could not think of a way to calm herself down without them.

***

Lunchtime came and went, but Alexa still did not return to the house. Sam was angry that no one had told him of the mood she was in when she stormed off. He jumped on his bike and sped off to the far end of the property and, sure enough, he saw her shoes dangling between the branches of a very large tree. That tree had always been her place to escape.

Sam made the ascent after filling his pockets with stones. He was not keen on heights and this tree was high. Halfway up the tree he began throwing the stones at Alexa, most hitting their mark, but she did not move. Three-quarters of the way up, he stopped and threw the rest of the stones, several hitting Alexa squarely on the leg, but she still did not move. He started to feel anxious, trying to see how her feet were hanging and if she had done something stupid.

Sam wanted to believe it was impossible, but he had never known one person to suffer so much. He climbed faster, forgetting his fears. When he finally reached Alexa, he saw she was asleep on a tattered cushion Pop had made her many years ago.

"I was wondering how long it would take you to get up here," smiled Alexa, slyly opening her eyes.

"You were awake the whole time?" Sam asked in a scandalised voice.

"It's hard to sleep when someone keeps throwing rocks at you," replied Alexa playfully.

"I'm going to kill you. Do you realise how high up we are?"

"You've been up here before."

"Yeah, and I was terrified then too," Sam replied honestly.

"I managed to distract you for a while," smiled Alexa seductively.

Sam's face coloured at the memory of that day. Alexa had dragged him to this very spot and sat him down on the cushion, positioned where the many large branches made falling almost impossible. She had climbed on top of him and they had made love in the treetops.

"That was a good day, wasn't it?" smiled Alexa.

"The best," Sam smiled, feeling his body warm at the memory. "If we're ever both single it could be a fun reunion."

"We are both single."

Sam moved in closer and kissed Alexa gently. His lips melted right into hers as she ran her hand over his back.

"We should go. Everyone's waiting for us," he said, pulling away.

It would have been so easy to continue. He spent half his days imagining moments like this.

"That would never've worried you before," replied Alexa, her hand still stroking his face tenderly.

"I know why you're doing this, but it won't make you feel better," Sam replied, closing his eyes, knowing he did not have long to enjoy this stolen moment.

They had snuck out last night and he had forced Alexa to confess all that had happened since the last day of school. He had cursed a lot. It was hard to believe the casual way she could detail those kinds of things, as if she did not care, when he knew she did.

"Maybe it will," replied Alexa with a smile. "Maybe you're the only one in the world who ever makes me feel better."

"If you weren't always so honest with me, then I might believe you," said Sam seriously. This was the part he hated the most. "Us, doing this, it'll only confuse you more. You love someone else," he said in an agitated manner, terrified of that truth. "And I don't love you that way, not really anyway."

"No?" queried Alexa.

"We all move on," Sam smiled gently. "Even from you."

It was true. He had finally found himself looking at other girls with a true interest in dating them. It had only been possible after accepting that part of him would probably always be tied to Alexa. He knew she believed their relationship was very one-sided, with her taking everything and capable of giving nothing, but she was the main reason he had coped with his parents' deaths.

"I love you. I always will," he reassured her, knowing she needed to be. "I just like the idea of other girls too."

"Promise me something?" Alexa asked seriously, the smile fading from her face.

"Anything," replied Sam sincerely.

"That no matter what happens you'll always be my friend."

"The fact that I am up this tree right now should be answer enough. I will never leave you, Alexa – unless you insist on staying up here."

Sam smiled and quickly started making his way down the tree. If Alexa needed more reassurance, she could come and get it on solid earth. A giggle alerted him to the fact that Alexa was moving, and he was not surprised to find her on the ground well before him. She had always been so agile.

Alexa's arms wrapped around him as she kissed his cheek and thanked him for his friendship, before begging to go for a ride on the bike. He did not care to go back to the house yet either, so quickly agreed and drove them to the dam furthest from the house.

They lay down with their feet dangling in the cold water. Lying in each other's arms, Sam felt Alexa pulling him closer, her legs entangling with his. When her lips pressed against his, it took him longer than it should have to pull away.

"Just for now. Just to be close," Alexa said softly, her eyes downcast.

Sam knew it was a bad idea, but rejecting Alexa would not make her feel better either. Stroking her cheek, he nodded and kissed her back.

***

The long, lazy days were easy to fill and Alexa was glad that there was no one in the house looking to wake her up early. Between relaxing in the house, swimming in the dam and trail-biking around the property, the hours moved quite swiftly and she was surprised when the week was almost over.

Bianca had made sure they spent as little time together as possible, with her and Chad often sneaking off alone somewhere. However, as much as Chad liked Bianca, it was clear he did not want to spend the whole week with her. Bianca and Ezra were not the adventurous types and had not really appreciated the level of laughter that had accompanied the attempts to teach them to ride the trail bikes.

That left Alexa with the boys when they wanted to ride, which suited her just fine. She was not keen on spending much time with Bianca either, though she knew she should try and heal the rift between them. It was just that every time she had tried to speak to Bianca and promise that she would keep the affair secret, Bianca had glared or snapped at her.

When everyone was together, Bianca made a point of being very close to Chad. She was always kissing him and hugging him, and not in the passive way Alexa often found herself in Sam's arms. Bianca and Chad's behaviour bordered on pornographic at times, and Alexa had the feeling she was not the only one it made uncomfortable when Chad became much more hard line about their level of intimacy in front of Gran and Pop.

"Stop it!" Chad hissed when Bianca moved behind him at the kitchen table, her hands stroking down his chest as her lips caressed his ear.

Bianca did not move and Chad threw her arms off him.

"I'm going to head out for a ride," said Chad in a low voice, pushing his chair away from the table.

"I don't see the issue," huffed Bianca, sitting down at the table. "I'm not allowed to do anything, but it's fine if she's sitting on his lap."

Alexa looked down. Pop had wanted to show her some old photos of the property and Sam's old place he had found since her last visit. Sam had not wanted to move, so sat her on his lap, his arm wrapped around her waist as they spoke to Pop. From the corner of her eye, Alexa noticed that even Mel was sneering at Bianca rather than her.

"You guys coming?" asked Chad, not looking Bianca's way.

Sam did not answer. He just grabbed Alexa's hand and pulled

her outside and on to the back of his bike. They drove out to the dam and jumped in, clothes and all. It was so hot they would be dry again in minutes anyway.

It was moments like these that Alexa had liked the best about her week. Thankfully, there had been enough of them that she had been able to ignore the less pleasant ones. Lying under the shade of the sole tree near the dam, she took a deep breath and forced herself to be grateful that there were any good moments at all.

"You know that anyone who gets to know you will understand what you did last year," said Chad suddenly, rolling over to face Alexa.

Alexa was confused for a moment, before realising that Bianca must not have remained completely silent about her opinions of her. She wondered what Chad saw in Bianca as she shook her head, wishing for a reason to release herself of the promise that now felt like a heavy burden on her chest.

"You didn't do anything you should be ashamed of," continued Chad. "If anyone should be ashamed, it's the guys who want to sleep with young girls. People pay for sex all the time – guys and girls. It's just guy prostitutes get to be called escorts and no one feels sorry for them, cos what guy wouldn't want to be paid to have sex, right?"

Alexa could only shrug. It was not as though she was not aware of the double standards society often held girls to. She was just too beaten down to fight. All she wanted was to survive.

"No offence, but you'd have to pay me to sleep with you," said Chad seriously. "And I don't know that I'd really enjoy it that much."

"Um, was this supposed to be making me feel better?" asked Alexa with bemusement, as Sam smiled and shook his head.

"Just pointing out that I've never liked you that way – like never," clarified Chad with a chuckling smile. "And I reckon you've never liked me that way either." Alexa smiled and shook her head. "Guys don't want to jump every girl they meet. Most of us want to be with someone special. Most of us want to fall in love. It's just not what we say in front of lots of guys. And most of us know the double standards for guys and girls suck. We can't change everyone's mind, but we won't all judge you either."

"How'd you find out?" asked Alexa, wondering if Mr Knight had broken his word and told people where Clinton had found her before he had raped her.

"Nick," replied Sam. "It was in the paper. It must've been Mr Marsh who put it out there – to discredit you, as if prostitutes can't be raped."

"So everyone knows?" asked Alexa, her stomach falling through her body.

"Yeah, but Chad's right," replied Sam, taking her hand and squeezing it. "No one's going to say it to your face, but we know – we know what people have said and they don't all judge you. Your life sucks. It's not fair what you and Bethany have had to deal with."

"Any decent person will think the same way we do," added Chad.

Alexa had to swallow the words that were pushing in her throat. It would be selfish to tell Chad about Bianca just so she could confess how much her words had stung. She already had his support, and Bianca was never going to change her opinion. Alexa would settle for small victories.

****

It was an early start on Sunday for the long trek to school. They were all up with the sun to make their train, with two trips into town required to get them all there. Gran made them each a big bag of food to keep them fed throughout the journey. Alexa hugged her and Pop warmly as they waited on the platform, feeling tears burning the sides of her eyes. She did not know when she would see them again, but knew they would only be older again when she did and the thought terrified her. They were some of the world's better people and the idea that that they could and would one day die was horrible.

Everyone sat together on the train into the city, chatting happily, trying to make the most of their last moments of freedom. No one seemed to notice how little Alexa and Bianca spoke directly to each other. Sam was concentrating his efforts on trying to make Alexa and Mel get along. Alexa tried for Sam's sake, but Mel was not playing ball. Mel still openly refused to believe that Clinton had ever raped her, stating that it simply could not be true. There was no denying that Clinton had strangled her – almost to death – when she had confronted him to try and lure him into a confession while wearing a wire, but Mel just said that was what she deserved for entrapping Clinton.

It was a relief when it all became too tense and Mel moved

away, though Bianca's snide smile as Mel spoke had not escaped Alexa's attention. Alexa tried to think of Mel as a victim of Clinton too, just one who had not learned the hard way what Clinton was really like, but with Mel intent on being so vicious it was a hard task. Mel had already done her best to make her life hell last year and she could only hope Mel's infatuation with Clinton quickly faded.

Ezra alighted the train prior to them reaching the city, where everyone else had to change trains, to make her way back to her suburban home. Alexa watched her wistfully, wishing she could go home each day. It made her wonder if she should have considered the Whites' offer more seriously. It would have been a trek, but perhaps she could have lived there and attended Redgrove as a day student. However, she was still not truly convinced that they had made that offer with the expectation that she would say yes.

Chad and Bianca moved seats as soon as the train pulled away from Ezra's station. Though the carriage was quite empty, Bianca walked them right to the other end, so they were about as far apart as the train carriage allowed, leaving Sam and Alexa together.

"Oh, hey, I got you a present," said Sam as soon as they were alone.

"What for?" asked Alexa with tender surprise.

"Just for being around. Here," replied Sam dismissively, pulling a rectangular box from his bag and giving it to her. "Just don't flash it around when you open it."

Alexa looked at Sam curiously then back at the box. She opened it and immediately understood his warning. It was a large pocket knife with a blade that folded down into the shiny silver handle. There were a couple of scratches and a few small dents in the blade, but it had been newly sharpened and was now lethal.

"It was mine," explained Sam. "Pop helped me fix it up and we cleaned the handle and sharpened the blade."

"What's it for?" Alexa asked curiously.

"Your protection. I know you trust Mr Knight, but I want to make sure you're safe – and it'll help keep creeps like Todd away from you as well."

"Thank you," said Alexa, reaching over and kissing Sam on the cheek, cursing herself for not loving him as she once had. He truly was an amazing guy.

"You'd better put it away and don't flash it around school, but keep it with you always, okay," instructed Sam firmly. "You attract too much trouble."

Alexa rolled her eyes, pushing the blade easily back into the handle and slid it into her bag. It was not something she ever wanted to use, but she did feel safer knowing she had it.

Chad and Bianca continued to sit away from them on the second train. Bianca was certainly not letting her brief affair hold her back with Chad, as they spent most of the train ride locked at the lips. The word overcompensation came to mind, but Chad clearly did not have any issues with the situation.

"Were we ever like that?" Alexa asked Sam, as she watched Bianca and Chad in interested disgust.

"No, you weren't big on public displays of affection," smiled Sam.

"Did that bother you?"

"No," Sam chuckled quietly, pulling her into an affectionate embrace. "You more than made up for it in private. Probably the way it should be, but it's also nice showing off your girlfriend."

"I don't think I'm big on affection of any kind," said Alexa, her body shivering slightly at the thought.

"I know." Sam was laughing now, but restrained himself when Alexa glared at him. "You just have no idea how long it took for you to hold my hand. I thought I was never going to get to kiss you, but then suddenly you were okay and it was all a rush after that."

Alexa smiled and rested her head on Sam's shoulder. They had been good times. She wondered if she and Sam would have fallen out of love if Clinton had never come along. She wondered if she would have seen anything in Mr Knight if she had never suffered at the hands of Clinton and been forced to put her trust in him. The problem was she was still not sure she really could trust Mr Knight. She had been wrong about people so many times before.

These thoughts made Alexa dread her return to school. As they walked up the hill from the train station, her legs filled with lead, but as soon as they passed through the school gates, much of the anxiety left her body. She was not looking forward to the year ahead, but Redgrove was essentially her home. The familiarity was comforting, if not soothing or welcoming.

"We'll meet you guys in five minutes to sign in," said Sam, when they reached the second floor of the dormitories.

"Okay," called Alexa and Bianca, as they kept trudging up the stairs.

When they reached their room, Alexa dumped her bags on her

bed and headed straight to the shower, running the cold water over her head and neck. She flicked her wet hair back and felt the cold water drip refreshingly down her spine and over her face and chest, taking her breath away.

"Nice," said Bianca condescendingly. "That should get all the guys' attention."

"What?" asked Alexa, completely confused.

"Nothing," muttered Bianca. "Are we going?"

"Wait. Look, I promised I wasn't going to say anything," said Alexa, making sure she kept her temper in check. "But if you're so worried about Chad finding out about Victor then why not just tell him?"

"Is that a threat?" questioned Bianca angrily.

"What? No, my God. I promised and I keep my promises," cried Alexa, tired of this year already.

"I don't need your promises. I just need you to keep your mouth shut," snarled Bianca before storming out.

***

Marcus sat anxiously at his desk, his eyes flicking up at every noise outside his door. He had been registering the arrival of the boarders all weekend and Alexa had still not arrived. He had hoped to hear from her foster parents, asking him to pick her up and bring her back to school, but the call never came. It was a ridiculous desire. He had spent the entire holidays with Jackie trying to repair their relationship and had been more successful than he had previously believed possible. Those weeks were some of the happiest of his life and he loved Jackie so much, but somehow it was not enough.

When Alexa walked in, Marcus knew he was doomed. She was beautiful and he thought he somehow loved her more now than he had six weeks ago, but she was holding Sam's hand – and smiling. Marcus forced a welcoming smile on to his face and hoped none of his disappointment showed on his face.

He had no right to be disappointed. They had agreed to forget about their feelings and move on with their lives. He had spent six weeks doing just that – and so had she. Marcus just hated that Alexa had been successful, as he realised just how woefully unsuccessful he had been.

Never before had Marcus thought it possible to be in love with two people at once, but that was his reality. The problem was that the one who he felt had true possession of his heart was the one he was determined never to be with. He would have to make sure he always loved Alexa enough to never reach out for her in a moment of pure selfishness.

"Miss Samson, your foster parents dropped you off?" Marcus asked, trying to be casual.

"No, I came with Sam. I spent the last week at his place," replied Alexa, her eyes wide with surprise.

"Were your foster parents aware of this?" asked Marcus, suddenly weary.

"You think she ran away?" asked Sam angrily. "She's here. She's on time. There're no cops."

"Mr Michaels, there was an agreement in place for Miss Samson's travel arrangements. I can't just ignore them."

"Great," sighed Alexa, throwing her hands up and turning away.

"I'm not trying to be difficult," said Marcus, desperate for Alexa to believe that and to understand that he would accept her moving on. "I just don't want you in trouble before school has even started."

"They let me go," said Alexa quietly, and Marcus wondered why she sounded so sad. Her voice pricked at his heart and he knew it was not his imagination, because Sam had her instantly in his arms.

"Then they must have just forgotten to let us know," said Marcus. He was not going to make trouble, not if Alexa was already hurting – again, still, always. "I will probably just have to call them, okay. If they're going to let you travel alone, then it will have to be recorded so you don't have any problems."

Alexa nodded and pressed herself further into Sam's arms as they bound her tightly. The sight was less torturous than Marcus expected. She was taken care of at least – and loved.

"You can go," said Marcus a little mournfully. "Enjoy the last night of your holidays."

***

Enjoyment was not what Alexa found that night. Bianca was still being distinctly icy towards her, but covered it with her continued and excessive interest in Chad. Alexa was profoundly grateful that Lizzie arrived just before dinner.

"So did you see Mr Knight? He's looking pretty good after the summer," said Lizzie, smiling at Alexa as they sat in the common room.

"Yeah, I noticed," smiled Alexa in return.

And she had. Mr Knight's skin was browner from the summer sun and his hair looked as soft as ever, falling freely over his forehead, directing her eyes to his. She had managed to look away before reaching them.

Alexa also noticed that Mr Knight had not doubted her word about being allowed to travel alone. He trusted her. In a way, she wished he did not, and then perhaps she would have a reason to dislike him. Instead, she realised that her feelings for Marcus – Mr Knight, she reminded herself for what had to be the thousandth time that day – were as strong as they ever had been.

"I think half of it's because things are going well with his fiancée," said Lizzie with a half-smile.

"How'd you know things were going badly to begin with?" asked Alexa, astounded by the type of information Lizzie could pull out of Mr Knight.

"I chatted with him for a while when I went to sign in. I think he found last year really stressful and the holidays were a good break. I think they even set a wedding date. He said it was after the finals, but didn't tell me the date."

Alexa was surprised that news did not hurt more. She knew the wedding was coming, but was relieved it would be after she had left Redgrove – after she had left him. The thought of Mr Knight marrying while they were still in each other's lives was much more painful. She did genuinely want him to be happy, and smiled at the image of him on his wedding day – quickly banishing the vision of her being the one walking down the aisle towards him.

"What's it like when he talks to you?" Alexa asked suddenly, truly intrigued.

"Normal, I guess. What do you mean?" asked Lizzie curiously. "No differently to the way he talks to you."

"Ha," laughed Alexa. "We don't talk. I get in trouble. We've never really talked – not like that."

"Well, he's just like any other teacher, but he doesn't talk down to you."

"I've never really talked to any teacher," smiled Alexa. "Trouble, remember?"

"Don't worry, this year will be good. You can't get in trouble forever," smiled Lizzie supportively.

"You would think so, wouldn't you? And why is everyone so

convinced this is going to be a good year?"

"It's our last year of school. We don't have to come back next year. I think that makes this year a good year."

"I think that makes next year a good year," Alexa replied, though she was not even sure she believed that. To date, no year had been a good year.

The official start of the school year did not bode any better for Alexa, only reinforcing her pessimistic view of the year to come. She was awoken early by yet another nightmare and could only be thankful that this time she had been woken by her tears rather than a scream. It was surprising the same dream could still affect her so badly after so many years.

Her heart had begun pounding as soon as she had seen her five-year-old body. Grabbing Bethany, she had tried to run fast, but at three, Bethany was almost as big as she was. With the bloody knife in her hand, Alexa had searched for a safe place to hide. She did not want to go back to the field of pipes. She knew it was not safe, but it never mattered how many times she had the dream or in which direction she ran, in the end, there was only ever one place left to go.

Cowering in the pipe, Alexa tried to convince herself that this time the ending would be different. Ben, the friendly, round-faced policeman, crouched at the end of the pipe as he called out to them.

"It's okay. You're safe now," Ben said kindly.

Alexa shook her head as panic spread through her body. "No, he's coming for you," she cried.

"Who? I can protect you, don't worry."

Alexa scrambled to the end of the pipe, grabbing Ben's hand to pull him to safety.

Sometimes she managed to pull him in. Other times he refused. It never made any difference. The shadowy man always found them, laughing mercilessly at her fear, and Ben always ended up in a pool of his own blood, his eyes staring lifelessly out at them.

The regularity and inevitability of the nightmare was horrible and continually tore Alexa violently from her sleep. The subtle permutations only contributed to the nightmare's disturbing nature. Once, during the holidays, Ben had even asked her about the baby.

"It's gone," Alexa had replied, looking mournfully down at her tiny five-year-old body. The little lump that had once resided in her dreamtime body had disappeared with her real baby.

"But the money. Didn't you get the money? I gave you the

numbers," called Ben, causing tears to stream down Alexa's face –
in her dream and in reality.

"I failed," she whispered, ashamed of that truth.

Alexa had looked up at the end of the pipe, fearful of Ben's
angry response, but he had already been shot. She would never
know how badly she had disappointed her dreamtime protector.

Those numbers, rolled down to her by Ben in marbles when she
had needed them most, had been just what Ezra had suggested –
the winning lottery numbers. Their amazing windfall had just come
too late for her child, and Alexa could now only hope that it would
not be too late for Bethany by the time she was able to collect it after
her eighteenth birthday.

When they all trudged up to breakfast, Bianca sat at Chad's table
and casually ignored Alexa. No one else noticed the snub. Chad and
Bianca's relationship bordered on nauseating for most people, so no
one was really surprised when Bianca ignored people when she was
with Chad.

"What's with Bianca? Is she mad at you?" asked Ezra as they sat
back down in the dining hall for their grade meeting after their start
of year assembly. Apparently, she was not as unobservant as their
other friends.

"I just asked her last night if she was sure she shouldn't tell
Chad about Victor. I mean, you don't think it's right what she's
doing, do you?"

"Not really, but I don't agree with lots of the things you do
either," smiled Ezra with slightly raised eyebrows. "I'm only still
your friend because I don't tell you what to do."

"But I didn't tell her what to do. And I only asked because she
doesn't trust me – no matter how many times I promise."

"She'll get over it. Just don't mention it any more. Let her handle
it her own way," suggested Ezra with a supportive smile.

Alexa nodded, prepared to try just about anything at this point
to make her life that little bit easier.

"Good morning, Year Twelve," said Mrs Taylor as she strolled
into the dining hall.

The grade groaned as one. If Mrs Taylor had come to their grade
meeting it meant only one thing – they had a new year advisor.

Alexa's heart sank. It was her fault and she knew it. She was the
reason Mr Knight had chosen not to take them on for a second year.

"I trust you all had a good holiday and are back ready to face
your last year of school and, most importantly, your final exams,"

continued Mrs Taylor cheerily.

"Isn't Mr Knight our year advisor this year?" asked Chad, looking between Mrs Taylor and the door.

"Ah, yes," smirked Mrs Taylor, suddenly smiling more broadly. "Mr Knight did advise us at the end of last year that we should look for another year advisor for this grade."

"Why'd he quit?" asked a voice from the back of the hall.

Alexa folded her legs on her chair and looked intently at her shoes. This was the point where it went from bad to worse.

"It's interesting, isn't it? This grade has tried to undermine every year advisor it's ever had, then suddenly you all find one you like, but it seems the memo to stop causing trouble never reached as far as Miss Samson."

"So we're all being punished because Alexa can't keep herself out of trouble?" asked Bianca harshly, throwing Alexa a scathing look.

The entire G7 and half of the grade turned to Bianca in shock, but many others nodded in agreement. Alexa continued to look at her shoes, twirling the laces between her fingers. She was not surprised that such a thing had been said – or even that is had been said out loud – but could not believe that it was Bianca who had said it.

Alexa could feel sadness and frustration building inside her to the point of explosion. She wanted to cry or scream or run away. She wanted to dispel the pain and her hand automatically curled around the razor in her pocket. Sam was trying to catch her eye, but she was intent on avoiding him. She now wished she had stayed with the Whites.

"That is the way Miss Samson generally likes it," replied Mrs Taylor in a sinister voice.

"So who's our year advisor, then?" asked Sam bitterly.

"After many searches and much pleading it turns out that we did not have a single teacher in this school willing to take you on."

"Do we have a year advisor?" asked Chris, as he and Stacey glared fiercely at Bianca.

"Yes, you do," said Mr Knight, striding forcefully into the dining hall.

Chapter Four

LOUD CHEERS GREETED Marcus's entrance. Every student in the room seemed to be smiling in response to his arrival. Everyone, that was, except Alexa. She was sitting with her legs crossed on her seat, paying her shoelaces an indescribable amount of attention.

"Sorry I'm late. I had some urgent family business to attend to this morning," Marcus explained, trying to control the frustration swirling in his chest.

"The grade was just debating your potential loss and its possible cause," smiled Mrs Taylor, her eyes flicking merrily in Alexa's direction. "I'll leave you to it."

"Okay. Let's settle down," said Marcus immediately, trying not to let his disgust in Mrs Taylor's actions show. She had known full well that he would be late to this meeting and that he had willingly agreed to take on the grade for another year. "I have your timetables here. Pass them around and let me know quick smart if you have any problems."

"Did you really quit?" asked Adrian, one of Chad and Sam's roommates.

Marcus tried not to let his gaze flick Alexa's way, but he had seen her when he had arrived and knew she had suffered because his poor decision-making and Mrs Taylor's vengeance.

"That topic is not open for discussion, Mr Curtis. I'm your year advisor for the rest of the year. That's all you need to know. This is a big year for all of you and no doubt a very tough one. If you have any problems my door is always open."

"Well, on behalf of the grade and the notorious G7," smiled Sam, rising from his chair. "We would like to say congratulations on being the first year advisor to make it back for a second year. As a reward, we will lay down our arms and from this point forth call an official end to all hostilities."

"Ah, thank you, Mr Michaels, I think," smiled Marcus. He knew from the way Sam's eyes had flicked towards Alexa that this comment was in part to distract the grade from her. "But I wasn't aware any of you had made a concerted effort to displace me."

"We didn't," said Nick with a hint of bitterness. "We acted no differently to almost any other year. Trouble finds us. We didn't always go looking for it."

"Thank you for the gesture all the same. I have nothing more to say, but I need to see the following people in my office: Mr Poulos, Mr –"

"What? Come on, Sir. I thought all that shit was over with," cried Sam, his voice losing its playful edge of a moment ago.

He was not the only disgruntled student. Chad, Stacey and Chris were also shooting daggers at him. Nick and Alan looked resigned, but this was really not about persecution.

"I need to see Mr Poulos, Mr Chan and Miss Samson in my office," continued Marcus firmly, his eyes fixed on Sam. "The rest of you are free to go."

***

Alexa ignored Sam's supportive hug at the end of the grade meeting. She barely even heard what he said to her as he walked with her to Mr Knight's office. They took their time and the office door was closed when they arrived. Murmured voices on the other side told them that Nick and Alan were already having their meeting.

"Want me to wait with you?" asked Sam, sitting down on the tattered lounge with Alexa. She just shook her head. "Forget Bianca, okay. She was way out of line and Chad's furious. We know this wasn't your fault."

"You should get to class, Sam," said Alexa. She was in no mood to be cheered up.

Sam hugged her and kissed the side of her head, not letting go of her hand until distance pulled them apart. Alexa curled up on the old and tattered, but comfortable lounge that had always lived outside the office. She closed her eyes and tried to clear her mind of everything, but could not conjure a single peaceful thought.

Eventually the door creaked open and Nick and Alan emerged looking happy and relaxed, but Alexa remained where she was.

"You're up," said Nick, smiling down at her. Alexa pulled her legs to the ground, sitting herself up, but did not rise from the couch. "Forget about this morning. Mrs Taylor was just trying to rile you up, knowing you couldn't say anything."

"She's a bitch. We all know that," said Alan spitefully, though his smile was supportive. "Don't worry, we're behind you."

Alan held out his hand and Alexa let him pull her to her feet. Nick wrapped his hand around hers and Alan's and they pulled her into a quick embrace before pushing her towards the door.

"He's fair," said Alan. "He's not looking for trouble."

Alexa nodded and entered the office without knocking. Mr Knight was sitting at his desk, looking out the window behind it. She felt nothing for him in that moment. She felt nothing for anything.

"I think, more than anything, I owe you an apology," said Mr Knight softly, turning to face her. "I spent the first week of the holidays deciding what I should do and how any decision I made would affect you. I quit, initially, because I thought it would be easier for you, but when no one else would take the job I didn't feel like I had a choice. I thought I would be a better year advisor than none at all."

Alexa listened to every word Mr Knight said, but did not show it. Only a very small part of her could care.

"I didn't intend for any of the students to find out that I ever quit. I should've told all those students who asked that I had agreed to come back. I wanted to surprise everyone," Mr Knight admitted with a half-ashamed smile and a shrug of his shoulders. "I wanted to walk in and see everyone's reaction. That was the plan. Mrs Taylor was never meant to be there. No one was ever supposed to know that I quit and you were never supposed to be blamed for anything."

Alexa could not help but roll her eyes at Mr Knight's last comment.

"Alexa, are you all right? I know what was said at the grade meeting this morning and you have every right to be upset, but I'd like it if you spoke to me."

Alexa did not want to speak. Everything Mr Knight had said sounded so reasonable and she did not want to like him again. She wanted to think of him like every other teacher and not be so grateful for his mere existence.

"I can't help you if you won't talk to me."

"You can't help me anyway," Alexa retorted immediately, only to see Mr Knight smile in response. "I guess you think you're good now," she said, only half in bitterness as she rolled her eyes and crossed her arms.

"That thought did cross my mind. How were your holidays? I spoke to your foster parents last night and they seemed pleased."

Alexa waited nervously, wondering what else Pam and Karl may have said, but Mr Knight gave no hint that he knew about what happened over Christmas.

"Why were you late this morning?" Alexa asked critically, to make sure the conversation was quickly turned away from her holidays, and to try and find some legitimate fault in Mr Knight's story. "You said you planned to be there."

"My grandmother died last night."

"I'm – oh, sorry – I shouldn't have – I didn't … I'm sorry. Why are you here, then?"

"She lives – lived – in England. It was sudden – heart attack. Better in some ways, I suppose. She didn't suffer, I don't think – not much, not like other ways."

Alexa could not respond. She did not know what to say and what she wanted to do was not allowed.

"Things will get better here," said Mr Knight after a few minutes of silence.

"Why does everyone believe that?" muttered Alexa in a voice she was not sure Mr Knight heard.

"Just hang in there, okay. And you can come and see me whenever you need – big or small. I'm here for you."

"I don't want to see you this year," replied Alexa and hoped Mr Knight understood why. "I can look after myself."

"As long as it's not the way you usually do. Otherwise you'll be seeing a lot of me," added Mr Knight sternly.

Alexa looked down at her cardigan and, with a brief smile, pulled it off to reveal smooth and slightly tanned arms.

"That's really good," said Mr Knight, unable to keep the relieved smile off his face. Alexa pulled her cardigan back on and picked up her bag. "I thought you only wore that when you were trying to cover your cuts."

"I guess you don't know me as well as you thought you did, huh?" Alexa smiled as she left, getting out before she found more reasons to want to stay.

***

Nick and Alan did their best to take the pressure off Alexa over the next few days. They told everyone who would listen what Mr Knight had told them; that the only reason he had quit as their year advisor was because of the guilt he felt over what Alexa had suffered at the hands of Mr Marsh and the little he had been able to do to prevent it. That Mr Knight confirmed their story when approached by students did much to sway the tide back in her favour. After all, whatever mistakes Alexa had made in dating a teacher, few could argue that she had deserved being raped and almost murdered.

It seemed the only person who would not be swayed to Alexa's side was Bianca. Convinced by Ezra, Sam and Chad that something else had to be going on for Bianca to be acting this way, Alexa tried to smooth things over, but Bianca was determined to hold a grudge.

"You talk to me about being there for you unconditionally, but when I ask the same from you it's too much to expect," spat Bianca as soon as Alexa tried to apologise.

"I've never asked you to choose between friends. Besides that, I haven't done anything to betray your trust," replied Alexa, unsure of what else she could do to redeem herself. "Despite what you say about me, I haven't told anyone what happened and I won't. What else do you want me to say? How many ways can I swear?"

Bianca did not answer and Alexa stalked off. She did not need this. She did not need more drama in her life. She did not even need her roommates taking sides over the issue. It became so hostile that, by the end of the first week, tensions in their room were at breaking point.

Martha and Bianca had been sniping at each other the whole week. Martha and Natalie were still livid over Bianca's comments on the first day of term, and Bianca was still glaring at Alexa every time she saw her.

"Hey, guys," said Lizzie in a soft and polite voice that only partially concealed her annoyance. "This is really crazy. Seriously, I've spoken to both of you," she said, looking between Alexa and Bianca. "You both want to be friends again and, Bianca, Alexa's apologised."

"Not that she has anything to apologise for," snarled Martha from her desk, earning her an exasperated look from Lizzie.

"It's really not fun in this room with everyone so angry," said Lizzie, continuing on the diplomatic pathway. "We all have to be here for the rest of the year. Can't you get past – whatever this is – and be friends again? For us?"

Lizzie's words seemed to have the desired effect. Bianca's shoulders dropped and she slowly looked up at everyone.

"I'm sorry for what I said on Monday. It was really unfair. I'm sorry, Alexa," said Bianca, her eyes dropping back down to the floor.

"It's doesn't matter. Forget about it," replied Alexa. She just wanted it to be over.

They continued working in that atmosphere of an unstable truce until six-thirty, when everyone closed their books to make their way to the dining hall. Bianca was slow packing up so Alexa waited, keen to dispel the rest of the tension between them.

"Alexa," said Bianca quietly when everyone else had left. "Can I talk to you about something?"

"Sure," replied Alexa hesitantly, seeing the look on Bianca's face.

"I think I'm pregnant."

Everything was still for a moment and Alexa wondered if this had been the real reason for Bianca's bad mood all week.

"To Chad?" Alexa asked automatically, though she had never supposed otherwise until the words had already left her mouth.

"I don't know," gasped Bianca desperately.

Alexa held her tongue and wrapped her arms around Bianca's heaving shoulders.

***

Marcus sat at his desk rubbing his temples. The headache that had started two days ago was now throbbing painfully behind his eyes. If he and Jackie had not had another fight, he would have just gone home. One week – that was all they had lasted. One week, one mention of Alexa's name and it had begun. He was glad Jackie suspected nothing more than an unhealthy obsession, but he could not really argue with the terminology. This week had been filled with nothing but Alexa.

It felt as though he had spoken to almost every student in the grade about her this week, leading off with Stacey and Chris. They were the first to abuse him for what Alexa had suffered in the grade meeting. Their defence of Alexa had surprised Marcus. He had never really considered them friends.

"We're not," said Stacey. "But you don't get lumped in together for six years without getting to know each other. Alexa, she doesn't deserve this – probably less than any of us."

"What do you mean?" asked Marcus.

"I mean, in the beginning, she never caused any trouble – ever – not on purpose anyway. She was just an easy target. Everyone knew her history. By the end of the first day we all knew about her mother and the foster families. Who knows who spread it, cos Alexa didn't speak. I don't even think she had friends for the first few months."

"Then how did she get into trouble?" asked Marcus quickly, wanting to know more.

"It started small," said Chris. "You could see that she just didn't know what to do. I remember seeing her. It was almost comical how foreign she looked – out of place. She got teased a lot and the teachers, they didn't help her. They just hammered her when she did stuff wrong – and it didn't have to be real wrong either."

"I feel bad now," said Stacey, looking truly ashamed. "I used to laugh at her – tease her too – none of us could believe that there was all this stuff she had never seen and done. Never used a computer. Had really old, daggy clothes that you could tell had never been bought for her. It wasn't fair how mean we were."

Marcus was impressed by Stacey's admission. Kids had always been cruel. The school yard was not the place where anyone wanted to feel ostracised, but as much as everyone could remember the times they were left out and slighted, it was a thousand times harder to look back and acknowledge that you had been responsible for making another person feel that way.

"The other thing was that Alexa never dobbed anyone in," said Chris. "People noticed that real quick when she got in trouble for stuff she didn't do. If the teachers asked, Alexa always denied it – unless she had done it. The teachers hated it when she denied stuff they thought she did."

"It was really horrible," said Stacey. "But no one wanted to get in trouble so they never stuck up for her – except for Sam," she added with a smile. "Alexa just copped the punishment and went on with everything. That was when some people who knew she would never dob them in started to use her to get out of trouble. But that didn't really last that long," she said fiercely.

"Why not?" asked Marcus.

"Because once they formed the G7, we looked out for each other," explained Chris firmly. "Especially Alexa. They really had it in for her after that."

"They?"

"The school," replied Stacey bitterly. "After that thing in year seven. They made the G7 – something that never existed – but we existed after that. We stuck up for each other, but mostly for Alexa. She's the one who needed it the most – especially after what happened that day."

Marcus waited anxiously for Stacey or Chris to divulge more, but when they remained silent he was forced to ask questions. That incident had been much spoken about over the years, but no one was really sure who or what to believe. Consequently, the G7 had remained a dividing force among the staff.

"We just all happened to be outside Mr Markson's office," said Stacey. "I think Sam, Chad and Alexa were in trouble. Sam had a rather annoying habit of trying to get himself kicked out of every class Alexa was. Nick and Alan were there to ask something. Chris and me were just there to sort out something – we don't even remember what any more. It was really just coincidence that we were all there at the same time.

"Anyway, when Mr Markson saw all of us, he just lost it and started telling us to go away. Told us he would have to deal with Sam, Chad and Alexa, but the rest of us would have to come back another time."

"We told him we didn't mind waiting," said Chris, when Stacey's pause continued on. "But he just went on about us leaving stuff to the last minute and not having the time to deal with all of us. When Stacey told him that he had already sent us away three times that fortnight Mr Markson started yelling and pointing his finger in her face – and I mean right in her face. Stacey pushed his hand away. That's when he grabbed her wrist. We could all see how tight he was squeezing it and twisting it. He then pulled her into his office. We were yelling, but it was Alexa who grabbed Stacey.

"She seriously just grabbed Stacey's whole body and wrenched Mr Markson's hand off her. Alexa stood there – in between Stacey and Mr Markson. She never said anything, just guarded Stacey. When Mr Markson took a step forward, Alexa pushed him back."

"Why'd he step forward? To grab Stacey again?" asked Marcus, his heart thumping as he imagined the scene. It did sound very much like Alexa.

"I don't think so," replied Stacey, looking sightly guilty about that fact. "But Alexa was just so protective. Mr Markson grabbed her and she struggled to pull free. When he let her go she fell and hit her face against his desk. She just jumped straight up and stood in front of me and asked me if I was okay."

"And that was when the others attacked Mr Markson?" asked Marcus.

"We never attacked him," replied Chris emphatically. "The

was yelling. There was abuse and threats, but we never laid a hand on him. Stacey and Alexa were both bruised, but still Mrs Taylor wanted to blame us for what happened. It was only because we stuck together and stuck to telling the truth that all this ever happened."

Marcus spent the best part of the next half an hour convincing Stacey and Chris that it had never been his intention for anyone to find out about him quitting as their year advisor. It was a story he retold many times that week as student after student came by to discuss something else, but always ended up asking.

If the students were going to ask their questions, Marcus decided he would ask some of his own. The answers were remarkably similar. Alexa was quiet and hard to get to know, but fiercely protective of her friends. The report from the school psychologist concurred on nearly every point.

Alexa is a mixture of defiance, distrust and defensiveness that makes her incredibly difficult to work with. She can be pleasant and interactive on topics of her own choosing and uses distraction and questions to move the conversation away from topics that are uncomfortable for her. When pressed, she closes off and regaining her trust is almost impossible. Sessions were discontinued after three sessions of complete silence on Alexa's behalf.

In one way, Marcus knew more about Alexa than he ever had, but for the most part everyone had just confirmed his own observations. Alexa had been a quiet and generally studious student in his year seven geography class. She had made no effort to distinguish herself and had always responded politely when asked a question.

Looking back, Marcus struggled to pull out any real memories of her from that class. His reports for her that year were fairly standard. It had been his first year of teaching and survival had been his main aim. It surprised him that once upon a time he had found Alexa so unremarkable. So much had changed since then.

That politeness had worn, and Marcus had borne the brunt of Alexa's defiance and defensiveness, but there was something he had gained. Amazingly, he had somehow gained Alexa's trust – and even her affections. He had managed to break down one of the biggest barriers between them and the pounding of his head was not made any better by the thought of how many other barriers he wished he could banish.

Realising none of the drugs the school nurse could dispense would do anything to ease his throbbing headache, Marcus grabbed his car keys and headed for the door. He knew he could, and should, just walk to the chemist, but his head was pounding and he just wanted relief. It was a dangerous move.

Pulling up in front of the chemist, Marcus could not even remember the route he took or if he had noticed the colour of the last set of lights he had driven through. He was in a complete daze until he felt himself slam into a poor lady who was just trying to leave the store. She stumbled as she tried to move around him and he quickly grabbed her shoulders to ensure she did not fall. Looking down to apologise, his heart suddenly stopped.

"Alexa! What the hell are you doing here?" Marcus asked, his heart now pounding out of time with his head.

Alexa's mouth opened, but she could not articulate an answer. Marcus noticed she was holding a bag and grabbed it out of her hands. He could not believe she could be this stupid – or arrogant – whichever it was.

Then everything stopped.

"Can you get back into the school undetected?" Marcus asked, barely able to breath.

"Yes, Sir," replied Alexa meekly.

"You will go straight to my office, no detours. Do you understand?"

"Yes, Sir."

Alexa turned and ran towards school. Marcus squeezed the bag in his hand tighter as he returned to his car, forgetting all about his headache. The strange and uncomfortable ache in his chest was the greater problem now. He tried to steady his breathing as he drove, desperate not to connect the dots, but they were so close together they virtually formed their own line.

Pregnant.

Alexa thought she was pregnant. But to who, he wondered.

Sam.

Hatred and anger boiled up in Marcus's mouth. That stupid, irresponsible slime. He could not believe Sam could be so reckless as to put Alexa in this situation – and then leave her to deal with it on her own.

Pacing back and forth in front of his office, Marcus tried not to think of how much he wished that if anyone had put Alexa in this position that it had at least been himself. He knew he could take

care of her, but he also knew that he could never have done it –
never have touched her that way no matter how he felt about her.

Pregnant again. Twice in two years. Marcus knew would have
to counsel Alexa on this. He refused to let her throw her life away.

When Alexa raced up the stairs, Marcus could only point to his
office. He noticed that Alexa flinched when he slammed the door
harder than he had intended.

"You had better have some remarkable explanation, Alexa, or
you're in some serious trouble," Marcus said, trying to contain his
anger.

Alexa looked straight into his furious eyes. She held his gaze
with the most tender look he had ever seen. He could that see she
was scared and was trying hard to hold at bay the defensiveness
that her fear always stirred.

"Why don't we start with these, then?" Marcus continued in a
softer and more comforting voice as he held up the pregnancy tests.

"They're not for me," replied Alexa simply, not dropping her
gaze.

Marcus went to speak, but stopped, thrown by Alexa's
statement.

"Then what the hell were you doing out there? If they're not for
you, then why were you out of school buying them? Who are they
for?" he asked finally, when the shock had worn off and allowed
him to think clearly.

"Does it really matter who they're for? They're not mine. That's
what you really wanted to know," retorted Alexa, the defiance
creeping back into her voice.

"Of course that's what I wanted to know. After what happened
last year, of course I wanted to know," Marcus replied, rubbing his
face in his hands, trying not to see the hopeless, dead look on
Alexa's face after he had pulled her back from the edge of the
platform. "But now I want to know who these are for. Don't you
understand? If it had been any teacher but me – if we had been seen
together, outside of school, with pregnancy tests! Damn it, Alexa, I
should expel you for this. You know I'm supposed to."

"You know I'm not pregnant, so why don't you?" asked Alexa
defiantly.

Marcus knew she was waiting for him to let her down and give
her a reason to distrust him.

"Because I have fought long and hard to keep you in this school
and it's clear that you were out there tonight for someone else," he

said passionately. "Why would you risk being expelled for someone else?"

"Don't you understand? If you hadn't been there, by some freak coincidence, I would've been in and out undetected. I wasn't running away, I was just trying to help a friend."

"What happened to you keeping out of trouble?" Marcus asked with a hint of desperation.

"I didn't think I'd get into trouble. I didn't want to do it, but I had to," replied Alexa, as though that were a reasonable explanation.

Marcus knew he had to be tougher on Alexa and demand better explanations, but she was answering his questions. It was so much more than he had received this time last year.

"Then tell me why you risked your place in this school for a person who just this week ridiculed and embarrassed you in front of the whole grade?" asked Marcus, finally putting all the pieces together.

"You don't understand," sighed Alexa.

"No, I don't. After what you went through, no, I don't understand."

"Listen, please just let me take the tests. If you want to make my life easier, then just let me give her the tests. I'll take whatever punishment you give me. Just keep everyone else out of it."

"I don't want to punish you, Alexa. I can't, not without tipping off Mrs Taylor. No, I will give you these," said Marcus, holding up the tests. "But I want you to promise me something in return."

"What?" asked Alexa warily, folding her arms and looking past him.

"That if this happens again – if you need something from outside of school, if you need to leave, if something happens – I don't care what it is or how you think I might react – you have to come and see me *before* you break the rules. I have fought too long and too hard for your place in this school and I don't want to have to punish you. I don't want to be the one to catch you and have to turn you in. Please, will you promise me?"

Alexa did not respond. She simply nodded her head. Marcus handed her the bag and indicated she could leave. She turned at once, almost rushing to escape, but then hesitated at the door.

"I'm sorry – for causing you so much trouble," she said, then closed the door behind her before he could respond.

***

The room was quiet and tense as Bianca dashed to the bathroom and slammed the door. Alexa sat at her desk and waited. She had wanted Bianca to take the test last night – given the trouble the trip had landed her in – but Bianca insisted that no one else could be around. Alexa had hoped that they would then just wait until everyone was at breakfast, but again Bianca was too paranoid that someone would return unexpectedly. Instead, they had waited until the whole school was filing into the hall for the usual Monday morning assembly, and Alexa knew there was no way they were not going to be late. This was hardly keeping her promise to Marcus – Mr Knight, she reminded herself again. Why did he have to continue being so nice and understanding?

"I'm not pregnant," sighed Bianca, walking out of the bathroom and sitting on her bed to face Alexa.

"That's really good. Now you can relax," replied Alexa, unsure if she was more relieved or annoyed.

"But I'm still late," added Bianca with consternation.

"It's just stress. I'm sure of it, but I bought a second test so if nothing happens you can do the test again next week or something," Alexa replied, pushing up from the desk.

"What if I'm still pregnant and the test just didn't pick it up?"

"We'll work something out. It'll be okay. Come on, we'd better get to assembly," said Alexa, though she noticed her response seemed to annoy Bianca.

Alexa and Bianca slipped into the hall under the watchful glare of all the teachers, none more so than Mrs Taylor, who was standing on stage with a malicious grin.

"I'm glad you could finally join us, Miss Samson. We aren't keeping you from anything, are we?" Mrs Taylor smiled nastily down at Alexa as she sat herself down in the last row.

Mr Knight was staring at her, before flicking his gaze to Bianca then back again. Alexa shook her head just slightly. His face transformed into a stony mask as he turned his attention back to Mrs Taylor.

"It seems five weeks of detention last year did very little for your manners, so why don't we try a week of cleaning the grounds after school," smiled Mrs Taylor viciously. "Miss Ross, you should join her, since you don't yet seem to have learned the trouble being associated with Miss Samson will get you into."

Alexa tried not to let the expression on her face change and continued to look straight ahead, but from the corner of her eye she saw Bianca angrily cross her arms and throw her a mutinous glare. Alexa closed her eyes and tried to block out her surrounds, hoping everything would be better when she opened them again.

"Looks like we're set for some fun in the sun this afternoon, huh?" said Alexa cheerily, catching up with Bianca after assembly, trying to put the best spin on the situation.

"Yeah, great fun." Bianca stopped walking and looked at her as though unsure whether she should speak or not. "If we'd come in separately, I wouldn't have even gotten into trouble."

"What?"

"You knew you were always going to get into trouble. You should've let me go in alone first and then I wouldn't have to clean this stupid school this afternoon."

"I risked my neck for you last night and stayed with you this morning for support," cried Alexa, unable to believe what Bianca was saying. "You know what, screw it. I'm over it. Don't bother asking me for help again."

Alexa stormed off before she could tell Bianca what she really thought of her. The day did not improve and all Alexa wanted was some time alone in the bathroom with her razor, but there was never a chance. When the bell rang for the end of class, she packed up her bags and walked slowly towards Mr Knight's office, wondering what he was going to say today.

"Hey, wait up," called Bianca. Alexa slowly turned to see Bianca jogging up to her with a half-smile on her face. "I want to apologise for this morning. I was just still really freaked out about the thought of being pregnant."

"But you're over it now?" asked Alexa, completely unconvinced.

"Yeah, definitely," smiled Bianca. Alexa looked at her with an air of distrust. "They came at lunch time. I'm definitely not pregnant."

"That's good," nodded Alexa.

"I really am sorry. I shouldn't have been so mean to you. You did do everything I asked of you."

Alexa was thankful Mr Knight was waiting outside his office for them with a pile of garbage bags so that she could delay her conversation with Bianca. There was so much she knew she should not say.

"Six-thirty, ladies," said Mr Knight sternly, handing them the garbage bags. "And I will want to talk to both of you afterwards."

Alexa took the bags without looking up, her heart stuttering with the fear of what Mr Knight might let slip in front of Bianca. However, when she walked out into the grounds, she was able to forget her concerns for a short while. The afternoon was so warm and bright that Alexa actually enjoyed strolling around filling her bags with rubbish. This was definitely one of her favoured punishments.

Bianca was not so easily convinced and their tentative truce was quickly broken when they came to yet another tossed bin and strewn rubbish. Bianca refused to believe that it was students helping them out and not causing them more grief. Truth was, without tossed bins, they never had enough rubbish to pick up and had always had to resort to emptying bins.

The sun was starting to lose its intensity as it rounded on six-thirty. Alexa did not want to return to Mr Knight's office alone, but she had not seen Bianca since she stormed off two and a half hours earlier. Alexa collected the five full bags of rubbish she had gathered and dragged them towards the year advisor tower, leaving them at the bottom and climbing the stairs to Mr Knight's office.

"Half a bag in three hours? What exactly have you been doing all this time?" yelled Mr Knight.

Alexa could only assume he was talking to Bianca, though she could not see either of them.

"This is stupid. I shouldn't even be here," said Bianca sulkily.

"You're here because you were late to assembly and this was your punishment," countered Mr Knight.

"Hi," interrupted Alexa. "Bianca's bags are downstairs. She wasn't feeling well so I said I would carry them for her." Mr Knight looked ready to challenge her. "I have three bags, Bianca has two and a half."

"That's all for three hours?" asked Mr Knight disbelievingly.

"We can't create rubbish that isn't there," Alexa replied defiantly.

"Fine, Miss Ross, you can go. Miss Samson, my office."

Bianca stalked off. Alexa watched her go with a growing feeling of emptiness. If not for Chad and Ezra, she was not sure she would speak to Bianca again.

"Now, are you going to tell me why you covered for Miss Ross – again?" asked Mr Knight as soon as they were in his office.

"Because she's my friend," replied Alexa automatically, though she was not sure that was entirely true.

"Really? After last week? After last night? After today? Did you even tell her about being caught last night?" asked Mr Knight in a passionate tone that Alexa did not find particularly teacher-like.

It was sweet that he cared about her welfare so much, but Alexa really did not need him fighting her battles for her. She had never brought people in over the top before and refused to now.

"I'm trying to keep my friendships, not destroy them. It'd help if you remembered that as well," Alexa retorted, though she knew it really was not his job to keep her rocky friendships together.

"All right. There is something else we need to talk about," sighed Mr Knight. He paused and the look on his face made Alexa's heart pound. "The police want to talk to you about Mr Marsh. The trial's set down for a few months and they need to discuss a few things with you."

Alexa felt the room spin sickeningly and had to hold on to the chair to make sure she did not fall. She had never given any thought to a trial.

"Are you all right, Alexa?" asked Mr Knight kindly.

"I'll have to testify, won't I?" she asked hesitantly.

"Yes. Peter Lam will be here tomorrow afternoon to talk to you about it. The police will be by after dinner."

"Will you be there?" Alexa asked, unsure if she wanted him to be or not.

"No," replied Mr Knight solemnly. "I have to testify myself and Peter wants to discuss things with you alone, but I told Peter you can use my office for your meetings. Nice to at least be somewhere familiar. Better than going to the police station."

"I don't think I want to do this," gasped Alexa, not able to appreciate the concessions Mr Knight had made for her.

"I know, but Clinton Marsh deserves to go to gaol for what he did to you," replied Mr Knight supportively. "You'll be just fine. Peter will meet you after you've served your detention."

"So I don't get out of it?" Alexa asked, looking up with a faint smile.

"Nice try, but no, you still have to clean the school," said Mr Knight, smiling back. It was nice the way he could make these horrible moments bearable.

The dining hall was beginning to empty when Alexa finally arrived. Sam, Chad, Bianca and Lizzie were all seated at one table.

Alexa did not want to join them, but knew it would draw more attention and questions if she sat at another table.

"I'm surprised you didn't try and have Mr Knight get you out of your punishment. I'm sure you could've persuaded him," said Bianca in a cool manner when Alexa sat down with her food.

Alexa had heard enough from Bianca that day not to bite back, and simply concentrated harder on her dinner.

"I don't know what your problem is," said Chad in amazement. "Alexa just covered for you after you've been nothing but rude to her all week and you still want to attack her. What's she done? I've been trying really hard to stick by you, but Alexa's been my friend since we started here and I've never known her to do anything to deserve the crap you've given her this week."

Bianca looked stunned and so was Alexa. It had only ever been Sam who had stood up for her so publicly.

"Well let's all hail Alexa," spat Bianca. "Looks like she has every guy wrapped around her little finger. She could get away with anything with all the men she has on her side. And she does."

Bianca stormed from the dining hall to the sounds of excited whispers. Alexa abandoned her dinner and marched after her.

"What did I do? What the hell did I ever do to you?" pleaded Alexa, flinging Bianca around when she finally caught up with her on the oval.

"You do whatever you want and never pay the consequences," replied Bianca angrily. "Everyone still stands by you. Everyone sticks up for you. You have the whole world on your side, yet you're still seen as poor little Alexa."

"What consequences do you think I've escaped?" Alexa questioned, unable to believe her ears.

"If I'd been pregnant, I would've lost everything. I would've been seen as the slut who couldn't stick to one guy, but you – the girl who's been with a thousand men – you would've been pitied by everyone."

Bianca's tone was so angry and accusatory that it could not help but strike deep. Alexa felt her lungs gasping as her body quivered.

"Our situations were completely different," Alexa replied, though her voice was barely more than a whisper. "You're not pregnant, you never were. How can you be angry with me for what might have been? I was pregnant and I didn't blame anyone for my situation but me."

"But nothing would've happened. Nothing ever does to you,"

snarled Bianca. "You get away with everything."

"What exactly do you think I get away with?" Alexa asked, trying to keep at bay the memories that were stinging her eyes. "I was the one that was almost killed for my stupidity in dating a teacher. What, do you think I should have been expelled or perhaps you think I should've died? Do you really think this way about me? I thought we were friends.

"I've never thought badly of you, at any stage, and if your boyfriend was not a good friend of mine there'd be no problem. But in the end I've stood by you and kept my word to you and risked my place in this school for you. So I don't really feel as though I have done anything wrong here."

Alexa turned and ran away, not remotely interested in any reply Bianca might have. If she never spoke to Bianca again it would be too soon.

"Alexa, wait," called Bianca, as she reached the dormitory doors. "I'm sorry. God, I'm so sorry. I have no idea what's wrong with me. I just keep getting so angry and I can't stop it. All these stupid things pour out of my mouth and I just can't stop them."

"I've been through more than you could ever know," Alexa cried, spinning around to face Bianca. "I've paid for the mistakes I've made, sometimes very dearly. I didn't just lose my child. Clinton killed it. He hit me until I miscarried," she finally confessed, hating that she was defending herself this way. "I know how scary it is to think you're pregnant, but don't you dare tell me that I haven't paid for my mistakes."

"I didn't know. I'm sorry. Please –"

"That's the point, isn't it?" snapped Alexa. "I don't want the world pitying me. I don't want everyone knowing about my life, but I've done my best to stick by you this last week and I've gotten nothing but grief."

"I know. I'm so sorry. Please forgive me and let me make it up to you. I can't say sorry many more times, but I am. I really am."

Alexa truly did not care if Bianca was sincere or not. She just wanted the fighting to stop. She had much bigger problems to face than Bianca's irrational anger. The fear of what was to come even saw he keep herself awake most of the night – just to draw out the time and prevent those hours from passing any faster than they had to.

"Hello, Alexa," said Peter, smiling as she entered Mr Knight's office after she had finished her detention.

No matter how hard she had tried, time had marched mercilessly on. Mr Knight had waited outside for her, but done nothing more than take her garbage bags from her and order Bianca to go and put them in the big skip bin.

"I doubted you'd be too happy to see me so I thought I would bribe you with some dinner," continued Peter with a somewhat sombre tone.

"You always knew the way to my cooperation was food," replied Alexa, trying not to let on just how unhappy she was to see Peter.

"Well sit down and we can start with the food, I guess."

Alexa did not have to be told twice. She ate heartily, thinking only about the food. The one thing she did like about Peter was that when he did feed her, it was always with good food. She did not even know what most of the food was that she was filling her stomach with, except that it was Asian and tasted good. Peter smiled warmly at her when she finished off the last of the food.

"Before we get started, I think I owe you an apology," said Peter as he cleared away the containers. "I feel in part responsible for what happened to you last year. I was here. I was listening to you talk to Clinton and we should've intervened earlier. It should never have been allowed to go on for as long as it did. You should never have been hurt the way you were."

"I don't blame you. It was the only option we had. I wanted him gone too," replied Alexa. She barely remembered what had been said that day and hated that Peter and Mr Knight had heard it all.

"I should give you an idea of what's happening," nodded Peter, switching into lawyer mode. Alexa always felt more comfortable when he spoke to her on a professional level. "Clinton wants to face the charges. He's saying he counselled you, admits taking you to his apartment and even admits that the relationship may have been a little inappropriate, but that it was never physical or sexual and that he never raped you. He will claim you made it all up to get out of trouble after running away. He obviously cannot deny the attempted manslaughter, though they will try to talk their way out of it."

"How's he going to explain trying to kill me?" Alexa asked tentatively, not sure she wanted the answer.

"As far as I know, they're going to claim that, because he never had a relationship with you or raped you, that he flew into a rage at your accusations."

"So he wants to say that it was all my fault."

"They'll try to," acknowledged Peter. "But you have to remember we do have the recording of the attack, and that is very much in your favour. The things he said – the way he acted – he never denied anything."

"But he never admitted anything either, did he?" asked Alexa, and Peter shook his head solemnly. "So there's no evidence for our relationship or the rape, is there?"

"No direct evidence, no."

Alexa was not sure she wanted to continue. The whole thing had been traumatic enough the first time and it had all been useless in the end. She did not want to be blamed for everything that had happened – tell her story just to have everyone call her a liar. She did not want to be told that she deserved everything Clinton had done to her.

"I don't want to do this. I don't want to go to court so that everyone can tell me it was my fault," she gasped, shaking her head.

"This isn't easy, I know, but you cannot give up now and let him get away with what he did to you."

"No, I only told Mr Knight so he could make Clinton stop," cried Alexa. "That's all I wanted. I didn't sign up for any of this. I can't do it."

Alexa rushed towards the door. Peter followed, placing a restraining hand on her shoulder as she tried to open the door.

"We can't make you do this and I won't blame you if you really can't handle it, but if Clinton Marsh goes free he will do it again. He'll just hurt another girl and she will have to go through what you're going through now."

Alexa thought of Clinton raping Mel and of Sam's anger at her for allowing it to happen. She did not want to imagine a world where Sam was not her friend, so slowly nodded and allowed Peter to lead her back to her chair.

The police arrived as Alexa sat trying to convince herself that she could do what was being asked of her. She had not spoken to anyone about Clinton since his arrest and had tried hard never to think of him. Now she was being asked to talk to the police and face a courtroom. It was a shock she should have expected, but she had been so happy that Clinton was out of her life that it never occurred to her that he would have to go to trial and that she would have to testify.

"Hello, Alexa," said Constable Banks pleasantly as he entered the office. Alexa could not smile, but was glad they had sent a familiar face. It made her wonder if they had assigned him the Redgrove cop and if everyone at his station hated him. "This is Detective Laura Mathews."

Alexa glared at them, hating the fact they were standing before her, knowing what they would ask. She just wished there was a way to punish Clinton without her having to talk about what he had done to her.

Peter ushered the officers into Mr Knight's bedroom to talk. They spoke in low voices so Alexa would not hear them, though she hardly bothered to listen. This was the last place she wanted to be and unless they were saying she could go, she was not interested. When they emerged, the officers sat on the opposite side of the desk from her, while Peter moved to the chair next to her.

"Are you up to answering some questions?" asked Detective Mathews.

"If I have to," replied Alexa, not looking up from her lap.

Detective Mathews obviously took that as a yes and immediately began her questioning. It was relentless. Alexa felt as though she was under attack. Detective Mathews and Constable Banks wanted to know everything. They asked questions about how her relationship with Clinton had started and why she had become involved with him in the first place. Alexa tried to remember what she had told the police the year before, but it was hard. She had purposely avoided thinking about it. All she knew was that she had never mentioned Ms Carter and her vicious assaults, or Clinton's promise to make them stop.

It was hard to come up with reasons why she would date Clinton without revealing that history. She would have been tempted to confess, except for the fact that Detective Mathews had already highlighted the problem her omission of the pregnancy in the original police interviews was going to cause. It was too late to set the record completely straight and Alexa did not want to talk about Ms Carter or the pain her cane had inflicted. Making out like there had been a conspiracy between Clinton and Ms Carter to get her to date him would simply sound too unbelievable.

Chapter Five

THE EVENING WAS more torturous than Alexa imagined, and she had expected it to be very unpleasant. When she was finally allowed to return to her room at nearly eleven o'clock, she was tired and angry. Even saying goodbye to Peter had been beyond her as she stalked out of Mr Knight's office. Walking into her room, Alexa was not pleased by the sight of Bianca waiting anxiously for her return. The last thing she wanted to do now was talk.

"Where have you been all night? Are you in more trouble?" asked Bianca, following her to her bed.

"I just want to go to bed. I'll talk to you later," replied Alexa, not looking at Bianca. She did not even want to say that much.

"Are you still mad at me?"

"No, I'm – look, I just had to talk to the police about Clinton," Alexa replied in a hurried voice, still refusing to look Bianca's way. "His trial's coming up in a couple of months. So please, don't get annoyed at me, because I really don't want to talk about it."

Bianca let her go and Alexa was glad. She did not have the patience to be nice, and did not need more fights.

When the morning came, Alexa's mood had not improved. She ignored everyone and kept her head down, so was surprised by just how nice everyone was being to her.

"You know?" Alexa asked softly, looking up between Chad and Sam.

They nodded and offered their support. Alexa was just thankful their support did not come with questions. Sam was the most comforting. Now that she had spoken, he moved to her side and pulled her into his arms. He continued to offer his shoulder at every opportunity and Alexa accepted it. She needed the security of his embrace.

Peter and the police came back twice more that week and planned to continue their thrice-weekly visits. Detective Mathews was unrelenting in her questioning, with the interrogation moving from Alexa's pregnancy, to her rape and through to her prostitution. By the end of the week Alexa was thoroughly depressed. She did not like talking about her failed pregnancy or reliving the rape, and did not feel the need to defend her decision to stay in the city to try and get Bethany clean. It was a decision she would make again.

There was nowhere in the world Alexa would rather be than with Bethany, irrespective of what she had to do to be there. However, she also knew that no one was going to let her go back, and if she left they would know where to find her. She was trapped, caged in now by more than bars and rules. It did not endear her to this life she was being forced to live.

So instead of spending her weekend studying as she needed to, Alexa wandered aimlessly around the school trying to clear her mind of the memories she was being forced to relive. As she rounded the corner to the back of the gym, the sight of Bianca and Chad in more than a passionate embrace greeted her. She backed away as quietly as she could, embarrassed to have witnessed such a sight.

"Cute, isn't it?" asked a disgusted voice behind Alexa, causing her to jump in fright. She turned to see Mel leaning against the side gym wall. "So in love. You have to wonder if he'd still want to screw her if he knew what a slut she was."

"*What* is your problem?" asked Alexa.

It was clear Mel somehow knew about Bianca cheating on Chad, and Alexa hoped that Mel would not use it to cause more trouble for her. It did not even matter that it had nothing to do with her. She knew Mel could somehow twist things so it affected her the most.

"The only problem I have is right in front of me," snarled Mel.

"Then get over it," Alexa retorted.

"No, not while Clinton's still in gaol and you're still out here enjoying your life. Do you know what's happened to him while he's been in gaol?"

"Nothing more than he deserves, I'm sure."

"Wrong answer," hissed Mel angrily, pushing Alexa and becoming more agitated by the second. "He was denied bail. He'll have to stay in gaol until his trial. You're the reason he's there and don't think I will ever forget that."

"He's the reason he's in gaol. I didn't make him rape me. I didn't make him wrap his hands around my throat and try and kill me."

"That was you! That was you trying to hide your filthy little secret. You'll pay for what you did to him – what you did to us."

"You can't still think that you and Clinton are a good idea. Don't you know what kind of person he is, what he'll do to you?"

"What you don't seem to be able to grasp is the difference between the two of us," replied Mel agitatedly, shoving Alexa again. "You're a slut, a worthless piece of crap and that's the way he treated you. Clinton and me have something special and I will stand by him."

"Then go and stand by him and leave me the hell alone," Alexa cried, pointing away from her, hoping Mel would just leave.

"I will never leave you alone until Clinton is free."

"Nothing I say or do could save him anyway," Alexa replied desperately. If it bought her peace, she would almost agree to set him free. "The police won't drop the attempted murder charge just because I ask them to."

"Really? They'll have nothing if you refuse to testify," retorted Mel.

"Why the hell would I do that? I'm not going to sit back and let him go free so that he can hurt someone else," said Alexa, trying to convince herself of Peter's logic.

"Your delusions are incredible. There's no one else in his life but me. You were nothing more than a failed project," cried Mel, before her voice became more threatening. "You'd better start thinking about how bad your life will be if you testify. You deserve everything you got."

"You can go to hell."

"Now, now, don't be like that," said Mel, her voice suddenly calm and sickly sweet. "You just remember to tell them that you won't testify or I'll make sure your life is a living hell."

Mel walked off, leaving Alexa shaking. She did not like to believe anything Mel said, but it was hard. Walking back around the rear of the gym, she was relieved to see that Chad and Bianca had left.

It had been a long time since she had lifted a razor to her arm. Mr Knight's revelation of his feelings for her the previous year had been able to halt the self-inflicted attacks, and the support of the Whites had been enough to cease them completely. Now, for the first time in many months, she examined her arm in minute detail. She put her hand in her other pocket and pulled out her razor.

"Shouldn't you be at dinner?" called a voice from the end of the gym.

Alexa quickly pushed the razor back into her pocket as she

looked up to see Mr Knight standing just a few metres away.

"It's before curfew. I can be anywhere I want," she sneered, hating that he had the power to tell her what to do, and seemed prepared to.

"Yes, but this is not a place I'm happy for you to be. Convince me that you weren't about to do what I think you were."

Alexa looked up at Mr Knight, trying her best to keep her face defiant. Mr Knight kept looking into her eyes until she could hold the stare no longer and hung her head between her knees. He sat down next to her, leaving a decent gap between them.

"How long's it been?" Mr Knight asked gently.

"Since last term – when you saw my arms," Alexa replied softly, not looking up.

"Is this really what you want to do? You could always give the talking option a go. I'm willing to listen."

"Talking won't solve anything," she muttered angrily.

"No, maybe not," replied Mr Knight quickly, and Alexa was glad he conceded that point. "But it will keep your arms uncut. That's motive enough for me. Just try me. I'm not offering to solve your problems. I'm just offering an ear."

The sun was starting to set as Alexa considered the value of talk. She did not want to tell Mr Knight about Mel, but was not sure how she would explain her feelings without doing so.

"You have to learn how to talk about things," said Mr Knight gently.

"Do you think I deserved what Clinton did to me?" Alexa asked, looking up briefly, but turning away before Mr Knight could meet her gaze. "I mean, not just at the end, but all of it."

"No," answered Mr Knight so quickly and forcefully that she had to look back up at him to see if he was lying. "That's the answer. No."

"But –"

"There are no buts," said Mr Knight over the top of her. "For a minute, let's just forget that he was your teacher and that the relationship itself wasn't permitted. There's nothing you did to deserve such treatment from a man, not any man. He was aggressive and uncaring even before his violent attacks."

"But I –"

"No, Alexa. There are no excuses," Mr Knight continued, refusing to let her make her qualification. "Nothing you did, nothing you have ever done could be enough to deserve such treatment from a man who was supposed to love you."

"He never told me he loved me," Alexa confessed, hanging her head. It had never been about love. It had been about protection.

"That's not the point," replied Mr Knight in a frustrated growl. "He was you boyfriend or whatever you want to call it. That means he was supposed to care about you and respect you."

"I just think that if I were a better person, he –"

"I don't ever want you to say anything like that ever again," Mr Knight snapped, grabbing her shoulders so that she turned to face him. "Clinton was a fool not to see what an amazing person you are. If you were mine, I ..."

Mr Knight turned away and let go of her shoulders. Alexa knew he would not finish the sentence, but she was touched by the sentiment. It was very sweet the way he saw something better in her, even if she could not see if herself.

"It is getting late. You should head back to your room," said Mr Knight in a flat voice that did not really seem like him. "There may be some dinner left if you want to try the dining hall."

"No, I want to stay here a while. I won't do anything to myself, I promise," replied Alexa, looking up into Mr Knight's eyes so he knew she was sincere.

"Do you want me to stay?"

"If you promise not to talk any more."

Mr Knight stayed seated and Alexa smiled softly at him. She was glad he wanted to stay. She tilted her head along the gym wall towards him. It was the closest she could allow herself be to him.

When the sun sunk out of sight Alexa curled her legs into her body against the sudden chill. Mr Knight – Marcus, she sighed internally – sat silently with his eyes closed and a slight smile upon his lips. She watched him in the fading light. She wanted to touch him, feel his hands and the warmth of his body. She wondered how a love so very wrong could feel so good and wished that there was some way they could be together.

"I'm going to go back to my room now," Alexa said, when Mr Knight opened his eyes. "Do you want to go first? I'll walk for a few more minutes before going inside."

Mr Knight nodded slowly, as if only then realising that they should not be sitting behind the gym together. Alexa smiled softly and thanked him before walking away, knowing that he would be the one against whom she would measure all other men in her future.

Despite everything Mr Knight had said to Alexa, it was Mel's voice that rang louder in her head and she seriously considered the idea of not testifying at Clinton's trial. Testifying was the last thing in the world she wanted to do. According to Mel, she was the only one Clinton wanted and he would never hurt her. Alexa decided to test the idea with her friends before suggesting it to Peter and the police, but they were all adamant she should testify and Clinton get the punishment he deserved. It was not what she had wanted to hear.

"Alexa, I hope you realise that we know how hard this is for you," said Detective Mathews when she returned for another round of questioning. It felt as though Detective Mathews had a complete spy network at the school. "Testifying against your rapist is very tough for victims and many cannot do it."

"I said I would, didn't I?" spat Alexa, folding her arms defensively. "Do I want to? No. I don't ever want to think about it again, but I said I would do it, okay."

"We just want to make sure you're all right," said Peter, placing a comforting hand on her shoulder.

"Can we just get on with it?" Alexa sighed, bowing her head.

Peter removed his hand from her shoulder. Alexa was glad he seemed to realise that to get through this she needed to disconnect from the world, and that even included the supportive parts of it.

"All right," said Detective Mathews, leaning forward to begin the interrogation. "You said Clinton's behaviour changed after an incident with your ex-boyfriend. Is that right?"

"Sam kissed me in class. I rejected him, but Clinton heard about it and was never the same after," sighed Alexa, refusing to meet anyone's eyes as she spoke.

"What changed?"

"He became really jealous. It was crazy. He was possessive and angry. That's when it stopped being nice."

"Was he violent?" asked Detective Mathews. Alexa nodded. "How?"

"It wasn't rape, but it wasn't nice any more," said Alexa, unsure of how to explain. "He was rough and wouldn't stop when I wanted him to. It felt like he made it hurt on purpose."

Peter closed his eyes and turned away, pinching the bridge of his nose with his fingers.

"What?" sighed Alexa. "What have I done wrong now?"

"You didn't want to have sex with him. He made you. He hurt you and he wouldn't stop when you asked him to. Alexa, that is rape," replied Peter in a soft voice Alexa had never heard before.

"No, I let him," Alexa replied, turning to Peter to urge him to understand. He had to know what she had allowed and what had been forced on her. Otherwise she feared everyone would believe she had asked for it all. "It would've been fine then if he'd just been nicer – not so angry. I didn't like it, but that wasn't when he raped me."

"Then why did you continue to see him? If you were no longer happy with him and he was hurting you, why not call it off?" asked Detective Mathews

"I was scared of what would happen," Alexa murmured, not daring to admit that she had had no idea how to call it off – how to walk away.

"Sam didn't know about Clinton?" asked Detective Mathews. Alexa shook her head. "But Clinton seemed to think that the baby wasn't his. Who'd he think the father was?" questioned Detective Mathews critically. "Sam?"

"Sam and Mr Knight were the only ones he ever mentioned," Alexa muttered, hating it when the questions circled back towards to her pregnancy.

"Mr Knight, your year advisor? Is there any reason why?" asked Detective Mathews in an intrigued voice.

"Clinton saw him taking me back to my room once when I was sick. Nothing happened."

"We need to know right now if there's anything going on between you and Mr Knight. Was the baby his? Was it Sam's? Are you sure it was really Clinton's?" questioned Detective Mathews, suddenly becoming very offensive.

"Of course I'm sure!" cried Alexa. "I know how babies are made and what you have to do to get pregnant. I wasn't with Sam then and nothing's going on with Mr Knight – then or now," she added desperately. "Do you think I go around fucking every goddamned teacher? Fuck."

"There's no reason to be so defensive, but we need to know. We can't go to court and find out that there's something going on."

"There's nothing going on," snapped Alexa.

"So if I start asking students and teachers about the two of you, they will all say it's the most ridiculous thing they've ever heard," queried Detective Mathews disbelievingly, her eyebrows raised. "This is not the first time Marcus Knight's name has come up in our investigation."

Guilt and fear began swirling in Alexa's stomach. The whole school was consumed by rumours about her and Mr Knight last year, and she was in love with him. He was engaged and destined for someone else, but she could not deny that Mr Knight cared for her.

"Alexa, we need to know. Whatever it is, we need to know," said Peter in a kind voice.

"Nothing ever happened between us, I swear," Alexa cried in a soft voice, looking up at Peter. "It's just that there've been rumours."

"And is there any truth to the rumours?" asked Detective Mathews, with a shake of the head and unimpressed eyes.

"I already said there wasn't. Fuck, are you dumb or something?" Alexa spat, turning to Detective Mathews.

Peter saw Alexa's rapidly swelling rage and quickly called a halt to the questioning.

"We're going to have to investigate this," said Detective Mathews darkly. "Are there any other rumours I should know about?"

"Go to hell," snapped Alexa, grabbing her bag and walking out, ignoring Peter's pleas to stay.

Detective Mathews and Constable Banks were regularly seen around the school over the next week, talking to virtually everyone Alexa had ever exchanged more than one word with. Bianca and Ezra were interviewed more than once, while Sam was grilled about the nature of his relationship with Alexa. Mr Knight was also a major target.

Suddenly, the focus of the investigation had switched from Clinton to Mr Knight, which only set the rumours swirling once more. By the time Detective Mathews finally resumed her meetings with Alexa, the rumours about her and Mr Knight were louder and more vicious than ever.

"You're quickly becoming the most incredible witness I have ever met," said Detective Mathews, skipping the pleasantries. "The defence will have an absolute field day with you. You allege that you were having a sexual relationship with Clinton Marsh, yet we can find no evidence to back your claim or any witnesses that saw the two of you together in that way.

"On the other hand, we have a whole school full of people, teachers included, who believe there is a distinct possibility that you and Marcus Knight are having an affair. Then of course we have your ex-boyfriend with whom you regularly share a bed. And let's not forget the fact that you were working as a prostitute at the time of the alleged rape."

"I have told you the truth," said Alexa, quivering with rage and fear.

"This is not about the truth."

"Then what the fuck is it about?" Alexa cried.

"It's about what we can prove and what a jury will believe, and right now I'm not sure they'd believe a single thing that comes from your mouth," replied Detective Mathews firmly. "And that's only the tip of the iceberg. You have misdemeanours running way back. You've been in and out of foster homes. You used to drink and steal. Your mother was a heroin addict. Your sister is a heroin addict. Then we go back to your father."

"Stop," said Peter jumping up from his seat. "There's no reason to bring that up."

"I think there is," retorted Detective Mathews. "She's been selective in her memories in this case and claimed not to remember anything about what happened during her father's trial. Is she going to have another sudden bout of amnesia when I put her on the stand?"

"She doesn't remember anything from back then. She still doesn't," said Peter in a warning tone.

"Then perhaps it's time to remind her, because right now she's going to be completely discredited. I can't risk this case by going into court with no idea what she's going to say."

"No! No one is going to force her to remember anything," said Peter in a low and dangerous voice, moving in between Alexa and Detective Mathews. "This case has absolutely nothing to do with that one and you know it."

Alexa slunk to the back of the room as Detective Mathews and Peter continued to argue about her. They seemed completely oblivious to her presence so she slipped out the door, not wanting to hear any more about how hideous her life was. The hallways were empty so no one stopped her as she ran out towards the oval, as though she could somehow out-pace her pain.

"Still considering testifying?" hissed Mel from behind as she stood heaving in the middle of the oval, unsure of where to go. "I met a lovely Detective. What was her name? Oh, that's right, Detective Mathews. It looks like she's my most recent convert to the 'Alexa is a Pathetic Piece of Trash' club. She was very interested in what I had to say about you considering how long I've known you."

Alexa turned to face Mel, who was smiling menacingly. It was a smile that reminded her so much of Clinton.

"Why don't you just get yourself a life and get the hell out of mine," Alexa screamed.

"You ruined my life and I will return the favour," replied Mel calmly. "You're going to be torn apart in court. Your whole horrid life will be laid bare for the world to see and by the end of it, it'll be clear to everyone that the person who should be locked away from society is not Clinton, but you."

Alexa did not want to believe Mel, but those words penetrated her deepest feelings of inferiority and worthlessness.

"The truth hurts, doesn't it?" snarled Mel. "How much support do you think you'll have after this trial? Everyone will know you for the slut you are."

"Get the hell away from me," cried Alexa, hunching her shoulders against Mel's attack, but for some reason she was unable to run away.

"They're not going to spare you a single bad memory, even the ones you've long forgotten. It seems you have a lifetime of people willing to testify that you're a pathetic, worthless piece of crap."

Alexa did not want to hear any more. Finally finding her feet, she pushed past Mel and ran towards the back of the gym.

"And that's just the trial," called Mel victoriously. "Just wait and see what I have ready for you here."

It was dark and lifeless behind the gym and bitter tears fell down Alexa's face at the memory of her afternoon with Mr Knight there against the gym wall. She knew it was the first place he would look for her so backtracked into the trees that lined the fence and climbed up into the branches of the tallest one.

Despite the cold breeze, Alexa yanked off her jumper and pulled out her razor. Without a second thought she pushed the blade into her left upper arm, beads of blood soon wrapping around and around her arm as she sliced into the skin. The familiar burn was like a drug and she welcomed the pain. When she reached her wrist she took the razor in her left hand and started on her right arm. By the time the blade reached the wrist of her right hand, anger and fear still pulsed through her body.

Unable to stop, Alexa pulled up her skirt and wrapped the razor around her leg. The virgin skin of her legs quickly prickled with pain, unaccustomed to this type of assault as the razor sliced through her skin, rapidly draining her of energy and emotion. It was not enough. She needed more. She needed to feel absolutely nothing. Leaning back awkwardly in the branches, Alexa pulled up her shirt and pressed the razor into her stomach. The cuts were long, deliberate and painful and after just four her hand was shaking with the effort of continuing.

Her white shirt spotted with blood, Alexa pulled her jumper over her red and burning arms, as her skirt clung to her bloodied legs. Slipping down out of the tree, she did not care that her body collected several more scratches as it scraped against the bark. She did not care about anything, thankful only for the empty and lifeless feeling that was consuming her and keeping her buffered from the world she did not care to be a part of.

The door to her room was open when she arrived, and she made her way straight to her bed, not sparing a glance for anyone in the room.

"Come on, Miss Samson. Come on, up you get. Peter's waiting for you in my office."

Alexa did not register the voice and did not comply until Mr Knight managed to turn her around and guide her towards the door. She could feel her feet moving below her, and her body moving forward even though she was not willing it to do so. When they reached Mr Knight's office, Alexa sunk immediately into the seat in front of his desk as Mr Knight closed the door behind them.

"Marcus, I wonder if I can talk to Alexa alone for a minute," said Peter in a calm, steady voice.

Mr Knight nodded and left, while Alexa sat silently, not caring what Peter had to say or that his eyes would not leave her legs.

"Are you going to tell me what you've been doing or should I take a guess?" asked Peter. Alexa looked down at her legs and realised the cuts were clearly visible. "Are they the only ones?" Alexa did not answer. She did not want to go back to the hospital. "All right, take your jumper off." Alexa shook her head slowly her eyes still on her legs. "I am your lawyer, Alexa. Nothing leaves this room unless you want it to. So, please, take off your jumper."

Alexa noticed that Peter took a deep breath as he watched her with a calm, unreadable expression on his face. Determined that she would keep Peter to his promise, she took her jumper off slowly to reveal her red and bloodied arms and shirt.

"You did this tonight?" asked Peter, his voice wavering slightly. Alexa simply nodded. "Did you have plans of taking it any further? Those cuts are pretty close to your wrist."

"Have to take care of Bethy. Can't go anywhere without her," Alexa muttered in a flat voice.

"And if she was not around?" asked Peter.

"Then what would be the point of me sticking around?" Alexa replied, trying not to properly consider such a situation. She never wanted Bethany to die, but right then she would have been thankful to shed her only tether to this horrible existence.

"You knew from the start that this trial was not going to be easy," said Peter, his voice pleading or frustrated; Alexa could not really tell.

"I said I would do it and I will," Alexa answered flatly. "You just let me cope with it my own way. They have every intention of destroying my life and credibility. Do you really expect me to smile as they do it?"

"No, but this can't go on either. You don't have much skin left to cut. What happens when it gets worse, because, at trial, it will be worse?"

"I don't know."

"You'd better go to bed. I want to talk to Mr Knight."

Alexa did not immediately move. She did not want to give Peter the opportunity to break his promise. This was not something she wanted Mr Knight involved in. She had already caused him enough trouble with this case. When Peter again urged her to go to bed, Alexa got up from her seat.

"Just remember, you're my lawyer," she said in a toneless voice that did not make it to demanding.

Alexa wished she could have said that he had to do what she wanted because she paid his bills, but she could not even claim that. With Peter holding on to the winning lottery tickets, she could not even risk arguing with him. All she was left with as she walked out was being forced to trust his word, something she had never been very good at.

Mr Knight was pacing outside his office when she emerged. He stopped and looked at her with concern, but Alexa knew she must have done a good job with her razor. She felt nothing as she walked past him without a second glance.

A week passed without any further visits or news from Peter or

Detective Mathews. Alexa did not ask where they were or when they were coming back. As far as she was concerned they could stay away forever. After a two-week absence, she was almost convinced they were never returning and they would hold the trial without her. However, midway through week seven Mr Knight brought her the bad news.

When the bell rang, Alexa felt her heart rise and stick painfully in her throat. She had promised Peter she would go through with testifying at Clinton's trial, but she was not sure how she would do it. The prospect of having her life laid bare was not enticing.

Standing outside Mr Knight's office, Alexa found it hard to move her feet those few steps forward, but the thought of perhaps seeing Mr Knight for even a couple of minutes was enough to propel her through the door.

"Oh, Miss Samson, Peter Lam rang. He's running late," said Mr Knight as she walked in without knocking. "He won't be here until after five. You can come back then if you like."

"Can I stay?" Alexa asked, feeling her voice shake unintentionally.

Mr Knight hesitated before answering and she wondered what Detective Mathews had put him through. It only made her more disgusted in herself.

"If you need to, you can stay," Mr Knight finally replied.

"I don't want to be thinking right now, you know?"

"Sit down," urged Mr Knight quickly, as he made her a hot chocolate and offered her some biscuits. "You'll be all right. I know this has been hard on you, but you'll pull through."

"I'm sorry you got dragged into it," said Alexa, looking down at her drink. "I had to tell them about the rumours. I just wish Detective Mathews believed me that there was nothing going on."

"She's not the only one who believes the rumours."

"This is why people should never get involved with me. I'll only make their lives worse."

"That's not true. I'm glad I met you and I'm glad I've been able to help you," said Mr Knight kindly. "No rumour will ever change that."

Alexa smiled weakly and curled her legs up to her chest, resting her head on her knees. She appreciated that Mr Knight was nice enough to lie to try and make her feel better. She watched him working until her eyes slid closed, unable to stay open against the weight of the situation.

The smell of food woke Alexa from her slumber. She lifted her head to see that Peter had replaced Mr Knight, and her heart sank.

"You don't have to look so disappointed to see me," said Peter with a half-smile. "I have pizza."

"I don't want to eat. When's Detective Mathews coming?" she asked, wrapping her arms around her chest to stop it from heaving in despair.

"She isn't. It's just you and I," replied Peter sombrely.

"Why? What's going on?" Alexa asked sceptically. "When does the trial start? I thought it must be soon because you came back."

"There isn't going to be a trial."

Peter's words shook the last remnants of tiredness from Alexa's body as she sat bolt upright.

"They settled on a plea bargain," explained Peter, though his eyes did not quite meet hers, making her nervous. "It means that Clinton wasn't sentenced to as long a term as he could've been if he'd been found guilty, but he will serve gaol time."

"I don't understand. Why now? Why didn't they do this before?" Alexa asked, annoyed by what they had put her through – presumably for their own amusement.

"They had every reason to believe they could get a conviction in the beginning."

"But I proved to have such low credibility that they didn't think that any more," she spat, her voice full of anger and bitterness.

"In part, yes. I won't lie. They were concerned about your credibility as a witness, but they were prepared to go to trial all the same. They still thought the case against Clinton was strong."

"Then why didn't they?"

"Because I didn't let them," sighed Peter, collapsing into Mr Knight's chair as though his body could no longer carry the strain of standing. "I wasn't going to risk your health and wellbeing just for you to testify. I thought I did the right thing convincing you to testify, but the ordeal you would've gone through would've been horrific and I could not allow it."

"But if I didn't testify how could they get Clinton to go to gaol?"

"Even without your testimony there was enough evidence to put him in gaol. You almost died when he attacked you," answered Peter emphatically. "Despite not being able to prove anything else, that much was clear. The state you were both in when we finally intervened – he'd torn your clothes and he was in a state of undress as well.

"We couldn't prove he raped you – or that he had been about to – but he couldn't make out like it was entirely innocent either. So he admitted to the attack and to inappropriate relations with you, taking you to his place and such, but he did deny ever sleeping with you or raping you."

"So what happens now?" Alexa asked, feeling her body start to lighten.

"For you, nothing. It's all over. You can put it behind you. Clinton was given a sentence of five years, but with parole and time served he'll probably be out in a little under two years. He will never teach again," explained Peter, though Alexa thought he sounded disappointed and she wondered about which part.

"But you said he refused to admit he raped me," she queried, still not quite ready to believe.

"He attacked and almost killed one of his students. No one would ever hire him. Alexa, what he did to you was horrific. In the eyes of the law alone, we can't prove his guilt about the rest, but everyone knows the truth," replied Peter passionately. "I know what he did to you. I know you weren't lying. It's not the punishment I would've chosen, but he will be punished."

"So it's really over? I don't have to testify? And you'll never bring Detective Mathews here again?" asked Alexa excitedly, not really caring as much about the length of Clinton's sentence as Peter.

"Yes on all counts," smiled Peter. "So why don't you help me celebrate and come and eat some pizza."

The relief Alexa felt could not have been more powerful. She had never been more grateful to anyone in her life. Perhaps Peter realised how much she wished she could have hugged him, because he smiled kindly at her as she jumped up from her chair and grabbed a slice of pizza.

It was good pizza too. Not the ordinary chain store pizza, but the gourmet kind, and three different varieties. It was a large amount considering how little Peter ate.

"I want you to know that my help comes with conditions," said Peter, once Alexa conceded defeat with the pizza.

"What conditions?" she asked warily, slumping back in her seat and folding her arms.

"That you don't lay another razor to you skin – not anywhere and not because of anything."

"I don't make promises I can't keep," Alexa replied firmly.

"Then you'd better find a way of keeping it," retorted Peter, his stance equally firm. "This is non-negotiable. I've offered my services to you and your sister free of charge for many years now and asked for nothing in return. You owe me this much."

Alexa felt a guilty knot tie in her stomach. She wanted to yell at Peter that he had no right to tell her how to live her life. Being dictated to was not something she generally accepted, but for what he had just done for her, she felt she had no choice but to agree.

"Okay. For no reason and under no circumstances," Alexa agreed softly, unsure how she was actually going to keep the promise.

"Good," said Peter with a triumphant smile. "I'd better get going. My wife will want to see me some time this year. Take the rest of the pizza. I'm sure you have a few roommates who'd appreciate it."

Alexa smiled. She knew Peter had bought extra just so she would be able to share the leftovers. It was very kind, because food this good was not a common experience in the dining hall. Sam, Chad, Lizzie and Bianca were suitably impressed, and despite eating their own dinners less than an hour before, devoured the rest of the pizza in a few minutes.

Waiting for them to stop eating, Alexa finally explained the source of the food and the reason behind the celebrations. However, none of her friends were as happy as she was with the outcome of the plea bargain.

"Two years for raping and almost killing you? That's pathetic," spat Sam.

"It's not very much, is it?" said Lizzie softly. "I mean, it's pretty obvious he tried to kill you."

"I don't care. All I care about is that it's over," replied Alexa dismissively, trying not to let their comments take away from the happiness she felt over the outcome.

"Don't you think you should care? After what he did to you, didn't you want to get into court and stick it to him?" asked Bianca.

"I wouldn't have stuck it to anybody," Alexa murmured unhappily. "You have no idea the things they were going to say about me."

"You mean about Mr Knight and Sam?" asked Chad. "Come on, no one really believes those rumours and, well, there really is no explanation for you and Sam," he smiled supportively.

"If it was just about those two, I would've been fine, but I have a life outside of here and it's full of things they would've used against me."

"Well here's to putting Mr Marsh in gaol," said Sam, raising his hand in a toast. "May he be raped a thousand times and castrated as well."

"Here, here," chorused Chad, Bianca, Lizzie and Alexa.

***

With the spectre of Clinton no longer hanging over her, Alexa found herself almost enjoying school. Easter was approaching and along with it Bianca's birthday. Alexa made Bianca a card for the occasion, not having the money or the means to buy her a present.

Bianca was up early on the morning of her birthday and had left the room by the time Alexa had made it out of the shower. Alexa left her card on Bianca's bed, not keen on trying to compete with Chad, knowing her present would appear very tokenistic in comparison. The thought made Alexa smile. It was tokenistic, but it had taken all her resolve to give Bianca anything at all. Despite Bianca being supportive in the lead-up to Clinton's trial, they had never really made it back to friends.

When Bianca and Chad were both absent from breakfast, Alexa knew Chad had started his day-long celebration of Bianca's eighteenth birthday. The plans were so sweet that Alexa could not help but think that Bianca did not deserve him.

Chad had asked his parents to buy Bianca's present and post it to him at school. It had arrived two days ago. The golden necklace with a small opal pendant was one of the most beautiful things Alexa had ever seen. Chad had been so excited that he had shown it to almost everyone in sight, only just avoiding showing it to Bianca. Alexa only hoped that he never found out about Bianca cheating on him.

Bianca was clearly pleased with her present. She showed it off to everyone she met during the day, while Chad sat beaming next to her. Chad made Bianca's day even better with a birthday cake at dinner. Bianca pretended to be embarrassed, but Alexa could see just how much she was enjoying the attention.

"He sure knows how to make sure he'll get some tonight," whispered Sam in Alexa's ear, smilingly jerking his head toward Bianca as she passed out the pieces of cake Chad was cutting.

"Yeah, cake is the way to a woman's heart," replied Alexa laughingly.

"You mean girls' hearts are down where a guy's brain is? Huh, interesting."

Alexa burst out laughing, elbowing Sam as he giggled next to her. He wrapped his arm around her, pulling her into his side as they tried to control their mirth under the unimpressed glare of Bianca. Turning away from Bianca, Alexa was surprised to see Mel on the other side of Sam, joining in the merriment.

"You're so gross," said Mel playfully to Sam.

Buoyed by the friendly smile and pleasantness of his sister's voice, Sam pulled Mel down to sit with them and handed her a slice of cake. It made Alexa wonder if Mel had seen the truth about Clinton now that he had been convicted, and was making the effort to move on from him. It had been weeks since Mel had threatened to make her life a living hell, and Alexa hoped the animosity between them was now gone, but that hopeful thought did not last long.

Mel continued to glare at her whenever Sam was not looking and more than once Mel gestured towards Bianca, reminding her of what she knew. It was a sickening thought. Now more than ever, Alexa did not want Chad to find out about Bianca's holiday fling, but she also could not risk exposing her and Mel's mutual dislike of each other. There was no way she could face that conversation with Sam. She never wanted him to find out about Mel's obsession with Clinton. So she smiled and played nice, ignored Mel's subversive threats, and took no notice of Bianca's complaint the next day that she had tried to divert everyone's attention away from her birthday by flirting with Sam.

With just under two weeks until Easter, a letter from the Whites arrived along with their invitation for Alexa to return their place for the holidays. It was annoying that she still had to go through the ritual of being invited back, but she supposed Redgrove had had too much experience with her foster care situation to assume any family would have her back.

Alexa had never been so excited about holidays before, particularly ones where there was no prospect of seeing Bethany. Everyone except Bianca was heading home for the holidays. Her parents would be out of the country so she had to stay at school. Chad decided to stay with her, though this time he made sure Bianca knew, after the debacle of the spring holidays last year.

At least the holidays provided Alexa a reason to legitimately go and see Mr Knight. She had barely seen him since Peter's last visit and liked the prospect of a few quiet minutes alone with him. She knew that was all it could be. They had been getting too close and she knew it had to stop, but it was just so nice to know someone who truly liked her.

As she walked into Mr Knight's office, the smile could not be kept from her face. She liked that he returned the smile.

"I assume you're here to organise permission to go back to your foster parents' for Easter," asked Mr Knight, although Alexa sensed his fear that she was somehow in more trouble.

"Yeah," Alexa replied, breaking her eyes away from the top of his chest, which was just visible through his open top button.

"How have you been?" Mr Knight asked as he took Pam's invitation and filled out her permission slip.

"Okay. Things are getting back to normal after the trial – well, non-trial."

"I'm glad. Are you ready for the exams next term?"

"Not really," Alexa replied with a playful scoff. "It's a bit harsh having exams the first week back. Hayley won't be happy with me having to study half the holidays."

"You're looking forward to going back?"

"Yeah, more than ever." Alexa saw Mr Knight's smile and realised just how excited she sounded. "I mean, it's better than staying at school."

Mr Knight smiled again and handed Alexa her form. They both sat in silence for a moment, just looking at each other, before the knock of another student sent Alexa on her way.

When the last assembly of the term finally drew to a close the following Monday, Alexa made her way to the library. With her and Bianca still not very close, she had taken to studying in the library, even during free periods. There was too much risk of seeing Bianca, saying the wrong thing or pulling the wrong expression. It was more stress than Alexa needed, and the reclusiveness of her study habits had seen her fall very much out of touch with the goings on in the grade.

Previously, always in trouble and right in the middle of things, Alexa had been one of the first to know about everything. Now she was one of the last. When she saw everyone chatting feverishly outside the chemistry lab as they waited for class to start, she realised just how out of touch she had become. There was another scandal brewing in the grade. Alexa could only hope it did not involve her or Mr Knight.

"What's going on?" Alexa asked Ezra as they sat down at their lab bench. "It's not me again, is it?"

"You didn't happen to tell anyone about Bianca and Victor, did you?" asked Ezra in a concerned voice.

"No," Alexa replied indignantly.

"It's just that everyone's talking about Bianca cheating on Chad and how bad it is after everything he did for her birthday."

Alexa's eyes began examining a chemical stain on their bench. She had no doubt that the rumours were Mel's doing, but knew that Bianca would never believe that. There was no reason for Bianca to ever suspect Mel, and Alexa knew she would look guilty even suggesting such a possibility. There was no one for Bianca to blame but her.

"I didn't tell anyone," Alexa said sincerely, hoping that Ezra at least would believe her.

"You'll have to convince Bianca of that. She's really upset. Chad doesn't believe the rumours, but he's pretty pissed off."

"He doesn't think I started the rumours, does he?"

"Nope," answered Ezra shaking her head. "And Bianca isn't going to say so or she'd have to admit that they were true."

"Does she really think I started the rumours?" asked Alexa, hoping for a way to clear her name. "Are the rumours about Victor or just that she cheated on Chad? Anyone could start a rumour like that. Wouldn't have to think it was true."

"I don't know, but we were the only people who knew the truth."

Alexa wished that were correct. She was tempted to ask if Ezra and Bianca had spoken much about it in the summer when they were alone together, because she did not believe Mel had been around when Bianca had made her initial revelation. However, she knew Ezra would convey her theory to Bianca, and Bianca would just see it as an admission of guilt.

By lunch, talk of Bianca cheating on Chad had reached fever pitch among the senior students. Alexa was not sure what the best course of action was. If she avoided Bianca, then Bianca would assume it was because she had started the rumours and that might even tip Chad off. Alexa did not really care about Bianca. Bianca was going to blame her anyway, but the last thing she wanted was to be the person responsible for telling Chad that Bianca had cheated on him.

"Heard the rumours?" asked Sam when Alexa sat down next to

him.

"Not personally," Alexa replied hesitantly. "I only know what Ezra told me. When'd they start?"

"Last night, this morning, I don't know."

Bianca sat against Chad's chest, his arms wrapped around her. Alexa avoided Bianca's gaze as Bianca stared hatefully at her. However, her trying to ignore Bianca only made Sam suspicious.

"Why's Bianca so mad at you?" asked Sam sceptically.

"I guess she's just angry about the rumours," Alexa replied, trying to sound innocent.

Sam looked at her intently, but said nothing more. A few minutes later he moved over to Bianca and Chad, leaving her with Ezra.

"Do you want to go for a walk?" Alexa asked Ezra, guilt twinging her stomach.

Even if she had not started the rumours, Alexa still hated the fact that it was her fault they had been spread in the first place. Chad really did not deserve this.

The walk was not a very long one. They had only reached the oval when Ezra asked her if she had somehow inadvertently let someone know about Bianca and Victor.

"How do I know it wasn't you?" retorted Alexa angrily.

"Because I'm Bianca's friend," replied Ezra simply.

"I thought I was too," Alexa snapped before storming off.

Halfway to her next class Alexa saw Sam and Chad arguing. Sam pointed angrily in her direction and they both made a beeline towards her.

"Alexa," called Chad, catching up to her. There was great pain in his eyes and she hoped he had not found out the truth. "What do you know about the rumours?"

"Nothing. I haven't even heard them myself. I only know what Ezra told me."

"Then why's Bianca mad at you?" asked Chad, clearly not believing her.

"I didn't know she was," Alexa lied, trying to sound ignorant. It did not work.

"Don't you think I know when you're lying?" asked Sam, who was standing right behind Chad. "You know who started the rumours and why. Was it you?"

"Why would I?" Alexa cried, stung by the accusation. "Bianca's my friend. Chad's my friend. I'd never do it to him."

"Are the rumours true?" asked Chad. Alexa tried to look away, but Chad was insistent. "Just tell me if the rumours are true."

Alexa looked Chad in the eyes, but could not respond. She could not lie, but she could not tell him the truth either. For Chad, her silence was answer enough. Tears began to well in his eyes before he stalked off. Sam scowled at her before running after Chad.

That afternoon was one of the worse Alexa had ever endured. Sam, Chad and Bianca all glared at her whenever they saw her. Ezra did not sit with her either, deciding that Bianca was in greater need of a friend that afternoon. Only Lizzie was prepared to stay with her as the rest of the grade whispered conspiratorially at the new developments.

Alexa kept her head down and tried to ignore everything that was going on around her, but it was difficult. Sam and Chad had never turned on her like this. Whatever rumours had swirled around her before, she had always had them and Ezra to support her. This time she was all alone.

When the final bell rang, Alexa rushed gratefully from the class and headed to a secluded corner of the library to study. It was nice to delude herself for a while that her solitude here was completely self-imposed, and not a result of peer hostility. If not for that, she was not sure she would have been able to focus on her work at all. However, when the curfew bell rang a sick feeling filled her stomach.

Alexa walked slowly back to her room, hoping not to encounter anyone on the way. The hallways were empty and, thankfully, Martha and Natalie were the only ones in their bedroom when she arrived. Sighing with relief, Alexa rushed towards her bed, hoping she could make it under the covers before Bianca emerged from wherever she was. However, she only made it halfway across the room before a slamming door alerted her to Bianca's arrival.

"You're such a bitch," yelled Bianca, as she strode angrily across the room towards her. "I thought you were my friend."

"I didn't start those rumours," replied Alexa calmly, turning to face Bianca full on. She refused to be blamed for this by her.

"You told Chad they were true."

"I didn't tell him anything, but I couldn't lie either," Alexa said in a determinedly even voice. "Besides, you're the reason he confronted me. Why would you ever suspect me unless the rumours were true?"

"No one else knew about Victor."

"The rumours weren't about Victor," Alexa pointed out. She had finally heard the contents of them in the last class of the day. They were so generic and malicious that she was surprised Bianca had even bothered reacting to them. "You don't trust me. That's why Chad found out. If you'd just denied the rumours, he would've believed you."

"If you hadn't started the rumours in the first place –"

"I didn't start the rumours!" snapped Alexa, finally losing her cool. "Why would I?"

"To get back at me," snarled Bianca.

"Get back at you for what? God, even if that were true, I wouldn't have said anything. Chad's my friend. I never would've done it to him."

"Everyone can hear you two," said Lizzie, slipping into the room. "There're people crowding in the hall to listen to you."

"I don't care. Let them all hear what a bitch Alexa is," said Bianca bitterly.

"I'm not the one that spread those rumours. I'm sorry that things were said about you, but you're not the only person who's had to deal with that," said Alexa, trying to stay calm. She had been the subject of much more vicious rumours than this and most of them had not been close to true. "But you did cheat on Chad and you can't blame me for that. That was all your choice."

Bianca took a step forward and slapped Alexa hard across the face. Martha, Natalie and Lizzie gasped collectively, but Alexa did not flinch. Bianca stared hard at her before turning and storming out of the room, the door slamming behind her.

Chapter Six

"WHAT'S GOING ON in here?" asked Mr Knight angrily, striding into the room just a minute after Bianca left. "Ms Carter's outside trying to disperse a crowd outside your room. They say there's yelling and fighting going on. I really expected more from you ladies."

No one spoke. Mr Knight looked between each of them as they exchanged sideways glances.

"So who's going to explain what's going on?" asked Mr Knight sternly, his eyebrows raised in impatient expectation.

Mr Knight immediately looked at Alexa, but she stared defiantly past him. As far as she was concerned, this had absolutely nothing to do with him.

"Bianca and Alexa were just having a bit of an argument," said Lizzie tentatively.

Alexa could have smiled at Lizzie's inability to refuse Mr Knight anything he asked for, but was really not in the mood. Lizzie's crush was not enough to dispel the shock of Bianca's attack.

"Bianca hit Alexa," said Martha angrily, looking straight at Alexa as though daring her to deny it.

Alexa could only roll her eyes and turn away. She really did not want to be used as a pawn in the ongoing quarrel between Martha and Bianca that had been going on since Bianca's arrival at the school at the start of last year.

"Miss Samson, is that true?" asked Mr Knight.

Alexa did not answer him. She could hear the horror in his voice and did not want him involved, so turned away and sat down at her desk, opening her maths textbook to some random page.

"It's true," said Lizzie, accompanied by nodding from Natalie, as Alexa continued to keep her eyes down.

"All right, Miss Samson, let's go."

Alexa tried to ignore him, but when his hand touched her arm she found her resistance dissolve. Once in Mr Knight's office she sat cross-legged on the chair, remaining silent. Just because she had followed him did not mean she would involve him.

Mr Knight examined her face without touching her, his eyes full of sadness and anger.

"What was the argument about?" Mr Knight asked, returning from his bedroom with an icepack.

"It was an argument. It doesn't really matter what it was about," Alexa replied flatly, refusing to meet his eyes.

"Why did she slap you?" Alexa did not answer. "I already know that she hit you. You remaining silent will not keep her out of trouble," continued Mr Knight more forcefully. Alexa still did not respond. "Why do you insist on protecting people that hurt you?"

"It's between me and Bianca. It has nothing to do with you," Alexa snapped, not appreciating his interference, despite how well-meaning it was.

"No one has the right to hit other people," said Mr Knight angrily. "Miss Ross could be expelled for this."

"You want to expel Bianca because of this? Would you want to do that if she had hit someone else?" Alexa asked. Mr Knight looked startled by the question, but did not answer. "If it was anyone else you wouldn't be so concerned. This has more to do with me than Bianca."

"That's not true," replied Mr Knight angrily, piercing Alexa's heart. She did not want to attack him. "I don't treat you any differently to the other students."

"Maybe, maybe not," Alexa retorted, though she knew the answer was definitely not. "I'm still at school even though you found me out of grounds. You didn't tell Bianca that you caught me because I asked you not to. You're still nice to me."

"Alexa, of course I'm still – how do you want me to react to this, then?" asked Mr Knight, conceding the point much quicker than she expected.

"Like I was the one who hit Bianca."

***

Marcus closed his eyes and nodded. He realised that Alexa's conduct would have to be his test for every punishment he metered out this year, because if the situation had been reversed, he would never have considered expelling Alexa. It was an uncomfortable position he had put himself in. He cared for Alexa too deeply, and if he continued to be so protective of her it would not be long before people realised he had feelings for her.

Walking Alexa back to her room without providing the comfort he had intended to, Marcus had to work hard to keep the look of disgust from his face when he saw Bianca walk out of the bathroom.

"My office, Miss Ross. Now," Marcus said before walking back out of the room.

It was a good thing Bianca took her time. It gave him the opportunity to compose himself, but he found it difficult to deal with Bianca as justly and even-handedly as he had intended.

"It's not my fault," cried Bianca as soon as she walked into his office. "She started the rumours. She's the one who broke me and Chad up. It's her fault."

Bianca's insistence on blaming Alexa sat in stark contrast to Alexa's determination to continually protect her. Having spent much of the last year defending the G7 when they were clearly innocent, Marcus found he had very little patience for Bianca and her sob story.

When the finger pointing did not work, having moved from Alexa to Chad, and even to her other roommates, Bianca tried tears. Marcus remained unmoved as he handed her a punishment much less than what she deserved.

"And your parents will be informed about this incident," Marcus added sternly.

Bianca did not take the news of her punishment well. "Yeah, and because Alexa doesn't have parents, she just gets away with everything," she muttered.

It took all of Marcus's self-control to hold his tongue. He had to remind himself that he was an adult and rebuffing Bianca's petulance would make little difference to her attitude. However, with Bianca continuing to try and shift the blame on to Alexa, he knew it was best that he escorted her back to her room to ensure that there were no more incidents. At the door, he decided to let Bianca know the extent to which Alexa had maintained her silence on the issue. Bianca said nothing. She just stalked into her room and sat sullenly on her bed. Marcus followed her in to see Lizzie, Martha and Natalie all waiting for further information. Only Alexa did not turn on his arrival.

"I have spoken to Miss Ross about what happened. She has admitted to slapping Miss Samson and will serve two weeks of detention after the exams next term," said Marcus in a stern voice. "I want this to be the end of it. No more arguments or fights. This is a very important year for all of you and I don't want you concentrating your efforts on disliking people when you should be concentrating on your study."

Lizzie, Martha and Natalie all nodded in agreement, although not without Martha throwing Bianca a look of deep disgust. Marcus found himself liking Martha more and more.

"Miss Samson?" asked Marcus.

"Okay," Alexa nodded quietly, still refusing to look his way.

Marcus knew he could expect little more. Though Alexa would never say so, he believed Bianca's slap had hurt more than just her cheek. Her shoulders were hunched and she appeared timid, as though hiding within herself. It made him want to throw his arms around her and pull her out of her shell with the promise that he would protect her. He had to settle for turning and leaving her to cope alone while he went to see Chad.

"I wanted to see if you were still happy to stay at school these holidays," asked Marcus once they had returned to his office and he had ascertained that Chad was coping well enough with the situation.

"Did Alexa put you up to this?" asked Chad, startling Marcus with such an enquiry.

"Why would she?" Marcus asked, trying to be innocently intrigued.

"Because we know that you'll accommodate her," replied Chad with a slight sneer.

"Excuse me?" asked Marcus, suddenly fearful that his secret was not very secret at all.

"You can't think that after everything you've done for Alexa – keeping her in school, saving her life – that we don't know you have a soft spot for her. No other teacher has ever been nice to her like that before. Why'd you think we brought her with us last year when I wanted to stay with Sam at the last minute? We just never realised how successful she'd be."

"Miss Samson made some good points last year and I will admit that they did help to sway me, but I didn't help you then just to please Miss Samson," replied Marcus, willing his voice to be steady and stern as his heart pounded erratically.

"I don't want Alexa involved," said Chad firmly. "I'm not having her indebted to any teacher for me. It's fine. I'll stay."

"Chad, I admire you for what you've said. I promise, Miss Samson had nothing to do with this – except that the points she made last year are still valid now. I can leave here whenever I want. You have four chances a year to escape. If you want to leave, we can try to arrange it. As long as I can get confirmation from your parents that you are allowed to leave and that there are provisions for you to be collected somewhere, then you can go home for the holidays."

Chad quickly agreed, and his return home for the holidays was arranged within half an hour, but the conversation left Marcus feeling decidedly unwell. Although Chad's comments were innocent enough, they were far too close to the mark. Marcus knew he and Alexa would need to keep their distance for the rest of the year and they could never be seen alone together except in the most official of circumstances.

***

The last few days of term were as painful as any Alexa had experienced at Redgrove. Bianca was ignored by virtually everyone, except for the continued spread of the rumours, which had only become more vicious since her assault on Alexa. Only Ezra stood by Bianca. That left Alexa feeling very alone, with Chad avoiding her and Sam still giving her angry stares every time he saw her. It was more than Alexa could handle and she knew she could not leave for the holidays with Sam and Chad as her enemies.

"Can I talk to you?" Alexa asked Chad quietly at lunch on the last day of term, as he and Sam sat in the dining hall.

"Do what you like," replied Chad morosely.

"I'm sorry about what happened. I always thought you deserved to know the truth," Alexa said, trying not to let her voice crack. "I just didn't think I was the one who should tell you."

"So you thought you'd let him find out by spreading rumours?" snarled Sam, stunning Alexa with his aggression.

"I didn't start those rumours," Alexa cried. "I had nothing to do with them. If you don't know that then nothing I say will convince you. When have I ever been involved in starting rumours?"

"I'm not angry at the rumours," said Chad, talking before Sam could. "But why didn't you tell me? All term she's been lying to me and you knew."

"I promised," Alexa explained weakly, knowing it was not a good enough excuse. She owed Chad so much more than Bianca. "I didn't want to, but either choice was going to be wrong and I wasn't sure that you'd even believe me. The whole thing was really eating Bianca up. I thought she'd tell you eventually."

"But she didn't and you decided to get back at her by doing

this," said Sam with a harsh glare.

"I had nothing to do with this!" cried Alexa, Sam's accusations cutting deep. "If you really want to know who's responsible then why don't you look a little closer to home."

Sam was immediately on his feet, towering over Alexa. It was intimidating and Alexa could not help but take a step back, though she refused to back down completely.

"Don't you dare accuse my sister!" said Sam in a slow, angry voice.

"Why? You're accusing me. Who's the only person outside the five of us that was at your place this summer? Mel loves causing trouble and starting rumours, so don't you dare blame me."

Alexa saw a flurry of movement at Sam's side. Chad was suddenly standing next to Sam holding back Sam's clenched fist. Alexa's heart broke in an instant.

"I never want to talk to you again," Alexa said in a flat, emotionless voice before grabbing her bag and walking away.

Sam had been the one person in the world she could always rely on, but now he was gone too. She did not want to cry or break anything. She wanted to die.

When the day finally ended, Alexa packed up all of her personal belongings. Without Sam, there was just no point in returning. She hesitated at the door, wondering whether she should say goodbye, but there was really no one left to say goodbye to – except one person.

"Come in," called Mr Knight in a tired voice.

"Hi," said Alexa softly as she entered his office.

Alexa felt tears burn the sides of her eyes, knowing that this would be the last time she saw Mr Knight. She closed the door behind her, but did not move more than a step into the office.

"Is everything all right?" asked Mr Knight, clearly concerned.

"I just wanted to say bye and thank you for everything you've done for me," Alexa breathed, not quite daring to meet his eyes.

Before Mr Knight could react, Alexa dashed from the room and ran towards the train station. She wanted to get away from Redgrove as fast as she could. She was almost at the bottom school gate when she felt her body being swung around. A breathless Mr Knight held her arm firmly and dragged her back towards the school.

"What are you doing?" Alexa asked, trying to pull herself free.

"Back to my office," said Mr Knight in a voice she barely

recognised.

Alexa pulled free, tempted to turn and run again, but she followed Mr Knight in silence, worried by his mood. She wondered what she had done. He did not seem angry, but there was something disturbing about the expression on his face. When they reached his office, Mr Knight quickly threw his belongings into a bag. She could see his hands shaking.

"I spoke to your foster parents. I'm taking you home now. We can talk about everything there."

Alexa could hear the quiver in Mr Knight's voice, despite his best efforts to control it.

When Mr Knight was packed, he finally looked up. Alexa could only stare back, confused by what was happening and hoping for an answer, but Mr Knight's only response was to rush to his bathroom to expel the contents of his stomach.

***

Marcus sighed deeply when he pulled up in front of the Whites' house. Alexa grabbed her bags and walked slowly to the door, while he followed a few steps behind. Pam opened the front door before they reached it and bundled Alexa inside.

"Hayley's waiting for you upstairs," Pam said in a slightly unstable voice, and pushed Alexa towards the stairs before guiding him towards the lounge room.

"What's going on?" asked Karl as soon as they walked into the lounge room. "Why the hell would you start claiming that Alexa is suicidal?"

"Because the last thing she did today was come and say goodbye to me," said Marcus with a hiccupping sigh.

"I don't see how that comment could get you so upset. It could've been completely innocent," said Karl. "She could've just been trying to be polite."

"I saw the look in her eyes when she said it," said Marcus softly, but firmly. If they had seen it, they would have understood, but it was not something he could describe, despite the vision continuing to float in front of his eyes. "It wasn't – it was a permanent kind of goodbye."

"What makes you think that she would try to kill herself? Don't you think that's a little extreme?" asked Pam, concern filling her voice.

"No," Marcus replied, shaking his head, realising he had no

choice but to confess. "Last year, on this very day, Alexa made a suicide attempt after school. It was very nearly successful. I only just managed to pull her back in time."

"What do you mean? How?" asked Pam.

"She tried to walk in front of a train. I'd been late leaving school. I noticed her walking towards the edge of the platform. I ..." Marcus stopped talking and the room fell silent.

"Why weren't we told about this?" growled Karl.

"I didn't inform anyone. I rode with Alexa to the city. I tried to get her to tell me what was wrong, but she wouldn't talk me."

"And you left her to catch a second train by herself and never told anyone!" cried Karl, jumping to his feet. "You should've informed the school, her social worker, us! My god, she was suicidal and you sat back and did nothing. What were you thinking? Why didn't you say anything?"

Marcus felt the room caving in on him. All of a sudden his actions seemed so foolish and incredibly selfish. He could not understand why he had put himself before Alexa.

"Because I threatened him," said Alexa, slowly walking into the room. "I told him that if he told anyone about the suicide attempt that I'd tell them that he made it all up because I wouldn't sleep with him."

"And you believed her?" cried Karl, flinging his hand out to point at Alexa.

"I wasn't bluffing and it would've been hard to prove I was lying."

"I should've told someone," said Marcus, feeling a little better for finally accepting responsibility for his actions. "But I was certain there was something very wrong and I didn't think telling people was the best way to deal with Alexa. I thought I could keep an eye on her."

"I remember that night," said Pam quietly. "You came home and went straight to bed. The next morning you looked as bad as I had ever seen you. You had a bruise on your face and looked rather ill." Alexa nodded to Pam. "What happened?"

"I was pregnant – to Clinton. I wanted to keep the baby, so I told him I would keep his name out of it if he gave me money to look after our baby. He hit me in the stomach and then kicked me to make sure I lost the baby."

It did not matter that Marcus already knew what Alexa had been through, hearing her speak those words was torture. She did not deserve to have suffered so much at such a young age.

"But why kill yourself?" asked Karl desperately.

"I let my baby die. I didn't think I deserved to live. I wanted to be with my baby," said Alexa softly, breaking Marcus's heart.

For the millionth time, Marcus cursed himself for not pushing for the truth at the time. He may not have been in a position to guess that Alexa had been pregnant, but he knew she had been injured by the red mark on her face. If he had taken her to the hospital then, they would have done tests and found out the truth. They would have been able to test the DNA of the child and prove what Clinton had done – all before he could have ever raped her. If he had just told someone.

"Why didn't you tell us?" asked Karl in an angry plea, looking at Alexa. "We would've helped you take care of the baby – or allowed you to consider your other options."

"I didn't know you guys that well. I just assumed you'd throw me out when you found out. I couldn't trust you. I couldn't trust anyone."

In the silence, a soft sobbing carried its way into the room. Karl looked around before collecting Hayley from the hall and sitting her on the lounge between himself and Pam.

"What about today?" asked Karl in a stronger voice, as he comforted his distressed daughter.

"I wasn't going to kill myself," said Alexa, turning and looking into Marcus's eyes, and he knew she was telling the truth. "I wanted to say goodbye because I was leaving. I'm not coming back next term. I wanted to tell you, but I didn't want you to try and change my mind."

"What do you mean you're not going back?" asked Pam.

"You guys said I could stay here permanently at the start of the year. Now I want to. I'm not going back to Redgrove."

The room fell into silence once more. Marcus felt his heart fall through his stomach. He would never see Alexa again. It was for the best. There was hardly a place on earth that was worse for her than Redgrove and he was pleased that its torture of her would now end. He only wished that he had had the chance to say a proper goodbye.

***

Karl promptly collected Hayley and Alexa and took them to the local shopping centre, where Brett was already hanging out with friends. Karl did not seem angry, but Alexa was not sure why they had been banished. Brett was just as agitated by the situation when she brought him up to speed about her decision to move in with them, though not the reasons why.

"Be cool having you round all the time," smiled Brett as they walked around the shops.

Hayley smiled and started bouncing happily, forgetting her previous horror at hearing about Alexa's suicide attempt.

"Hey, is that that girl you were dating last year?" asked Alexa, sticking her chin out at a girl a few shops away.

"Yeah," smiled Brett.

Alexa grinned mischievously before calling out. "Hey, Kathy!"

The girl turned, despite Alexa knowing her name was Karen. Alexa waved and put her arm around Brett's shoulder. Laughing, Alexa snaked her other arm around Brett's neck, and allowed him to lean down and kiss her. Alexa felt almost deviant kissing Brett, but it was clear he had had a lot more experience kissing girls in the year since they had first pulled this prank.

Brett's mobile started vibrating in his pocket before it rang loudly, pulling them apart. "It's Dad," he said, hanging up after thirty seconds. "He's coming to pick us up."

Brett slipped his arm around Alexa's shoulder and walked her towards the exit, holding her close, as Hayley took her other hand.

"Probably have to stop doing that when you start at my school though," smiled Brett.

Alexa was relieved, thankful she had not stirred deeper feelings in Brett this time. Although Brett had been very gentle, it had felt a bit like kissing her brother and thought he might feel the same way.

Karl did not answer any questions on the drive home, leaving Brett and Hayley quite annoyed as they sat down on the lounge. Alexa was more nervous, worried she had misinterpreted their invitation.

"So what happened? Is Alexa staying or not?" asked Brett impatiently as his parents sat down on the other lounge.

"I called Brett's principal and he agreed to come over and the four of us discussed Alexa's wish to leave Redgrove," said Pam. "It was agreed by everyone that leaving Redgrove would be in your best interests, in one respect."

"What does that mean?" asked Brett.

"Mr Lawson, Brett's principal, thought that Alexa may have a few problems changing schools at this late stage. She would have to start anew, make new friends, possibly start all new work," said Karl.

"There's also the living arrangements to consider," said Pam. "Alexa, how long has it been since you lived with a family full-time for more than a few weeks?" Alexa dropped her head and crossed her legs under her body. "I'm not saying that you wouldn't be welcome here, but I think it would put a lot of pressure on you – trying not to do the wrong thing, having Hayley around twenty-four–seven. I just don't think you understand how different it would be."

"It's okay. You don't want me to stay. I understand. You only asked me before because you were sure I would say no," said Alexa, rising from the lounge.

"We didn't say that," snapped Karl, before returning to a calmer voice as he made Alexa resume her seat. "If you really want to stay here and go to Brett's school it will happen. We just want you to listen to some other options first."

"What other options?" asked Alexa warily.

"First one is that you have a break these holidays and decide you want to go back to Redgrove and everything stays as it is," said Karl. Alexa crossed her arms and legs and rolled her eyes. "The second option, and the one favoured by everyone, is that you return to Redgrove, but you come home every weekend instead of just every holidays."

"So I would spend the weekends here and not at school?" asked Alexa cautiously.

"You would come home on Friday night and return to school on Monday morning. So you would spend three nights a week here and four nights at school," explained Karl. "How does that sound?"

"Do you mean it? Every weekend?" queried Alexa, sure it was too good to be true.

"Every weekend, no matter what," smiled Karl.

"Promise?"

"Yes, we promise, Alexa," said Pam. "We are as excited as you by the prospect. Hopefully, we will get to know each other better this way and you will know that you can trust us – for anything."

"But really?" asked Alexa, still not daring to believe.

"Just say it's what you want and it will happen," said Karl.

Alexa looked over at Brett and Hayley, who were nodding furiously.

"It's what I want," Alexa replied, her voice barely above a

whisper.

"It's what we want too," smiled Karl, looking around the family. "I think this requires a celebration. Go get changed, all of you, and we'll go out to dinner."

Alexa could not believe how holidays destined to be so horrible could possibly turn out to be the best she had ever experienced. After a long awaited sleep-in on Good Friday, Pam and Karl decided to take them all to the Easter Show. Brett and Hayley were ecstatic, while Alexa could only smile blankly.

"You'll enjoy it, don't worry," chuckled Karl.

Alexa had heard of the Easter Show before, but had never been and was almost overwhelmed by the sight. There were people everywhere, thousands of them. Alexa often had to cling to Brett or Hayley to stop herself from being separated from them. Hayley loved the idea of being able to show her things she had never seen before and dragged her to every corner of the show. The animals, the rides and the show bags, it was all a sensory overload.

"No, no," said Alexa, when Karl handed her fifty dollars to buy show bags. "I don't need anything. You've spent too much already."

"We'll sort her out," smiled Brett, grabbing the money and pulling Alexa into the show bag pavilion.

Brett and Hayley tried hard to make Alexa buy something, but there was nothing that she needed. She had always been so cautious with money that it was almost impossible for her to throw it away on junk.

"Get some chocolate ones to take back to school with you," suggested Brett. "You can share them with your friends."

Alexa could only shake her head, tears burning in her eyes at the knowledge that she no longer had any friends at Redgrove.

Brett shrugged as he handed the money back to Pam and Karl, and Alexa was glad when they did nothing more than joke that they wished Brett and Hayley were more like her. Alexa hoped they understood that just the experience was magical enough. Sitting and watching the fireworks as they ate overpriced fried food, Alexa could not help but wish that she could one day show Bethany all the Easter Show had to offer.

Easter Saturday was a quiet day, everyone thoroughly exhausted, but it was perhaps one of the nicest days Alexa had ever experienced. More than once Karl expressed how nice it would be to have her home on the weekends. Alexa was not sure she truly believed him. He and Pam had been forced into the decision by their reckless comment at the end of last year. It made her desperate to hear their whispered conversations when they thought the rest of the house was asleep.

"I just don't understand why no one told us it was possible beforehand," Karl muttered to Pam in the kitchen, while Alexa eavesdropped on the stairs. "I would've been happy to try it at the start of last year. If she'd been allowed to come home on the weekends, she could have seen her sister more often. She might never've had to run away. That brute might never've … are we really doing the right thing letting her go back there?"

"Alexa seems happy with the arrangement," replied Pam. Karl muttered in reply, but Alexa could not make it out. "Well we'll only have to wait a week to ask her. Every weekend from now on she'll have the chance to stay."

"We'd never let Hayley step foot in that place."

"No, and like Alexa said, if she'd come here from the start … I almost wish we were able to take her sister. We considered it, but I just don't think – I wish we were strong enough for that."

"Next year we might have to be. Alexa won't come here, not without her sister. We'll have to start thinking about ways we can help Alexa take care of her. I don't want Alexa back on those streets."

Alexa did not get to hear any more of the conversation, rushing up to her room to quiet the heaving sobs in her chest. The idea that she could have been at home with the Whites every weekend since the start of last year tore her heart apart. If she had been able to see Bethany every weekend, perhaps Bethany would never have run away. Perhaps Pam would have discovered her pregnancy the way Bianca had, and she would never have had to face Clinton. She would never have tried to kill herself and she would never have cared for Mr Knight.

That last thought was strangely painful. It no longer felt like a good thing to have never loved Mr Knight. Closing her eyes, Alexa tried to forget all that could have been. She would not let the Whites give her any more than they had. If the money came through as she hoped, she would be able to give them back all she owed them.

When Alexa awoke on Easter Sunday to find a large basket of chocolate eggs outside her bedroom door, it made the amount she owed the Whites balloon out catastrophically. It was more chocolate than she had seen in her lifetime. Pam and Karl could only laugh at her reaction. It was certainly not the way Brett and Hayley responded to their Easter gifts.

"You're making us look bad," joked Brett.

"We can always take some to your sister, if you'd like – if you can't eat it all," said Karl.

Tears immediately began to slip down Alexa's face at the idea of walking away from Bethany again.

"I can't do it," Alexa explained meekly, Hayley's arms around her shoulders. "And she doesn't need chocolate."

"No, she doesn't," mused Pam sadly.

The next day, Pam took Alexa shopping and helped her buy things Bethany did need. They put together a pack of toiletries and other basic items and boxed it up. Alexa was sure the other people in the post office thought she was insane as she cried writing Bethany's address on the box.

"Every little bit helps," said Pam reassuringly.

Alexa nodded, then hugged Pam tightly. It was the first hug Alexa had ever given Pam and she had to pull out of it quickly, but she needed Pam to know just how much she appreciated what she and Karl kept doing for her. However, beyond that, what Alexa really needed them to do was stop.

"No, no, no," said Alexa rapidly, as Pam smilingly explained what they were doing next. "No, you've done too much. I can't. You can't. You've bought me all this already today."

"Shampoo and tampons don't count," laughed Pam. "It's coming up to winter. You need some warmer clothes. Come on, I need to get some clothes too."

Pam dragged Alexa to the shops before pulling out some gift cards, explaining that they had been given to her and expired soon. If they did not use them, they would just go to waste. It was the only thing that got Alexa to comply, though it was still Pam who made the decision to ultimately buy the clothes. Alexa could never bring herself to say she wanted something, but was quite vocal when she thought Pam would be completely wasting her money.

"Ah, so when you stay silent, you actually really like it," smiled Pam, putting a jacket back on the shelf and going back to the one Alexa had liked the most.

Alexa felt sick seeing Pam pick up all the items she had truly desired. History had always told her that nothing this good came without catastrophic consequences, and she feared how much these clothes would truly cost her. However, as she held the bags in the car, Alexa could not help but feel amazingly blessed by the array clothes she now owned.

When they walked into the house, Karl could not hide his surprise over how much they had bought. Alexa's face burned with shame, as she wondered how she could have let Pam give her so much.

"We used those gift cards that were about to expire," said Pam pointedly, making Karl smile broadly.

"I won't fall for that again," scowled Alexa, realising how they had tricked her.

Karl just laughed as he walked over and hugged Pam tenderly. Pam shrugged and kissed Karl, as Alexa stomped to her room.

"For the rebel child you sure do the saint act good," smiled Brett, seeing her disgruntled face. "They'd been planning that trick on you for weeks – even before you decided to stay."

"What?" cried Alexa, only feeling guiltier.

"So shouldn't tell you it was my idea then, huh?" smirked Brett, before openly laughing as Alexa's mouth fell open. "Ha, it was worth it just for that face."

Brett rushed over and grabbed the bags from Alexa's hands and threw them on her bed before wrapping her in a very brotherly embrace.

"Chill. You're one of us now," he said kindly. "We're gunna take care of you."

Alexa smiled as she pushed gently out of Brett's arms. Being taken care of was not a concept Alexa was used to, and she found it strange having a whole houseful of people caring about her and her welfare. It was not even the big things that touched her the most. It was all the tiny, insignificant details no one had ever cared to notice before, like her love of peas and dislike of beans, or her acceptance of cauliflower and hatred of broccoli.

Even on Tuesday, when Alexa had to forgo holiday leisure for endless hours of study, the Whites took care of her. Hayley was not too pleased with the disruption to her holiday plans, but Karl and Pam made sure Hayley let her study, charging Brett with taking care of Hayley for most of the holidays.

Alexa loved that Hayley liked her enough to be upset, so promised to make it up to her the first weekend after her exams finished by doing anything she wanted for the entire weekend. That was enough to cheer Hayley up and have her practically wait on her as she studied. It was very sweet and only mildly disruptive.

Alexa's frantic study schedule resulted in the rest of the holidays passing as a continuous blur of textbooks and practice essays, which were broken only by meals, sleep and calls from Sam. He first started calling on Wednesday. Hayley answered the phone, but Alexa was in no mood to talk to him, even if he was calling to apologise. Sam called twice again on Thursday, catching Brett and the answering machine. After that, Alexa stopped answering the phone.

The next time Sam called, Hayley answered the phone, but was quickly booted off by Brett. Alexa sat next to him so she could hear Sam's voice on the other end of the line.

"I want to speak to Alexa," said Sam desperately.

"Alexa doesn't want to speak to you and I suggest you stop calling," said Brett angrily.

Brett had finally made her tell him why she had wanted to leave Redgrove and he had not been very impressed by the answer. Though he was two years younger than her, Brett was already much bigger and was taking the role of protective big brother to her and Hayley very seriously; so seriously that he had been close to telling Pam and Karl the truth. It had taken all of Alexa's persuasive skills to stop him. She had been successful – just – but that event made her doubt that she really could survive living with the Whites full-time, not if they were going to be so good to her all the time.

"Who are you anyway?" retorted Sam in an unimpressed manner. "It's got nothing to do with you. Just let me speak to Alexa."

"I'm her brother. So I'm warning you, stop calling her. And when she gets back to school you'd better keep your hands off her. If you lay a single finger on her, you'll have me to deal with."

There was silence and Brett hung up. Sam did not try and call again. It left Alexa feeling very uneasy about her return to school and she tried desperately to draw out the hours until that moment.

However, when Monday morning came, Alexa was up early to shower and dress. Karl was already eating breakfast and smiled at her arrival downstairs. He had agreed to give her a lift to the station. Her stomach was churning nervously. She had an exam that afternoon and it was the first time she had had to worry about making it to school on time.

"All ready?" asked Karl. Alexa could only shake her head, as she poured herself a coffee. "I was talking about going back to school, not your exam," he smiled, before laughing when she thought he was serious and tried to throw out her breakfast. "Just wanted to check you had packed."

"Should I take everything?" Alexa asked tentatively.

"Only what you need for the week," replied Karl, half-answering her real question.

"You're definitely going to let me come back on Friday?" whispered Alexa, not daring to look up.

"If anyone stops you from trying to come home on Friday afternoon, you call us and we will be at that school as soon as we can get there. Then you can pack everything, because you won't ever be going back," answered Karl, his voice determined. "Now let's get you to the station so you can get to school without any stress before your big exam," he continued in a lighter voice.

Hayley and Pam were both up in time to say farewell. Brett had said his the night before, stating that since she was now part of the family she no longer warranted the special effort of rising early. Alexa had found it a very warming gesture and it made her smile as she hopped in the car with Karl, Brett's window still determinedly dark.

"Good luck for your exams," said Karl as they reached the station. Alexa could only nod, feeling more nervous by the second. "And see you Friday night," he added with a broad smile, tucking her hair behind her ear before pushing her gently out of the car.

There were no disasters with the trains and Alexa made it back to school on time without any hassles. Lizzie was in the dining hall and Alexa decided to join her for a much more relaxed second breakfast. It did not last long. Sam took only five minutes to come over and try to talk to her, but Alexa had no interest in him, not any more. Leaving her half-eaten breakfast, she grabbed Lizzie by the hand and headed off towards the hall for assembly.

"Can you give me a minute?" Alexa asked Lizzie, noticing Mr Knight's open door as they walked past his office.

"Okay," said Lizzie with a smile and sat down on the couch outside the office.

"Hi," said Alexa, smiling gently at Mr Knight as she closed the office door behind her. "Lizzie's waiting outside. I just wanted to say thank you for letting me go home on the weekends."

"I thought you should've changed schools," replied Mr Knight seriously. "But under the circumstances, I guess this is the best option. There's not much left of the year."

"You wanted me to leave?"

"I wanted to you to be safe, happy," Mr Knight answered sombrely. "Your brother's principal asked why you couldn't be a day student, why you had to be a boarder. I don't know why you were made to board here in the first place, but the comment made me realise there was no reason to keep you here.

"Mrs Taylor's not too happy with the arrangement," he added with a roll of his eyes. "But I got your foster parents to write a letter demanding the change. The school has no reason or right to deny their request."

Without thinking, Alexa moved around to the other side of Mr Knight's desk and stood next to his chair. He swivelled around to face her. There was still so much sadness in his eyes when he looked at her.

"I'm sorry I upset you – for last year as well," Alexa said with soft sincerity. "I never really bothered to think about how it affected you. I wasn't dead so I didn't think much about it. Well, I tried hard not to anyway."

"I'm all right, Alexa. You don't have to worry about me."

Alexa moved her hand to sweep the hair off Mr Knight's face, but pulled back before she touched him.

"Sorry," she said, backing away towards the door, keeping her hands clasped firmly together for fear of what they might do.

It was dangerous just how comfortable she found Mr Knight's company and just how much his welfare now meant to her. All through the holidays her thoughts had swirled around how her actions had affected him. She did not want to be the person responsible for causing him pain. Even now it took all her concentration to focus on studying and not on him.

That task was made easier by her first exam. Staring down at the questions, unsure whether she could answer them correctly or not, Alexa found her mind snapping into gear. It helped her create a routine of study, punctuated by exams, that was strangely comforting.

She made sure she spent the majority of her study time outside of her room, virtually claiming a corner of the library as her own. Everyone seemed to know to leave her alone while she was there. The truth was that there was no one left to really bother her. At meal times only Lizzie, Martha and Natalie sat with her. Even Sam did not try and speak to her again.

However, school was one thing Alexa did know how to endure, and she was surprised by just how quickly the weekend seemed to come around when it had felt like one of the longest and loneliest weeks she had ever lived.

"Miss Samson," called Mr Knight on Friday morning as she left the dining hall.

Alexa expected him to walk back towards his office, but he just moved to the other side of the corridor and waited for her to join him.

"I just wanted to let you know that you can leave right after the final bell this afternoon," Mr Knight said softly. "It's all arranged. You don't need to get permission each week to leave – not unless the situation changes."

"Really? You promise? I won't get in trouble if I just go?" asked Alexa, still not quite believing.

"Only on Friday afternoons," replied Mr Knight with a chuckle. "Standard rules apply the other days. But, yes, I assure you, Miss Samson, you can leave this afternoon. Now, do you have an exam this morning?" Alexa nodded. "Then you should get going. Good luck, Miss Samson, and we will see you back here on Monday."

Alexa felt her body practically skipping away from Mr Knight. The prospect of going back to the Whites' that afternoon made the exam that much easier to endure, though the excitement of her impending release did make it a little difficult to study in the afternoon. The second the final bell went, she sprinted back to her room and packed a small bag.

"Is this a new tactic?" asked Martha as Alexa swung her bag over her shoulders. "Don't you usually wait til dark to run away? How long are we trying to cover for you?"

Alexa could not help but smile at the casual way Martha approached her disappearances.

"I get to go home for the weekends," replied Alexa happily.

"Aw, what? Way to make us jealous," cried Martha with true disappointment, as Natalie just stood with her mouth hanging open. "You realise that is like the luckiest thing to ever happen to any of us."

Alexa could only agree, smiling and nodding joyously.

"If only you were eighteen, your weekend escapes could be useful for more of us," muttered Bianca, but no one paid her any attention.

Alexa was glad. She knew from Ezra that Bianca was not happy about being stuck in school when she was now old enough to claim their lottery win, but Alexa was adamant they needed to wait until they were all eighteen. The fact that she had the winning tickets locked away with Peter Lam made it hard for them to argue, but it apparently did not make Bianca any less bitter.

Arriving home in time for dinner, Alexa gave Pam and Karl a rundown of her first week of exams. Hayley was dismayed by the fact that there was still another week of them.

"But I had plans!" Hayley cried.

"Next weekend, okay, I promise," replied Alexa. "I want to hang with you too, just can't do it this weekend."

And that was the last moment of relaxation Alexa had that weekend. The rest of it was spent in a pile of books and notes. Pam refused to let her eat in her room, forcing her to the table for meals, but Alexa only ever scoffed her food before excusing herself back to her desk. There was so much to learn and so little time. The problem was that it was not just work from this year that she had to learn. Her lengthy absences during previous years were starting to show and the basic knowledge everyone else was building on was often absent from her mind.

"Time for bed," said Pam, closing all of Alexa's books ten minutes after midnight on Monday morning. "There's no point studying to all hours. You need your sleep just as much, if not more. You still have to get to school yet."

"I'll be fine. I can function on less sleep than this," smiled Alexa, reaching out for her books.

"Yes, but after studying so hard, why risk it all by not getting enough sleep? You won't beat me on this," added Pam, her hand pressing firmly down on the books Alexa had tried to reach for.

"Okay, I'm going to bed," conceded Alexa, not really wanting to argue with Pam over something so insignificant.

Pam smiled, but did not move until Alexa did, and was back ten minutes later with Karl to make sure she had complied with her request.

"Is this what parents do?" Alexa asked, when Pam and Karl bade her goodnight.

"Yes," replied Pam with a slight smile.

"It's a little annoying," admitted Alexa.

"Teenagers do say that about their parents," replied Karl coyly.

Alexa nodded and closed her eyes, before snapping them open again in fear. "You'll keep doing though, right?" she asked.

"Absolutely," replied Karl seriously, before closing her bedroom door.

Chapter Seven

BY TUESDAY NIGHT Alexa had just one exam left and by Thursday lunchtime it would all be over. It was blissful the way time was moving now that she could spend the weekends away from school. It made the five days in between, with few friends and too many enemies, that much easier to handle.

To everyone's surprise, Bianca joined Alexa and the rest of their roommates at the breakfast table on Thursday morning. Bianca did not speak to her more than to smile a brief greeting. Martha scowled back in a rather unhelpful manner. Alexa hid her smile, because despite knowing she and Bianca were never going to be close friends, there were too many reasons for them to try to be friendly. It was just a bad day to start. Alexa was too concerned about the impending biology exam to make a genuine effort. The best she could do was to wait for Bianca to finish breakfast so she could walk with her and Lizzie to the exam.

Three hours later, the exam was over and Alexa allowed herself to finally relax. All the information she had forced into her brain over the last month suddenly flooded straight back out, leaving nothing but blissful emptiness. Exams were over and she was free for the entire weekend – every weekend. And she hoped this one would be longer than the others.

"Hi," said Alexa happily, walking into Mr Knight's office, while he sat behind his desk with a worried look on his face.

"Oh, Miss Samson, what can I do for you?" asked Mr Knight, sitting forward with a look of mild concern.

"You told me to come and see you after my exam. I want to go home tonight, not tomorrow. I gave you Pam's note on Monday."

"Oh shit, I'm sorry, I forgot all about that," replied Mr Knight, looking completely flustered and embarrassed.

Alexa quickly closed the office door behind her and sat down. "You forgot about me? This has to be good," she said, thoroughly intrigued. "When has there ever been major trouble without me being involved."

"Oh, Alexa, I think I would cry if I have any more trouble with you. No, there's been a cheating issue. It looks like there're a few people involved and then of course we'll have to talk to all their friends, who may not have been silly enough to make their cheating so obvious."

"So major trouble, and I'm not involved. This is good," smiled Alexa.

"I wouldn't be too confident just yet. You know what Mrs Taylor's like. She'll find some way to accuse the seven of you of being involved. Just tell me that you didn't cheat."

"You're kidding, right?"

"I'm afraid not. The way it's looking, I'm going to have to ask the entire grade the same question. I just believe you when you answer me."

"I never cheated," said Alexa solemnly, her heart glowing at Mr Knight promising to trust her word, though he only smiled weakly at her response. "Does this mean I have to wait until tomorrow to go home?"

"No, go and pack. I'll call your foster parents at work. There were issues with the note." Mr Knight waved his hand dismissively and Alexa knew issues meant Mrs Taylor. "I'll come down with your permission slip to leave today in about ten minutes."

Fifteen minutes later Alexa was waiting at the train station and an hour and forty minutes later she was almost home. Hayley was walking down the street towards home at the same time Alexa was and screeched in excitement at the sight of her.

With the stress of exams over, Alexa decided to cook dinner for the family. Hayley bounced with excitement at the idea and begged to be able to help. Alexa searched the cupboards until she found a full three-course dinner she could make with the food in the house. Hayley helped her prepare the food and washed up as dishes and baking trays began to pile up around them. It really was a mismatch of dishes, but Hayley thought it was going to be the best meal ever.

Pam and Karl looked a little concerned when they each arrived home, but were ordered from the kitchen. Alexa wanted it to be a big surprise. She had to repay them for all they had done for her over the last year and a half.

"Okay, the main and entrée are ready at the same time. I hope that's okay," Alexa said nervously, as everyone sat waiting at the dining table.

"I think we can cope with that," smiled Karl.

Alexa returned to the kitchen and brought out two plates of

mini pizzas and a large baking dish of chicken pasta bake.

"This looks awesome, Alexa. How come you don't cook like this, Mum?" asked Brett as he started piling food on to his plate.

"If I had to cook every day you wouldn't be getting this either," laughed Alexa.

Her cooking became much more basic when it had to be repeated often, but it had been a long time since she had had the opportunity to really cook.

"Thank you, Alexa," smiled Pam.

Alexa watched everyone as they ate, barely touching her own food. She was worried they were just being kind as they consumed the food and were really trying not to gag.

"That was very good, Alexa," said Karl, pushing his empty plate away from him as he patted his stomach.

"All I did was throw a few things together and I had Hayley's help," Alexa replied dismissively, as she ate more eagerly, feeling confident enough that they were not completely lying about liking the food.

"Are you going to cook like this every weekend?" asked Brett, who was still helping himself to more food.

"I don't know. I think the novelty would wear off pretty quick. I haven't cooked a big meal like this for a long time. The last big meal I really cooked was ten courses," Alexa said with a reminiscent smile.

"What was that for?" asked Hayley.

"Bethany's tenth birthday. Since she was four I used to cook a course for every year old she was. The ten courses were hard to do. We were both living with the Christies then. We hadn't been there that long. They went out in the morning and I started cooking. With ten courses it more like a whole day feast. We were up to course seven when they returned. They weren't very happy, but I finished the rest of the courses all the same."

"Why weren't they very happy?" asked Hayley, who clearly thought her idea was one of the greatest ever.

"The kitchen was a bit of a mess and the cupboards were fairly empty afterwards. I spent hours cleaning the kitchen after Bethy went to bed, but Mrs Christie was really upset. She ..."

Alexa could still remember the sting of the slap Mrs Christie delivered. She had hit Mrs Christie right back across the face. The look of fury on Mrs Christie's face was burned into her mind forever. Mrs Christie flew into a rage, grabbing a wooden spoon and hitting her continuously across the back as she huddled in a corner.

Mr Christie had pulled his wife off her to find out what was happening. When he was told that she had hit his wife, he had pulled Alexa up by the collar and turned her around. The slap from Mr Christie did not sting like the one from his wife had. It had felt as though she had been hit in the side of the head by a brick.

"… well, I got in a bit of trouble, but it was Bethy's birthday. She was worth it," finished Alexa with a shrug of her shoulders, determined not to dwell on the fallout that had resulted from the day.

"You could cook me eleven courses for my birthday. That would be really cool," smiled Hayley.

Alexa could not answer. She felt as though the air had been sucked right out of her lungs. It was strange that Hayley's birthday would pick up right where Bethany's finished. It seemed impossible that they had been separated for so long.

"I think that's asking a bit much," said Karl, sparing Alexa a response. "And we don't expect this sort of thing from you every week either."

"Wait, we haven't had dessert yet," said Alexa, running into the kitchen and returning with a cheesecake. She was glad she had something to turn her thoughts away from Bethany.

"Ah, but you might be able to change my mind about the cheesecake though," laughed Karl. "I could definitely eat this every week."

When everyone was well and truly full, Alexa collected all the dishes from the table and took them into the kitchen. She could hear Karl ordering Brett and Hayley to help clean up as Pam walked into the kitchen behind her.

"Here, I will do this. You've done enough tonight," said Pam, reaching around Alexa from behind to take the dishes out of her hands.

Despite knowing Pam was there, Alexa was startled by her touch. Jerking away, she dropped the dishes and they crashed heavily on the floor.

"I'm sorry," said Alexa softly, dropping to her knees to quickly gather up the shattered pieces of crockery.

"What's happened here?" asked Karl boisterously, as he walked into the kitchen. "Come on, Alexa, leave that. I'll clean it up."

Alexa paid no attention. Karl bent down next to her to take the broken dishes from her hands.

"I'm sorry. I'll have it cleaned up real soon. I'm sorry," Alexa muttered anxiously, gathering pieces more quickly as Karl tried to help. Her breathing hitched as her hands shook with the effort of trying to work faster.

"Come on, Alexa, get up. It's all right."

Karl tried to pull her to her feet, but she remained crouched. He pulled her more forcefully and turned her to face him. She refused to look into his eyes. She did not want to see this slap coming.

"I said it was all right."

Karl's left hand was grasped around her arm and he moved his right hand towards her face. The closer he moved to her the more her body shook. He released her, but she continued to shake, terrified the next touch would not be so gentle. When he did not move again, Alexa bent down to continue collecting the broken plates.

Alexa cleaned the kitchen without further interruption. Though no one dared to enter, her body continued to shake, fearing the reprisals for her clumsiness. Part of her brain was trying to reason that she did not have to worry – that Pam and Karl were not mad at her – but she had too much experience of life to trust such arguments.

When the kitchen was spotless, Alexa headed towards her room, hoping that the quietness of the house was a good indication that she would make it there without encountering anyone. However, when she made it to the hallway, she heard Karl and Pam talking softly in the lounge room and moved to the doorway to listen.

"I thought we'd moved passed all that. She's still petrified of me. I wasn't going to hurt her," said Karl in a shaky voice.

"I know that and I think she knows that as well. I just think she's been through more than we know about. She's not reacted like that for a long time, but it only ever happened in certain situations and we avoided them after that. Perhaps this is just another situation we have to avoid."

"I just wish I knew what I was doing wrong. I kept my distance from her for a long time because of things like this, but lately she's been a lot better and I thought we were starting to connect. I thought she was connecting with the whole family."

"I think she is and I don't think we should let this set us all back," said Pam tenderly.

"I just don't like her being so scared of me," said Karl sadly. "I still remember the day I walked into our bedroom and she was there returning something for you. The way she looked at me. You would have sworn she thought I was going to … I would never hurt her."

"I know that and I really do think she knows that as well. Let's just see how she is tomorrow. We'll talk to her then if she hasn't recovered and is still really jumpy."

The night passed slowly as Alexa sat by her window looking out at the starless sky. She had not meant to upset Karl. Those were the kind of situations she could not control or predict and it was not really Karl she saw before her. It was the shadowy darkness of the scores of men who had hurt her in her life and it no longer mattered who was around. She just knew that she should be scared.

These episodes had never made her feel sorry for anyone but herself, but she had gotten to know Karl and knew that he would not harm her. He was a wonderful father to Hayley and Brett, and she knew he had been hurt by her actions, involuntary though they were. There was just no way she could talk about what happened or explain how she felt when, at the time, she had been sure Karl had been about to hit her. Now she knew he never would have, but that did not change the fear she had felt. The best she could manage was a note apologising for what she had done, which she slid it into Karl's briefcase in the middle of the night.

The next day was very quiet. After sleeping in until well after everyone had left, Alexa decided to be useful. She cleaned the house top to bottom, though the kitchen was still pretty tidy from the night before. It helped pass the time, but she was glad when Hayley came home from school and wanted to hang with her.

Pam arrived home around six, immediately starting on their dinner. Alexa offered to help, but was not surprised when Pam told her to relax.

Dinner was a quiet affair. Karl was working late and would not be home until after nine o'clock, and Brett was going out, so ate quickly before returning to his room to get ready.

"Have you decided what you want to do for the weekend yet, Hayley?" asked Alexa, as they finished up their dinners.

"I want to go into the city," replied Hayley happily. "We've never been in there together. There's so much to see and do. We can just pick when we get there. Then on Sunday maybe we can see a movie or just go for a ride around the park, if the weather's good."

Alexa realised why Pam and Karl had not wanted Hayley to talk about her plans last weekend. The last time Alexa had been in the city was to give Bethany her Christmas present and she had not wanted to leave. The thought of going back was not enticing. The parts of the city Alexa knew best were not parts she wanted to introduce Hayley to, and she did not know how to be in the city without looking for Bethany.

"You don't have to do everything Hayley wants to," said Pam cautiously.

"I know. It's okay. We can go where she wants," replied Alexa, trying to sound confident in front of Hayley, but she could see that Pam was still concerned.

Thankfully, Hayley did not sense Alexa's uneasiness and was almost happy to go to bed early so she could be rested for her big weekend. Alexa escaped to her room, trying to conjure a plan for their trip into the city. It would have been wiser to just to tell Hayley they had to do something else, but it was not something she knew how to explain to her.

"Can I come in?" asked Karl, standing in the doorway.

"Sure," nodded Alexa, automatically pulling her knees into her chest.

She noticed Karl stutter, seeing her recoil, but he continued to move forward and sat down at her desk.

"I hear Hayley talked you into taking her to the city. Do you think that's wise?" he asked.

"No, but what should I tell her?" Alexa replied honestly. "How do I explain to her the parts of the city I know best? This is where my sister regularly shoots up heroin and here's where I worked as a prostitute."

Karl's face twisted awkwardly, though Alexa could tell that he was trying hard not to react. He shifted as though he was going to sit on the bed with her, but stayed where he was.

"You don't have to take everything on your own, you know," said Karl, but Alexa could only stare at him blankly. "Why don't I come with the two of you? I know the city quite well – the other parts," he added with a kind smile. "Then if something happens, I'll be there to help, and you can just relax."

"You would do that?" Alexa asked curiously, not really believing.

"For my daughters, I would do that and so much more. It would be nice to spend the day with the two of you."

"Okay," nodded Alexa.

Karl smiled as he left and Alexa was glad he did not wait for some kind of thanks. She loved that, despite all their arguments and her inability to commit to them, they continued to see her as a genuine member of their family. She would never be able to tell them just how thankful she was, and was glad they never expected her to be able to.

Hayley was almost bouncing off the walls when she found out Karl would be coming with them. Karl worked hard and frequently long hours. Before Alexa came to live with them, Hayley often resented Karl and threw tantrums when he could not spend enough time with her. When Alexa first arrived, Hayley had directed all her attentions Alexa's way, pushing Karl, and often the rest of the family to the sideline. With Alexa's acceptance of, and newfound closeness to, the rest of the Whites, came an improvement in relations between Karl and Hayley.

Alexa was grateful for Karl's presence. Even before they reached the city, she began to panic. It was made worse when Hayley insisted on knowing where she wanted to go, and she had to admit that she did not know.

"But you come to the city all the time. You must know heaps of things to do," argued Hayley.

"I only know the bad parts, Hales," replied Alexa softly.

Hayley seemed to understand that explanation and looked up at her father. Karl smiled and took Hayley's hand.

"That's why I'm here, to show you two around, let you discover this place together," he said kindly.

Although Hayley was still a little wary, her excitement quickly returned when they started walking around the harbour foreshore. It was a beautiful, clear blue day that made the harbour simply sparkle. It was hard not to admire the beauty.

"This is where I used to bring your mum when we were dating," smiled Karl. "We used to walk through the Botanic Gardens."

"Can we go there, Daddy? Can we?"

Karl looked over at Alexa with a worried look and she was sure he was thinking what she was; Bethany loves parks. When Alexa nodded, she was not sure if she was being heartless or reckless. Part of her was almost desperate for the chance to see Bethany again, but she was sure Karl would have to drag her away to get her to leave this time. Another part wondered what Bethany would think if she saw them without them spying her.

Alone and in a drug-affected state, Alexa could not imagine

what Bethany would make of her being with the Whites. Karl and Hayley were laughing and smiling, drawing her into their happiness more often than she thought possible. She hoped it would make Bethany realise what she was missing by staying on the streets, but knew that was unlikely. If Bethany saw them now, she would feel betrayed and abandoned.

It made Alexa grateful that Hayley's stomach started growling and they were forced to leave the gardens in search of food. Karl kept them away from parks after that.

"You're doing great," Karl whispered to Alexa as they sat down at the pancake parlour Hayley had chosen for lunch.

Karl was breaking all the rules and allowed Hayley to have sweets for lunch, while he and Alexa shared a pizza.

"Where are we going next?" asked Hayley, as Karl finished off her chocolate pancakes that she had only been able to get halfway through.

"I want to get a present for your mother," replied Karl, stroking Hayley's hair. "And then we should probably start making our way home. Don't want to be late for dinner."

If it had just been her, Alexa knew Hayley would have argued against such a proposal, but she did not dare argue with Karl. Hayley's unhappiness at the plan disappeared completely when Karl asked for her help selecting a present.

"See anything nice?" asked Karl, standing behind Alexa at the jewellery store. Alexa shook her head and stepped back from the cabinet, looking anywhere but at the jewellery. "For Pam," he added, putting his hands and her shoulders and moving her forward.

"You should pick these sorts of things," replied Alexa, still shaking her head.

"I have expensive taste. If Pam knows I bought it without input from anyone, she'll say I wasted money. We're trying to save."

"What for?" asked Alexa guiltily, worried about how much she was costing the Whites.

"Holiday. We want to take the whole family, so help me find something simple, beautiful and less than fifty dollars."

Hayley was like Karl and had to be continually directed away from the expensive, diamond-studded jewellery. Knowing the budget, Alexa did not find it anywhere near as difficult to find suitable suggestions. Selecting between three different options, they eventually all settled on a pair of silver drop earrings.

"Perfect," smiled Karl, looking down at the earrings as he handed over the money.

After a desperately needed coffee, they boarded the train back home. Alexa shook slightly as the train pulled away, tears stinging her eyes at the thought of leaving Bethany once more. Karl's hand reached out to stroke Hayley's hair, forcing his arm to sit behind Alexa's shoulders as she sat between them. Karl just smiled reassuringly when she looked up at him.

Alexa held it together until after dinner, when she could not stop herself from escaping to her room. With tears slipping down her cheeks, she curled up in bed with the photo album Pam and Karl had given her for Christmas. Although the photos of her and Bethany were interspersed with the ones of the Whites, she could not reconcile her two families so easily. To be with one was to abandon the other and she did not want to choose. There was no choice. She could only hope that a way to keep the Whites in her life next year soon developed, because she wanted Bethany to know what it was like to be loved by a family, even if it had to be coupled with the terror of continually thinking she would lose it.

***

With exams over and normal classes due to begin again, Alexa became more anxious about returning to school. There would be no way of avoiding Bianca, Chad and Sam now. Walking into the dining hall for her traditional second breakfast, Alexa found the year twelve boarding students looking very sombre and, most unusually, all seated around just one table. Lizzie was with the rest of their roommates, not too far from Sam and Chad. It was not the welcome Alexa had hoped for.

"What's going on?" Alexa asked Lizzie quietly.

Sam looked up at her as she joined the table. His face was grave and serious, like everyone else's, but he did not try to talk to her.

"A whole heap of people got caught cheating in the exams. Apparently, the answer sheets were photocopied and sold," said Lizzie

"And guess who they think's responsible?" asked Chad angrily.

Sam kept looking at Alexa, watching her reaction. Alexa was glad she had some forewarning of the issue. It would have been a terrible start to her week otherwise. If it had become this serious so quickly, there was no way she would not be implicated with the rest of the G7.

"Us, I assume," Alexa replied casually. "Who got caught though?"

"We don't know. We haven't heard anything. It all came out on Friday, but Mr Knight wouldn't tell us anything. He's been here all weekend," said Lizzie.

At nine o'clock the anxious boarders were joined by the curious day students in the library, with the usual whole-school assembly cancelled to deal with them. Mrs Taylor arrived with Mr Knight and the heads of each subject. It was the greatest congregation of teachers the grade had ever amassed.

Nobody spoke as they were told that the answer sheets – all the answer sheets – had been stolen. It was followed by a pained silence when it was revealed that each of the answer sheets had incorrect answers on them to identify anyone who had tried to memorise the answers. This was not the first time answer sheets had been stolen and the school had learnt from their mistakes.

Those involved were being threatened with expulsion. For the students who cheated it was a serious situation, but for the members of the G7 it was dire. If any one of them was found to be involved, all of them could be expelled.

"There are enough suspected cheats that each of you will be friends with at least one," said Mrs Taylor. "Therefore, every single one of you will face a meeting with the heads of each subject and myself. The onus will be on you to prove you did not cheat. Mr Knight will remain out here if any of you wish to confess. Alphabetically will do fine, Mr Knight."

Mrs Taylor and the heads of subject moved in to a small room inside the library. Mr Knight did not look at ease with the arrangement and Alexa was sure it had been planned without his knowledge.

"Kylie Adams, you're first," said Mr Knight in a low voice. "Make your way in to see Mrs Taylor. Richard Allen, you're next. Wait outside the door."

Alexa made herself comfortable at one of the tables in the corner of the library. With the entire grade to question it was sure to be a long day. Ezra and Lizzie soon joined her.

"Can I sit with you guys," asked Bianca timidly.

Lizzie and Ezra turned to Alexa, and from the look on Ezra's face, Alexa thought this might have been a premeditated plan.

"Sure," said Alexa, shrugging her shoulders. She really did not need more issues this year and it was easier to pretend to be friends with Bianca than to actually be her enemy.

"We need to talk," said Nick, arriving minutes later with Alan, Chad and Sam, all looking very grave.

Alexa nodded and followed them to a quiet section of the library. The stony looks on the boys' faces did not bode well. It made her wonder if this was the inevitable event that was required to counteract all the good she had been experiencing with the Whites and to set her life back in balance.

"We're in trouble," said Alan. "It looks like Stacey and Chris both bought copies of the answer papers."

"Please be joking," said Alexa, sighing in defeat. "Of all the things I could be expelled for it'll be the one I had nothing to do with. Did they tell you who they got them off?"

"They're keeping that to themselves. Please, just tell me that none of you three bought any of the answer sheets," said Nick.

"No," said Chad and Sam in unison.

"Me either," said Alexa.

"Good, then it's the five of us," said Nick, smiling slightly.

Alexa felt like the G7 had officially become the G5. It was a strangely natural grouping and one she would have actually chosen to be a part of.

"Alan Chan, you're next," called Mr Knight from across the library.

"Wish me luck," smiled Alan, holding his fist up for Alexa to tap.

Alexa smilingly complied, doing the same with Nick as he left with Alan, but her smile faltered when she realised she was alone with Sam and Chad and that they were no longer her friends.

"I'd better get back," Alexa said, turning quickly away from them.

"Wait," said Sam, grabbing her by the hand.

"Look, you made it pretty clear what you thought of me last term," Alexa replied, her voice breaking at the memory.

"I was wrong, okay?"

"No, Sam, it's not okay." Alexa could feel her voice cracking despite her efforts to control it. "You wanted to hit me. How is that ever supposed to be okay?"

"I would never hit you."

"Chad seemed to think you would."

"I know. I was angry and I took it out on you."

"It seems to be a good pass time around here."

"I was wrong, more wrong than I could ever say," said Sam sadly. "Mel had been in my ear for weeks, just dropping little hints about you planning something to get her in trouble. She said you were mad at her for disliking you and objecting to our friendship. I know you never start rumours – and that she does – but it fit what she'd said about you wanting to blame her and when you did … I never thought she could be so manipulative. I wanted to believe her. She's my sister. Please. Forgive me."

"Sam, I …"

"I know you didn't have anything to do with the rumours, okay. I was wrong. Please forgive me. I will beg if you want me to." Sam fell to his knees and took Alexa's hands in his. "Please forgive me for being the biggest bastard in the world."

Alexa could not help but smile, though she did not want to. She did not want to let Sam off so easily after the hurt he had put her through.

"Why should I forgive you?" Alexa asked seriously. "Would you forgive me if it was the other way around?"

"Yes, in an instant," replied Sam solemnly.

"I don't know. Am I forgiven?" Alexa asked, turning to Chad.

"I don't blame you for what happened," said Chad sincerely. "I was just upset. It wasn't your fault. You didn't cheat on me, and I don't know that I would've wanted to tell you if I knew Sam had ever cheated on you. We're cool. Just don't expect me to talk to *her* ever again."

"As long as you talk to me," replied Alexa, almost wishing she could cut her ties with Bianca so cleanly.

"So we're all forgiven?" asked Sam.

"Yes, all is forgiven," Alexa nodded, daring to smile just slightly.

Sam jumped up to his feet and hugged her tightly, his head in her neck. Alexa was not sure she had done the right thing by forgiving him, but knew he was sincere when she felt his tears soak into her shirt.

"I really am sorry," Sam said softly. "You're the one person I could always count on. I shouldn't have treated you so badly."

Sam brushed the hair off Alexa's face and stroked her cheek gently. It made her heart ache. She had missed him so much more than she realised.

"Just don't do it again, okay," Alexa said in a tortured voice. "You broke my heart."

"I know. I promise I won't ever hurt you again," replied Sam sincerely.

Alexa smiled, trying to believe him completely, but it was difficult. Sam had never hurt her like that before and she had never believed he would. It made hanging with him awkward, and she was glad when an excuse came up for her to go back to sitting with Ezra and Lizzie.

The day passed slowly as student after student was called in to see Mrs Taylor. By lunchtime nearly all the day students had been spoken to. Everyone came out of their meeting looking stressed and nervous, though it was clear from the whispered conversations that they weren't outing the cheaters in the meeting and many were still hoping they would get away with their indiscretion.

Stacey was the last of the day students to be questioned. Once she was called in for her meeting the rest of the grade was allowed to go to the dining hall for lunch.

"So what happened? What did they ask you?" Chad asked Alan and Nick when Alexa arrived at their table.

"They just asked us about our answers to some of the questions on each exam, but after that Mrs Taylor grilled us on if we copied the answer sheets or knew where they were kept," said Nick.

"Were any of you offered the answer sheets?" asked Alexa, after finding out Ezra had been, but refused.

"Nope," said Nick and Alan, while Sam shook his head.

"Yeah," said Chad. "I thought they were joking. I was complaining about all the work and how after Bianca I thought I was going to fail big time."

"Who offered them to you?" asked Nick.

"Adrian."

"As in our roommate?" asked Sam.

"Yeah," nodded Chad. "I thought he was joking and I didn't want them anyway so I didn't ask him any more about it. I just told him that I'd be right."

"We can't just dump Adrian in it because he was dumb enough to cheat. Just because he had the answer sheets doesn't mean he stole them," said Sam.

"Maybe not, but do you realise how screwed the four of you'll be if you're expelled?" asked Alexa, thinking this might be the one time they should try and save their own skin. "You're all top of the grade at the moment and this isn't some stupid prank. This could really mess things up for you guys."

"What about you?" asked Sam.

"I know how to screw up my life all by myself. This really doesn't make much difference to me," Alexa shrugged. She was almost thankful for the excuse to go and live with the Whites full-time. She was getting a bit sick of this routine.

Sam placed his hand on her face and rubbed her cheek gently with his thumb. Alexa rose from her seat without looking at Sam.

"You guys decide what we're doing. I think without saying something we're a good chance of going down for this," she said. "But we've never ratted on anyone before. It's up to you guys. I'll go along with whatever you decide."

The questioning of the students continued after lunch and when the bell rang at the end of the last period the day students were allowed to go home and the boarders who had already been questioned could go back to their rooms, leaving Alexa and Bianca together in the library.

"How were your holidays?" asked Alexa cautiously, hoping that she could call an end to all hostilities that day, but was not given the chance.

"Bianca Ross, you're next," called Mr Knight, and Bianca rose and moved outside the door where the meetings were being held.

"Miss Samson," said Mr Knight softly, sitting down across the table from her when Bianca moved into the interrogation room. "You're up next."

"Thanks," she said, giving him as a soft smile.

"I need you to keep your temper in there," Mr Knight urged desperately. "You know the purpose of these meetings and since you didn't cheat you should have no problems with the teachers. Mrs Taylor, on the other hand, will try and find any way of expelling you. Please just keep your temper under control. I doubt I can work any more miracles for you."

Alexa could see the toll the day was taking on Mr Knight. This was perhaps the only thing she could do to ease his pain and she did not want to let him down.

"Not a single unpleasant word will leave my mouth, I promise," she smiled and moved to the door where Bianca was being interviewed.

Twenty minutes later Alexa strolled to the dining hall for dinner with a slight smile on her face. It had been an interesting meeting. She had kept her word and been pleasant the whole way through, though Mrs Taylor had tried to make it as difficult as possible. The teachers had started with direct questions about whether she had cheated in any or all of her exams, but Alexa never let herself be pushed into losing her cool. The attention had then been turned to her exam papers. All had been marked and Alexa had been thankful to see that biology had not been as disastrous as last year.

Alexa had then been asked to explain her answers to questions she had done both very well and very poorly in. In fact, she had found that section of the meeting very useful in identifying the weaker aspects of her exam performance. She almost smiled at how helpful the other teachers were being, and from the slight smirk on Mr Pollock's face, she was sure the other teachers were trying to make the best of this situation too.

"Did you copy and distribute the answer sheets to your fellow students?" Mrs Taylor had asked, once the analysis of Alexa's exam answers ended.

"No, ma'am," Alexa had answered firmly, but politely.

"Do you know where the answer sheets are kept before exams?"

"No, ma'am."

Alexa could see Mrs Taylor was becoming increasingly frustrated with her two-word answers and it had only made her more determined to continue.

"Do you know anyone who does?" asked Mrs Taylor in a disbelieving tone.

"No, ma'am."

"Do you realise I think you are lying?"

"Yes, ma'am," Alexa had smiled, refusing to temper her unimpressed stare.

Mrs Taylor had glared at her before finally waving an irritated hand to dismiss her. Mr Knight had watched her leave from the corner of his eyes and she had given him a sneaky thumbs-up to reassure him that she had done everything he had asked of her.

Alexa's joy at that minor victory did not last long, tempered by the dozens of anxious faces in the dining hall. Dinner was a tense affair as they discussed what might come next, but it was nothing compared to the mood in the library the next morning. The heads of each subject were absent, but the sour faces of Mrs Taylor and Mr Knight were all the students needed to keep them fearfully quiet.

One by one the guilty students were named, including the five innocent members of the G7. In all, they totalled almost a fifth of the grade. There were so many that the school could not possibly expel them all. They would be suspended and receive a mark of zero for all the exams they cheated in. Nick, Alan, Chad and Sam groaned as one, their heads falling into their hands in disbelief. Alexa wished she cared more, but she had been resigned to this outcome since yesterday. She just hoped Pam and Karl would come and pick her up today.

The rest of the grade was allowed to leave and return to normal classes. Alexa waved Ezra and her roommates goodbye and moved between Sam and Chad, her arm around each of their shoulders to comfort them.

"All your parents have been called to explain the situation," said Mrs Taylor. "The suspensions will be effective as of today. Arrangements are being made for all of you to return home by the end of the school day. If your parents are not able to pick you up, you will be sent home with a note they will have to sign."

"You five," said Mr Knight, pointing to the newly designated G5. "You need to go to my office. You will be dealt with separately."

Mr Knight accompanied the guilty students to Mrs Taylor's office, leaving the innocent G7 members to wait outside his office on the couch.

"I guess we're not suspended yet," said Chad glumly, as Nick, Alan and Sam all took seats on the lounge, while he and Alexa sat on the armrests.

"I think yet is the operative word," said Alexa.

Sam curled his arm around her waist and hugged her, rubbing her thigh tenderly. She stood up off the armrest and moved out on to the landing. Sam quickly followed.

"What's wrong? You still don't think I'd hurt you, do you?" asked Sam, as they stood alone on the landing.

"No, it's not that," Alexa replied somewhat dishonestly. "It just doesn't feel right any more, you touching me like that."

"Is this about *him*?" Sam asked with barely masked contempt. "I thought you said that anyone that doesn't understand us isn't worth it."

"I did, but this isn't for him. It's for me," replied Alexa. "I love him, Sam, I really do. He's the one I want to put his hand on my waist, not you. I know you're just trying to comfort me, but I don't want to be comforted like that any more. We're getting older now. I just don't think it's appropriate. You know you couldn't do it when you get another girlfriend."

"I guess," shrugged Sam, making Alexa realise that he would

probably never truly accept her feelings for Mr Knight. She wanted to tell him he never had to worry about anything ever happening between them, but she still hoped that one day that might not be true. "Just let me give you one last kiss, okay."

Alexa smiled and nodded, wondering if she would ever be able to deny Sam anything. Sam moved in and kissed her gently on the cheek. It was warm and tender. Her arms wrapped around his neck just as Mr Knight rounded the corner. Sam was still holding her cheek to his lips and Alexa could see jealousy and sadness flicker in Mr Knight's eyes at the sight, but her eyes remained unapologetic.

"Thank you," Alexa said, hugging Sam gratefully.

"Inside," said Mr Knight gruffly, opening his office door.

"What's going on?" asked Nick. "We being suspended? This isn't fair. We didn't cheat."

"I know," sighed Mr Knight. "The teachers know that too. I need to ask. Do any of you have any information about this? Do any of you know who copied and distributed those answer sheets?"

No one turned to look at each other. If they were going to dob, they would have decided to before now.

"No," they replied in unison.

"Okay," nodded Mr Knight, though Alexa realised he did not seem his usual self and was refusing to look her way. "This is what is going to happen. You won't be suspended. Your marks will stand, but Mrs Taylor is sending your parents a note explaining that she believes you were involved, which they must sign and return."

"Who are they sending my letter to?" asked Alexa. "My social worker?"

"Your foster parents," replied Mr Knight softly, still not meeting her eyes. "I've already spoken to them, as well as Mr Michael's grandparents. I will phone the rest of your parents tonight to explain the situation."

"That's it?" asked Chad, his voice somewhere between annoyed and thankful.

"No. The police have been called. Cheating issue aside, it was a serious breach of security just accessing the exam answer sheets. It has huge implications for other exams like your trials and finals. We need to know the papers can be held securely in the school."

"So I guess that means Alexa's at the top of the interview list," joked Alan. "Surely the way she can sneak in and out of school undetected is as big a security breach."

Mr Knight groaned in a way that suggested Alan's joking was

not far off the mark. Alexa could only shake her head as Alan smirked apologetically.

Neither the school nor the police were able to glean any information from any of the suspended students. That left Mrs Taylor only more convinced that the G7 were involved. As Sam and Chad were the only two people in their room who had not been suspended, they were the first of the G5 to be interviewed by the police. Alexa actually smiled and waved at Constable Banks as he waited with another officer outside Mr Knight's office.

Constable Banks smiled and shook his head.

"You're on my list," he said, pointing at her as she walked past.

"How else do I get to spend time with you?" laughed Alexa.

The joking continued when she, Alan and Nick were called to Mr Knight's office for their interview. They were just thankful they got to do it all together.

"Can you tell us anything that might be useful?" asked Constable Banks, finally getting down to the issue at hand.

"We didn't cheat, we were never offered the answers," replied Alexa seriously. "We know people who were, but most never told us who by and the rest we know is just from rumours. And I refuse to tell you those. I know how untrue they can be."

"Then let's just run through this list of questions so we can say we asked," sighed Constable Banks.

It was clear Constable Banks found this process as useless and tedious as they did, so they cut him as much slack as possible and kept their sarcasm to a minimum.

"They hate you, don't they?" said Alexa as they finished up. "Your workmates. This is their way of torturing you, sending you back here all the time."

Constable Banks smirked slightly.

"I'm the school liaison officer. It's part of my job," Constable Banks replied, before frowning slightly. "But I can't say that I've ever had so much trouble at one school before, or been forced to deal with the same students so often. Apparently, if your year advisor stopped defending you and accepted you were to blame I would never have to be involved."

They all gasped slightly at the revelation and Constable Banks put his finger to his lips, warning of the trouble he would get in if they spread that confession. However, it explained a lot about the difference in their punishments since Mr Knight had been their year advisor.

"Right, well we need to go and speak to more useful people than you three," smiled Constable Banks as he stood up to leave.

Nick, Alan and Alexa took the opportunity to escape and went to find Chad and Sam, but they refused to talk about their interviews. Chad, in particular, seemed more worried and downhearted than ever. It made Alexa nervous. She, Nick and Alan had expected to be laughing and joking with them over their respective interviews and the ridiculousness of the situation, but Sam and Chad were taking it very seriously.

"What's going on?" Alexa asked Sam, the day before the suspended students were due to return.

Chad was still refusing to talk to her, but she knew he had told Nick and Alan what was happening, because they were now intent on keeping her in the dark too.

"Nothing, it's okay," replied Sam dismissively.

"No, it's not. Neither you nor Chad has told me what happened with the police and Chad seems really upset. What's going on? I might be able to help."

"Chad had to tell the police that Adrian offered him the answer sheets," sighed Sam, looking at her warily, as though gauging how much more to say. "I think Adrian may have been involved, but now Mr Knight's really angry because he didn't mention this before. He's even talking about suspending Chad to make an example out of him."

"I'll talk to him. Nothing will happen. I'll make sure of it," Alexa assured Sam instantly.

"We didn't want you to do that," hissed Sam urgently, grabbing her hand. "We don't want Mr Knight having that sway over you. I don't care how much you trust him, it's not enough. We don't trust him, okay. Just leave it be. We'll handle it."

"Okay," Alexa nodded, and squeezed Sam's hand. She did not tell him that she suspected Mr Knight's anger had more to do with her and him than Chad, or that this was not something she was going to let slide.

Mr Knight had barely left the school since the cheating situation arose so Alexa was sure he would still be in his office. The door was open, but he was not behind his desk. She entered without knocking to find him standing at the window, peering out at the grey skies. He did not hear her enter and stood unmoved as she sat down.

Alexa watched him scan the sky. It was nice to be able to just sit and look at him. After almost five minutes he turned his back on the window and sat at his desk.

"Oh holy shit," gasped Mr Knight, jumping from his chair at the sight of her seated before him. "Alexa, how long have you been there."

"A little while."

Alexa was trying hard not to laugh, causing her cheek muscles to cramp painfully as Mr Knight slowly resumed his seat. His eyes softened as he watched her.

"What brings you here?" he asked kindly, a slight smile on his face.

"Chad."

"That has nothing to do with you," replied Mr Knight firmly, the smile slipping from his downturned lips.

Alexa stood up and closed the door before resuming her seat.

"It has everything to do with me," she replied firmly. "Do you think I don't know why you're considering suspending him? I bet you wish it was Sam who'd been offered the answer sheets." Her tone was not accusatory, but soft and deliberate. "So because you can't get to Sam directly you thought could punish him through Chad."

"I think you misunderstand the situation, Miss Samson. I told everybody that I had no tolerance for cover-ups. Mr Olsen knew more than he said."

"Yes, and he told the police," Alexa pointed out. "Everyone who was suspended kept their mouths shut. Chad didn't cheat. He refused the offer of the answer sheets even though he was going through a rough time and probably really wanted them. You should be praising him and yet you're trying to suspend him. Why would anyone not cheat when refusing to cheat has the same consequences?

"You let jealousy guide you. Sam gave me a kiss, on the cheek, and I let him. Why? Because I put an end to physical contact between the two of us. Do you see me getting all angsty when you go home and fuck your fiancée? The reality is that you are engaged and I am your student. 'We' don't exist."

Chapter Eight

IT WAS NEVER clear if Alexa was the reason why Chad was spared further punishment. Alexa made sure she did not come close enough to Mr Knight over the next week to find out. She also did not dare tell Sam that she had confronted Mr Knight; not with him, Chad and the others just as intent on maintaining their silence on the issue. When all the suspended students returned to school, the whole grade seemed determined to not speak of it again.

The only student who did not return was Adrian, after the police indicated that he would be their main suspect – though that did not change Mrs Taylor's belief that the G7 had put him up to it; something she told them to their faces. Adrian's older brother, Edward, had been suspected of stealing answer sheets when he had been a student at Redgrove, but it had never been proven. That previous incident was the reason incorrect answers were included on the answer sheets. Most of the students wondered why the school did not just find a better place to store the answer sheets, but logic never had been a defining attribute of Redgrove College.

As the drama over the cheating scandal subsided, Alexa started to fear what would replace it. It made her thankful that she had sorted things out with Sam. She was not sure she could have handled having him as her enemy again. That left Bianca as the most obvious threat to her peace, but somehow even that situation calmed down to the point of civility.

Bianca's icy glare had slowly thawed as the term progressed. Alexa had the feeling it was a combination of Chad and Sam confronting Bianca about blaming her for starting the rumours, and letting Bianca know who did start them, and Bianca finishing her two weeks of afternoon detention. However, friendliness never extended to an apology and a large part of Alexa was actually grateful for that. She was not sure she could forgive Bianca for the way she acted, though she could certainly move on from it. If Bianca had asked for forgiveness she might not have been able to give it and that would have surely spelt the end of their shaky friendship.

With her friendships back intact and the weekends being spent at home with the Whites, life had never been so easy for Alexa, although Karl had not taken the arrival of the letter from Mrs Taylor very well.

"You had better be able to explain what the hell is going on," said Karl angrily once Brett and Hayley had gone to bed on the Friday night after receiving the letter.

"I didn't cheat, I swear," replied Alexa sincerely, hoping they would believe her.

"I know you didn't cheat!" cried Karl. "I want to know why you're being accused of it when there's no proof. It's clear they were able to prove the other students cheated. Why are they accusing you of being the mastermind ringleader?"

Alexa found Karl's outrage endearing, but her attempts to placate him by explaining that that was just the way Redgrove was did not work very well.

"Give me one good reason why we should let you go back there on Monday," Karl stormed.

"Because it's too late in the year to change schools, I'm used to all that crap, and my friends are there," Alexa replied, before deciding to throw in some extra reasons to placate him. "And it's never been more bearable than it is now. Being able to come home every weekend, and not having the stress of starting a new school or making new friends. This set up is almost perfect."

"I've already told your year advisor I don't accept this," said Karl more calmly. "We won't sign it. I'll send it back saying I've read it, but I won't sign it. If they kick you out, I'll take them to court. That place has put you through enough already."

Alexa tried to joke the next day with Pam about Karl's anger, but she was surprised to find that Pam was angrier than Karl about the letter. Pam did not yell the way Karl did, but Alexa had never seen her so furious as she explained, point-by-point, just how wrong and unjust the situation was.

"I'm not that happy with you either," said Pam, turning on her. Alexa could only stutter her surprise. "That incident with the bombs last year, that was serious and we felt we understood why they were taking precautions. It was your friend's brother that was hurt, after all. But you knew then, you knew all of last year that you were being persecuted there.

"Alexa, we signed up for this whole thing so that we could help make a difference. We wanted to give another child a chance to experience all the opportunities our children take for granted. If you had let us, we could have given you so much more than this, spared you things like this."

There was no way Alexa could respond. Every week Pam and Karl seemed to go that little bit further, envelope her that little bit more, and she knew that if she was not careful they would soon possess her completely. Part of her wished they would, but she was also fearful of enjoying this peaceful life too much. Life with Bethany, life on the streets, did not resemble this family life, and Alexa did not want to become so soft as to not be able to face the world to which she truly belonged. She could not abandon Bethany for her own comforts.

It was a balance Alexa was trying hard to strike, but it was not the only one. The weekends were no longer so long and boring, and without the stress of exams hanging over her, she found it hard to muster the motivation to study when she was home with the Whites. The only way she could justify spending so much time away from her books was to work doubly hard during the week.

Up early on school days, Alexa managed to squeeze in two hours of study in the mornings and was often the last in her room to leave her desk in the evenings. It was tiring, but strangely rewarding. For perhaps the first time in her school life, she felt like she understood what was happening in most of her classes. She paid attention to the teachers and worked hard in class.

When Alexa made it home on the weekends, her books nearly always remained in her bag under the bed. The main occupation was now Hayley's upcoming eleventh birthday three weeks before the end of term. Hayley was so excited that her birthday fell on a Saturday and that Alexa would be home for it. All their conversations now revolved around what they would do on her birthday weekend and the parties they were having.

"Hales, I don't think I can help you out with planning your birthday party," confessed Alexa tentatively at dinner on Saturday night. "I've never had a birthday party. I've never even been to one."

Hayley's face fell as silence reverberated around the dinner table. No one knew what to say, though from the corner of her eye Alexa could see that the awkward tension was starting to make Brett crack. Seconds later he burst out laughing. Pam scolded him, but he could not stop.

"I'm sorry, but you're so weird," Brett laughed, making Alexa smile. Whatever he thought about her, it was not cruel. "You've done so many extreme things, but never been to a birthday party."

"Brett," warned Karl sternly.

"What? It's true," continued Brett smilingly. "And isn't it better we get to be the ones teaching her how to throw a birthday party rather than how to shoot up crack?"

"Smack," replied Alexa automatically. Everyone stared at her. "We learned how to shoot up smack, not crack, at home."

"See," laughed Brett.

Karl finally cracked a smile, but it was followed by a heavy sigh and a shake of the head. Alexa noticed Pam was struggling to see the lighter side, but she liked the way Brett could make fun of her life. It was never mean and he did have a point. Her life was very backwards.

"I can throw you a birthday party for you this year," said Hayley excitedly. "Your first one. It'll be awesome."

Alexa just managed to squeeze out a smile. Her birthday had never been a day of celebration and she had had no plans for changing that, but there was still plenty of time to have that conversation. For now, Hayley was smiling and that was all that mattered to Alexa.

The weekend before Hayley's birthday was chaotic. Hayley would not leave Alexa's side as they tried to get everything prepared. Hayley had not allowed any final decisions to be made until Alexa arrived home, which meant that Friday night was spent frantically organising. A family day was finally organised for the next Saturday, with a birthday party for Hayley's friends planned for the Sunday.

When everything was sorted, Pam ordered Hayley to bed with barely concealed frustration.

"I'm sorry," said Alexa meekly as Brett laughed.

"It's not your fault," sighed Pam. "We're really happy you're involved. I'll just be glad when next weekend is over. I fear for what Hayley intends to plan for your birthday now she's found out it's your eighteenth. She's been talking about that almost as much as her own birthday."

"You don't have to do anything," replied Alexa solemnly. "It's really not a big deal to me."

"It's a big deal to us," replied Karl in a flat, tired voice, before smiling softly and ordering them to bed.

It took all Alexa's strength not to try and imagine what they would do for her birthday, but her heart warmed at the knowledge that they would do something. Dinner at a nice restaurant, perhaps. Or a day at the beach. Alexa quickly pulled herself away from those thoughts. It was too much to ask for and more than she deserved. She could not continue to let the Whites give her so much.

Pam had to practically sneak Alexa out of the house the next day so they could shop for Hayley's present, but Hayley saw them leaving and rushed to Alexa's side.

"But she can't go out. We have to choose birthday cakes," cried Hayley, grabbing Alexa's hand.

"You chose them last weekend and you're not changing your mind," replied Pam firmly.

"But I haven't decided what to wear," Hayley tried next.

"That's okay. I can stay," replied Alexa, looking over at Pam. "We don't have to do what I planned."

It was almost comical the way Hayley's eyes widened and her head swivelled between Alexa and the house.

"You'll help me pick clothes later?" asked Hayley, her voice wavering.

Alexa nodded and Hayley finally conceded, running back into the house.

"She seems very excited. Has she always been this excited about her birthday?" Alexa asked Pam, as they drove to the local shopping centre.

"She's always liked her birthday, but I've never seen her this excited. This is off the scale, even for Hayley," smiled Pam. "I think it has more to do with the fact that you're going to be here. She used to ask last year about you coming home for family things, special events. I wish we'd considered it more closely. She really looks up to you."

"Does that worry you?" asked Alexa. It worried her.

"It used to, but I don't think she aspires to be as troubled as you. She sees the other side of you. Given everything you've been through, it's a surprise you're still so polite and unjaded, I guess you would say."

"I don't feel unjaded, or polite for that matter, a lot of the time," laughed Alexa, surprised that such descriptors were being applied to her by people who had borne the brunt of her very jaded and angry side.

"We think you're doing very well, given the circumstances."

"I'm trying – I – I don't want to make trouble for you guys."

"We know," smiled Pam. "We're trying too. It's just as hard for us to know the right things to say and do sometimes."

"What do you think Hayley would like for her birthday?" asked Alexa, quickly changing the subject. "I was thinking of buying her a necklace. Do you think she'll like it?"

"I think she'll wear it until it falls apart."

After shopping, there was no escape for Alexa. For the rest of the weekend, Hayley peppered her with questions, insisting she give her opinion on every single detail. They were not the big sister duties Alexa had been used to performing and by Sunday night she was exhausted.

"Next weekend, when I come home on Friday night, you're going to have to let me do my homework, okay," Alexa said to Hayley before bed on Sunday night.

Alexa had not done a single minute of study this weekend and the workload was only increasing as the weeks went on.

"I want to be able to spend the whole weekend with you, so that means I have to have all my homework done. Is that a deal?"

"That's a deal," Hayley said, wrapping her arms around Alexa's neck.

But even as Alexa lay in bed, she tried to set out a new schedule in her head for the week so that she could complete her homework before the weekend. Deep in thought, worried it would not be possible, Alexa jumped when she heard her bedroom door creak open.

All the lights were out in the house. Alexa's heart started to thump erratically. Karl had never crept into her room before and she wondered if this was when her misplaced hope and faith would finally let her down.

"Can I sleep with you tonight?"

The little voice was so soft and sweet. Alexa's heart stammered guiltily as she lifted her quilt to let Hayley into her bed. Hayley snuggled close and wrapped her arm around Alexa's body. Alexa reciprocated, kissing the top of Hayley's head as she closed her eyes and promised herself she would not think so ill of Karl again.

***

Marcus watched Alexa take her seat at assembly on Monday morning. They had not spoken in weeks, not since she had confronted him about Chad, and he was grateful. However, he did still enjoy these moments where he could observe and admire her from a distance. The soft, contented smile that sat on her face as she laid her head on Sam's shoulder was so beautiful. It sat in stark contrast to the girl who had walked into his office at the start of last year.

No one had ever seen Alexa as excited as she had been over the previous few weeks. There was the smile that sat calmly on her face, despite the tiredness that often accompanied it, and the liveliness Marcus had never seen before. All her teachers had noticed the difference as well and were open in their praise of her new attitude. Barely a day went by when one of Alexa's teachers would not mention just how surprised and impressed they were with her. Alexa was working hard in class and had even started to answer questions and participate in discussions. It was like a different girl had returned to the school this term.

There was no doubt in Marcus's mind that the change was due to the Whites. He could not believe such a small alteration in Alexa's living arrangements could have such a profound effect, but realised that was arrogant and naïve. He had grown up in a loving, stable family. Of course he could not fathom the huge impact such an environment had on him. He had only ever seen its flaws, yet the things he had complained about then – and now – seemed so petty and unimportant compared to what Alexa had experienced.

Walking towards his office at the end of the week, Marcus was almost bowled over as Alexa bounded down the stairs towards the dormitories. He grabbed her to stop her from falling and set her right on her feet. Alexa looked up at him with the most serene smile he had ever seen. He could not help but stop and watch her as she raced away.

It was in that moment that Marcus was able to catch a glimpse of Alexa's future. It was a future he knew could not and would not involve him. Free from some of the burdens of her life, Alexa was finally able to act her age. She could be the seventeen-year-old girl she was, not the adult she had been prematurely forced to be.

Marcus was glad that he found that reality more beautiful than heartbreaking, and for the first time he was truly at ease with his feelings for Alexa. They finally had a purpose. For the rest of this year, his role would be to protect Alexa from all that Redgrove could throw at her, and help set her up for life beyond school. She had the talent, if not the marks, to go to university, but there was much within his reach that could remedy that. He would help her receive the concessions her situation deserved and he would help her see that her future would be a successful one.

Then, at the end of it, he would watch Alexa leave, never trying to find out where she was going and never trying to follow. He would seal that part of his heart and hold it dear for the rest of his life. Marcus knew that Alexa's future happiness probably lay with Sam and felt a little guilty that they were being kept apart because of him. However, he also knew that he had deliberately set his wedding date for after the school year – after Alexa had left Redgrove – for the very same reason.

He could not marry Jackie while Alexa was around and the part of his heart that belonged to Alexa continued to grow. Once it was closed off, he would dedicate everything that was left to Jackie.

Sitting at his desk with the photo of Jackie in his hands, Marcus was almost willing that time to come. He loved Jackie and wanted to be able to devote himself to her the way he had before Alexa had come so forcefully into his life. Although he could find some purpose in his feelings for Alexa, he could still find no comfort. Alexa was a child and under his care. There were no excuses for how far things had gone already and he knew that the chances of this coming back to haunt him one day were huge, and yet somehow he could not pull himself back. It was simply beyond him. Alexa was like no other. Marcus hoped to God she was like no other. He had never been attracted to a student before her and hoped he would never be again.

Picking up the phone, Marcus called Jackie to let her know he would take her out to dinner that night – somewhere special. He owed her that much.

***

Alexa raced from school, managing to catch the earlier trains she usually missed and was home half an hour earlier than expected.

"Hey, Hales, what do you want to do tonight?" she asked Hayley excitedly, as Hayley tidied her room.

"What about your homework?" asked Hayley.

"I finished it all before I came," replied Alexa happily.

"But I have to do cleaning tonight. Mum said I have to have the house really tidy before my friends come over on Sunday."

"And right she is. I can help you. I know how to clean," smiled Alexa, so excited that even cleaning was a happy prospect.

"Thanks, Alexa," cried Hayley, wrapping her in a hug that made Alexa feel like she had just offered Hayley the world. "I'm so glad you're my sister. Brett would never help me clean."

Alexa tried to rope Brett into cleaning as they ate dinner, but he was having none of it. He thought she was a sucker, but she slyly pointed out that she had helped him out before in awkward situations, making him blush fiercely as Hayley laughed loudly.

"Do we want to know?" asked Pam warily.

"No," replied Alexa, Brett and Hayley with varying levels of anxiety and amusement.

The memory kept Hayley and Alexa smiling through the rest of dinner as Brett continued to blush intermittently. It made Alexa feel young and carefree, a different person to the one who belonged to her real life – her life with Bethany. Those holidays where she had pretended to be Brett's girlfriend to make his ex-girlfriend jealous seemed strangely disconnected to the present, even though that was one of the last times she had felt this way.

It was as if her time with the Whites was a fantasy – a miraculous escape from reality – dreams at the end of excessively long, torturous days.

After dinner, Alexa and Hayley cleared the dining room table, and then moved into the lounge room. Before they began cleaning, Alexa rifled through Pam and Karl's music collection and turned the music up loud.

"What's going on?" shouted Karl.

"We're cleaning," smiled Alexa.

"What's with the music?"

"Bethy and me used to do everything to music. Music makes everything bearable, even cleaning."

"How about I turn it down just a little before the neighbours complain?" replied Karl with a slight smile as he dialled down the volume.

It took Hayley a while, but she was soon swinging away with Alexa in the lounge room. There was much more dancing than cleaning going on, but they were having fun. They moved from room to room, listening to old music from Pam and Karl's collection, much of which Alexa had listened to as a child. Pam and Karl were also enjoying the trip down memory lane and started picking the music. Brett, unenthused by selections and sick of the cleaning he had been forced to do, escaped to his room at the first chance he found.

They had almost finished when Pam changed the CD. Alexa felt her insides suddenly turn to ice. Fear gripped her body as the music snaked through her. It was almost paralysing, but she forced herself to break its bonds. Ripping the CD out of the player, it took all her strength not to break it, having just enough consciousness to realise that whatever was happening to her was not real.

Pam and Karl stood motionless as she fumbled with the CD, looking for its case. Her arms were shaking so violently that she could barely grip anything.

"Here, let's try this one," said Karl gently, taking the CD from her trembling hands and placing another in the stereo. "This one okay?"

Alexa did not recognise the music and nodded slowly. She could see Hayley staring at her with wide, frightened eyes.

"I think we've done a pretty good job," said Pam, her voice shaking just slightly.

"Haven't done the downstairs bathroom yet," said Alexa, her voice soft as her brain started to slowly unfreeze, though her body still ached with fear.

"Do you want to do that quickly while Hayley and I make some hot chocolate? Then we can have a nice supper before bed. I think we'll need something to sustain us through this weekend."

Alexa nodded and walked towards the bathroom. She was surprised that Karl followed her. They usually left her alone when she flipped out. Karl did not talk. He just helped her clean as he sang along to the music, never on key, always off-pitch and often singing the wrong words, but it was soothing in a way nothing else could be. Alexa was surprised that she even managed a smile when they were finished.

"Thank you," Alexa squeezed out as they walked to the kitchen.

"Baby steps," replied Karl, rubbing her shoulder briefly.

***

"Happy Birthday, Hayley! It's not eleven courses, but I thought you might like it all the same," said Alexa as she sat down on Hayley's bed the next morning with breakfast for the two of them.

It was probably the first time Alexa had ever been up before the rest of the household, but to see Hayley's sleepy eyes grow wide with excitement was more than worth the effort. It reminded Alexa of what Bethany had been like when she had been very young, and it panged at her heart. Life had stopped being wondrous and exciting well before Bethany's eleventh birthday.

Hayley shuffled up the bed so that Alexa could sit down with her and insisted that Alexa eat as well. Alexa had made a lot of food and they were still eating when Pam and Karl came in to wish her a happy birthday.

"We were wondering why it was so quiet," laughed Karl.

"Happy Birthday, Darling," said Pam, planting a kiss on Hayley's forehead.

"Happy Birthday, Sweetie," said Karl, also kissing his daughter on the forehead. "Well, it looks like we don't have to worry about cooking you a special breakfast."

"I'm sorry," replied Alexa anxiously. She could not believe that she had not thought to ask Pam or Karl about their plans. "I didn't know you had anything planned. I –"

"It's okay, Alexa. We didn't have anything planned," said Pam gently, while exchanging concerned looks with Karl.

"So what are we doing today, Daddy?" chirped Hayley excitedly.

"You know what we're doing," smiled Karl, ruffling Hayley's hair, knowing that Hayley just liked hearing about their planned celebrations. "We're going to Grandma Sophie and Grandpa Ken's place for lunch. Everyone's going to be there – just for you. Then we're having dinner here at home. So don't eat too much at your grandparents' or you'll never fit in the cake your mother's making you."

Hayley could not remove the grin from her face as she bounced happily into Alexa. It was clear she loved the attention that was being lavished on her.

"You're coming, aren't you, Alexa?" asked Hayley for what had to be the hundredth time.

"Nothing in this world could stop me," replied Alexa, stroking Hayley's hair tenderly. It was true. Not even the horrible ache in her heart was enough to let her contemplate breaking Hayley's.

By eleven-thirty they had arrived at Karl's parents' home. This was only the second time Alexa had attended a whole-family function and her breath hitched at the thought of that fateful Christmas. It was a testament to just how much she loved and cared for Hayley and the Whites that the prospect of seeing the whole family again had not fazed her until now.

All the aunts and uncles were already there, including Todd. It was obvious that Todd's presence was not expected, or welcome. Alexa could almost see the steam hissing out of Karl's ears. It was not a development she was happy about either, but she did not want to be the reason Hayley's birthday was ruined.

Karl clearly had other ideas about what constituted a ruined birthday. He stormed straight up to Todd as the family watched on in horror, his hand clenched in aggravation, leaving Alexa little choice but to intervene.

"What the hell are you doing?" huffed Karl, as Alexa rushed in between him and Todd. Karl's fist was still raised in readiness, but Alexa refused to move.

"It's Hayley's birthday. Don't do this to her," Alexa pleaded softly, placing her hand over Karl's fist until he lowered it. "We can all handle this. Let her be happy for one day."

"You stay away from my family, especially my daughters," snarled Karl in a low and dangerous voice, pointing at Todd viciously over Alexa's shoulder.

"But it looks like Alexa doesn't want to stay away from me, doesn't it?" said Todd with a slimy smile, his hands sliding over her hips.

Karl's fist rose instantly, but before he could strike, Alexa spun around to face Todd. Todd's hands moved swiftly over her bottom. She ran her hand across Todd's middle and below his belt, sneering at his sleazy grin. Then she grabbed and twisted.

There was a pained squeal as Alexa spoke in a low, forceful voice that still shook more than she wanted it to. "If you come anywhere near me or Hayley again I will make sure they'll never be able to reattach your balls. Got it?"

Todd nodded meekly and Alexa released him. She was sure Todd would have hit back, except this time Karl stood between her and Todd and glared angrily at him. The rest of the family stood in shocked horror as Karl led Alexa back to Pam. Only Brett was smiling broadly.

"That was cool," he said with an approving nod. "Just don't ever do that to me."

"You'd never give me a reason to," Alexa laughed, before hugging a slightly dismayed Hayley. "It's okay, Hayley. This is going to be a good day, I promise."

Alexa was surprised that she was able to keep her promise. No one said anything about the incident, and Todd kept a low profile through the rest of the visit. Karl made sure she and Hayley sat next to him as they ate lunch, and that Todd was kept well away from them. It was awkward and tense at times, but Uncle Matthew and Aunt Linda's two-year-old twins did much to lighten the mood.

Hayley bounced excitedly after lunch as everyone gathered to give her their presents. Pam and Karl insisting that she wait until after dinner for her presents from them had been a slightly sour point that morning. It resulted in a wide, enthusiastic smile sitting on Hayley's face as she happily tore the wrapping paper off her presents.

"And this one's from me," said Uncle Todd, handing Hayley her last present.

Hayley sat paralysed as Todd continued to hold out his present to her. Pam and Karl both nodded encouragingly, though could not manage smiles, while Brett was barely able to contain his agitation. In the end, Alexa had to take the present from Todd and hand it to Hayley, who opened it cautiously, her eyes flicking between Karl and Brett.

"You like it?" asked Todd, when Hayley revealed the girly photo frame and pink journal.

Alexa kept a hand on Karl's arm, feeling him silently fume, though the she noticed that Pam actually looked angrier.

The visit did not last long after that. There was enough time for Grandma Sophie to bring out a cake and for them all to sing happy birthday, but once the cake had been eaten, Pam and Karl were moving them towards the door.

"You're being rude," hissed Karl's mother.

"I told you I didn't want him near my family again. You knew that. You were the one who insisted he be here," growled Karl in a low voice to keep the conversation from Hayley, who was with Brett saying goodbye to the rest of the family.

"He's your brother."

"Who forced himself on my teenage daughter! Or did you forget that part?" snapped Karl angrily. "I know what happened. I know what he did."

"She's not your daughter. I think you've forgotten who your real family is," replied Karl's mother in an angry hiss.

Karl looked over at Pam, who nodded and took Alexa by the hand and led her out to the car. Hayley, Brett and Karl joined them minutes later. No one said anything as they piled into the car. It was a quiet ride home. Quieter than usual, Alexa realised, when she noticed they did not have the radio on. She assumed it was because of her and was both thankful that they were so considerate and sorry that they had to be.

The moment they walked in the front door, Brett grabbed

Todd's present from Hayley's bag and threw it in the garbage bin. Hayley watched with a disappointed face, but did not complain or try to stop him.

"Do you want that present, Hayley?" asked Alexa.

"Not really," Hayley replied, though the downhearted tone was not convincing. "I mean, it was a nice present, but I don't want anything from him."

"If you want the present you should have it," urged Alexa, even as Brett glared at her.

"Would you want it if he hurt me?" questioned Hayley.

"No," Alexa replied emphatically, before realising where Hayley was coming from.

"So why should I be different? I don't like him because he hurt you and I wish he didn't come, but I liked the way you twisted his nuts."

Alexa smiled and wrapped her arm around Hayley's shoulder, allowing Brett's scowl to finally slide from his face.

Dinner was a small but noisy affair. No one wanted to dwell on earlier events and everyone was determined to be happy and light-hearted for the rest of the evening.

When they moved to the lounge room after dinner to shower Hayley with more gifts, Alexa could not help but realise just how amazingly happy she was. She really did feel like she was part of the family. As she, Brett and Hayley sat on one lounge, it felt as though they had been siblings their whole lives. It was something she never wanted to give up and started to hope she would never be forced to.

By the end of the year, she would have enough money to take care of herself, and hopefully enough money to get Bethany clean. Perhaps Pam and Karl really would be willing to open their arms, if not their home, to Bethany. If Bethany could feel the love and support of such an amazing family who did not want to tear them apart, perhaps staying clean would not be so much of a battle.

"So who's going first?" asked Karl, as they all held their presents.

"I will," cried Alexa.

If she went first there would be nothing for her present to compete against. Hayley opened the present with shaking hands, squealing at the sight of the pouch that clearly indicated the present was some sort of jewellery. Tipping the contents out on to her hand, Hayley barely looked at the necklace before she was tugging at

Alexa to put it on her.

Alexa was worried that Hayley may not actually like the present. She still had not really looked at it and kept it covered with her hand and she opened her other presents one-handed.

"Should we have the cake now?" asked Pam, smiling at Alexa and nodding slightly towards Hayley who was still touching her necklace.

"Yeah," nodded Hayley excitedly, jumping to her feet.

"I'll get it," said Alexa, rising quickly and telling Hayley to sit back down.

They did not usually eat in the lounge room, but Karl had decided the occasion was worth making the exception for.

"The candles are in the cupboard," called Pam as Alexa left the room.

Alexa rummaged through three cupboards before finally finding the candles. She placed eleven evenly around the cake and had lit eight of them when there was an unexpected knock at the door.

"I'll get it," called Alexa.

She faltered slightly, wondering whether to light the rest of the candles or answer the door first, before deciding to quickly blow the candles out so the cake did not end up covered in wax. They could easily be relit once she got rid of their uninvited guest.

As she opened the door, Alexa froze.

Before her were three men. Two she had never seen before, but the third and the clear leader, she recognised. It took a moment to reconcile the sight with reality. If she had been on the streets in the city it would never had taken so long to realise the danger.

"What? Not going to invite us in?" asked Leo, Bethany's drug-dealing boyfriend, in an exaggeratedly friendly voice.

Alexa quickly tried to slam the door shut, but the two thugs on either side of Leo moved swiftly forward and barged their way inside.

"Get out, get out now," Alexa cried, as she continued to try and push the men back out the door, to no effect.

Leo stepped forward, closing the door behind him as his thugs pushed Alexa back into the kitchen. He had a knife and pointed it straight at her face.

"No, no, no," said Leo, waving the knife in front of Alexa's eyes. "Bethany has told me a lot about this family of yours and I would like to meet them."

"Get fucked," spat Alexa.

Leo nodded and the two men grabbed Alexa. She wrestled against them, but it was pointless. They were so big and strong that she had no chance.

Karl and Brett were both standing when Leo pranced calmly ahead of them into the lounge room. Alexa stopped fighting and the thugs allowed her to stand on her own feet, locked between them.

"I'm sorry," Alexa said as her foster family watched on in stunned silence.

She had never felt so separate from them as she did in that moment. It was like a sick joke that just minutes before she had considered herself a true member of their family.

This was her life intruding into theirs. This was the violence and the horror that had typified her existence, and she had now brought it into the Whites' peaceful, loving world.

"So this is the family," said Leo. "And this must be Hayley. Bethany never told me how pretty she was. And whose birthday is it? Hers? I could give her a present she would never forget."

Leo stepped towards Hayley and brushed her cheek with the back of his hand.

"Get your fucking hands off her," cried Alexa, breaking free of the two men and pushing herself between Hayley and Leo.

Rage tore across Leo's face as he slapped Alexa hard. Her cheek burned, but she would not move. She would die before she let her world destroy Hayley's innocence.

"What the fuck do you want?" Alexa asked bitterly.

"It seems your sister has gotten herself into a bit of debt. I'm here to be repaid," replied Leo calmly, his face twisting into a horrible smile.

"How much?" asked Alexa, trying not to cry.

"Three thousand dollars."

Tears welled in Alexa's eyes as she shook her head. She had nowhere near that amount.

"I have a bit. You can have all of that now and I can get you the rest later."

"I can give you the money," said Karl, stepping forward. "I have it all in the bank. We can go now and you can leave my family alone."

"No thanks, Pop. I don't want *your* money. I might have a bit of your daughter though. A few days with her should cover the debt."

Leo stepped forward but again Alexa pushed him back. She would not let him touch Hayley again.

"Isn't that sweet," snarled Leo. "Bethany always said you were the protective type."

"You stay the hell away from her," growled Alexa.

Alexa had the knife Sam had given her in her pocket and looked around the room, constantly hoping for a chance to use it. Brett looked like he was prepared to fight, but he was still just a boy and no match for Leo or his muscled thugs. Even Karl would provide little physical resistance, despite his more solid build. He was in a state of shock and clearly not busting for a fight. Alexa knew that if they fought and lost, it would be Hayley who would pay the ultimate price.

"This is between you and me. I'll go with you and give you the money I have. After that, we'll work out how I'll pay the rest of the debt," said Alexa defiantly. "I have to go upstairs to get my wallet and I'm taking the kids with me."

Leo did not move as Alexa walked backwards to the lounge room door, keeping herself between him and Hayley. She collected Brett, pushing him out first, followed by Hayley.

"What about Mum and Dad?" sobbed Hayley, when they were safely in Alexa's room.

Brett hugged Hayley tight to help stem the flow of her tears. He looked terrified.

"They'll be okay as long as they don't try anything stupid," replied Alexa, trying not to think about what could be happening downstairs. "Brett, when I go, lock this door and don't open it for anyone unless you're sure they've left and not come back. If *anyone* tries to get to Hayley, kill them."

"What are you going to do?" asked Brett, trying to keep his voice steady.

"Just what I said. I'm going with them to try and keep them away from here."

"But they will –"

"Listen to me, Brett," Alexa said urgently, needing him to understand. "You know what Leo wants. He doesn't want me. He wants Hayley. She's eleven. Do you think she'll understand or recover from that?" Brett shook his head and tightened his grip on Hayley. "Take this." Alexa pulled her knife out of her pocket. "Kill anyone who tries to hurt Hayley. And I mean it, Brett. Kill them."

Brett nodded solemnly as he took the knife and Alexa knew he would do as she asked. Seeing him pull the blade out of the handle, she felt like she watched him aged two years and wished she had not been responsible for destroying his childhood. But she knew they would both agree that it was better they suffer than Hayley.

Alexa heard the door click locked behind her as she made her way back down the stairs. She was petrified. All she knew was that if she did not face what Leo had planned for them, Hayley would have to.

Returning to the lounge room, Alexa was horrified by the sight of Karl curled up on the lounge. His mouth and nose were bleeding and there was a bruise near his eye, which was already blackening. Pam sat next to him as Karl tried to shield her with his body.

"Are you okay?" asked Alexa, kneeling by Karl.

"Don't go with them. They will kill you," he slurred.

"Better me than Hayley," replied Alexa, knowing they would never argue with that logic.

With one last look, Alexa stood up and threw her bag over her shoulder.

"Let's go."

"Wait, take these," said Karl, pulling Alexa back by the hand. He pulled out his wallet and quickly scribbled the PINs on the back of two bank cards. "Give them all the money you can and get away from them."

Chapter Nine

MARCUS LOOKED UP at the ceiling contemplating his future. Jackie lay next to him pretending to sleep. Her uneven breaths were all he needed to know that she was as confused as he was about the present state of their relationship. This time they had not even made it one night before it had all come undone.

He had managed to book them a table at an expensive restaurant overlooking the harbour on Friday night. They had both dressed up for the occasion, Jackie looking absolutely stunning. They talked for hours over dinner, and not just about the mundane things either. They connected in a way they hadn't since the Christmas break.

Drinks and dancing had followed, and for the first time in almost eighteen months Marcus had felt like himself again. Away from school, away from teenagers and their adolescent issues, he had felt his adult-self revitalise.

"I've been spending way too much time at work," he said, kissing Jackie as they danced close. "It's messing with my head. I don't care. I'm just going to start leaving when the bell goes."

"Yeah right," replied Jackie, but she was smiling. It was the first time she had truly smiled at anything he had said for such a long time.

That was when Marcus realised that he had forgotten just how beautiful Jackie really was.

"I need to take you home," he whispered in her ear.

"We don't have to go that far," she whispered back conspiratorially.

Marcus smiled and shook his head, taking Jackie by the hand and leading her out of the club.

Once in the sanctuary of their bedroom, Marcus had revelled in Jackie's beauty. It was blissful being released from the bonds of Redgrove and indulge in the life he had once cherished. Stripping off Jackie's clothes, Marcus had tried hard not to wonder what Alexa's body looked like naked, but it was a pointless battle. The image of Alexa's swim-suited body from their stolen day at the beach last year floated across his eyes as he continued to worship Jackie's body, the fantasies of that day returning as he kissed Jackie more intensely. Jackie's passionate whispers flooded Marcus's brain, merging with the forbidden images of Alexa swirling in his mind. However, the resulting visions had stopped him in his tracks; his body suddenly limp, no longer able to fulfil his desires, as his mind conjured images of himself and Alexa in the most intimate of embraces.

"What's wrong?" asked Jackie, feeling the change.

"Nothing, it just – I don't know," stammered Marcus, unable to tell the truth.

Never before had he let himself indulge in those fantasies while he was with Jackie, and it shocked him that the conclusion of them would be so repulsive to him. In one way it was a relief. He had been worried where stolen moments might lead him and Alexa, but he now realised that he would never be physically able to have sex with her. It was just too wrong.

"Great," sighed Jackie. "Bet if it was one of your students you wouldn't say no to them. You never say no to them," she muttered as she stomped out of bed.

The resulting fight was their worst ever. Marcus was indignant that his own fiancée would imply such things, and they had come close to calling off the engagement then and there. It did not matter that he was guilty of feeling way too much for one of his students. He was not the type of man to sleep with a child, and refused to be accused of such a thing – even the possibility of such a thing.

The silence that followed had been deafening. Jackie finally apologised the next morning, but Marcus had struggled to accept it, and so the silence had continued on.

The phone trilled violently in the still air. Jackie answered it immediately, confirming the falsehood of her slumber.

"Hello?" she said in a sad voice. "I'll just get him." Jackie handed the phone to him without saying a word.

"Hello?" said Marcus, yawning. "What? Wait, slow down. What happened?" Jackie sat up at the change in his voice. "I'm on my way."

Marcus hung up the phone and jumped from the bed, his heart pounding.

"What's wrong? What happened?" asked Jackie anxiously.

"Someone broke into the school. Held a gun to the matron's head. I don't know much more than that. They broke into the dorms

– a room of year twelve girls – so I have to go and see if they're all right."

"Why would someone want to break into the dorms?"

"I don't know."

Marcus was out of the apartment in less than five minutes. All he could think about was Alexa. He did not know what room had been broken into, but his gut told him that it was hers. She was the only student who could attract this much trouble. Marcus was just grateful that she was with the Whites and was spared this ordeal. He was not sure how he would have withstood the drive to school if he thought something had happened to Alexa.

"What happened? Is everyone all right?" Marcus asked breathlessly, striding quickly towards the police officers. They were standing outside Alexa's room.

"They're a little shaken, but otherwise they're all right," said Constable Banks at the door. Marcus walked in and saw Alexa's roommates huddled together on the centre bed.

"Are you ladies all right? Can I get you anything?" Marcus queried, wondering which of them this drama centred on.

"Have they found Alexa yet?" asked Bianca softly.

Marcus felt his heart skip a beat.

"What do you mean? Miss Samson's at home with her foster parents," replied Marcus. The look on the girls' faces clearly told him that she was not. He turned back to Constable Banks, who had moved into the doorway. "What happened?" he asked desperately.

"There was a home invasion earlier this evening at Alexa Samson's foster parents' house," replied Constable Banks gravely, making Marcus's stomach roll over.

"So why's Alexa missing?" Marcus asked desperately.

"She left with the three home invaders. It appears her sister had a drug debt that needed repaying. We think it was her sister who came here to tip her off, but it looks like the debt collectors had a better idea of where she was," explained Constable Banks. Marcus grasped the door frame as he tried to digest what he was hearing. "I don't have all the details, but it appears Alexa left with the men to protect other members of the family. We have a lot of people out looking for her. We're still hopeful of finding her."

Marcus tried to control his breathing. This was not the time or the place to lose it. Right now they had to concentrate on finding Alexa, though he had no idea how such a task was to be accomplished. As he spoke to officer after officer, demanding information they did not have, he tried desperately to keep his mind off what could be happening to her.

When detectives came to speak to Alexa's roommates, Marcus insisted on sitting in. He wanted to know what had happened here. Detective Shepard showed Alexa's roommates a photo of a young girl with a slim face, long brown hair and deep blue eyes.

"Is that Bethany?" asked Marcus.

Detective Shepard scowled before nodding and looking up at Alexa's roommates. "Is this the girl who came looking for Alexa?" he asked.

"Yes," said Martha, as Natalie answered with an emphatic, "No."

Lizzie and Bianca were undecided.

It was clear that the girl who had terrorised their night did not look like the clean-cut, pretty girl in the school photo. When Marcus examined the photo, he saw, despite the smile, the same haunted, experienced look in Bethany's eyes as he saw in Alexa's and wondered if she had suffered as much as her older sister.

"It's her," said Bianca eventually after she and the other girls had spent five minutes examining the photo.

Detective Shepard nodded solemnly, walking out of the room, leaving his partner to question the girls further.

"What does that mean?" asked Marcus, following Detective Shepard out of the room.

"It means I want to find Alexa sooner rather than later," replied Detective Shepard gravely.

Although Detective Shepard refused to say much else, Marcus understood how seriously the police were taking the situation Alexa was in and what that meant for her welfare. It seemed impossible that one life could be filled with so much trauma and he feared how much Alexa was suffering again.

***

The world blurred hazily and pain seared through every inch of Alexa's body as she lay battered on a strange bed. Her face burned and her body ached. She tried to manoeuvre herself into a comfortable position, but the bindings around her ankles and wrists dug painfully into her skin with every movement. Through her battered and swollen eyelids she tried to survey her surrounds, searching for anything to distract her mind for even the briefest second.

The two men who had accompanied Leo had kept her covered on the floor below the back seat as he drove. She had tried to remember each turn, but after five minutes had been utterly directionless. After some incalculable amount of time, Leo had pulled her out of the car to withdraw the money. The streets were deserted. Alexa had looked around for some sign of what suburb she was in, but recognised nothing. She withdrew all the money she could from her own as well as Karl's accounts, managing to give Leo two thousand dollars; the daily withdrawal limits keeping her from being able to clear the debt in its entirety. When she handed Leo the money, she snapped all three cards in half.

"You bitch," Leo screamed, throwing her by the hair back into the car.

Alexa still wondered how stupid that one act was. It was spiteful and thoughtless, but she knew this had never been about money. If she had been able to give Leo all the money, she might have also given him a reason to take her home. Then she would have had nothing to entice him away from Hayley.

They had driven again for what felt like an hour, but it could have been ten minutes. Time really meant nothing any more.

"Now remember to keep your mouth shut, because I can easily go back for that sweet little girl you were so desperate to keep me from," growled Leo, as he dragged Alexa out of the car and pushed her up the stairs to an apartment on the third floor.

Inside the apartment, Leo hauled her into a bedroom and slapped her hard across the face. Her knees weakened beneath her, but she stood her ground.

"That's for ruining my plans. I was looking forward to getting to know that adorable little girl, but I suppose you'll have to do – for now."

Leo pulled Alexa towards the bed and ripped at her clothes. She had tried desperately to pretend that he was just another client, that this was just sex, but it wasn't. She did not want to do this. She had already been raped once in her life and fear gripped her mercilessly at the thought of it happening again. It had only been vision of Hayley in this situation that had kept her from trying to run.

Despite that, Alexa had no intention of giving Leo what he wanted without a fight. He pulled at her legs, trying frantically to pry them apart, but she had held strong, even as a barrage of punches attacked her body. Her resistance had only been broken by the arrival of Leo's thugs, who pulled at her legs, while Leo continued his beating.

Alexa had been sure her battered body could not possibly feel any further pain. She had been very wrong.

"For that little stunt everybody gets a go," growled Leo, as he climbed on top of her, his two thugs tightening the binds around her ankles, keeping her legs spread.

Hands pinned above her head, Alexa had been powerless against Leo's violent thrusting. She tried her hardest to block out what was happening, but no other thought could compete with the blinding pain surging through her body. She did not scream. She refused to give Leo the pleasure of hearing her pain and fear.

When it had finally ended, Alexa rolled her body on to its side, curling into the foetal position, trying desperately to ease her aching body. Her efforts were futile. As soon as Leo was off her, the first of the thugs pulled at her for his go. Alexa fought against him until they tied her hands to the corners of the bed leaving her spread open, completely defenceless.

Despite the earlier invasion, this attack was been no less painful. Alexa rolled her head backwards, away from the pain and the sight of her attacker, concentrating all her energy on the imperfections in the wallpaper.

As the second thug climbed on top of her, a figure walked next to the bed and sat down beside her. He held her hand and gently brushed the hair from her face.

"It's all right. I'm here and I won't leave you until it's all over," said Mr Knight in a soft voice.

Alexa turned her head and looked deep into his chocolate eyes. Mr Knight smiled and squeezed her hand, the image only broken by a thunderous slap across her face. Pain surged though her head, making existing sickening, but amongst the laughter of Leo and his thugs, Alexa heard another voice and felt a gentle hand turning her head back to the side of the bed.

"I'm not leaving you. Hold on, Lex. I'm right here, just hold on," said Mr Knight, his voice gentle and soothing, but determined.

He kept his promise. Mr Knight stayed by her side until the three men had finished with her, leaving her there, tied to the bed. Naked, filthy and powerless.

When the sun slowly penetrated the curtained windows, the light burned painfully at Alexa's eyes, which were now little more than slits. Her face was a sickening mixture of blue and red, swollen almost beyond recognition. She wanted to stay awake, to observe her surroundings by the light of day in the hope of finding out more clues to her location, but her body could not stand it and she was soon in a deep sleep.

The peace of her blackened sleep was broken abruptly and violently. Alexa woke to see Leo once again on top of her. Looking desperately to the side of the bed where Mr Knight had sat the night before, Alexa hoped he had not left her. She did not want to have to go through this alone.

"I've got you," said Mr Knight, appearing by her side and placing his hand on her forehead.

Alexa breathed deeply and flailed her bound hand until Mr Knight took it in his. She squeezed it tightly. He could not block out the pain completely, every one of Leo's thrust as excruciating as the last, but Alexa held on to Mr Knight's hand, too scared to face it alone.

"If you agree to behave, I'll untie you," said Leo, as he pulled up his pants.

Alexa nodded slowly. "I need to go to the toilet," she choked, her throat dry and sore.

Leo untied the ropes that bound her to the bed before yanking her to her feet. Alexa stood unsteadily, too terrified to move without permission.

"You're so much like your sister," said Leo sickly, tenderly stroking the side of her face. "Threaten something you love and you're both prepared to give me anything to save it. That little girl still worth it?"

Alexa said nothing and Leo grabbed her arm, dragging her through the apartment to the bathroom. She paid close attention to the layout of the unit as they walked. Four men sat in the lounge room watching TV near what she thought was the front door. There was no way she would be able to out run the five of them. She doubted she would even make it to the door.

Left alone in the bathroom, Alexa's body shook with the effort of every movement. She did not want to stay and face any more, but knew Hayley would not have survived the previous night. Standing before the mirror, she could barely recognise the figure staring back at her, all resemblance to the image of the girl she held in her mind were gone. That girl was dead.

Alexa tried to drink water from the tap, but found her body could barely function and managed to only swallow a few mouthfuls before she was dragged back into the bedroom.

"How much more til the debt's paid off?" Alexa asked defiantly, though her voice was barely more than a hoarse whisper.

"Oh I think the debt is all but clear," smiled Leo, stroking his finger down the middle of her chest. "The rest is just for fun."

Leo locked the door behind him when he exited, leaving Alexa alone with her terror. Despite the pain moving caused, she walked around the room, examining it for any source of weakness and possible escape route. It was a pointless exercise.

The only exits were the locked door and a barred window that had been painted shut. With little energy, Alexa had no chance of forcing the window open, though she tried, collapsing on the floor from the effort.

Locked inside the room, there was no way for Alexa to know if Leo was at home or not. She could only hope that Pam and Karl had taken Hayley far away from their house. She did not want all this to be in vain. She did not want to wake to the sound of Hayley's screams.

The day dragged on and Alexa was left alone as the apartment fell into silence. She wrapped her naked and battered body in a blanket and curled up in a darkened corner of the room, the sun excruciatingly painful on her tiny slits of eyes. When she looked beside her, Mr Knight smiled back and wrapped his arm around her shoulders, giving her the peace she needed to rest, sleep finding her intermittently.

Alexa awoke later in the day to the sound of clinking of glass. The men had returned and were becoming louder as they hours drew on. She knew they were getting drunk and knew it would not be long before they called in to see her. Her only hope was that Mr Knight would stay by her side.

When the room fell into darkness, the men in the lounge room unlocked the door and pulled Alexa off the floor and on to the bed. She did not resist this time, but it made no difference. They were as violent as the night before. With each drink came an upsurge in the force with which she was hit. Left untied, her arms took the bulk of the violence as she tried to protect her head and face.

It was a barrage of such intensity that Alexa did not know if Mr Knight made it to her bedside. Her left eye was swollen shut and she could not take her arms away from her face for a second, fearful the next hit to her head would claim her life.

When the sun finally rose and the men departed, sleep came swiftly, as Alexa's body began to shut down. With no food or water, the effort required to keep herself awake and alert was too much, and she no longer cared to try. As she slept, fevered and broken dreams taunted her, but always by her side sat Mr Knight, with a gentle hand and smile. It was the only vision that kept her alive.

The sun set again to the sounds of clinking glass and cheering men. Alexa knew this night would be no different to the one before. The men stumbled through the door for her body, but she could no longer mount any form of defence. She remained limp on the bed, her body useless, but her mind far too aware of what was happening to her. Despite the days of violence, every new rape tore at the few remaining pieces of her soul, but by her side, holding her hand, though she had no strength to squeeze it, was Mr Knight.

"Hold on, Lex. It'll be over soon. I'm here. Don't give up yet," he kept repeating softly in her ear.

When the last man left, Alexa rolled on to her side, wanting to feel Mr Knight's arms around her, but he disappeared and she fell deep into the darkness. This time her sleep was not peppered with broken and fevered dreams. It was completely black.

Her body became limp and lifeless and her breathing shallow. She could feel herself falling deeper and deeper into darkness that was enveloping her and it felt good.

The next time Alexa opened her eyes, Mr Knight was by her side. A short, muffled scream escaped her, knowing that the men were back. That night however, she felt nothing. Men came and went with only the slightest flicker of recognition from her as she slipped in and out of consciousness.

Alexa no longer had the energy to hold on to reality and let herself slide deeper into the silent darkness that encased her. She did not care that she could no longer feel the men violate her body, or that she felt nothing when Leo pushed her off the bed, her body broken and filthy, covered in the vile fluids of half a dozen men. All she cared about was that the pain was disappearing and soon it would be gone forever.

***

The clock ticked over to three. Marcus was not sure what it was about that exact moment, but in his heart he knew it was over. Alexa was dead. After five nights, he could no longer stretch his faith and hope, and grief flooded him in a way he had never known before.

The misery of Alexa's absence had nearly paralysed him and

now he fell to his knees, pain tearing at his chest as tears streamed down his face. Every breath was a painful gasp. He searched, desperate for some source of renewal for his hope, but could not find it. Clasping his hands in prayer, he knelt beside his bed, focusing every molecule of his mind on Alexa.

"Please, God. Please, God. Please."

He did not even know what to pray for. He wanted Alexa back, but more than anything he wanted her to be at peace and no longer in pain, because wherever she was, he knew she was not having a good time. Detective Shepard had been back to the school and Marcus had forced him to answer questions of his own. The answers had been as shocking as they had been predictable.

Marcus tried to stifle the cry that was tearing through his chest at the thought of what Alexa might be suffering. He wanted the grief that was consuming every part of his body to leave. He wanted a miracle, but knew it would not be granted. There was no point in hoping beyond reason.

Collapsing on his bed, Marcus tried to find comfort in the fact that Alexa would finally be at peace. If she was dead, then at least this world's torture of her was finally over. They would lay her to rest and he would hold on to his grief – and his love – for the rest of his life; an eternal flaming tribute to her life.

Dressing slowly, Marcus was not sure what part of his mind was forcing him through the day. He had no will to face anything and there was no one to share his grief with. There was no way he could he ever disclose the loss he was experiencing when he should never feel the way he did about Alexa. He could never express his grief without confessing his love.

Trudging along the corridors, Marcus's sorrow was only matched by that of Sam's. Although Sam had insisted on continuing on with his classes, he had spent the last five days in perpetual stony silence, broken only by the occasional rogue tear. His roommates had confessed that Sam's composure only held while he was in class. In his room, he was a broken mess.

Sam and Alexa's closeness had once been a source of intense jealousy, but Marcus was not jealous now. In their brief meetings, Marcus had wanted to tell Sam that he knew exactly how he felt, to confide in him and share their loss. Instead, he had just offered to let Sam skip any classes he needed to.

"I don't need more time alone thinking about what's happening to her," Sam had replied in a broken voice.

It was a stark contrast to Bianca, who missed two days of classes, holing herself up in her room in tears. Marcus had little time for her grief, knowing the pain she had caused Alexa this year. Nor did her roommates. They had come to his office to vehemently condemn his approval for her absence from class. Martha's annoyance and the addition of Chad's disapproval did not surprise Marcus. What he needed was a less-biased view.

Pulling Lizzie aside and asking for the true state of the situation had not turned out to be the best idea. Her answers to his questions made Marcus's blood boil. That anyone would question the danger Alexa was in was simply incredible. Bianca remarking, apparently seriously, that all this was a cover story and that Alexa had skipped town with some fanciful bounty of cash was absolutely beyond comprehension.

It had made Marcus's comments to Bianca on the third day much harsher than he intended, but if Sam could keep going to class, then so could she.

Passing Bianca on the way to his class, Marcus noticed her glare from behind her dark glasses. Ezra walked next to her, looking drawn but composed. The faces waiting outside his classroom were a similar mixture of distress and stoicism.

"Have you heard anything, Sir?" asked Lizzie, her voice breaking as she spoke and tears running down her face.

Marcus could only shake his head, words not forming, as the girls in his class hugged Lizzie supportively. Sam turned away, Chad's hand on his shoulder, squeezing tight.

"Got a video to start with today," said Marcus quietly. There was just no point giving them lots of work at the moment, none of them were taking anything in.

Lights out, Marcus started the video and walked over to the window at the back of the class. He pretended he was watching as he looked out over the suburban skyline.

"Come back, Alexa. Please come back to me," he gasped silently, fresh tears falling down his cheeks as his students stared blankly ahead.

***

Bright light filled the room. Alexa brought her arm up over her eyes. A breeze flowed across her skin, making her shiver. Pulling her arm down slowly, she looked over at the window. It was open.

Alexa tried to climb out of the bed, but struggled to unwrap herself from the quilt that had been thrown over her body. If she could make it to the window, then maybe she could call for help. She might make it out of here after all. But when she eventually made it to the window there was no one in sight – nothing but nothingness.

"Lex! This way, Lex."

Alexa turned. Mr Knight was standing in the open doorway.

"They're gone, Lex," said Mr Knight, stepping forward as she stood still, not comprehending. "We can escape."

Alexa took a step forward and stumbled. Her body felt so heavy. Suddenly she did not care for escape. All she wanted was to curl up and sleep.

"Come back to school, Lex. You're free now. Come back with me. I will keep you safe. I'll protect you."

Opening her eyes, Alexa saw Mr Knight kneeling by her side, lifting her gently to her feet. It was a struggle. Her body was heavy and unsteady, but Mr Knight persevered. He held her close to his body, supporting her weight as he walked her slowly towards the door. Alexa sighed as they passed through it and kept her eyes to the ground as they walked. She did not look at her surrounds. She did not care where she was as long as she was with Mr Knight.

It was tiring, but Mr Knight walked slowly. His arms were wrapped around her body, but it did little to protect her from the cold wind swirling around them. Mr Knight quietly reassured her that he would find her warmer clothes. Continuing to hold her tight, Mr Knight changed their direction and led her into a large store. He grabbed a trolley, leaning her tired body against the handle as he pushed it down the aisles from behind.

Mr Knight grabbed food off the shelves and piled them into the trolley.

"Cold," gasped Alexa, shivering violently.

Warmth immediately spread through Alexa's body as Mr Knight selected from the racks of clothes in front of them. He picked the most beautiful outfit in the store, pulling it off the rack and dressing her tenderly.

"My Queen," he said affectionately, as he hugged her tight. "Now let's go eat."

Taking her hand, Mr Knight led her out of the shop and walked them towards the cliff-top park. The sound of the waves breaking softly on the rocks below was beautiful and Alexa was sure it would always represent the sound of freedom to her. Mr Knight walked her down the steps and down to the rock ledge where they had spent their forbidden day together.

Alexa wished she had the energy to swim, but though she was warmer now, her body still felt slow and lethargic. Mr Knight kept hold of her as they walked, before sitting her down on the rocks and wrapping her in his arms. It was soothing, and she could not help but close her eyes and rest against Mr Knight's strong, protective chest.

"Lex, wake up. You have to eat, Lex," said Mr Knight softly, rousing her from her sleep as he gently stroked her face.

Alexa liked that Mr Knight was able to comfort her while she slept, and that she did not flinch away from him as she did with everyone else. It was nice to know that he was different. Mr Knight sat her up straighter and placed small amounts of food in her mouth. Every time her eyes grew heavy, he stroked her face or arm and encouraged her to continue to eat a little bit more.

"That's okay. That's enough for now," said Mr Knight softly when her stomach rolled sickeningly. "Rest now. I'll wake you when it's time to eat more. Rest now."

Alexa did not need to be told twice. She closed her eyes as Mr Knight's arms wrapped around her, and she fell back into blissful sleep.

A distant, cracking sound made Alexa's head snap up. She looked around, disoriented by her surroundings. She was sitting up against a tree on the edge of a reserve. There were a few houses in the distance, but the cluster of trees surrounding her kept her hidden from sight. Then she realised she was all alone. Panic started to course through her body, causing horrid visions to flicker through her mind.

Concern over the mystery of where she was and why did not last long. Alexa found her mind quickly diverted towards the sickening hunger rumbling through her stomach. Looking down, she noticed a plastic bag at her feet with a strange collection of foods. She reached into the bag and pulled out an opened packet of biscuits. Stuffing a handful into her mouth, she chewed vigorously to try and dispel the relentless hunger that was now tearing through her body.

Rustling through the plastic bag, Alexa was grateful to see a bottle of brightly coloured drink. She opened it and washed down the biscuits, but almost as soon as the food and drink hit her stomach, a wave of nausea washed through her. Turning her head, she just managed not to vomit over her legs and the plastic bag that sat in front of her.

Pain rippled angrily through every part of her body. It was agonising, but strangely grounding. Maybe she was awake. Perhaps this was real. She was outside. Free. It was such a soothing thought that Alexa's eyes immediately slipped shut. She would die free.

"No, Lex. You need to eat."

Jerking her head, Alexa forced her eyes open. Though she could have sworn she had heard Mr Knight's voice, there was no one around. His voice swirled in his head again, urging her to eat. Her stomach rumbled painfully in response, forcing her to comply. It was horrible, and she could only handle allowing small chunks of food to disintegrate in her mouth, but she wanted to do as Mr Knight asked.

When she had finally eaten just enough to subdue the anger in her stomach, Alexa rested her head back against the tree and closed her eyes. She did not know what she was supposed to do next. There was rumble of a train in the distance and Mr Knight suddenly appeared by her side. He put his arms around her shoulders and rested her head in his neck.

"Come back to school, Lex," he said gently as he stroked her hair. "I'll protect you."

"Train. School," Alexa mumbled.

"Come back to me, Lex."

Alexa nodded. Mr Knight helped her to her feet. She started walking forward, struggling to keep herself upright. The guiding sound of the train had gone, and she could only turn in confused circles, wondering which direction to walk in.

"This way, Lex," said Mr Knight. He was walking ahead of her, his hand outstretched reaching back for her.

Alexa forced her feet forward, her hand reaching out for Mr Knight's, but he remained out of her grasp. Her body ached with the forced movement. It made her sick, but she knew she had to keep going. She had to make it back to school. Mr Knight would keep her safe there. Maybe he would even let her stay in his office and hide in his sanctuary forever.

After what seemed like an eternity, a flash of silver greeted Alexa's eyes. She had found the tracks. Mr Knight was walking far ahead of her, calling for her to continue on to the train station. Spurred on, she walked faster until the station was finally visible. Then her legs gave out. Her lungs were gasping as the world spun hazily. Holding on to the fence, she managed to fall somewhat gently to the ground, but she could not go on.

"I'm sorry, Lex," said Mr Knight in a desperate voice as he sunk to his knees beside her.

Cradling her in his arms, Mr Knight rested her head against his shoulder and urged her to find something she could eat.

Alexa barely had the energy to comply, but she forced her arms to open the plastic bag and pulled out the bottle of coloured liquid. It instantly revitalised her, but she could not take more than a sip without risking vomiting it back up. Placing another piece of chocolate in her mouth and letting it melt, Alexa slowly felt her strength return, but not before she watched two trains rumble by.

"It's okay," whispered Mr Knight. "We'll catch the next one," he reassured her tenderly, stroking her hair. "Don't worry. I'll stay with you. I'll get you back to school."

Mr Knight was as good as his word. He helped Alexa to her feet and held her tight to his side as they walked slowly to the station. He guided her to an empty seat on the platform, occasionally feeding her food when her concentration started to wane.

"Can't make it," gasped Alexa when the pain and exhaustion became too great. All she wanted was to close her eyes and be at peace.

"Almost there, Lex. Don't give up. Come back to me."

The sound of an approaching train helped Alexa make up her mind. She pushed up herself off the bench and on to the train. Warm arms immediately wrapped themselves around her body as she sat down in the closest available seat. She closed her eyes and rested her head in the crook of Mr Knight's neck. It was soothing being so close to him. He continued to tend to her during the trip, placing small amounts of food in her mouth without requiring her to open her eyes.

Mr Knight allowed Alexa to continue to rest during the trip. She was vaguely aware of movement in her body at times, but she did not care to think too much about it. The trek to school on the train was one she knew so well it did not require conscious thought.

"Lex!"

Alexa's eyes burst open to see Mr Knight standing on the platform and the train doors closing. Her heart gave a frantic lurch as she pushed her body forcefully off the train. Pain screamed through her body as she stumbled on to the platform. Knowing she did not have the energy to keep moving, she crawled under the nearby stairs as her lungs gasped desperately for rejuvenating air.

"Lex, I'm at school. You're so close. Don't give up."

Mr Knight's voice swirled in the air. Alexa wished she had the strength to comply. Realising how close she was, she reached into her plastic bag and pulled out the drink. She forced herself to drink slowly despite her aching thirst. Daring to eat something more solid than chocolate, Alexa was glad when her stomach did not instantly rebel, but she knew she could not risk eating more. She was alert enough now to compel her body to move through the pain. Mr Knight was close. She could survive this last trek.

Everything suddenly felt more dangerous as Alexa pulled herself up the station stairs. So close, she was terrified that it was about to be ripped away. It made her desperate to get back to school before it all disappeared in a cloud of blackness.

The hill up towards the school had never felt so steep. Alexa clung on to the fences that lined the street to pull herself along, never looking up, just continuing to put one foot in front of the other. It was a desperately hard walk, but ahead stood the towers of Redgrove College and inside one of those towers was Mr Knight. She could hear him calling her forward. It kept her feet moving despite the agonising pain tearing through every joint in her body.

The stairs of the year advisor tower took a lifetime to climb, and as Alexa rounded the first corner she felt the floor spin. Her stomach churned uncomfortably, forcing the food she had eaten back out of her body. She turned her head, but did not stop walking. She knew where she needed to go and it was not far away.

Mr Knight's office was now just metres away. The door was shut, but Alexa did not care. Her legs became sluggish as if they were stuck in mud. She refused to look down, her eyes focused on her destination as she all but crawled the last few metres and collapsed on the lounge outside his door.

Curled up on the warm, comfortable cushions, Alexa let her eyes slide closed. Mr Knight would be here soon. He would protect her.

"Alexa!"

Alexa slowly opened her eyes. Mr Knight stared back at her. One of his hands was holding hers as the other stroked her face to keep her eyes on him. He was not smiling. This was not the face of a man happy to see her. He had come back to her bedside. It could only mean one thing. The men were back.

A tear trickled slowly down her cheek as she gasped

desperately. It had been a dream. All those broken moments of freedom had just been a dream. It was more than Alexa could face. She did not want to live through another night of this.

Closing her eyes for what she hoped would be the last time, Alexa wished for a quick death.

Chapter Ten

"ALEXA, CAN YOU hear me? Alexa?"

Marcus did not want to risk moving her too much. He was barely able to recognise her with such heavy bruising on her face. Her eyes flickered as he spoke, but she did not respond. He did not want to leave her side, but knew he had to call an ambulance. Releasing Alexa's hand, he unlocked his door and grabbed his mobile from his bedroom.

"I need an ambulance at Redgrove College immediately."

Marcus held the line and answered the operator's questions as he sat on the ground, his hand gently cupping Alexa's battered face.

"I think she's conscious again," he said into the phone. "Alexa, can you hear me? You're all right. You're at school. I won't let anything happen to you now."

Alexa's eyes looked as though they were trying to focus on him, but they were so swollen it was hard to tell what she was looking at. Marcus tried to smile and reassure her, but she turned away from him, looking down towards her feet before letting out a shuddering sigh. Her head turned slowly back and Marcus could see her eyes widening as her hand stretched tentatively out towards his face.

Marcus could not stop himself from grabbing Alexa's hand as soon as her soft fingers touched his rough stubble. He held her hand against his cheek and closed his eyes for a moment. When he opened them, he thought he saw a slight smile on Alexa's face before her eyes closed and her body went limp.

The wait for the ambulance was excruciating. Marcus checked his watch when they arrived, prepared to lambast them for their tardiness, but it had barely been five minutes. The police arrived moments later.

"Where is she?" asked Detective Shepard, pushing through the crowd of students that had gathered. "Get these kids out of here!"

Marcus did not move. He stayed on the landing, watching as the ambulance officers stabilised Alexa. They put an oxygen mask on her and placed a drip in her arm, before examining the rest of her battered body. He hated to think how bad her internal injuries could be, seeing the extent of the external ones. If Marcus had not known Alexa so well, known every curve of her body and the strength of her spirit, he was not sure he would have recognised her.

"Alexa! Alexa!"

The sound of scuffling turned Marcus around to see Sam struggling against several officers who were holding him back from the scene.

"Let me through!" yelled Sam.

"This is not a freak show," snarled Detective Shepard.

"Mr Michaels is Miss Samson's best friend. If anyone is going to be by her side at this time, it will be him," replied Marcus firmly.

Marcus was not sure what Alexa had been put through, but knew that, besides Bethany, Sam was the one person she would want with her in her final moments.

Sam pushed the officers away and rushed towards the lounge, but Marcus put his arm out to stop him getting too close.

"Let them do what they need to do," Marcus said softly in Sam's ear. "I'll make sure you get to see her before they take her to hospital."

Sam nodded and Marcus lowered his arm. Then they just waited. Alexa's eyes remained closed. It made her look like she was dead, but Marcus had to assume she was still breathing as they patiently checked her over and placed her on the gurney.

"Alexa," cried Sam, when they started to wheel her away. He rushed forward and grabbed her hand, squeezing it tight. "Alexa, you've got to get better, okay. Please. It's me. Please. Can you hear me?"

"We need to take her now," said the ambulance officer.

Marcus stepped forward, but he did not need to intervene. Sam nodded and stepped back, though he still had hold of Alexa's hand. When the ambulance officers started to move, Sam released her hand. It fell lifelessly by her side. Looking at Alexa's face, Marcus feared this would be the last time he saw her alive.

Sam was suddenly surrounded by the rest of the G7 and Alexa's roommates. It was clear they too feared for Alexa's life. Though all Marcus wanted to do was follow Alexa to the hospital, his duty of care extended beyond her and he quickly ushered the students into his office. The only problem was that now that Alexa had returned, they wanted answers that no one could give them. Their demanding state eventually left Marcus no choice but to send them on their way.

"What's this?" asked Detective Shepard, pointing down at a plastic next to the lounge as Marcus leaned heavily against his office doorframe.

"Don't know," Marcus sighed, reaching down to grab the bag, but Detective Shepard yelled at him and slapped his hand away just before he touched it.

Leaning down, Detective Shepard opened the bag with his pen. There were bits of food in there and a wallet. The sight made Marcus's heart thump erratically. It obviously had the same effect on Detective Shepard, as there was a flurry of activity, with gloves being passed around and the contents examined more carefully.

"You find this person. You find out how they're involved and you do it now," commanded Detective Shepard, pointing at the licence in the wallet. "This may be the only real clue we get. Track it in every direction. I want every single person involved."

Marcus knew he should have cared more about the police investigation. He did want the monsters who had hurt Alexa so badly arrested and gaoled, but right then all he cared about was Alexa and seeing her again – perhaps for the last time.

The drive to the hospital was slow in the peak hour traffic. It frustrated Marcus, thinking that these delays would steal his chance to say goodbye. He remembered last year when he had tailed Alexa to the hospital after Clinton's attack, only to arrive and find out that she had died twice in that time. If she died this time, he could not convince himself that they would be able to revive her.

It was horrible to believe that Alexa might even be better off dead. What she had already suffered was bad enough. It was the thought that her future would be filled with similar horrors that truly haunted Marcus.

When he arrived at the hospital, he was directed straight to a waiting room. And that was what he did. He waited – with no information and little acknowledgement of his presence. It did not matter. He was not leaving until he knew what was happening.

"She's been taken to Ward Six East," said a kind nurse two hours after he had arrived.

Marcus was immediately comforted by the fact that Alexa had not been taken to intensive care. She would be okay, he thought happily. Then he saw her. The sight of her asleep, with tubes and wires flowing out of her body was one of the most horrific things he had ever witnessed. He had to fight hard to stop himself breaking down completely.

Alexa looked just as young and fragile as she had the year before when he had stood over her hospital bed. However, this time he was not wracked with guilt over his feelings for her. There was nothing in the world that came easier than loving Alexa. Marcus only wished he could have stayed with her, but was ushered out after just half an hour, as the ward closed for the night.

Walking towards the exit, his fingers pinching the bridge of his nose, Marcus was greeted by Detective Shepard.

"Have you seen her?" asked Detective Shepard in a slightly anxious voice. It was a far cry from the anger he had displayed at the school.

"I was just kicked out," replied Marcus. "But she looks a thousand times worse than I've seen anybody look in my life."

"I heard they tore her up pretty badly."

Marcus was sure he could see tears welling in the detective's eyes. It made him wonder which part of Alexa's story touched Detective Shepard the most. Trying to answer that question himself only made his blood boil.

"Have you caught the bastards that did this to her?" asked Marcus in an angry growl.

"We're not even sure who did this to her. We need to talk to Alexa and find out who they were. We're positive that she knew the leader and we have a tentative identification of him, but how long it takes us to catch them will all depend on how much she's willing to tell us."

"You don't think she'll tell you what she knows?"

"I know Bethany is involved. That means we may never know what happened, at least not from Alexa."

"But I thought Bethany was just trying to warn Alexa, but she never found out that Alexa was going home on the weekends," said Marcus, his heart beating frantically at the possibility that Alexa was betrayed by her very own sister.

"I don't think Bethany would've needed the gun to warn Alexa, and Alexa was never the main target of the home invasion. I don't think the two instances were linked the way it was first assumed," replied Detective Shepard.

"When are you planning on talking to her?" Marcus asked anxiously.

"Tomorrow, if possible. The earlier the better. I want to get to her before she tries to make herself forget."

"I want to be there when you talk to her. She's not to be spoken to without me. Do you understand?" demanded Marcus. Detective Shepard looked at him curiously. "She might be seventeen, but she is still a child and she will feel like she's being interrogated. She deserves to have someone with her that she knows."

There was no way he was going to let Alexa face a second of this torment alone.

"I will call you as soon as we're allowed to see her," nodded Detective Shepard, before walking off.

The night was cloudless and cool as Marcus walked up the deserted stairs to his office. He could still see Alexa's battered body lying on the couch. He had never known such contradicting emotions in all his life. Part of him had been ecstatic at the sight of her, while the rest of him had been almost paralysed by her nearly unidentifiable face and the thought that, although she had made it back to him, she may still die.

As Marcus moved closer to his office, he noticed there was still a shadowy figure lying on the couch outside his office. He turned on the light, startling Sam from his sleep.

"Mr Michaels, what are you doing here?"

"Is she okay?" asked Sam, his voice shaking, as fear and desperation filled in his eyes.

"She's stable," nodded Marcus in soft reassurance. "She doesn't look very good. I didn't get to spend much time with her. I'll know more tomorrow."

"But she's not going to die or anything, right?"

Marcus heard Sam choke on the word 'die' and felt nothing but sympathy towards the boy.

"She'll be all right," Marcus replied gently.

"When will she be back at school?" asked Sam, though his voice was almost commanding.

"I think it's a bit early to be thinking about that. She may not be out of hospital for a while. She's really not in a very good state."

"When she does come back, I'm going to look after her," said Sam intently. "I just want you to know that. It won't change anything for her, but she needs someone there for her and right now no one else can be."

Marcus turned and looked Sam in the eyes. It was clear that Sam knew how he and Alexa felt about each other. For the first time, Marcus was grateful for Sam's presence, grateful that he did not appear to disapprove of their feelings and that he would look out for Alexa while he could not.

"Thank you. I'm really glad you'll be there for her," said Marcus softly. "She's going to need your support."

Marcus arranged for other teachers to cover his classes the next day so he could return to the hospital. Mrs Taylor was not impressed and tried to make him stay, but on this he had the support of the other teachers. Although Alexa had not been named, her ordeal had been reported in the media, and Marcus was not above going to the press if Mrs Taylor wanted to make an issue of the situation.

For all intents and purposes Redgrove College was Alexa's home and Marcus had responsibility for her welfare. He knew he was neglecting his other students, but he refused to let Alexa lie in hospital alone. She had to know that he was there for her.

Walking up to Alexa's ward, Marcus was surprised by the sight of Detective Shepard asleep in the hallway outside her room. His eyes were closed, but Marcus could see that one hand was resting on his gun.

"Have you been here all night?" asked Marcus, startling Detective Shepard.

Detective Shepard's hand grabbed at his gun and Marcus quickly moved to the side, before Detective Shepard looked up and released his grip.

"Yeah," Detective Shepard replied, stretching his body out of its twisted position. "I wanted to make sure Alexa had no unwanted guests. Are you going in to see her?"

"I was hoping to," answered Marcus warily.

"Good, well if you're going to be with her, then I might go and get some breakfast."

Marcus watched Detective Shepard leave, wondering what he knew about Alexa's attackers and what danger she was still in. It made him sick to think that her ordeal might not yet be over.

***

Alexa slowly turned her head and opened her eyes. Mr Knight stood next to her, staring mournfully. Her heart began pounding painfully, as her breath hitched. Things seemed different somehow, yet she was not prepared to believe that this was not the beginning of another night. Mr Knight took her hand as he sat down. She squeezed it back, feeling the pressure and heat of his touch burn through her hand.

Releasing his hand, Alexa reached out towards his face, desperate for him not to disappear. Mr Knight grabbed her hand again and held it to his cheek. His other hand moved to gently cup the side of her face, stroking her cheek softly with his thumb. A tear slipped from her eye. It seemed real, but she had dreamed of escape before.

Daring to glance down at her body, Alexa let out a gasping sob when she realised there was nothing but blankets on top of her body. When she looked around the room, there were walls of white and everything appeared clean and sterile, not squalid and filthy.

"You're in hospital. You're safe now," said Mr Knight, still holding her hand tight. She turned back to look into his eyes. "I promise."

It was real. She had escaped that nightmare. She had survived Leo.

That reality hit hard. Alexa found her body sobbing uncontrollably. Mr Knight released her hand, and she curled her body into a ball, covering her face with her arms, as though it would somehow keep the sight from each of them. She felt his gentle touch try to soothe her, but that only reminded her of why she never wanted to be touched again. She was glad when he sat down and rested a simple hand on her head.

It took a long time for Alexa to compose herself. Mr Knight handed her tissues. She gently wiped her eyes and face, feeling the sting of bruising with every touch. When she had finished with the tissues, Mr Knight grabbed them and threw them in the bin, seemingly unconcerned about touching her contaminated fluids. It was a strangely intimate gesture that she could not help but appreciate.

"How are you feeling?" asked Mr Knight tenderly when she had been silent for several minutes.

Alexa tried to reply, but it was too painful. Her throat was dry and sore, preventing her from talking. Mr Knight touched her hand softly, promising he would be back soon, before he left to collect some ice. He returned quickly, but not fast enough. As soon as she was alone, Alexa had started to panic. Her body shook, but her mind remained paralysed, unable to determine what she should do.

Thankfully, Mr Knight did not seem too shocked by tearful state on his return. Though he rushed back to her bedside, he simply handed her the cup of ice, with another handful of tissues, and sat down silently beside her.

"I'm okay," Alexa replied gingerly, after several minutes of sucking on ice to recompose herself. "Everything hurts."

"I thought we'd lost you," said Mr Knight with a broken voice, tears suddenly tumbling down his cheeks. He quickly wiped them away, trying to smile.

Alexa wanted to feel sorry for his pain, but she was too exhausted to feel anything except the bruises covering her body. When she lay back down, she curled her body towards Mr Knight, her right hand resting near the edge of the bed. She was thankful when Mr Knight took it in his, allowing her to rest without the fear of being transported back to that horrid place.

"I want to go home. I want to get out of here," she said forcefully, looking into Mr Knight's eyes as he watched her.

With her bodily wounds being treated, every minute saw her mind becoming more active and, with it, her memories more vivid. Stuck in an unfamiliar bed, it left the hospital feeling like another prison she had to escape.

"I think they'll want to keep you in a bit longer. You've been hurt very badly," replied Mr Knight in a tender voice.

"I don't care. I don't want to be here. I can lie in a bed anywhere. Please, get me out of here," pleaded Alexa, her voice breaking.

Mr Knight nodded, but did not leave immediately, unwilling to leave her alone again. When a suited man entered, Mr Knight acknowledged him with a nod and promised her he would talk to the nurses. She tried to smile her appreciation, but couldn't.

Watching Mr Knight leave, Alexa finally turned her gaze away from the empty doorway. She did not really care who the man in the suit was and was prepared to ignore him – until he moved forward, close enough for his face to come into focus.

Alexa pushed herself up in her bed away from him, suddenly worried that she really was dreaming. The man did not move. He just stood at the end of her bed looking at her, his eyes appearing to fill with tears. Alexa lay back down slowly, never taking her eyes off him. She waited for him to speak, but he just stared silently.

"They have to run a few tests before they can let you go, but they said if everything comes back okay they might be able to let you leave this afternoon," said Mr Knight, retuning to Alexa's bedside. He looked worriedly between Alexa and the man. "Is everything all right?"

"I was waiting for your return," answered the man in the suit, his voice making Alexa's heart beat erratically. "You told me not to question her without you present."

"I'm not answering any questions while I'm here," said Alexa in a soft, but determined voice. She was not going to do anything else on anyone else's terms. It was her way or no way. "You want to talk to me, you get me out of here."

"I'll see what we can do for you," smiled the suited man, before leaving the room.

"Was he bothering you while I was gone?" asked Mr Knight.

"No," said Alexa, absently shaking her head.

Mr Knight sat down, but he seemed uneasy.

"I don't want you there when they question me," said Alexa after fifteen minutes of silence, her mind finally turning from the man in the suit. Mr Knight looked shocked by the comment. "You won't like me if you hear all that. I don't want you to have any more bad images of me in your head."

"I want you to look into my eyes," said Mr Knight in a low voice, so no one else could hear. It was impossible not to comply. "Nothing I hear could change the way I feel about you. Nothing. When you come back to school I won't be able to be with you when you need me, but I can be with you through this. I want you to know that you can face this because you have me there beside you. You don't have to do this alone."

Alexa's resolution faltered in the face of Mr Knight's support. She still did not want him to hear what had happened to her – what she had willingly done – but she did not want to face it alone either. Her hand twitched and he instantly took it in his, squeezing it reassuringly. There was so much comfort in his touch, and yet somehow nothing more.

***

Alexa was taken for tests just before lunch. Marcus took the opportunity to drive back to school to pick up some clothes and personal items for her. He pulled Bianca out of class for the task, hoping it would force her to realise the depth of Alexa's suffering. There were some genuine moments of concern from Bianca, but Marcus also knew what Bianca had been saying between her tears. Along with her fanciful stories, Bianca had also openly questioned Alexa's decision to leave with her attackers and whether the whole situation had just been a set up to gain attention and notoriety.

Those who knew Alexa's protective nature had been terrified of her situation. When Stacey had heard that Alexa had been protecting her foster sister, she had become so distressed that she had to be excused from class.

"Is Alexa coming back to class tomorrow?" asked Bianca when she had finished packing Alexa's things.

"No," snapped Marcus angrily. "She has been beaten to within an inch of her life. Do you really think she will be coming straight back here to school?"

Marcus did not pay attention to what Bianca's tearful reply was. Instead, he apologised for snapping and forced all the right words from his mouth. When Bianca requested leave from her afternoon classes, he wrote the note without complaint.

Driving back to the hospital, Marcus found himself questioning his recent resolution to play no role in Alexa's future life. Right now, he never wanted to contemplate his life without her in it. The knowledge that he could be with her, love her, and never want to be anything more than a friend made him more confident that that future was possible without him becoming yet another man who would hurt and abuse her.

There were several police officers, including Detective Shepard, talking to a doctor outside Alexa's room when he arrived back at the hospital. It was clear Alexa had been continuing to press her insistence on leaving the hospital in his absence, as Detective Shepard was urging the doctor to understand their need to get a statement from her.

Slipping past them into her room, Marcus noticed Alexa was sitting up in bed anxiously watching the proceedings outside her door.

"Can I leave?" she asked forcefully as soon as she noticed him.

"I don't know," Marcus smiled, loving that not everything had been lost in this latest attack. "They'll be finished talking soon. I had Bianca pack you some clothes and things for you."

Alexa took the bag, but her attention did not leave the congregation outside her door. After several impatient minutes ticked by, the party finally moved over to her bed.

"Your tests have come back. You have mild concussion and extensive bruising, but no broken bones," the doctor said, watching Alexa carefully. "You were severely dehydrated and suffering from hypothermia, but appear to be recovering well from both. You are very lucky, and I would prefer to keep you in for observation. You have been through a tremendous ordeal. We want to make sure that you have physically recovered before we release you."

"But what will I do here that I can't do at home? There's nothing wrong with me. If all I can do is rest then let me do it at home. I'll leave today whether you want me to or not."

Marcus noticed Detective Shepard smiling at the doctor, shrugging his shoulders as though he had expected Alexa's reaction. Marcus found it strange that Detective Shepard had gleaned so much about Alexa's personality in such a short period of time. However, the way Detective Shepard had spoken about Bethany had made Marcus believe that he had had previous encounters with her. Maybe he had encountered Alexa before too.

The doctor sighed and waved her hand in defeat.

"We will discharge you today, but you will have to take it very easy. You are not to return to school for at least two weeks and I want her back here at the slightest hint of trouble," said the doctor firmly. "Anything doesn't feel right, you come back and we'll investigate."

Alexa nodded, her eyes suddenly flicking nervously around the room then back at the doctor. She looked terrified.

"I don't want to be pregnant," said Alexa in a soft voice.

Marcus felt sick. Her comment confirmed what he had feared on first hearing the news of her abduction.

"We will take care of that," replied the doctor compassionately. "We will also organise medications to try and prevent infections."

"So I can go?" asked Alexa timidly.

"Yes, once we sort all that out for you. But you really have to take it easy, and that includes you lot interviewing her as well. No more than an hour at a time and at least a fifteen minute break in between," said the doctor in a reluctant voice, as though she were still doing this under duress.

The doctor ordered everyone from room. Marcus watched as Alexa's eyes flicked his way. He knew she did not want him to stay for this, but he could also see how terrified she was about being left alone with strangers.

"We're going to be just outside that door, okay," said Marcus, touching his finger to Alexa's hand.

Alexa nodded stoically as a single tear slipped down her cheek. Marcus had to hold on to the sobbing gasp that erupted in his chest at the sight. All he could do was smile and nod supportively as he followed the police out into the hallway.

Marcus positioned himself near the officers, trying to listen to what Detective Shepard and his partner were saying. He heard

Alexa's name spoken several times, but they made sure the rest remained unheard. When the doctor finished treating Alexa, she made her way over to the detectives and they spoke conspiratorially again. Marcus tried to act detached – as if he was just Alexa's teacher – but it was harder than he imagined. Right then he felt so attached to Alexa that nothing could tear them apart.

Everything took longer than Marcus thought it would to finalise, meaning it was after four o'clock when he pulled up outside the police station. He had picked up some food from the hospital café before they left the hospital, but Alexa had barely touched it. It was not quite what he had expected. Her forcefulness earlier in the day had given him hope that she would continue to come out of her shell, but the opposite had occurred. When he looked over at her, he noticed her body was trembling.

"Are you all right?" Marcus asked gently. Alexa nodded slowly as she released a shuddering breath and stepped out of the car.

Constable Banks led them to an interview room. Inside sat Detective Shepard and his partner Detective Parker.

"Sit down, Alexa," said Detective Parker in a pleasant voice. "We're just waiting on a female officer before we start the interview. Would you like a drink?"

"I don't need any chick here to talk to you. The whole police force could be female and I wouldn't want to answer your questions," replied Alexa in a soft, but cynical voice.

"Shall we start, then?" asked Detective Parker, looking around the room, then back at Alexa.

Alexa shrugged her shoulders and looked at the wall. She did not move. Marcus had to step forward and place a guiding hand on her shoulder to usher her towards the seat. Detective Shepard and Detective Parker sat opposite her while Constable Banks stood against the wall behind them.

"What can you tell us about Saturday night?"

Alexa did not answer. Marcus watched her from the side, where he was leaning against the wall, as she stared intently at a dark spot on the table, giving no sign of recognition to Detective Parker. Marcus wanted to be closer, but part of Alexa had truly not wanted him here and he had to accept that much of what she was going to say would be easier without him in her line of sight.

"We know that three men entered your foster parents' home at approximately eight pm. We know they alleged that your sister, Bethany, owed three thousand dollars to one of the men. We know that your foster father offered them the entire amount, but the offer was refused. Instead, they wanted to take his daughter, Hayley, at which point you offered yourself and took Hayley and her brother upstairs out of danger. We also have a pretty good idea of what happened to you after that by the medical report."

"It seems you have it just about sorted, so what do you need me for?" asked Alexa in a small, broken voice, not looking up at the detectives.

"We want to know who the men were. We want to catch them and put them in gaol for what they did to you," explained Detective Parker passionately.

"They didn't do anything to me," replied Alexa matter-of-factly.

"So you punched and raped yourself?" asked Constable Banks.

"I left with them and I agreed to the deal we made. There's nothing to charge them with."

Everyone in the room, except Detective Shepard, looked at Alexa in amazement. Marcus could not believe that she had somehow found a way of taking the blame for what had happened to her, but Detective Shepard looked as though he had expected nothing less. Marcus supposed he should have too, but he did not want to. He wanted Alexa to realise just how wrong it was that she had suffered so much. He wanted to be able to wipe those events from her existence and bring back the lively, beautiful girl he had watched dance away from him on that fateful Friday afternoon.

"The scary thing is you seem to believe that. Do you think they were really there for money?" asked Detective Parker. "Why don't I tell you about something else that happened that night? Back at your school, everyone was asleep and happy until about ten pm when an alarm went off, signalling that one of the external doors in the dormitory had been opened. Your matron, Ms Carter, walks down presuming that a student has tried to leave or enter the building.

"Instead, halfway down the stairs she is met by a girl with a gun. This girl holds the gun to her head and forces her back up the stairs. This armed girl then walks with her until they find your room. Inside, she throws Ms Carter to the floor and walks straight over to the bed next to the window. This bed, as you know, was empty.

"The girl becomes panicked, turns on the light, waking everybody in the room, and starts tearing apart the room looking for money she is convinced is hidden somewhere. No one in the room has seen this girl before and everyone is a little confused until she starts pointing the gun at their heads and asking where you are. Can you think of who this girl might be?"

The stillness of Alexa's body was the only indication that she was even listening to Detective Parker. Marcus watched her intently and thought he saw her eyes widen, but could not be sure.

"Bethany will be arrested and charged whether you give us any information about what happened to you or not. She broke into a school and physically assaulted a teacher," said Constable Banks.

"What are you talking about?" asked Alexa, looking up briefly.

"Throughout her raid of your room, Bethany continually beat Ms Carter. She also verbally abused her, but none of the students heard what she said and Ms Carter seemed far too shaken to repeat any of it."

Alexa's head fell on to the table as she traced the dark stain with her finger, but she said nothing. Detective Parker tried a couple of times to get Alexa to answer his questions, but Detective Shepard put a stop to it. It had been almost an hour, so the interview was halted for fifteen minutes.

"Would you like something to eat or drink?" asked Detective Parker.

Alexa nodded slowly, but could not articulate what it was she wanted and was almost in tears trying to do so. It was sickening to watch, and Marcus hated that it took the officers so long to understand that they needed to choose something for Alexa, not continue to press her for a decision.

"Can I go to the bathroom?" Alexa asked tentatively, as if actually asking for permission.

Detective Parker gave her directions, but Alexa just sat glued to her chair as her body quivered. She took one look at the door and shook her head.

"I'll take you," said Marcus, stepping forward, feeling ill.

Alexa shook her head again, hunching her shoulders and curling her arms into her chest. Constable Banks moved forward and offered to show them where to go, but she still did not move. When Detective Shepard told her to go with them while he got her something to eat, she finally rose to her feet.

Constable Banks opened the door to the women's toilet for Alexa. She took one step in before quickly retreating.

"Someone in there," she gasped.

Constable Banks beckoned a female officer to clear the

bathroom. They smiled at Alexa as they left, but that only made her shake more.

"Can you come in?" Alexa asked when Constable Banks held the door open once more. He nodded solemnly and started to follow her. "Both of you?"

Marcus felt his heart crumble. He and Constable Banks stood silently waiting, until Alexa asked if they could talk to each other. Topics of conversation were hard to come by until Constable Banks mentioned that he had just become a first-time father. It was easy to keep him talking after that.

When they eventually returned to the interview room, Marcus noticed that they had taken his suggestion of hot chocolate seriously. There was a mug for each of them and a plate of biscuits.

"It's been a long day," said Detective Shepard.

Alexa passed one of the mugs to Constable Banks before giving one to Marcus. Marcus could not help but smile in response. In the midst of all her turmoil, she was still the most kind-hearted person he knew. When Alexa started offering everyone biscuits, he knew she was working on her diversionary tactics. It seemed like Detective Shepard knew that too, but he let her go on until there was nothing left for her to offer.

Detective Shepard leaned forward and Marcus could see that Alexa was trying to avoid his eye. Detective Parker was sitting back and it was clear they had decided to change tact for the second hour.

"Do you remember me, Alexa?" asked Detective Shepard.

Alexa nodded slowly as she gazed up at his round face. "You're in my dreams," she replied softly.

"What do I do in your dreams?"

"You die."

Marcus felt his heart stop as Detective Shepard smiled wryly and threw his head back mirthlessly.

They knew each other.

Alexa's nightmares had long been a source of concern for Marcus, but all she had told him was that she had had the same dream since she was a child. He had never learned what the dream was about, and not once had he considered that she would be dreaming about something real.

"I remember that day too," said Detective Shepard, looking back at Alexa.

"I don't," replied Alexa in an emotionless tone.

Detective Shepard considered her answer for a moment, before nodding solemnly. Much to Marcus's frustration, Detective Shepard said nothing more about the dream, but what he did manage to do was get Alexa talking.

"You're a good sister. You protect Bethany, don't you?" said Detective Shepard, leaning back in his seat casually, but keeping his gaze fixed on Alexa.

Alexa slouched back and crossed her arms in an almost defiant manner, but she answered his question with little hesitation. "I try," she said, her voice cracking.

"And then she does this to you."

"It would've been okay. I could've given her the money," said Alexa softly, her voice suddenly more controlled, but much less emotional.

"But they didn't want the money," stated Detective Shepard.

Alexa shook her head slowly.

"She wanted money. He – he didn't care," she said hesitantly, her voice breaking. "He wanted Hayley. She gave her to him. She told him where they lived."

Everyone looked dumbfounded as Alexa continued to answer Detective Shepard's questions freely. No one else spoke or interrupted for fear of stopping the flow of information.

"What makes you think Bethany was after money?" asked Detective Shepard curiously.

"The gun. She wanted to make sure I didn't try and change her mind. He knew she was going after me and took the chance to get Hayley."

"Why'd you go with them? Why not fight them? There were two adults and Brett's a fairly solid boy."

"He's a child," spat Alexa contemptuously. "It was her eleventh birthday. What if we couldn't fight them off? We couldn't have beaten them. I knew what he would do to her. I couldn't let that happen."

"If he really wanted Hayley then why'd he take you?" asked Detective Shepard, sitting forward slightly.

"I'm Bethy's sister. He knew how much I hated him. I think the chance to make me give – take … and I think he always planned to go back for Hayley."

Alexa's voice had become colder with every word, until it was icy and free of any emotion. It was as if she was recalling times tables, rather than recounting a horrific week in her own life.

Marcus could hardly believe it was the same girl he was in love with. He had forgotten what Alexa sounded like when she spoke in her coldly rational manner.

"Do you think Hayley is safe now?" asked Detective Shepard.

"No," Alexa replied, shaking her head. "She was the one he wanted."

"You haven't asked about your foster family, how they are, what happened to them. Why not?"

"Because I don't want to hear that he went back and found Hayley anyway and I wasn't there to protect her," replied Alexa, her voice barely above a whisper.

"Do you really think it's your job to protect her?"

"When it's my fault she was put in danger, I do," answered Alexa flatly.

"How is what happened your fault?" asked Detective Shepard conversationally. Marcus could only admire his ability to stay so calm. He would have been pleading with Alexa for reason by now.

"I'm Bethy's sister."

"You cannot be held responsible for her actions, much less the actions of her boyfriend."

"She's fifteen. Who is responsible for her? I should've stopped all of this," cried Alexa, finally showing some emotion. It seemed she was still completely capable of hating and blaming herself. "I put other people in danger all because I wanted ..."

"You wanted a life. You wanted to be happy. You cannot blame yourself for wanting those things," replied Detective Shepard, his voice also showing some passion, perhaps in response to Alexa's.

Alexa did not reply. She laid her head back on the table and started tracing the spot again.

Marcus was sure that they had heard all they would from Alexa as they took their second break. Alexa did not move from her seat and ignored the food that was placed in front of her. She did not even show any sign of recognition as Detective Shepard and Detective Parker sat back down across the table from her. Detective Shepard indicated again that he was the only one to speak.

"What happened when you left your foster parents' house?"

Alexa did not answer. Detective Shepard waited patiently as Alexa ran her finger around the dark spot on the table. She sighed deeply, but no words came out. Still, no one spoke.

"We drove," she said eventually.

Marcus could hear the strain in Alexa's voice. He wanted to

throw his arm around her and comfort her. He wanted to take away every horror she was being forced to relive.

"They put me on the floor of the back seat," Alexa continued, the emotion draining from her voice with every word, until there was hardly a drop left. "I couldn't see where we were going."

"Where did they take you?" asked Detective Shepard, returning his voice to the casual conversational tone that had worked so well during the previous hour of questioning.

"To a flat."

"Do you remember what it looked like?"

"Yes. It was unit eight on the third floor and the building was number ninety-seven. It was brick with ugly box metal balconies," replied Alexa, surprising Marcus with the kind of details she remembered. He had been prepared for her to remember nothing of her ordeal.

"What about the inside, do you remember what that looked like?" asked Detective Shepard as Detective Parker scribbled notes furiously. Alexa nodded and pulled the pen and paper from Detective Parker's hands. She carefully drew the layout of the unit on the paper, naming the rooms she knew. "What did they do to you when you arrived at the apartment?"

Alexa hesitated before answering. Marcus was sure she was blocking all the emotion from her memories to enable her to speak. However, Marcus could not block his emotions the way she could as she recounted the attacks. Alexa did not give detailed descriptions, but the sheer violence and volume was enough to have Marcus holding his hand over his mouth. Even Constable Banks and Detective Parker seemed nauseated by the account. Detective Shepard simply closed his eyes for long periods as if meditating.

"Do you know how you made it back to school?" asked Detective Shepard when Alexa's memories of the attacks went black.

Alexa raised her head slightly. She looked confused by the question. "You didn't find me?" she asked.

"No," answered Detective Shepard solemnly. "We still don't know where you were taken. We know where you took the money out of yours and your foster father's accounts. We think we know where you were left after the attacks and we know you eventually made it back to your school."

"But I thought you said I was hurt really bad," said Alexa, as if doubting that fact. "How could I make it back to school?"

"We don't know," replied Detective Shepard. "You have always had amazing skills in evasion, navigation and self-preservation. I don't know many people who could have done what you did. I just need me to tell me what you remember. Even the smallest thing could make the biggest difference."

Alexa hung her head in her hands. Marcus thought he saw her look back at him under her arm, but could not be sure.

"I remember Mr Knight helping me," she said tentatively.

"That would have been when you got back to school," said Detective Shepard immediately, but Alexa only shrugged, as though she was unconvinced by that fact. "You caught the train there. Do you remember that? We have some CCTV footage and some witness accounts. Do you know where you caught the train from?"

Marcus found Alexa suddenly looking at him as though he could answer that question for her. When she comprehended his confusion, her whole body slumped slightly as she slowly shook her head.

"That's okay. We should be able to work that out. Do you remember anything else? Anything. Doesn't have to seem important."

"I remember the water. That's where I rested," said Alexa, her voice still soft and tentative, as though unsure she saying the right thing. When Detective Shepard nodded, smiling just slightly, she continued. "It was by the ocean, small bay – not big waves, but soothing sound. Sat on rock –"

Alexa stopped talking at the very moment Marcus's heart stopped beating. That place sounded exactly like where he had taken her to swim last year. It seemed impossible that she could have been dumped at that very same spot.

"We believe you were left near a river," said Detective Shepard softly. "Do you remember how you got there? You remember driving? Walking?"

"You think after I had enough fun with them, I just went for a stroll and hung out by a river?" asked Alexa scathingly.

"No," replied Detective Shepard casually. "We're trying to work out how far away from where you were held that you were dumped. I don't believe that you wrapped yourself in a blanket and jumped off a bridge into a shallow river."

Marcus gasped. The contempt with which Alexa had been treated by these men was inhumane. It was the kind of thing that only happened in movies or the seedy underworld of society. It was a world away from the life he had known up to this point and he hated to believe that that world was one that Alexa belonged to.

"Don't know how I got anywhere," muttered Alexa.

"You had a wallet on you when you returned to school. We interviewed the person it belonged to, but we're pretty sure they had nothing to do with what happened to you," said Detective Shepard. "They live near the river we believe you were dumped in. We think you snuck into the house, stole the wallet, clothes and some food. Do you remember that?"

"Why? You going to charge me?" asked Alexa in a flat, defiant voice.

Marcus wished he could have been certain the answer was no, but could understand the defensiveness of her question. The world had a way of kicking Alexa when she was down.

"No," answered Detective Shepard emphatically. "You are not in trouble. This isn't about finding some way of punishing you. Alexa, the fact that you survived is a miracle in itself. Yes, we have some information on how you got back to school, but what you did – it shouldn't be possible. All I want is to understand."

"I don't know," Alexa cried softly, her forearms pulling back to cover her ears. Her eyes were scrunched closed and her arms were pressing hard into the sides of her head. "I don't know."

"Okay, Alexa. It's okay," said Detective Shepard quickly. "You've done really well already. It's our job to figure out the rest. You've given us everything we could expect."

Marcus watched Alexa's eyes slowly unscrunch, releasing tears down her cheeks. It was a heartbreaking sight, and he hated that there was nothing he could do to make this whole ordeal any more bearable. He knew these interviews were tantamount to torture for her, but the idea that these men would get away unpunished for their crimes was obviously too much for everyone else to consider granting Alexa her unspoken wish.

The best Detective Shepard could do was offer Alexa another break before starting on their final session.

Chapter Eleven

ALEXA LAID HER head down on the table and closed her eyes. She could feel Mr Knight's eyes on her. While she was so glad that he was close by, part of her brain still tried to pretend he was not there. She hated that he had heard so much.

When Detective Ben Shepard returned to the room, he promised again that this would be the last session. He sat down next to her with a large photo album of known offenders and urged her to identify her attackers, but she found it hard to concentrate. Her eyes kept flicking up to his face, trying to compare it to the friendly saviour in her dreams. His face was no longer so round, but his voice was familiar and just as soothing and gentle as she had dreamt.

"Are you real?" Alexa whispered, briefly flicking her eyes up at Ben then back down at the photos.

"Yes," Ben replied equally softly.

"And you know who I am? Before this stuff, you knew me?" asked Alexa in a gasping voice. Ben nodded solemnly. "I knew you?"

"We met when –"

"No, just answer – don't want to know – I just … I'm not crazy, right?"

"You're not crazy," answered Ben solemnly. "I understand your situation and I know how much you love Bethany and want to protect her, but this is not the way to do it. If you want to protect her, then you help us arrest her boyfriend. Help us get him away from her."

"She's still going to be in trouble but, isn't she?" asked Alexa, her voice breaking at the knowledge that she could not protect Bethany from this. Ben nodded slowly. "Can you ring my lawyer? His name is Peter Lam. Can you tell him what happened? If you find her, promise me you'll call him. He's her lawyer too."

Alexa noticed Mr Knight slip a piece of paper on the table before walking away. It had Peter's phone number on it.

"You've spoken to him?" asked Ben, looking up at Mr Knight.

Mr Knight shook his head. "You find the people who attacked you and I'll do this for you."

"But what if they're not in here?" asked Alexa desperately, reaching for Peter's number as she shook her head. "I'll call him. You're not allowed to not let me call him," she said frantically.

"I'll do it, okay," replied Ben quickly, grabbing Alexa by the shoulders to restrain her. "I'll do it now. You look through the photos and I'll call him right now."

Ben left immediately. Detective Parker took his seat next to her and opened the book of photos.

"Just take a look," said Detective Parker gently. "You'll be surprised how they jump out at you. Don't stress."

Alexa nodded and took a deep breath. Detective Parker was right. Most of the photos were just pictures of faces, but when she found Leo's it jumped out at her so violently she was not sure she would have been able to stop herself from pointing at it.

Despite looking at all the photos twice, Alexa was not able to identify any of her other attackers. In her mind they all looked the same and she had tried not to look close enough to see any distinguishing features. She never wanted to be able to recognise any of them again. She did not need more men haunting her dreams.

"It's okay," reassured Detective Parker. "We were able to get some DNA evidence from your body."

"But I thought you said I was dumped in water. Wouldn't it have washed off?"

"The doctors took internal samples as well as some external ones. We also think we found the blanket you were wrapped in when you were dumped. We are gathering evidence. It won't come down to you picking them by sight. I promise, we won't let them get away with what they did to you."

"I want to go home," sighed Alexa, putting her head back down on the table.

Detective Parker put a hand on her shoulder and left her alone. Mr Knight immediately took his place. Alexa was glad he did not speak. He rested his arm next to hers, but did not take her hand. The heat of his touch was comforting in a way nothing else could be, like a tether to this life she no longer wished to live.

"We've contacted her foster parents. We have them in a safe house. They're expecting her," said Ben, walking back into the interview room just before nine o'clock.

"I'm not going back there," said Alexa in a dull voice, closing her eyes, her head still on the table.

"Where else is there for you to go?" asked Ben.

"Home. I'm going back to school," Alexa replied flatly.

"You're still too sick to go to class, Alexa. You should go back to your foster family until you're better," said Mr Knight in a soothing voice.

"I'm not going back there," Alexa said, her voice more determined and angry as she sat up and glared at Ben.

"You'll feel better when you see them. They don't blame you for what happened. They want you to come back," said Ben, trying to calm her.

Alexa's heart strained with the desire to be with the Whites again, but all she could think about was Hayley's screams as she was attacked over and over, beaten and violated. It was something she could never allow to happen.

"I'm not going back there," repeated Alexa firmly, desperate to block out those images.

"Alexa, you have to –"

"No!" she screamed, fear filling her body. She could not be responsible for hurting the Whites, for hurting Hayley. "I'm not going back there!"

Ben stepped forward and Alexa stumbled away from him. When he kept approaching, she picked her chair and held it out between them.

"Alexa, –"

"NO! I'm not going back there. What part of that don't you understand?"

Ben hesitated, but continued forward as Detective Parker and Constable Banks entered the room and moved towards her. They came at her from all sides. Alexa thought she heard Mr Knight speak, but could not make out the words over Hayley's desperate screams. They were trying to force her into hurting Hayley and she would not do it.

Using the chair as her weapon, Alexa tried to escape, flailing it around her and taking out anyone who dared to come near. They continued to surround her and she swung the chair violently again. She did not know who it was that cursed in pain, but she cried out when arms locked around her torso and the chair was wrestled from her grasp.

Ben's voice echoed in her ears as she felt her body collapsing to the ground.

"I'm not going back there," Alexa said softly, as Mr Knight crouched down in front of her. Ben was still restraining her from behind, his arms locked around her chest. "I want to go home. Please, take me home," she said with pleading eyes.

"It's okay. I'll take you home," said Mr Knight, cupping her cheek so that she was looking in his eyes as he nodded his assurance.

Alexa could not stop herself from lunging into Mr Knight's chest. She felt him sigh heavily as he held her close, his hand cupping her head as if he could and would protect her from the world. There was nothing inappropriate about the way he held her. It was almost paternal. He kept holding her as she gripped his shirt, terrified of being torn away from him and his promise.

He would take her home. He would protect her. She wondered if she would ever want him to touch her the way she had once thought she would desire, but the idea of being with him that way made her body shiver violently. Mr Knight held her tighter, resting his chin on her head as he whispered reassuringly that everything would be all right soon.

***

Alexa sat quietly as Marcus drove them back to school. He wished he could take Alexa home with him. He did not want to take her back to Redgrove. That place was not good for her, but in so many ways, he guessed she was right. It was her home. For the past five and a half years, it had been the most permanent home she had had.

The problem was that Marcus could not take care of her at school. He could not be there for her. He was not even sure if they could protect her at school. If those men found Alexa there, threatened her there, then he knew that she would not hesitate to give herself to them again to save her friends. She would put herself forward to suffer more to protect them. At least if she was with him, he knew he would give his life before anyone ever hurt her.

"You must be hungry. Do you want to stop somewhere for food?" Marcus asked.

"I don't want to go in anywhere. I don't want to be with people," replied Alexa quietly. Her voice was so sullen that Marcus wished to hear that defiance he once hated back in her voice.

They pulled into the car park of a fast food outlet. Alexa had immediately disclaimed the bright lights of the drive-through. Her eyes were still bruised and swollen and Marcus imagined the bright lights against the dark night would be immensely painful.

"Do you want me to park and run in and get something?" he offered, already undoing his seatbelt.

"No! Don't – please don't leave me alone out here," replied Alexa, panic etching her voice.

Marcus looked back over at the drive-through, suggesting it would be the easiest option. When he handed Alexa his cap, she nodded, pulling it down low over her face. However, when he stopped at the menu, the simple task of choosing something to eat had her in silent tears. It was a horrible sight.

Marcus had thought that he would never see Alexa brought as low as she was after Clinton's attack, but this ordeal looked as though it had sucked the very life out of her and he was not sure that the defiant, vibrant girl she had once been would ever return.

Ordering the first thing he saw on the menu, Marcus got them through and back on the road as fast as possible. Alexa ate quickly as they drove. Marcus was worried that he had not bought her enough food. She had eaten so little during the day and he was glad to see she had her appetite back.

"Shit. Pull over," said Alexa as she held the last of the food near her mouth.

Marcus quickly pulled the car to the side of the road, allowing Alexa to jump out. She rushed to the back of the car before vomiting in the gutter. She moved further down the street and sat on the edge of the road with her head between her knees.

"How are you feeling?" asked Marcus, sitting down beside her, though he made sure he was not too close.

"I don't want to know," Alexa sighed mournfully, resting her head on her knees.

"I want to help you. I don't want to see you hurt like this," said Marcus, though he regretted it as soon as the words were spoken. He had no right to desire an easing of his pain.

"You already helped me. You saved me, you know," said Alexa looking over at him. She was not smiling. "You sat with me. No matter what they did or how many times they came back, you sat next to me and held my hand. That's why I had to make sure you were really there at the hospital. I didn't want to be back there. I didn't want it to be happening again."

Marcus felt the contents of his own stomach rebel at such a

thought and had to push it down.

"You did the same thing when I found you at school," he recalled, not comforted by the memory. "I ... I don't know what I can say to make things better."

"Nothing, there's nothing you can say. I don't need you to make things better, nothing can. Just take me home."

Marcus nodded, helping Alexa to her feet and into the car. The rest of the drive was spent in silence. She did not even speak up when they arrived at the school. It was the first time she had not argued with him when he had insisted on walking her to her room.

Alexa did not turn back to look at him as she entered her room and Marcus knew he had to let her go, even though all he wanted to do was keep her close and safe. When she disappeared into the bathroom, he warned her roommates not to question or harass her. Whatever they felt about Bethany's attack was to be kept to themselves. Alexa was here to rest and recover. They were not to discuss school work with her or let her worry about what she missed.

"If you think something is wrong, then come and see me," Marcus added in a low voice. "Big or small, I don't care."

Alexa's roommates nodded. Marcus could hear the water from the shower running and was desperate to know if Alexa had any razors in her room. He did not want to come back tomorrow to find her dead on the bathroom floor. In the end he had no choice but to trust that she retained some will to live.

Walking back to his office, Marcus knew he could have gone home. He should have, but while Alexa was here, he knew he would be too. It never even crossed his mind to call Jackie. All his thoughts were for Alexa, but as he stepped under the hot water of his own shower, the emotions that he had been holding in check since Alexa's return spilled over.

The ordeal that she must have gone through. The pain. The suffering. Her strength and bravery. The very miracle of her survival. His desires raged within him, tearing his insides to shreds, but he almost welcomed the pain. This would be nothing to Alexa's suffering, but if she was hurting so should he. Yet that thought unleashed the images he had been trying desperately to keep at bay.

Stepping out of the shower, Marcus dashed to the toilet and threw up. The concept of Alexa holding on to his image while she was raped pierced through his body, causing him physical pain. It did not matter that it had not been real. He hated the idea that he could just sit by her side, hold her hand and do nothing while men violated her. However, what bothered him the most was the knowledge that, in Alexa's mind, his image would always be associated with her rape.

Lying on his bed, Marcus thought about his desire to hold Alexa in his arms and keep her safe from the rest of the world. Nothing could justify such a future, no matter which way he considered it. He would always be ten years older than her and he would always have been her teacher. They were insurmountable objections. He simply no longer cared.

If Alexa wanted him, he would take her. He hoped she never wanted him that way, because he really was not sure he could be with her like that, even if they wanted to be. However, he could be her friend. He would look out for her and protect her in every possible way. There was just one thing he now refused to do, and that was walk away from her.

***

Word quickly spread of Alexa's return, though few people actually saw her. Mr Knight arranged for food to be available in the dining hall for her when the rest of the school was in class. She did not speak to any of her roommates and none of them forced her to. They simply smiled when she looked their way and carried on with their days.

Sam came up every night. Using the secret passage they had found the year before that linked his bathroom, two floors below, to hers, he crept into her room after curfew. He did not talk or try to slide into her bed. Instead, he sat against the wall in the small gap between it and her bed.

"I just want to stay nearby, okay," Sam said the first night when Alexa had continued to stare at him. His voice broke slightly as he spoke.

Alexa wanted to reach out to hold his hand, but couldn't. That level of physical contact was still beyond her. Realising that Sam would not leave her side, she nodded and went to the bathroom to find him a spare pillow and blanket. He smiled brightly and laid himself down to sleep.

Although none of Alexa's roommates ever saw Sam arrive, they saw him every morning when they woke. Lizzie screamed on Wednesday morning, again startled by his perpetual presence. They always quizzed him about when he came in, but Sam never answered their questions. Alexa hated the fuss and wished Sam would learn to wake up earlier, but it was not in his nature.

By Friday morning the bruising covering Alexa's body had subsided, though it was still often quite painful to move. She wondered if it was normal or if she should be feeling better by now, but was not willing to ask the question. She feared the answer too much.

Waking early, with the intention of kicking Sam out before her roommates woke, Alexa looked down and watched him sleep. His body was contorted in a strange, twisted way in the small space he had to sleep. He did not look comfortable in the slightest and it made her smile.

"I was starting to wonder if I would ever see that smile again," said Sam sleepily, as he pulled himself up into a seated position. Alexa's smile quickly faded. "You look a lot better today. Do you feel it?" Alexa shook her head. "Can I sit up there with you?" She nodded and moved across the bed.

Sam sat down and lifted his arm until Alexa moved back in towards him. He reached around her shoulder, interlocking his hand in hers. She had to repress a shudder as his hand touched her body, but she forced herself to move in closer to him. She would not let anyone make her afraid of Sam.

"Did Marcus tell you everything?" Alexa asked softly, her voice crackling through lack of use.

"You'd better not call him that around here," replied Sam softly, startling Alexa. She had not realised what she had said. "You don't need any more trouble, but yeah, he told us enough."

"So you won't need to ask any questions."

"I have one. Why didn't you use the knife I gave you?" asked Sam desperately.

"I gave it to Brett so that he could protect Hayley," Alexa replied softly, burying her head in Sam's neck as she tried to block out those memories.

"But when is someone going to be there to protect you?"

"I don't need protection. I can take care of myself."

"I hope one day you'll change your mind about that. Are you going home tonight?" asked Sam, changing the subject slightly. Alexa thought he was probably trying to be kind, but the answer was torturous to confess.

"No. I don't have a home any more. This is all I have," she replied softly.

"They didn't kick you out, did they?" asked Sam in a horrified voice.

"No, I … you'd better go before everyone wakes up," said Alexa, her body quivering as she thought about the Whites and her intense desire to see them again. All she wanted was to go home to them and pretend that she was one of them, pretend that the life she truly belonged to was not with the filthy, violent underworld of sex and drugs.

Thankfully, Sam complied with her request without further questioning. He squeezed her hand and kissed the side of her head before jumping out of the bed. When his eyes flicked back to her, she knew he had felt the shudder of her body, rebelling against the intimacy of his touch.

"I'll see you tonight," he smiled as he stroked her cheek tenderly. She loved that he did not take her fear personally.

Once everyone was safely in class, Alexa strolled slowly towards the dining hall for breakfast, but food was no longer the friend it used to be. Since being released from hospital she had not managed to keep a whole meal down. The large stacks of toast were now a thing of the past. She could only keep down a maximum of two slices and that could take her over an hour to eat.

This was something Alexa knew she should tell someone about. She had already lost a lot of weight, but she was not prepared to go back to the hospital. Aches and pains were something they could treat at the school. This was something she feared would result in her being admitted.

If she was going back to hospital, she was going back to die. If she was not dying, she refused to go back.

With the time required to eat, rest and successfully evade all company, the day passed quickly. When her roommates returned to the dormitory at the end of the school day, Alexa remained where she was on her bed with the curtains pulled back. She did not acknowledge their arrival. Lizzie dropped her bag at her desk before moving tentatively towards her.

"Um, Alexa, Mr Knight asked me to tell you that he wanted you to come to his office tonight at six-thirty."

"Thanks," replied Alexa, looking up at Lizzie, who seemed heartened by the response and sat down on her bed facing her.

"Are you feeling any better?" asked Lizzie hesitantly.

"I couldn't feel much worse, could I?" Alexa replied flatly.

Lizzie gave her an unsure smile. Alexa knew she was trying to find the right thing to say and knew that she never would.

At six-thirty Alexa walked out of her room with the rest of her roommates as they headed for the dining hall. She did not feel bad about missing dinner, having already thrown up her lunch. It was not a process she cared to repeat.

The door to Mr Knight's office was closed when Alexa arrived. She knocked and waited for his reply. A moment later he appeared at the door and ushered her inside. Something about the way he had opened the door struck her as odd and she soon realised why. There, in the corner of his office, stood her foster family. Karl and Pam stood at the back, each with a hand on Hayley's shoulders, while Brett stood to the side. She had not been prepared for this.

"They wanted to come and see you and talk to you," said Mr Knight, sitting down behind his desk.

Although Alexa wanted to stay near the door, she could not trust herself to be so close to her foster family. Moving to the opposite corner, near the window, she crossed her arms and pretended not to care for anything they had to say.

"We want you to come back home with us. We're selling our place and moving somewhere else. We want you to come with us," said Pam.

It took many minutes for Alexa to muster the strength required to resist the offer. If it had just been her, then she knew she would have given up everything else, including Mr Knight, to be a part of their family, but she could not give up Bethany.

"I'm not coming back. I'm staying here," Alexa said firmly.

"We're not angry at you. None of this was your fault. You're part of our family," said Karl in a firm, but tender, loving voice.

Alexa tried not to look at Hayley who was beginning to cry. Hayley did not deserve this pain and Alexa began to regret ever being placed with the Whites. She had only done them harm.

"I won't come back," Alexa replied, almost choking on the words as her body tried to prevent her from speaking them. "I have a sister who, though I probably should, I will not abandon and if I see her again I will tell her exactly where she can find me."

"If Alexa coming back is going to put Hayley in danger, why should we ask her back?" asked Brett passionately.

The whole family turned to Brett with scathing looks, but Alexa could not help but look at him with pride and admiration. He at least understood the situation for what it really was.

"No, shut up, Brett," cried Hayley, stepping forward. "Please,

Alexa, please come back. I'm sorry."

Alexa fought to hold back her tears as her stomach turned to lead. The last person in the world she wanted to hurt was Hayley, but she knew it was what she would have to do to keep her safe.

"Do you know what happened to me, Hayley? Did Pam and Karl tell you what happened to me?" Alexa asked more harshly than she had ever wanted to speak to Hayley. Hayley shook her head slowly, never taking her eyes off Alexa. "That man that came to the house, he didn't want me. He wanted you. Do you know what he would have done to you?"

"Alexa, no –" interrupted Mr Knight, but she continued unrepentant.

"They would have taken you to a strange house and put you on the bed. Do you know what they wanted from you, Hayley? They wanted to rape you. And if you tried to resist, those two big men would've held you down and pulled your legs apart and held you there while he climbed on top of you and raped you."

Hayley cried loudly as the room fell silent in shock.

"Then after that, the other two men would have raped you as well."

"Alexa, please –" pleaded Karl, stepping forward and hugging the now sobbing Hayley tight.

"No!" Alexa screamed in reply, desperate for them to understand just how much danger she would put Hayley in. "Do you know what they would have done to you after that, Hayley? Each night a group of men would've come around and gotten really drunk and they would've come in to see you, one after the other, the whole night – raped you, the whole night. And the drunker they got, the more it would've hurt and the harder they would've hit you. By the end you would've been wishing to die and, you know what, they would have granted you your wish.

"Don't you understand, Hayley? I took that for you and I don't regret it for a single second." Alexa struggled to control the emotion in her voice as she spoke, but not a single tear fell from her eyes. "I would never have let that happen to you and, if I had to, I would do it all again to spare you. I would. Nothing in this world would stop me from protecting you, but I don't think I could go through that again.

"If I come and stay with you, then he will find out where we live and he will come back for you. I would give my life for you if I had to, Hayley. Please don't ask me to."

Silent tears fell from the eyes of everyone, bar Alexa. She turned her back on her foster family and stood at the window watching their reflection. They milled in the corner for a minute, waiting for her to turn back around. When they realised she wouldn't, Karl wrapped his arms around his family and walked them out the door.

As the door clicked closed Alexa felt her heart crumble. She opened the door to Mr Knight's bedroom and dashed into the bathroom, collapsing in tears on the floor.

She had just lost her one true chance to have a family.

***

Marcus sat on his bed waiting anxiously for Alexa to emerge. He was not sure how long to wait before forcing open the door. He did not want to push her, but he was concerned what damage she may do to herself if left alone.

"Alexa," he said, knocking on the bathroom door. "I'm coming in, all right."

Marcus unlocked the door and entered the room. Alexa sat in the corner with her head buried in her knees. Beside her were several of his shavers that had been pulled apart to extract the razors, along with several bottles of pills. They were only vitamins, but he knew what she had been looking for. He quickly pulled her to her feet and out into his office.

"I cannot imagine how hard all this is for you, I really can't, but you cannot think that killing yourself is an option," said Marcus passionately, terrified by the possibility. "You're one of the strongest people I know. By all rights you should be dead by now, but you're not. You've fought so hard and given up so much. Don't let all it be for nothing."

"It is all for nothing," cried Alexa savagely. "What's there left for me to fight for? I have nothing."

"That's not true. You have friends who care about you. You have people that love you, please don't forget that," Marcus replied, stopping short of confessing how deeply he felt for her.

"I have nothing," Alexa murmured as she made her way to the door.

"Alexa, please, don't do anything stupid. I'll be here if you need me. I'll be staying at the school for the rest of the term."

"Go back to your fiancée. I don't need you," Alexa replied coolly. "I don't want you."

Alexa walked out of the office, the door slowly clicking shut behind her. Marcus stepped forward to follow her, but stopped himself at the door. He no longer knew where the line was between him and Alexa and he could not let himself get near it, let alone cross it.

He did not want her to want him. Alexa was better off feeling nothing for him, but he was still determined to do everything he could to make sure she not only survived Redgrove, but had somewhere to go and a life to lead when she did leave. That would be his role. If, later on, she wanted a friend, he would be that too.

Until then, he would do everything he could to take care of her from afar and cause her as little distress as possible.

****

Sam returned to Alexa's bedside on Friday night after all her roommates were asleep, but she did not make him sleep on the floor. She shuffled over, allowing him into her bed. Sam smiled and placed his pillow at the foot of the bed, gently kissing her goodnight before hopping in.

When they woke on Saturday morning, Sam refused to leave until Alexa agreed to come to breakfast with everyone, which again led to his discovery. This time they confessed to how he could sneak so easily into their room without being noticed.

Everyone except Alexa gathered in the bathroom to watch Sam disappear down into the secret passageway between their rooms. She waited until they had all satisfied their curiosity and jumped in the shower. It was difficult to convince herself that she should even bother. She did not want to go to breakfast or be near people, but she also did not want to be alone with her own thoughts either – especially not with the memory of last night's encounter with the Whites still swirling in her mind.

Sam waited for her at the door of the dining hall and walked her through the hushed crowd with his arm firmly around her waist as she pressed her body closer to his. She did not care much for the stares and whispers of the students as she walked between the tables. She was paying more attention to Mr Knight, who was standing in the corner, watching the students eat. He did not seem jealous or angry that Sam was holding her and he even smiled at her as she continued to stare at him.

After breakfast Sam led Alexa out on to the oval and held her hand in silence, the cold wind blowing around them.

"Thank you for everything you're doing for me," Alexa said

eventually. "And thank Chad too. It's nice being able to sit with you all on one table again."

"He's trying, but I don't think he finds it very easy. He keeps asking how we managed to stay friends."

"I guess the fact that I never cheated on you made a difference."

"I don't know," smiled Sam, seemingly unconvinced by her explanation. "I still don't know why you really broke up with me. But it doesn't matter any more. We're friends and there's no point dwelling on all that. Besides, I'm seeing someone else."

"Who?" asked Alexa, trying to feel curious.

"Natalie Wang."

"My roommate? For how long?"

"Not that long," replied Sam, looking uncomfortable at the question.

"Is this a real relationship or messing around?" asked Alexa, suddenly feeling scared that she might be about to lose Sam as well.

"Probably more messing around, but she's a cool chick," replied Sam with a casual shrug of his shoulders.

"That's why she was so interested in the passageway?" mused Alexa. She had no right to continue to claim Sam, but right then she could not let him go either. "Just have her come to you. It's not something I want to walk in on."

Sam blushed and they both giggled. It felt strange to be laughing and she quickly stopped, her heart aching at the memory of why she hated her life so much.

"You can laugh, you know. Just because everything's going wrong doesn't mean you can't laugh when there's something to laugh at. I know it won't fix anything, but you're allowed to feel good occasionally."

Alexa stopped walking. Sam stood in front of her and watched as the tears welled in her eyes, before pulling her into a tight embrace. It would take more than a smile to make her feel good again.

Over the course of the weekend Alexa saw Natalie disappear into the bathroom a couple of times and not return for almost half an hour. She did not find it so strange that Sam was with another girl, but odd that she knew exactly when. However, things became much stranger on Sunday night when both Natalie and Martha disappeared into the bathroom together. When they finally emerged they were both smiling happily and headed straight to their desks to finish their homework.

The next morning Alexa packed her bag and made her way to breakfast. It would be her first day back at school for two weeks and she was not looking forward to it. She knew the doctor had made her promise not to return to class for another week, but she could not stand the thoughts she was left with when she was on her own with nothing to do.

Her melancholy was not matched by the rest of the school. It was the last week of term and everyone else was buoyant at the looming prospect of escaping Redgrove for two weeks.

Alexa made sure she was up early enough to finish breakfast before assembly, and though she arrived in the dining hall over half an hour before her roommates, she was not finished eating until well after them. Everyone waited for her, but the immense number of people was suddenly overwhelming. She was grateful that Sam understood and that he, Chad, Natalie and Martha all left her alone.

Ezra, Bianca and Lizzie all continued to stay with Alexa during the day. While Alexa appreciated it, she could not show it. She did not care for her life any more. There was no part of it she wanted to engage in. Nothing could motivate her to listen in class, study at her desk with the rest of her roommates or even talk to her friends at lunch. Just existing was excruciating enough.

At dinner Alexa noticed Martha and Natalie sitting on either side of Sam at the next table. The whole situation was still beyond her comprehension. Sam saw her looking and grinned happily. Chad was up getting himself a second serve of dinner so Alexa excused herself and walked over to him.

"So what's going on? They aren't really a threesome, are they?" Alexa asked Chad with a distorted look on her face.

Chad looked over at Sam and smiled. He looked like he was about to laugh, but held back.

"Do you really think he's that kind of guy?" asked Chad seriously, though he was still smiling.

"No, but –"

"How many girls are there?" he asked.

"Two," Alexa answered tentatively.

"And how many guys are there?" continued Chad.

Alexa looked confusedly at Sam then looked back at Chad, who was nodding and rolling his hand as though to help continue her thought processes.

"So you and Martha?" Alexa asked, not trusting her ability to work out anything. Chad smiled as he nodded. "This is so odd."

"Well, commitment sucks. Look, I don't think Sam should've told you, not with everything you've been through," said Chad, his hand reaching towards her shoulder before pulling back. "We're just mucking around and having a bit of fun. Sometimes I wonder if you could ever want to have sex again, but when you do, just remember that you deserve someone better than either of us. You only ever deserve the best from now on and don't let yourself settle for anything less, okay."

Chad smiled supportively at her and walked back to his table. Alexa returned to her own table and watched them from the corner of her eyes. It was true. She was not sure she would ever want to have sex again, but she did wish she could be close to someone. It would just never be possible. She was far too dangerous for anyone to get involved with her.

Despite the support from all her friends, the rest of the week passed in a painful blur. In every new class Alexa was given notes on all the work she had missed. She appreciated the effort all her teachers had made to help her catch up, but she still could not find any motivation to do so. She did not listen in class and barely wrote. It was only when her mind focused on unwanted things that she chose to pick up her pen.

Sam tried to convince her to spend the holidays at his place and she was more than tempted. In the end it was Mel who tipped the balance. Alexa knew there was no way she could handle any taunts from Mel right now, and was not convinced that Mel would believe that she had sufficiently paid for all her sins to leave her alone.

The surprise was Mr Knight. After keeping his distance for most of the week, he started trying to talk to her, asking her to come to his office. Knowing he would never force her against her will, Alexa walked away from him as if he did not exist. Then the notes started coming to class. Her teachers always sent her on her way, but she never went to see Mr Knight, finding different places around the school to hide until the bell went. On the last day of term, the note changed.

Mr Pollock called Alexa to his desk and made her pull up a seat as he looked through a stack of papers. He talked, but she did not listen. She did not care what she was being asked to do. She just filled in whatever form Mr Pollock put in front of her. When it was over, she went back to her desk and laid her head on her arms until the bell finally rang.

Walking past Mr Knight's office on the way back to the

dormitories, Alexa was glad that her body shied away from his door. She would not hurt like this again. She would not love him or any other again.

***

The school was all but deserted. It was the first time Alexa had ever stayed at school during the holidays. She had not heard anything from her social worker and assumed Mr Knight had told them that she preferred to stay at school. The thought of being placed with yet another foster family was not appealing and she was glad she had never been given the option.

Bianca was once again staying at school for the holidays, making them the only year twelves remaining at school. The rest of the grade's boarders had taken the opportunity to leave, since very few went home for the holidays before their final exams. Alexa could only hope that she and Bianca would get along.

For the most part, they did. However, Alexa knew that was partly because they spent very little time alone together. Alexa had hoped that she would find something other than homework to keep her mind occupied during the holidays, but in the end the need to think of something other than her life was enough incentive to start catching up on all the work she had missed. Bianca worked steadily through the holidays as well, but Alexa needed to get out of their room, so spent most of her days in the library.

All alone, Alexa found it easier to concentrate on studying, though rarely an hour went by without her mind wandering back to the events of Hayley's birthday. At dinner and in the evenings, Alexa would talk to Bianca for a while before drawing the curtains closed around her bed and pulling out the photo album Pam and Karl had given her for Christmas.

For the first few nights Alexa had sobbed softly as she traced her finger over the faces of Bethany and Hayley. After that she stopped opening the album, instead she simply held it to her chest and fell asleep with it in her arms.

Despite her initial reservations, Alexa found herself becoming closer to Bianca than she had ever been. As the holidays went on, she started spending more time studying at her desk rather than in the library. Bianca was generous with her time and spent hours helping her understand some of the more complex work she had missed.

"Thanks for your help, Bianca," said Alexa, as they walked to lunch on the second Wednesday of the holidays.

"That's okay. I kinda feel like I owe you that much. Part of me always wanted to think that you made your problems sound worse than they really were so you could remain the centre of attention. But I couldn't imagine having to go through everything you've been through. I acted really stupid this year."

"We all do dumb things," replied Alexa softly, hoping this conversation was not leading towards questions or discussions about recent events or past fights.

It did. Bianca wanted to talk about Chad and Martha. She was resentful and thought Chad was just dating Martha to get back at her. Alexa could not say what she was thinking, not when Bianca had been so nice to her, and she still needed her help to catch up on the rest of the work. So she was forced to politely listen to Bianca's complaints, realising they inhabited two very different worlds, but it did keep her mind occupied and for that she would be thankful. And when Bianca was not feeling sorry for herself, Alexa actually found her quite considerate.

By the last weekend of the holidays, Bianca had helped Alexa catch up on nearly all her work. Alexa was still not sure that she understood anywhere near half of it, but it meant that her work load at the start of term would be a lot more manageable. With their trial exams coming up in only five weeks, it was a huge weight off her shoulders.

However, as the weekend wore on and the dormitory began to fill, much of the peace Alexa had found was replaced with people. Lizzie and Natalie arrived on Saturday night, while Martha arrived back on Sunday morning. Alexa could feel the chill between Bianca and Martha and tried to make sure they were kept as far away from each other as possible. Martha did not deserve Bianca's wrath, but Alexa also felt sorry for Bianca. Martha never made any attempt to make things easier for Bianca. Alexa at least had the ability to tell Sam to keep his relationship out of her face, a luxury Bianca did not have.

When it all became too much, Alexa escaped and walked aimlessly around the school. She was not surprised to find herself drawn towards Mr Knight's office, but was not happy with the ache in her heart when she thought about him. She did not want to like him any more.

The office light was on and the door was slightly ajar. Alexa was tempted to go and see if her anger and fear were still overriding her love for Mr Knight, but deep down she knew she just wanted to see him and take sanctuary in the comfort of his company.

There were no students around so Alexa continued to stand on the stairs, looking at the door to Mr Knight's office. Every few minutes she decided to leave or go in, and so her feet remained glued to the spot.

At nine o'clock the curfew bell rang. Alexa realised she had not moved for well over an hour. Mr Knight appeared at the door and spotted her immediately. He did not try to speak to her. He simply smiled and nodded, before closing his office door and turning off the light.

***

"Did you all hear about Mr Knight?" asked Lizzie at breakfast the next morning, trying to break the growing tension between Bianca, Martha and Chad.

Alexa turned her head slightly to look at Mr Knight as he strolled across the other side of the dining hall. He saw her looking at him and kept her gaze. He did not smile, but it felt like he did. His gaze was warm and supportive, as though he was trying to hug her with his eyes.

"What about Mr Knight?" asked Martha, causing Alexa's head to turn slowly back around.

"Oh, it wasn't very interesting," said Lizzie, biting her lip slightly as she stared confusedly at Sam. "I was just talking to him about his holidays. He said he went up to Queensland and laid on the beach for a whole week."

"Why would we want to know that he spent a week on the beach?" asked Martha in a confused tone.

"I would want to know if he was going to be topless anywhere," replied Lizzie sheepishly. Alexa could not help but allow a shadow of a smile creep on to her face, while Sam and Chad laughed. "You think he's cute too," accused Lizzie, looking at Alexa to diffuse the attention on herself.

"I know," shrugged Alexa. "But I don't say those kind of things out loud."

"You two are hopeless," said Martha, shaking her head. "I don't know what everyone sees in him. I mean, he's nice and it's a change having a year advisor for more than a year, but he's not that good."

Alexa and Lizzie turned to smile at each other and in that moment Alexa knew there was no way of purging her feelings for

Mr Knight. She would just have to accept that he deserved to be loved, and though she did not think she would ever be able to let him possess her body, her heart would always belong to him.

The group made their way to assembly, meeting up with Ezra outside the hall. As the hall filled, Alexa held out her hand to Sam. He promptly passed her his music player and she pushed the earplugs into her ears. Making it through the day was getting slightly easier, but that in no way made Alexa prepared to listen to an hour of Mrs Taylor's voice. Mr Knight may have achieved the miracle of keeping Mrs Taylor off the G7's backs, but Alexa knew her temper was not up to another encounter with her Principal.

Music loud in her ears, Alexa was able to block out the world, but she had to be careful not to let her thoughts wander. More than once, tears welled in her eyes as the music took her back to places she needed to forget. Pulling herself out of another painful memory, Alexa suddenly realised the hall was strangely silent. Mrs Taylor had stopped talking and all the teachers had stunned looks on their faces.

Pulling the earphones out of her ears to ask Sam what was going on, Alexa heard a stunted cry from the front of the hall, drawing everyone's eyes to the door near the stage.

"Lex!"

The scream tore through silence of the packed hall.

"Lex!"

Alexa hurdled out of the row and sprinted down the aisle towards the front of the hall. Skidding to the stop in front of the stage, she had just enough time to take in the wild, frantic looking in Bethany's eyes as she raised the gun in her right hand and stormed towards her.

"Bethy," gasped Alexa. "What are you doing?"

Bethany pressed the gun hard into Alexa's forehead. Alexa looked into Bethany's eyes and knew straight away that she was wasted. This was not the best time to try and reason with her.

"Oi! Close that fucking door!" screamed Bethany, looking back at the door she had entered through, the gun still pressed hard against Alexa's head.

Mrs Jackson had tried to usher a few of the year seven students out of the hall, but their panicked exit had been too noisy to ignore.

"No one moves or I will shoot her in the fucking head," screamed Bethany.

Everyone stood still except for Mr Knight. Alexa could see him moving slowly across the back of the hall and down towards the front. With Bethany's back to him he managed to get to where he could see Alexa's face. Alexa thought he looked like he was preparing to intervene, but she hoped he stayed out of it. This was between her and Bethany and no one was ever going to come between them.

"What are you doing, Bethy?" asked Alexa softly.

"They found him. They found him and took him away."

"Who?" Alexa asked, not comprehending.

"Don't pretend that you don't know. You fucking slept with him. He was my boyfriend!"

The anger that Alexa had been harbouring towards Bethany suddenly boiled up inside of her. She had been prepared to help Bethany now irrespective of what had happened before, but she would never let her defend Leo.

"He's a paedophile!" cried Alexa, her chest tearing apart with the pain of thinking about Leo. "You're fifteen and I couldn't stop him from getting to you, but she was eleven. Damn it, Bethy. You gave him Hayley! How could you ever think I would let anything happen to her?"

"You weren't supposed to be there. You were supposed to be here," cried Bethany desperately.

"How does that make it any better? You protect me, but give him Hayley. Eleven, Bethy, eleven. Don't you understand what he would've done to her? I'm glad I was there. I'm glad it was me he took and not Hayley."

Alexa watched Bethany slowly take in what she said. Behind Bethany, Mr Knight was staring at her in stunned horror. She wished that she had spoken to him last night, wished that she had let him know that she still loved him.

A second later Alexa's attention was diverted as she felt the pressure of the gun release from her forehead. She sighed with relief, thinking Bethany finally understood the vicious thug Leo was. Then she realised that Bethany had not given up, she was just directing her frustrations in a different direction.

"Put the fucking phone away or I will shoot you in the head," said Bethany to a boy in the second row, pointing the gun at him between the heads of two girls in the front row.

Alexa's heart began to thud erratically, realising she might not have the time to talk Bethany through her high. She grabbed Bethany's arm, swinging it away from the terrified ninth graders and back towards her own head. Bethany jerked at her forceful touch. The sound of a gunshot broke the silence of the hall. With a stunted gasp, Alexa's hand fell from Bethany's arm as blood began to spill over the floor.

The girl sitting in front of the boy Bethany had threatened clutched her stomach as blood flowed on to the seat. Alexa could not hear the screams of the girl's friends as she watched the blood drip on to the floor. With Bethany slightly off guard, Alexa pulled at Bethany's hand and pointed the gun back into her own forehead.

Alexa's heart pounded as her chest constricted painfully. Of all the things she had experienced in her life, she had never watched someone die. She gripped the gun tightly so Bethany could not move it from her forehead.

"Someone get her the fuck out of here! Get her out and call an ambulance," cried Alexa, as teachers stood motionless.

Mr Pollock moved shakily forward, lifting the girl into his arms and carrying her from the hall.

"You know the police are going to be here soon, Bethy. They'll shoot you if you don't give up," said Alexa, her voice shaking, but her hands steady.

"I do give up," replied Bethany, her voice weak and her eyes wide with terror. "I tried, Lex. I promise I tried."

Bethany pulled a piece of paper from her pocket and held it out. Alexa recognised the letter immediately. It was the letter she had sent Bethany last year after finding out about the lottery win; the letter she had sent just before Bethany had run away.

"I couldn't wait for you there. I couldn't wait there without you. I'm sorry. I don't want to wait any more."

A single tear fell down Bethany's cheek. Alexa moved one hand off the gun and wiped the tear from her cheek. As her hand moved down Bethany's face, she noticed the locket she gave Bethany for Christmas was still around her neck.

"Oh, my Angel, it's okay," said Alexa, moving her hand back up on to the gun. It was now clear the reason Bethany had come to find her. One would never live without the other and if Bethany could not face living any longer, neither would Alexa. "I'll go with you. We'll be together. It'll be okay."

Alexa smiled at Bethany, who nodded slowly.

"What if you go to heaven and they send me to hell?" asked Bethany softly.

Alexa could not help but smile. It may have only been for the last few moments of their lives, but at least she would die with her true sister and not the foreign drug addict who too often inhabited Bethany's body.

"I won't let that happen. Not even God can take you away from me," Alexa promised.

"But what if they won't let me come with you?" asked Bethany sincerely, demonstrating just how similar their greatest fears were.

"Then I will come to hell with you."

Alexa squeezed Bethany's hand and gave her a reassuring smile. She was not even sorry to die. Seventeen years of her life was more than enough. The end was almost welcome. It was only the sight of Mr Knight, his eyes wide with despair, that tugged at Alexa's heart. She was sorry that they would never have the chance to be with each other, even for just one stolen moment. Looking deep into his chocolate eyes, Alexa said her final goodbye.

"I love you," she mouthed, before moving her eyes back to Bethany. "Okay, let's go."

Alexa held Bethany's shaking hands steady, closed her eyes and waited for an instant of pain before the peace of death.

Chapter Twelve

"PUT THE GUN down, Bethany!" screamed a voice from the door.

Alexa's eyes jolted open and she saw over a dozen police officers enter the hall, their guns all pointed towards Bethany.

"Bethy, they will shoot you," cried Alexa desperately. "We made this deal, Bethy. We go together or not at all." Bethany's hands shook in Alexa's. "I love you. I will take care of you, I promise. Don't let them take you from me."

"Put the gun down, Bethany. This is your last warning."

Alexa looked over Bethany's shoulder and saw the police moving in on them, Detective Parker and Detective Ben Shepard at the front. She knew that if they killed Bethany, she would force them to kill her too, but was scared of what she would have to do to push them to that point. If it was going to end now, it was going to end badly.

Her eighteenth birthday was now only months away. The time when she would have the means to take care of them was closing in rapidly. With that pinprick of hope for a better future, Alexa knew it was the time to act before she lost Bethany.

With Bethany's hands still shaking, Alexa was sure Bethany would not pull the trigger to kill her. Alexa pushed the gun down and towards the front of the hall. With one hand still on the gun, she wrapped herself around Bethany, putting her body between the police and Bethany, then quickly put her other hand back on the gun and pulled Bethany to the floor.

"It's going to be okay, I promise. I'm going to take care of you and we're going to be a family again," Alexa whispered in Bethany's ear, as they rocked slowly back and forth.

Behind them, Alexa could hear the hurried exit of the rest of the school from the hall. As they rocked slowly on the floor, Alexa continued whispering in Bethany's ear until her grip on the gun loosened. When the gun finally fell from Bethany's hands, Alexa held it out behind her for the police to take.

Alexa sat on the hall floor whispering to Bethany for over half an hour, holding her tight as they rocked slowly. No one tried to arrest Bethany or break them apart.

"They're going to take you soon, but I won't abandon you," Alexa said, holding Bethany tighter, hating the knowledge that they were going to be torn apart again. "I'll help you and make sure you're okay. I'll make sure you don't get in too much trouble. It'll be okay. I'll take care of you, I promise."

Bethany nodded slowly as Alexa lifted them to their feet. When they turned around, they saw almost twenty officers standing near the exits to the hall. Detective Ben Shepard stood at the front of them with Detective Parker.

"We have to take her now, Alexa," said Detective Parker in a kind and gentle voice.

Alexa nodded and two officers from the door moved forward and handcuffed Bethany. They were not rough, for which Alexa was thankful, and Bethany did not resist. The officers led Bethany to the door, but Alexa hated the sight of her leaving again. Running after her, Alexa wrapped her arms tightly around Bethany's neck.

"I love you, Bethy," she said, as tears fell down her cheeks. Bethany bent her head into the crook of her neck, pressing softly.

"Come on, Alexa," said Ben, pulling her from Bethany and back into the hall.

Alexa fell to the floor as tears streamed silently down her face. Ben sat down next to her, gently patting the top of her head.

"They would've shot her. They would've killed her," Alexa gasped, reliving the last hour, though imagining very different endings.

"She had a gun to your head. She was going to shoot you," said Detective Parker, pulling up a seat next to them. "She wanted to kill you because we arrested the man who raped and beat you half to death."

"No, she wanted to die," explained Alexa, desperate for them to understand the truth. "And if we don't go together, we don't go at all. She was just coming to get me. She was just keeping her word."

"Alexa, you can't make those sorts of deals," said Ben in horrified desperation.

"She's all I have in the world. Without her, I don't exist," Alexa explained mournfully, only just stopping herself from explaining just how little she cared to exist now anyway.

Ben and Detective Parker sat with her until her tears ran dry. Around them, police were taking photographs and talking to teachers, who were pointing at different parts of the hall.

"We will need to get your statement," said Detective Parker.

"Why? What will you use it for? Against Bethy in court?" Alexa asked anxiously, her body tensing. They did not answer. "No. I won't say anything."

"They will subpoena you," said Ben gravely.

"And I won't answer their questions – or I will just explain the way it really was – that it was my fault, not Bethy's."

Ben put his hand on Detective Parker's arm and shook his head slightly to silence him. They looked at her for a moment before rising to leave. As they walked away, Alexa's mind immediately turned to Bethany's fate and how she could spare her as much as possible.

"Ben," Alexa called as he walked towards the hall exit. "I need you to look after Bethy for me, make sure she's okay and that nothing bad happens to her."

"I'll do what I can, Alexa, but she's in a lot of trouble," replied Ben gravely, not quite meeting her eyes. "The girl she shot is in a serious condition in hospital. They had to do emergency surgery and there's still the matter of the break and enter."

"I don't care," replied Alexa angrily. "Please, just make sure she's okay. You have to. You owe us."

Ben's eyes widened at the comment. Alexa knew it was because it was such a blatant lie. In her dreams, Ben had already done so much to help protect her and take care of Bethany. To ask more of him now was the height of selfishness, but to look after Bethany, she would be as selfish as she had to be.

"I also need you to contact my lawyer, Peter Lam, and let him know what's happening," Alexa added quickly to her list of demands. "Did you talk to him before? And make sure Bethy doesn't answer any questions unless he's there. Tell him that I'll give him the money when I get out of here. Please, Ben."

Ben met her steely, defiant gaze. She tried to hold it, but blinked first. When she looked back at him, all she was left with was pleading desperation.

"All right, Alexa. I'll take care of it," nodded Ben, looking away.

"You swear?" Alexa asked firmly.

"I swear," Ben replied solemnly. "Anything you need, anything Bethany needs, I'll do it. I promise. I'll let you know what happens, okay."

Alexa nodded and watched Ben leave. Following him out of the hall, Alexa looked around, wondering what time it was and what class she was supposed to be in. Reaching for her timetable, she realised her bag was still in the hall and went to walk back in, but was stopped by the uniformed officers.

"It's a crime scene," the officer explained gruffly.

Alexa tried to argue, but they would not let her enter.

"Miss Samson, what's wrong? What are you trying to do?" asked Mrs Jackson, walking up to her as she continued to argue with the officers.

"I need my bag. I don't know what class I'm supposed to be in," Alexa replied, shocked to feel her voice break and tears well in her eyes just because she could not remember her timetable.

"Classes have been cancelled. You can go back to your room," replied Mrs Jackson. "Don't worry about your bag. If it's still in there, we'll bring it to you. You just go and take it easy."

Alexa was surprised by the way Mrs Jackson's voice crackled, and was even more astonished when Mrs Jackson offered to be there if she needed to talk. It was not an offer Alexa would ever take up, but it was very nice that it had been given.

Everyone was in the seniors' common room when Alexa returned to the dormitories. Sam hugged her tight when she walked in, but released her to sit back down with Natalie. It was strange. Sam had always been there for her when she needed him. It left her feeling very alone despite the fact that she was surrounded by friends.

They all rubbed her shoulder or smiled reassuringly whenever she looked at them, but it was like they did not really exist. It was like nothing existed any more. Alexa could barely comprehend what had occurred, but knew that this day would be the one that decided if she lost or saved Bethany. She only wished there was a way of telling the future, because that outcome would decide her own fate.

The uncertainty was too much for Alexa to bear. There was no way she could explain it to her friends. They would never understand her pact with Bethany. Heading to bed early in the hope of ending this horrid day as quickly as possible, Alexa found herself frustrated and annoyed as she tossed and turned restlessly, never finding the peace of sleep. At a quarter to midnight she finally gave up trying.

Lying awake, staring at the ceiling, Alexa decided to have a hot shower to try and settle her. It would help pass time, if nothing else. The room was dark and the curtains were drawn around everyone's bed. Alexa walked into the bathroom and closed the door behind her before switching on the light to avoid waking her roommates.

A horrified squeal emanated from Natalie when the room was flooded with light and she tried to cover her naked body. Alexa jumped in fright, backing into the door, but could not immediately move. It felt as though her heart had been torn out and thrown back at her. Sam looked at her as if pleading for forgiveness. Fumbling with the door, Alexa finally managed to escape, only to collapse on the bed, her body convulsing with tearless sobs.

"Alexa, wait," called Sam the next morning, chasing her as she walked across the oval. "Alexa! I'm sorry."

"Sorry for what, Sam?" Alexa asked spitefully when he finally caught up with her.

"Sorry for what you saw."

"Don't be sorry, Sam. You're not my boyfriend. You can screw whoever you want, wherever you want," she spat, hating the anger and bitterness that was coursing through her and shooting out her lips.

"I know how you feel. I didn't expect to feel like this either," said Sam guiltily.

"I asked you. I asked you just to make sure the door was locked. Why couldn't you do that?" Alexa cried, seeing that Sam did look as bad as she felt.

"I'm sorry. I really am, but this isn't real – what we're feeling."

"I don't know what I'm feeling," cried Alexa angrily.

"Anger, hurt, jealousy, everything you'd feel if we'd been going out. I feel like I've betrayed you and we're not even dating," said Sam, accurately detailing everything she was feeling about what happened last night.

"Sam, I just don't understand. I …"

"It's okay," he said, pulling her into a tight embrace. "I'm sorry. You don't need this now. I should've been there for you last night, not Natalie."

"She's your girlfriend."

"And you're my best friend. No girlfriend of mine, or boyfriend of yours, should ever stop us being there for each other when we need it the most and last night I should've been with you."

"I just don't know what's wrong with me," Alexa whispered, her voice shaking.

"You had a gun held to your head by your sister. If that's not enough to mix you up, I don't know what is."

"I don't know what to do. I don't want to be mad at you. I just don't know …"

"You just have to survive," said Sam seriously, taking Alexa's face in his hands so their eyes met. "Your life will get better. Things will get better than this. You just have to make it through to see that I'm right."

"I don't know if I can," Alexa replied truthfully as tears began to slip down her cheeks. "I just want it all to stop. I want to close my eyes and not open them until it's all gone away. I can't do it any more, Sam. I can't."

"Yes, you can. You can and I'm going to be by your side whenever you need me. You'll get through this even if I have to carry you through myself."

Alexa nodded and Sam wrapped her in his arms, probably knowing as well as she did that he would need to keep that promise. In too many ways she regretted the way things had turned out yesterday. If she had not protected Bethany, if Bethany had not hesitated, it would have all been over by now.

Much to Natalie and Martha's annoyance, Sam and Chad decided to sit at the same table as Alexa, Lizzie and Bianca at dinner. Alexa only picked at her food, but so did nearly everyone else. It had been a very quiet, sombre day of classes.

"Oh, hey, Alexa," said Lizzie, pushing away her half-eaten dinner. "I heard today that the girl that was shot is going to be okay. She's in a normal ward and everything."

"That's good," nodded Alexa. She knew it was a good thing, but there was no getting around what Bethany had done and that it was partly her fault it had ever happened.

"You can't blame yourself. You were trying to stop her shooting someone. It wasn't your fault," said Bianca, as if reading her mind.

"Bianca's right. It wasn't your fault," said Chad. It was the first time Alexa had heard Chad say Bianca's name since they broke up.

"Miss Samson, can you come to my office when you're finished your dinner, please," asked Mr Knight from behind, causing her to jump slightly.

"I don't need to talk, Sir. I'm fine, really," replied Alexa, forcing herself not to turn around.

"Detective Shepard is here to talk to you. I thought –"

Mr Knight could barely keep up with Alexa as she pushed her food away and rushed towards his office. She did not speak or even look at him as he trailed behind her. She did not want to remember how much her heart had softened for him in what she thought were going to be her final moments.

Ben was standing by the window when they entered and turned as soon as he heard them, a half-smile sitting awkwardly on his face.

"What's going on? Is Bethy okay?" Alexa asked anxiously.

"She's fine. Why don't you sit down," said Ben, directing her to a seat.

"I'm fine," she replied forcefully, hating that Ben's police-like manners made her feel like she was being interrogated. "Just tell me what's going on."

"Peter has agreed to represent Bethany and said he doesn't want you to worry about the money," said Ben, accepting that she would not sit.

"Is that all?" Alexa asked, pacing the room anxiously and stopping only when Ben spoke.

"No. Bethany didn't apply for bail. There wasn't really anywhere for her to go. She'll be remanded in juvenile detention until her trial, which will be at least a couple of months away."

"How long is she likely to get?" asked Alexa, trying to keep her voice steady. It would be naïve to think that gaol was not a likely outcome.

"It could be a few years," said Ben. Alexa gasped. She had been hoping for months. "It may depend on how she pleads, but she's in serious trouble."

"Is she okay?" Alexa turned her back on Ben and Mr Knight as she asked the question, her voice breaking. Tears welled in her eyes as she traced invisible lines on the wall.

"She's not the best. She's going through withdrawal," replied Ben in a low voice.

"Are they helping her?"

"Yes. She'll enter rehab as soon as she's gone through withdrawal. There are doctors looking after her. She'll get treatment. She wants it too. She knows what happened – what she's done. She understands she'll be punished for it."

Alexa nodded slowly and wiped away the tears in her eyes before turning back to face Ben.

"Can I see her?" she asked, though tried to make it more of a command. It did not work.

"I don't think that's the best idea right now, for either of you. She's not ready."

"Will you keep seeing her – keep an eye on her for me?" asked Alexa, her eyes wide with desperation. She did not know Ben – only his face from her nightmares – and she was not sure why she trusted him, but she needed him. She needed someone who could take care of Bethany, given the poor job she had done.

"I promise," replied Ben solemnly. "Do you want me to – I can come and see you every week or every fortnight to let you know how Bethany is doing."

"Every week," Alexa answered forcefully. She would have preferred every day, but knew she and Bethany would not rate that high in Ben's life.

Ben smiled and nodded, before his eyes flicked down to his watch.

"I'd better go. I'll come back next week."

Ben placed a hand on Alexa's shoulder, squeezing it gently, before leaving. Alexa did not look up at him. The room felt as if it was shrinking. When it was just her and Mr Knight remaining, there did not seem to be any space or air left between them.

"Are you all right, Alexa?" asked Mr Knight tenderly, making her heart ache that much more.

Alexa felt the emptiness inside her spread through her body, consuming every part of her. Tears welled in her eyes as the feeling of loss grew. She did not want to lose any more. She could not bear to be so close to Mr Knight, knowing that she would never be with him.

Mr Knight rose from his desk and moved next to her. Alexa could feel the warmth of his body and was so desperate to curl up in his arms. She wanted to be loved and be a part of something special, but she knew the consequences of those desires, and refused to suffer them again.

"Alexa, –"

"Please don't," she whispered, finally finding her feet and rushing out the door.

He did not try to stop her.

The next morning brought a hollow numbness to Alexa that would not dissipate. She felt distant from the rest of the world, as though she was encased away in her own lonely bubble. No one could reach her and she did not want to even try to reach them.

Ben came every week to update her on Bethany's situation and how the case was progressing. He often had very little new information to give, but Alexa was glad he came. She liked Ben. She liked the familiarity of his face and voice, and liked the way he seemed to know her – know what not to ask and what not to say.

Although all Alexa knew about Ben was that he was the policeman from her nightmares, she never asked him more about that dream or her past when he came to see her. She did not really care why Ben had always died in her dreams or why he was even there in the first place. He was alive now, so the dreams could not be a true recollection of their past, and she knew enough about her life to know that any answers Ben gave her were unlikely to be happy ones.

Occasionally Ben would ask her questions about her life. He was curious about the number of foster families she had lived with and her scholarship to Redgrove College. Alexa liked that he accepted her short answers. When he asked about Bethany, she could not stop herself from detailing her failings. That information Ben needed to know. He needed to understand that what Bethany had done was not her fault, but was the result of her poor care.

Those stories were easier to tell now that Mr Knight no longer sat in on their meetings. A messenger simply came to tell Alexa when Ben arrived. She never saw Mr Knight leaving or arriving back at his office. In many ways, he had almost disappeared. Alexa knew he was doing it for her, to keep her from becoming so distressed, but she wondered if he understood what it was about his presence that made her so upset.

It was in this torturous manner that the weeks managed to crawl by, bringing the trial exams agonisingly close. The whole grade was suffering under the stress of their approach. Only Alexa remained immune. Although she sat at her desk while her roommates studied, she did not open a single school book. Instead, she poured out her heart in letters to Bethany. She had sent a letter a day since Ben's first visit. There had been no response, but Alexa did not give up. She knew that Bethany would read them. And, in spite of everything, Alexa knew that Bethany was the one person in the world she could tell anything to; the one person who would not judge or criticise her.

Despite the passing time and the activities that kept her days, if not her mind, occupied, Alexa could not pull herself out of the numbness that still encased her away from the rest of the world. She liked the company her friends and enjoyed listening to their conversations, but she could not bear to feel close to anyone any more. As they spoke incessantly about the upcoming trials, she just sat and listened, wondering if she would ever care about such mundane things again.

"You're bound to do better than the girls in our geography class," said Lizzie in response to everyone's stress. "Ever since they found out Mr Knight was single, they've been trying to find ways of getting him to notice them."

Alexa kept her head down, but started listening much more intently to the conversation.

"I thought he was engaged," said Bianca.

"No, he broke it off," said Lizzie.

"And they really think he's going to go out with a girl from our grade? As if," scoffed Bianca.

From the corner of her eye, Alexa saw Ezra and Sam exchange concerned looks before they both turned to her. She kept her eyes averted as the news swirled inside her.

"Where are you going?" asked Sam as Alexa pushed her half eaten lunch away and rose from the table.

"I just remembered something I have to do before class. I'll see you guys in English," Alexa replied in a soft voice.

Only Sam and Ezra appeared suspicious of her departure. Everyone else just waved her goodbye. Her behaviour of late had been erratic enough to let her get away with almost anything.

Alexa climbed the stairs to Mr Knight's office. The door was ajar so she walked straight in without knocking.

"Oh, I'm sorry," she mumbled, as she noticed a group of three year ten girls standing around Mr Knight's desk.

"It's all right, Miss Samson. I will only be a few more minutes if you want to wait outside," said Mr Knight, looking as flustered as she felt.

Alexa waited outside as the girls chatted and giggled. Mr Knight was doing his best to get them to leave, but they seemed just as keen to stay. It was so odd. Despite the feelings Alexa had for Mr Knight, she had never just come and chatted to him. It made her wonder if she was just another student to him.

"Come in, Miss Samson," said Mr Knight from the doorway, as he showed the year ten girls out of his office.

Alexa followed him in, but could not sit down. Her heart was beating erratically as guilt saturated her body, remembering why she had come to see Mr Knight in the first place. This was not what she wanted to do, but she had do try and make things right.

"What's wrong?" asked Mr Knight with deep concern as she

slowly paced the room.

"Was it because of me? Because of what I said? I wouldn't have said it, but – I thought – I don't want it to be my fault."

Alexa continued to pace in ever smaller circles her eyes glued to the ground.

"What don't you want to be your fault?" Mr Knight asked in a slightly panicked voice.

"Your break up," Alexa replied in a barely audible voice. "You need to get back with her. You can't break up with her because of me. I don't want that to be my fault too."

Mr Knight lowered his head and buried it in his hands. Alexa realised then that he had done it because of her and she felt sick.

"Sit down, Alexa," he said in a muffled voice. Alexa shook her head and continued to pace. "Nothing that happens in my life is your fault," he said firmly, looking in her eyes. "I broke up with Jackie because I didn't love her the way I needed to – to marry her. She deserves a lot better than I've given her over the last twelve months."

"Because of me?"

"Because of *me*," cried Mr Knight passionately. "I am responsible for my own relationships, not you."

Alexa stopped pacing but could still not sit down. She wanted to believe him, but was not sure how to. In the end, things always ended up being her fault.

"But what I said to you in the hall, that made a difference, didn't it?" she asked, her body shaking.

"No. I ended things with Jackie during the holidays," replied Mr Knight in a deliberate voice, keeping her gaze. "Before that day. That was why I wasn't around during the holidays. It wasn't an easy thing to do."

Alexa moved towards the chair, wondering if she should dare to believe. She would not put it past Mr Knight to lie to her about something like this – just to try and make her feel better.

"Sit down, Alexa, please. You're not responsible for everything that happens. Do you want me to tell you that you played a part?" he asked with raised eyebrows. "You did. You helped me realise how selfish I was being and that I needed to make a decision about my life and that's what I did. I made a decision. It wasn't easy. I hurt someone I care a lot about, but there's no blame to be had. If there ever was, it should be worn by me and no one else."

The bell rang in the background and Alexa turned to the door.

Now she had to make her decision. Up until this point, she had always tried to choose the right path and do the right thing, and it had always brought her grief. She had never felt so safe or free with anyone as she did with Mr Knight. It was wrong, but she no longer cared. She had lost everything – everyone but Mr Knight – Marcus. In less than six months he would stop being Mr Knight forever and she wanted to be with him when that time came. If she had lost everything else, she would hold on to the only thing she had left.

"I didn't mean to say what I said to you in the hall," Alexa said quietly, her heart rate rapidly increasing as she turned around. "I mean, I did, I just never expected to see you again."

"I understand, Alexa, I do."

"I meant it, though. I just wouldn't have said it normally."

"For me too," said Mr Knight quietly. Alexa smiled slightly and felt the numbness that had encased her these last four weeks start to fade away. "But that doesn't change the situation we're in," he added in a stronger voice.

"Not now, but that's only until the end of the year," said Alexa, hoping he understood.

When a broad smile slowly spread across Mr Knight's face, Alexa knew he realised what she was suggesting and that he was willing to throw everything away for her too.

"I should probably get to class," Alexa said with a soft smile.

This went completely against her original plan, but in making the decision to be with Marcus, she had given herself something to hope for and a future to look forward to.

"I'll write you a note. You don't need to find yourself in any more trouble," said Mr Knight, though she noticed his voice trembling slightly. "How are your classes going? Are you ready for the trials?"

"I don't know what's going on most of the time. I don't think it matters if I catch up or not. I've missed so much, I don't know what I'm doing."

"You still haven't caught up on the work you missed last term?"

"No, I did. Bianca helped me in the holidays, but I just can't care any more."

"Alexa, I know this hasn't been an easy year for you and you mightn't like what I'm about to say, but this year is important – not the be all and end all, but it is important," said Mr Knight earnestly, and Alexa could see he was trying hard not to preach. "You don't want to do so badly that there's no point in you being here – or that you have no choice but to repeat. You have nowhere else to be and nothing else to do. Your sister is somewhere she can be helped and there's nothing more you can do for her right now. You need to do something for yourself. You need to start thinking about your life and what you want to do."

"I don't know what I want to do," Alexa replied flatly, trying not to sound too hopeless.

"Because you've spent your entire life worrying about everyone but yourself," countered Mr Knight. "Now is the time to be selfish and do what's right for you."

Alexa managed to conjure a half-smile. She was not sure how she would do what Mr Knight – for now he had to remain Mr Knight – had said, but she wanted to try – for him more than herself. It felt nice that he cared, and that next year they would be together.

"Do you know the park in the Rushcutters Bay?" asked Alexa. "It's where all the boats are moored and it looks out on to the water and the harbour. I used to go there a lot when I was living in the city." Mr Knight nodded his head cautiously. "It looks like a really great place to watch the New Year's Eve fireworks from." He nodded again, but looked confused. "It does get really packed, but if you stick around it empties out pretty quickly. It's usually a really nice sunrise."

Mr Knight was still nodding, and Alexa was not sure he understood.

"Sounds like it might be worth checking out," he replied slowly. "I'll be alone this year, but New Year's Eve is a pretty magical night. You never know who you'll meet."

Alexa smiled broadly and took the note from Mr Knight's outstretched hand. It was the perfect plan, even more so because it gave her time to set herself up outside of school and after that they could pretend they met as normally and as innocently as any other couple.

***

Nerves and anticipation filled the air outside the hall as the grade anxiously awaited the start of their first exam. Mr Knight walked among them, offering his usual words of encouragement and support. Sam kept close to Alexa. She noticed he did his best to be closest to her whenever Mr Knight looked over, but Sam never managed to solicit a jealous look from him.

Mr Pollock opened the hall doors to allow the students in. Everyone stood up and prepared to make their way inside. Alexa stayed where she was, eyeing the hall fearfully.

"Are you coming?" asked Ezra, as they moved forward towards the hall.

"Yeah," nodded Alexa. She picked up her pens and walked slowly towards the hall, taking long, deep breaths to try and slow her painfully pounding heart.

With every step, the images of Bethany and the wounded girl became clearer and clearer in her eyes until she stopped five metres from the door, unable to take another step forward.

"Miss Samson, are you all right?" asked Mr Knight. His voice sounded a thousand miles away as she watched blood drip on to the hall floor.

Mr Knight physically turned her and walked her away from the hall as the grade watched on curiously. The movement pulled Alexa out of her trance and she noticed her hands shaking.

"How do you feel, Miss Samson? Do you think you're up to doing the exam?" asked Mr Pollock.

"I can't go in there," said Alexa, clamping her hands between her knees to try to stop them shaking as she sat on the steps staring blankly at the hall.

"She hasn't been in there since the first day of term," Mr Knight said to Mr Pollock. "Is there somewhere else she can do the exam?"

Mr Pollock organised the rest of the grade before taking Alexa to a small room under the hall where she could sit the exam. Convinced that she had failed anyway, Alexa made her way leisurely through the exam, writing down whatever came to mind. She knew she had promised Mr Knight that she would care, but right then it was just too hard.

Alexa did not give up though. That was only one exam and there were still plenty more to try to keep her promise with. It really was just something to fill in the time. She would work and try, but found caring far too difficult. The only thing that made the process possible was the routine created by the hours of study and occasional examination.

It gave Alexa short-term focus and release. It was also a great distraction. With all the study she needed to do for each exam, there was little time left for her to think about the events of the last few months, though they were never far from her mind. There were just too many reminders that she refused to part with.

The clothes that Pam and Karl had given her, which once fitted perfectly, now hung loosely from her body as a result of the dramatic weight loss she had suffered since Leo's attack. Her Christmas photo album sat on her bedside table, though she no longer opened it, holding it to her chest every night as she fell asleep; and the bracelet from Hayley and Brett remained around her wrist. It had not left her arm since the day she opened the present and she vowed that it never would.

When the exams finally ended and normal classes resumed, so did Ben's weekly visits. He had stayed away during the trials and Alexa was anxious to know what was happening with Bethany, as she had still not answered any of her letters.

"So what's happening? Is Bethy okay? Can I see her yet?" Alexa asked, as soon as she walked into Mr Knight's office.

"I'll leave you guys to it," said Mr Knight, walking to his desk and gathering some papers.

"I don't care if you stay. I just want to know what's going on," said Alexa.

Mr Knight exchanged looks with Ben before sitting down at his desk. Alexa knew Mr Knight would want to know what was going on almost as much as her – perhaps even more so now if he was going to be a part of her life. Ben sat her down on a chair, seating himself next to her.

"Listen, Alexa, this is not a fast process. There are still many things that have to happen before a court date is set or anything like that. Things have also been slower as we had to wait until Bethany was out of rehab before we could interview her," said Ben in a calm voice.

"So you've got no news for me?"

"Not on the progress of your sister's case, no. I can tell you that she's doing much better now. She's been through rehab and has started some of the courses they have to build life skills."

"Do you know why she won't reply to my letters?" Alexa asked, her voice much calmer, but also much sadder. Perhaps, now that Bethany was clean, she was angry that she had been sent to gaol rather than letting them die as they had originally planned.

"I think she needs some time to adjust. There's very little chance that she'll receive a non-custodial sentence. That might take her a bit of getting used to, but I know she loves getting your letters. Keep writing. She'll come around soon."

"I want to see her," said Alexa, trying to sound demanding.

"I know and I will take you there myself when the time is right," nodded Ben.

"When will that be?" Alexa asked angrily, hating continually being told when she could and could not see Bethany.

"I know this isn't easy for you. I just need you to trust me," said Ben. Alexa stood up and walked to the corner of the room. She turned back to face Ben with a hateful look on her face. "Then just believe that there is no personal gain for me here. I'm just doing what you asked me to. I'm looking out for Bethany, but I'm also looking out for you. I don't think either of you realise the fragile states you're in right now."

"I'm not fragile. I can handle anything I have to –"

"Alexa, I know, maybe better than you, what you and Bethany have had to handle," said Ben forcefully. Alexa could see the strain on his face from trying to contain his anger and it kept her silent. "I don't want to burden either of you any further. I don't think you deserve to have to handle anything else right now. Please, I will be here the instant you can visit her. I'm trying to help the both of you."

Alexa did not answer and did not move from the corner as Ben rose and said goodbye. When he closed the door behind him she slid down the wall, sitting herself cross-legged on the floor.

"I think he means well," said Mr Knight, as she picked at the carpet. "I think you should trust his judgement."

"Can I stay here for a little while?" Alexa asked softly, choosing to ignore Mr Knight's comments.

Mr Knight made hot chocolate and left her cup on his desk. It was a ploy to get her to sit up off the floor and she knew it, but she did not mind being closer to him. He smiled as she sat up on the chair and passed her some biscuits he had in his drawer.

"It's all my fault, you know," said Alexa, looking sadly into her hot chocolate. "The way everything is – the fact that Bethy's in gaol."

"Alexa, that's – you can't think like that. Bethany made her own choices."

"But see, she didn't. She was born addicted to heroin. She never had the choice. She watched my mother shoot up and craved it, even as a little girl. I tried to keep her away from it as much as possible. I guess I raised her in a way. From as far back as I remember I was the one who looked after her. And then I left her and came here."

"Why did you come here?" asked Mr Knight with genuine curiosity. Apparently, that was one of the few things they chose not to detail in her file.

"I was shipped around a bit after our mother died, while Bethy spent a few months in hospital recovering from her overdose. We were eventually sent to the Christies. They loved Bethy and Bethy really liked them. I didn't get on so well with them. They thought I was a bad influence. They just didn't really like me. In the end they asked the department to remove me, but I wasn't going anywhere without Bethy.

"Our social worker got me the scholarship here and I was told I could come back and stay during the holidays. I didn't want to go, but they told me that Bethy would join me in two years and she was happy for the first time in so long. I thought I was doing the right thing."

"What went wrong?"

"They went back on their promise. The Christies wouldn't let me return. They wouldn't even let me see Bethy. I ran away from every foster family to try and see her. Some had me back, most didn't. I can't even remember how many I've been to. It was a few weeks after I didn't come back for the first holidays that Bethy started using drugs again. They didn't even tell me until it became so bad that they needed me to find her."

Mr Knight did not immediately answer and Alexa did not look up from her hot chocolate to see the look on his face. No one ever looked happy when she talked to them about Bethany and their childhood.

"This doesn't make what's happened your fault. You were just a child. You did the best you could," said Mr Knight sincerely.

"No, I should never have left her. I should've known. She was just ten. I should've taken her with me, done anything but left her."

"It was still her choice."

"She had no choice. I should've left here. When I managed to find to her I could always get her off the drugs. I should've left while I could've helped her. I could've stopped all this."

"She's getting help now. You've done more for her than you realise," said Mr Knight tenderly. "There aren't many people that would put themselves in the line of fire of a dozen police officers to protect someone else."

"She was high. I doubt she'll even remember what happened. I couldn't let her die."

"Even though she was going to kill you?" Mr Knight asked incredulously.

"It was over anyway. We were both dying that day," Alexa sighed, trying not to wish that they had. She really needed to focus on being alive. "It was a pact we made last year after I tried to kill myself. She was really upset with me and said that I couldn't go without her. I could never kill her so I knew I could never try and kill myself again."

"But she could take your life."

"No, I don't think she could," said Alexa quickly, desperate for Mr Knight to understand. "She had all the time in the world, but she didn't shoot me. She was so desperate to end her life that she came to find me. In the end it was what saved us both."

"But what if she had shot you?"

"Then we would've died together – and that would've been okay. I would rather that than –" Alexa saw the look of horror in Mr Knight's eyes and decided not to finish that sentence. She loved him, but he could never have a greater hold on her heart than Bethany. He would have to know that to be a part of her life. "I won't let us be separated again," she said firmly, laying down the challenge before they got too involved.

Chapter Thirteen

MARCUS SAT BACK in his chair and rubbed his hands against his face. The way Alexa could talk so rationally about her life unnerved him. He could not believe everything she took upon herself. He wanted to reason with her and show her the errors of her thinking, but in many ways, her thoughts and decisions made sense. He could see where desperation had pushed her, but he could also see the desperation still there in her eyes and he knew that any life with Alexa would involve a life with Bethany and he tried hard to not think the worst of her.

"Were you scared?" Marcus asked after a minute of silence, deciding the rest could wait for another day.

"Scared of what?" asked Alexa, appearing genuinely confused.

"Dying," he answered.

"I've died before. Do you want to know what it's like?"

"No," replied Marcus quickly, horrified at the thought. "But you didn't know that was coming. Weren't you scared waiting to die?"

"No. I knew I would be with Bethy. I'm not scared of dying. I've come close a few times. I fought back because I could, but in the end it's out of my hands. I'm not scared of things I can't control."

"Are you scared of anything?" Marcus asked incredulously.

"I don't know. No, I don't think so," replied Alexa with a thoughtful look. "What are you scared of?"

"Heights – and snakes, and spiders."

Alexa smiled at him as he shivered. She probably picked up spiders with her bare hands.

"Why?" Alexa asked curiously.

"I don't know really," Marcus answered hesitantly. He had never even thought about why. Everyone was simply allowed to be scared to those sorts of things.

"Why be scared if you don't even know why you're scared?" asked Alexa, as though he was a bit of an idiot.

"Doesn't anything just frighten you? Haven't you been scared of anything?" he asked, smiling at the bemused look on Alexa face, though he was not convinced there was nothing she feared. "What about sleep? Aren't you scared of your nightmares?"

"No. I can't control them. I don't fear anything I don't have control over. I've had them since I was little. They're mostly bad dreams now anyway, not even nightmares," shrugged Alexa, trying to look unaffected, but Marcus was not sure the truth was so clear cut.

"That's good to hear, I guess," he smiled, not challenging her answer. It was not as though he wanted her to be scared of her nightmares. They tortured her enough.

Marcus briefly considered asking Detective Shepard about the dream next time he came to the school, but knew if Alexa wanted him to know more, she would tell him. She had the right to privacy. Clearly not reading his thoughts, Alexa's smile was full and amused as she took in his pensive silence.

"Children are afraid of nightmares," she laughed. "They're dreams. They can't hurt me no matter how scary they are. Anyway, I'd better get to dinner. It still takes me an hour to eat."

Marcus smiled and nodded as he slouched back in his chair.

"Alexa," he said as she reached the door. "You are right. If there's one thing you're not, it's a child."

"I'm just a girl," she replied dismissively.

"You're the most amazing woman I have ever met."

***

The weeks started to rush by as the term neared its end. Alexa worked as hard as she could, discovering every revision lesson more work she had missed. It was not that she particularly cared, but it many ways it gave her something to do. For every subject she now had a checklist of topics she had to write revision notes for to ensure there was nothing she missed. It made the time pass, and that was pretty much all she cared for.

Ben continued his weekly visits, though he brought little new information. It was frustrating and disheartening. Alexa also hated Ben's insistence that she and Bethany were not yet ready to see each other. It took all of her limited self-control not to lose her temper and tell Ben where he could stick his useless visits. She needed him, but she was losing faith in him and herself. Her reasons for trusting Ben had always been flimsy at best and she had let him near Bethany. She would never forgive herself if Ben hurt Bethany.

With no end to the stalemate in sight, Alexa was determined to be released for the next holidays – to another foster family if that was necessary – and from there she would visit Bethany every single day. Whether or not she would return was another matter. She would be eighteen by then. She had the winning lottery tickets and would go and claim it on behalf of her, Bianca and Ezra if she needed to. No one was going to continue to force her to stay in school and away from Bethany.

At the end of each of Ben's visits, while Alexa was formulating those plans, she stayed in Mr Knight's office. Mr Knight would always make her a tea or hot chocolate and leave it on the desk until she had calmed down enough to join him. She liked that he did not try to talk to her until she was ready.

They could talk for as little as fifteen minutes or as long as two hours. It all depended on her moods and the questions Mr Knight asked. Some questions were easier to face than other, but for the most part she wanted Mr Knight to be the one answering the questions rather than asking them.

"So tell me about your family. You know all about mine," said Alexa, walking casually around his office.

"You've only told me about you and Bethany. You've barely mentioned your mother and not said one word about your father," replied Mr Knight, though his voice displayed no agitation.

"You won't find out anything about them if you don't tell me something about you," Alexa countered light-heartedly.

Mr Knight smiled as she stood staring at him defiantly, her eyebrows raised and the corners of her mouth slightly curled. She liked that she had some power over him.

"I have a sister, mother and father. We grew up in the suburbs and I don't think I ever wanted for anything. My childhood was happy and the rest of my life has been as well," answered Mr Knight simply.

"What's your sister like?"

"Rhianna is a free spirit," smiled Mr Knight indulgently, and Alexa liked the affection in his voice as he spoke about her. "I guess that's the best way to describe her. She travels, picking up work here and there. I don't think she's ever held a job for more than six months."

"You don't approve?" Alexa asked, a little fearful of how judgemental Mr Knight was.

"I don't understand. Don't get me wrong, I think it's amazing what she does and I sometimes wish I could do the same. She's just twenty-four and has seen so much – so much more than me," explained Mr Knight with a slight wistfulness.

It was something Alexa could empathise with. There had been many times in her life where she had wished her nature had allowed her to make different decisions.

"You like security, there's nothing wrong with that," she said, deciding against telling Mr Knight how much she craved it too.

"I like stability. We had a very stable life, almost boring she would say. Rhianna always wanted more excitement, more drama. I was happy with the stable, steady life. The few pieces of drama I've had to face I could've well done without."

"Like what?" Alexa asked, trying not to be sceptical of his level of suffering.

"Apart from you?" smiled Mr Knight, before continuing to her unamused face. "I guess the worst was when I was fourteen. I went camping with a mate from school and his family. It was my first trip away without my parents. I was so excited. Anyway, on the second day we camped by a dam or waterhole – water, anyway. James and I decided to go for a swim. I never liked heights so I just waded into the water, but James climbed up this cliff face and dived in. We'd seen other people doing it and nobody got hurt. He must have struck a rock or something, dived too deep. By the time we found him he'd stopped breathing. They never revived him."

Alexa sat down on the chair watching Mr Knight's face as emotion swept over it.

"Not quite as dramatic as anything from your life," he smiled, waving his hand dismissively, even though she could see tears in the sides of his eyes.

"Do you really think that I reckon your pain is less valid than mine?" Alexa asked angrily. "Pain is still pain. I know what it's like to lose people. I didn't say anything because I know what it's like to have someone spout crap at you, thinking they can make things better. I think it would've been a terrible thing to have to go through."

"I didn't mean it like that. I just –"

"Bad things happen to everyone. Just because more things happen to one person doesn't make your pain any less real."

"I know. I'm fine now. I just prefer less drama. It makes me wonder why I like you. Since the start of last year my life has felt like nothing but drama."

"Sorry," Alexa murmured, wondering how it was possible that Mr Knight liked her enough to even talk to her let alone plan to be with her.

"It hasn't all been your fault," said Mr Knight, shaking his head. "My grandparents were killed in a car accident at the start of last year. It was a massive shock. Besides James, they were the first deaths I'd had to deal with. It was harder than James. I think I had reached the age where it really hits you what it means for someone to die. And then my other grandmother died this year. It's been a lot in a short period. I haven't coped that well."

Alexa sat in the chair with her legs crossed, realising that she did not know the first thing about consoling other people.

"You take everything in your stride. All this drama came as a bit of a shock to me. I expected a rowdy, trouble-making grade. I wasn't ready for you."

"Am I really that bad?" asked Alexa sincerely.

"You're not bad. I just wasn't ready. You caught me off guard in every way. You had me intrigued from the first day. I remembered you as this little girl from my year seven class and that was not the girl who walked into my office. Your confidence and complete disregard for me – it amazed me. You got under my skin and I still didn't know how."

"I barely noticed you," smiled Alexa sheepishly.

"I know," replied Mr Knight with a solemn nod.

It made Alexa wonder how there could have ever been a time when she did not notice or admire Mr Knight. Love was something different, but she was surprised she had not always realised just how amazing he was.

***

The third-last week of term brought Alexa's birthday, and with it an increase in her resolution to see Bethany. She had continued to write a letter a day, but so far Bethany's only response had been silence. Alexa's imagination liked to believe that Bethany would make an exception today, but she tried not to get her hopes up. Bethany's priority would not be her birthday.

Alexa never celebrated her birthday, not even with Bethany. Their mother had never cared for the day, and neither had any of their foster families. The pain that had caused Alexa in the early years made her determined to never let Bethany suffer in such a way. Consequently, Bethany had grown up loving her birthday, never truly understanding why she did not feel the same way.

It seemed like an easy concept, to just celebrate her birthday, but it was never that simple, especially not this year. Even acknowledging the existence of her birthday made her think of Hayley and the Whites. They had been determined to celebrate the occasion, and Alexa knew they would have kept their promise. She was still terrified of what they would have given her. Part of her was even paralysed by the hopeful fear that they would still not let the day go unnoticed.

Clutching her chest as she lay in bed, trying to conjure the will to face this day, Alexa knew that fear was pointless. The Whites were nowhere celebrating her birth. If they were thinking of her at all, it would be to rue the day she came into their lives, destroying the peaceful, happy family they had once been.

Alexa's thoughts became darker as the minutes ticked by. It made her wish for Bethany. It was wrong to take away Bethany's chance to make something of her life, but right then she would rather die. Those thoughts were so tempting that Alexa had to quickly turn them in another direction.

This birthday was different, she assured herself. She was finally eighteen. It was a milestone she had been waiting for since her mother's death. It was supposed to have been the age that she took responsibility for Bethany and saved them both from the world of foster care. She had always imagined having to kidnap Bethany until her sixteenth birthday later in the year. After that, no law could keep them apart. That was what she had believed.

The law was now threatening to keep them apart well beyond Alexa's eighteenth birthday, perhaps even beyond Bethany's eighteenth birthday. It strengthened Alexa's resolve to get out of school and see Bethany. They needed to work on Bethany's defence. She would not let Bethany be punished for her mistakes.

Strengthened by her purpose, Alexa made her way to breakfast. No one said anything to her as they sat down to eat. Since she had never celebrated her birthday, most of her friends had no idea when it was, let alone that it was today. She was glad. The last thing she needed was people coming up to her trying to make out like it was a happy day.

As Alexa started making her way to class, she noticed Sam and Chad rushing towards the dining hall to grab some breakfast before it was packed up. She waved her greeting, wondering at their inability to turn up to breakfast on time. It had to affect their digestion, scoffing food that quickly. Sam suddenly changed course and rushed towards her. He grabbed her hand and pulled her into a corner of the dining hall.

"What's up?" asked Alexa, wondering if Sam wanted her to eat another breakfast. He had commented more than once on her weight loss. Sam just smiled, kissed her on the cheek and engulfed her in a crushing bear hug. "What's this for?" she asked, hugging him back. It was impossible not to.

"Nothing. It's just a good day." Sam smiled, hugging and kissing her again before releasing her.

"Thank you," Alexa smiled. She loved that Sam knew her well enough not to even say the words.

Besides Sam's morning greeting, the day passed as blandly as any other. It made it much easier for Alexa to pretend it was nothing special, but when she slouched towards her desk at the end of the day she was sorry that her homework could not disappear for her birthday. She had been trying hard to keep her promise to Mr Knight and had even tried thinking about future careers, but as yet nothing had come to mind. Besides the obvious professions of teaching, law and policing, she really did not know what most people did for a job. She had never even asked Pam or Karl what they actually did for work.

"Oh, Alexa, did you get your mail?" asked Natalie as they started to pack up for dinner. "I put it on your bed."

Alexa rushed to her bed. She almost never got mail, not recently anyway. Bethany had never been the greatest pen pal, but her letters had always been the best. The hope that they still would be filled Alexa's chest as she picked up the two envelopes. The writing on the bottom letter was instantly recognisable. Tossing the other letter aside, Alexa tore open the envelope as her heart pounded in her throat.

It almost did not matter what was in the envelope. Anything from Bethany would be precious. The simple, hand-made card that was inside was perhaps the greatest gift Alexa had ever received. It was a piece of cardboard folded over. A picture of a rose had been cut out and stuck to the front. The inside was blank but for a few scrawled words.

Happy Birthday Lex!
Love Bethany

Alexa knew it would have looked thoughtless and tokenistic to anyone else, but she understood how much thought Bethany would have put into it. Whatever Bethany's reason for her silence, she had broken it with this gesture and it meant more to Alexa than everything else she had ever been given.

Grasping the card tight in her hands, Alexa was unable to stop reading those few words over and over again. Her chest was so swollen with happiness she felt as though it might burst.

"Are you okay, Alexa?" asked Lizzie.

"I'm more than okay," replied Alexa, her voice barely more than a gasp.

"What happened?" asked Bianca.

"Bethany wrote to me."

Knowing they would not understand or care, Alexa jumped off her bed and rushed out the door. She ran down to the common room to find Sam, but he was not there. Since it was almost dinner she back-tracked up to the dining hall, but he had not yet arrived. Her excitement was too great to sit down and eat. She wanted to jump and scream with joy.

After turning in circles a few times, Alexa decided to go down to Sam's room. She needed to share her good news. Then she saw Chad and Sam walking up the corridor with Martha and Natalie. Sam sprinted up to her as soon as he saw her, stopping just a foot away.

"She wrote?" he asked, his eyes wide with anticipation.

Alexa could barely speak as she nodded. Sam pulled her into a tight embrace, twirling her jubilantly as he kissed the side of her head. When Sam set her back on her feet, they stood in each other's arms, their foreheads resting against each other as they smiled happily. Alexa loved that Sam was able to understand just what this moment meant to her.

"I'm not sure this is going to get either of you fed," said Mr Knight in a light voice, startling Alexa and Sam.

Alexa let go of Sam and turned to Mr Knight, her face still full of joy and excitement. Mr Knight automatically smiled back, but Alexa was sure she saw the briefest flash of disappointment in his eyes when she turned around.

"Bethy wrote to me," she said, so excited she was almost breathless.

"That's really great news," said Mr Knight, smiling again. "So it's been a good day, then?"

"Better than I ever expected."

Mr Knight smiled and nodded before walking into the dining hall, though Alexa was sure his face paled slightly as he walked away. When he walked to the other side of the dining hall his face turned stony and grave. Part of her hoped that he was jealous, upset that it could not be him who was enjoying this moment with her.

"We'd better go in otherwise you'll never finish your dinner," said Sam, guiding Alexa into the hall by the waist.

"Um, perhaps you should go and see Natalie," said Alexa, catching a glimpse of Natalie as she sat next to Martha and Chad, her face full of anger and hurt.

"Shit, she's going to make a big deal out of this. I probably won't see you until tomorrow," muttered Sam, before hugging her, then pulling back and cupping her cheek so her eyes looked into his. "I'm really glad Bethany wrote to you and I'm so happy you had a good day."

Alexa smiled and Sam kissed her gently on the cheek before slouching off towards Natalie. She noticed that Natalie looked somewhat appeased when Sam sat down next to her, allowing her to sigh with relief. It might have been strange watching Sam date someone else, but she never wanted to break up his relationships.

Bianca had an alternative motive for her actions, but Alexa refused to listen to her muttered conversation with Lizzie on the other side of the table. Alexa was so good at appearing as though she was in her own world that they did not bother to really keep their voices down, although she suspected Lizzie had a different reason for that.

"She's not flirting," said Lizzie. "Sam's just happy for her."

"Yeah, well I wouldn't want my boyfriend being that happy for her," hissed Bianca before settling into a thoughtful silence.

"Have you guys done Shakespeare revision in English yet? There's still a section I don't get," said Lizzie, clearly thinking the previous conversation was finished.

"Maybe that's why Chad broke up with me," replied Bianca, this time in a softer voice. "Chad started getting all defensive and protective of Alexa in the summer. She got all high and mighty about me cheating on him, but that was probably just to cover what they were doing. They were always going off together at Sam's place."

"No, I don't think so," replied Lizzie in a stuttering voice.

Alexa could have smiled at the horrified look on Lizzie's face. If Alexa had been lulled into a false sense of friendship with Bianca over the past couple of months, she might have been offended. However, that conversation and Bianca's warm smile and friendly chatter on the way back to the dormitory pretty much epitomised the strange dichotomy of their relationship.

Lizzie and Bianca went straight to their desks, but despite the dinner-time conversations Alexa was too excited to study. She went to her bed to write to Bethany and thank her for the card, hoping that this would be the trigger for more detailed communications.

Sitting down on the bed, Alexa noticed the second envelope that she had neglected in her excitement. Her stomach churned uncomfortably as she wondered who it could be from. She wanted it to be from Hayley and the Whites, but was terrified by the prospect. She needed them to forget her. She needed them to be safe.

The writing on the front of the envelope was neat and strangely familiar, but Alexa could not place it, making her heart beat with fear. She opened the envelope slowly to reveal a card with a picture of a beautiful beach sunset. It was clear now that it was not from the Whites, and she felt her heart pounding with anticipation as she opened the card. A small, blue velvet pouch fell out. Alexa picked it up and looked back at the card. The writing was not as neat as on the envelope, making it suddenly recognisable.

Happy Birthday Alexa

Three simple words. Alexa felt her heart melt. She opened the pouch and tipped out the contents. Lying in her hand was a beautiful gold chain with a pendant of sapphire and diamond. She now understood the look of disappointment on Mr Knight's face when he had seen her. He had expected her to be wearing the necklace.

The golden chain sat weightlessly around her neck. She held the pendant tight in her hand as she wrote to Bethany, thanking her for her card and describing, in minute detail, every aspect of the necklace and pendant Mr Knight had sent her.

As Alexa laid herself down to sleep, she clasped the pendant tight and imagined Marcus's arms – because he would be Marcus then – wrapped lovingly around her. With that thought, new warmth spread through her heart and she fell peacefully to sleep.

The joy and warmth Alexa had felt the night before did not dissipate the next morning. She could not stop touching the necklace or holding the pendant and soon everybody noticed it hanging around her neck.

"Where did you get that necklace?" asked Bianca, as she sat with

Alexa, Lizzie and Ezra before class started.

"Oh – um – I … um, I've always had it. I've just never worn it. It was my mother's. I had it packed away. I never felt that comfortable wearing it, but I thought it was time to get over that," Alexa lied.

Bianca and Lizzie seemed to believe her. They had no reason to think it a lie. It was Ezra who saw through it. Though she smiled and nodded along with Bianca and Lizzie, Ezra had too much knowledge of her life and pure loathing of her mother to believe such a thing, but Alexa doubted Ezra would realise it was from Mr Knight.

Alexa did not have any trouble selling her story to anyone else that day, as one-by-one people noticed her necklace. The only person who would know it for an absolute lie was Sam. He did not even smile. His jaw stiffened and his eyes grew hard, before he just turned away and started a conversation with Nick. It made Alexa glad they did not spend all their time together. She did not need his disapproval over this. Mr Knight's love was about the only thing getting her out of bed in the morning.

With the weather warming up, Alexa suggested they eat their lunch outside in the sun. It had the added advantage of getting them away from more people who would ask about her necklace. She had not realised how horrible she would find speaking her mother's name. It had been such a simple lie and yet now it was associating a woman she despised with necklace she loved.

Alexa stayed out of the lunchtime conversation. Stretching her body out in the sun, she imagined she was free, lying in the park with Bethany. Clasping her hand over her pendant, she envisaged Marcus there with them. It was a beautiful daydream, broken only by the arrival of Sam and Chad. They both looked very disgruntled and Sam was cursing as he sat down next to her.

"What's with girls?" queried Sam angrily, throwing his hands out to them as if begging for an answer. "What do you all really want? I mean, you say you want one thing and that's what we give you, then you expect something completely different."

"Are we going to get the non-cryptic version of these complaints?" asked Alexa as she sat up, taking Sam's hand and squeezing it tenderly.

"He told Natalie not to compare the two of them with you and him, that you and Sam have something special and that they were just together for the sex," said Chad.

Lizzie and Bianca gasped. Alexa pulled her hand from Sam's

and used it to cover her face. She really did not need this, and she had never wanted to come between Sam and Natalie – or hurt Natalie. Natalie had never been anything but nice to her, and Alexa hated to think that this would turn Natalie and Martha against her.

"You didn't really say that, did you?" asked Ezra.

"Not in those exact words," said Sam defensively. "But it's essentially true. That was the whole thing when we hooked up. We discussed it. It wasn't supposed to be a serious relationship. She agreed!"

"I think Natalie agreed to that so you'd go out with her and hoped you'd really like her," said Ezra in a tone the girls knew was simply pointing out the obvious.

"How am I ever supposed to know that? She didn't tell me. No wonder you're never satisfied and whinge about guys all the time."

"Girls give guys more credit than they deserve," said Bianca. "We assume you can work these sorts of things out for yourselves."

"And guys assume their girlfriend won't cheat on them because they're absent for more than a week, but it turns out we're mistaken about that too," replied Chad harshly, glaring at Bianca with deep bitterness.

Alexa knew that jibe was meant to strike deep and was aimed not just how Chad and Bianca had broken up, but how they had gotten together. The resulting silence was tense and awkward, everyone looking at each other from the corner of their eye, wondering what to say next.

"So does this mean that you and Alexa are getting together again?" asked Lizzie in a hopeful voice, trying to ignore the growing tension between Chad and Bianca.

"No!" cried Sam and Alexa simultaneously, their frustration evident.

However, when Alexa noticed Lizzie's eyes flick Chad's way, she realised that Lizzie may have had other reasons for asking that question.

"I suggest we change the topic," said Chad quickly, avoiding Bianca's gaze, which was suddenly switching between him and Alexa.

"So what about you and Martha, are you two still together?" asked Lizzie hesitantly.

"Apparently, I fell into the same trap as Sam. I just had the sense not to say anything like what he said. I have to agree with Sam, though. You girls are an absolute nightmare."

"Unfortunately, girls only become more sophisticated as they get older," said Mr Knight, walking around to the front of the group. "What have they done to you this time?"

"Why do girls say one thing and expect another?" asked Sam bitterly. "I mean, if they just tell us what they want, they'd have a much better chance of getting it than if they make us guess."

Alexa could see Mr Knight trying hard not to laugh as the girls chuckled silently.

"Unfortunately, women tend to be fairly good mind readers. I think they expect us to be just as good, but they're far too complex for any mortal man to understand. You'll be right, Mr Michaels. The trick is just to find one that's worth the pain and frustration."

"Gee thanks, Sir," said Bianca, slightly put out by the assessment, though it was fairly close to what she had suggested.

Mr Knight turned towards Bianca, but caught Alexa's eyes first. She could not help but look down and his eyes followed hers. When she looked back up, he was still staring at the chain around her neck with an indescribable look on his face. She hoped he was not upset about her wearing it – or regretting giving it to her.

"Are you all right, Sir?" asked Lizzie, trying to keep her face from blushing.

"Yes, sorry, Miss Chatri. All this talk about girls and I forgot why I came down here. Miss Samson, Detective Shepard rang and said he won't be able to come to see you this week. He wanted me to tell you that he was sorry and he'll make sure he sees you next week."

Alexa nodded her head slowly.

"It's not like he tells me anything new anyway," she said, trying to keep her voice light and upbeat as she made her resolution. If Ben did not say he was going to take her to see Bethany when he next came, she would ask Mr Knight to get her out of school for the holidays – foster home or no foster home.

"All right, well enjoy the rest of your lunch," said Mr Knight, walking quickly away.

"He was acting a little odd, don't you think?" Lizzie asked Chad.

"I can't believe he was listening to our conversation," replied Chad, clearly disgusted by the idea.

"Sam, Alexa and me really need to talk to you for a minute," said Ezra, catching Alexa by surprise.

Alexa assumed it was about what Sam had said to Natalie and

so followed Ezra and Sam away from the group.

"Are you two trying to make things obvious to the whole school?" asked Sam, his voice soft, but stern.

"What? I thought this was about you," said Alexa.

"No, it's about you," said Ezra in a low voice. "I just didn't want to make it more obvious, as they don't seem to have seen what happened."

"You're going to have to stop wearing the necklace. No one's going to buy that story about it being your mother's if Mr Knight keeps looking at you like that," said Sam, Ezra nodding in agreement.

"Wait a minute, how do you even know?" Alexa asked Ezra. They had definitely never had that conversation.

"Seriously, how would I not know? I'm the one who pointed it out to Sam," said Ezra, looking quite proud of herself. "You'll admit shit to him." Alexa just stared at her. "The others aren't very observant, but someone will be and then it'll be all over the school."

"But there's nothing going on. We like each other. That's not a crime," replied Alexa desperately. "It's not like anything will ever happen between us."

Alexa did not add the qualification that followed in her head. It was not worth the fight, and right now was probably beside the point.

"No one will be interested in the truth. No one will believe that the two of you are in love and waiting until next year to act on it," argued Sam, speaking the qualification for her. "They'll believe that the two of you are in a relationship and that'll make things very hard for you and it could ruin his career."

"I'll fix it," Alexa said quickly, suddenly thumping back to reality. She could not allow Mr Knight's life to be ruined in any way because of her.

"Good," said Ezra with a smile. "So back to you," she added, turning to Sam. "What the hell were you thinking saying such a thing to Natalie? Surely you didn't think she was going to take that well?"

"But it's true," cried Sam defensively. "Alexa and me do have something special. It doesn't mean we want to go out with each other. I'm just sick of everyone picking at us and making more of what's really there."

"I hate to break this to you," said Ezra solemnly. "But I know you two and what's going on and sometimes I'm confused. I know you're just friends, but when the deepness of that friendship goes on public display it looks like a lot more. I mean, who else goes around hugging and kissing their ex?"

Neither Sam nor Alexa answered, but Alexa went to bed that night with a lot on her mind. She and Sam would have to have a good look at their friendship. Natalie had spent much of the evening on her bed in tears. It was a horrible sight and Alexa had forced herself to go and apologise. She had not been sure if Natalie's silent response was an acceptance or an accusation.

"She doesn't blame you," said Martha, suddenly appearing at Alexa's bedside. "Not really," she added with a grimace. "It's not like you've been chasing Sam. It's just that the affection he displays for you is pretty endearing and it sucks when you can't emulate it."

"But we've been friends for years. He didn't always treat me like that," said Alexa, trying to ease her own guilt more than anything.

"He won't admit it, but Sam was smitten with you from the minute he met you. I remember. I think half the reason he got in trouble was to have the chance to see you. Natalie knows that. It's just that she's had a crush on Sam since about that time too. I warned her it would end badly, but she wanted to take the chance. She'll get over it – eventually."

"What about you?" asked Alexa tentatively. "You know, with Chad."

Martha smiled brightly, her gaze flicking to Bianca then back again. It looked like Martha was struggling not to laugh.

"I knew what I was doing," replied Martha, her smile even broader now. "That was just for fun. I may have made a bigger deal out of it for Nat's sake at lunch today, but it wasn't an issue. I only broke it off cos it would be too awkward now she and Sam have split. Felt pretty bad."

Alexa could not help but smile. She knew she was supposed to be Bianca's friend, but what Bianca had done to Chad was so horrible that she could not be upset that he had taken some revenge, especially now that she knew Martha had not been hurt in the process.

"I actually found him tonight – explained," added Martha in a conspiratorial whisper. "He was pretty thrilled I wasn't pissed at him. Bit hard to be when we were having so much fun. We both knew it wouldn't be anything outside of here. We're so different. But we do have the chemistry."

Alexa felt her eyes widen as Martha chuckled. She really was not sure if she should be laughing or not. Martha's hand suddenly reached out for hers and squeezed it tenderly.

"You doing okay?"

Tears started stinging the sides of Alexa's eyes as she slowly shook her head. It was not normal for her to answer that question truthfully, but this time she could not stop herself.

"Me and Nat, we can't do much, but we'll do anything you need us to. You just say the word. None of this other shit will ever change that. No one deserves the crap that you've been through."

Martha seemed to know that she could not respond to that and smiled softly before leaving her to sleep. Taking a deep breath, Alexa forced herself to turn her lips into a very slight smile. Everything Martha had said was very kind and did help to assuage much of her guilt over Sam and Natalie's break-up. It was nice to think she would not lose any friends because of it.

Closing her eyes, Alexa wrapped her hand around her pendant. Turning her thoughts away from the day's troubling events, she thought about Marcus and imagined his arms enveloping her body. It was warm and safe in that place, allowing sleep to swiftly find her.

***

"Caitlin. Come here, Caitlin. You don't think you can get away from me, do you? If I can't have you, Caitlin, no one will."

Alexa woke with a start, her heart pounding and her body covered in sweat. Her stomach churned sickeningly as fear pulsed through her body. With two steps she was in the bathroom with her head over the toilet.

The continued violent retching soon woke her roommates, who stared worriedly from their beds.

"Are you okay?" asked Bianca. Alexa nodded as she sat on the bathroom floor. "Do you want me to turn the light on?"

"No. I'm okay," coughed Alexa, her voice hoarse from the vomiting. "You go back to bed. I'll be out in a minute."

Bianca went back to bed and Alexa closed the bathroom door. She stood in the dark, her body trembling violently.

"It's just a dream," Alexa said softly to herself. "It's just a dream."

Her body still trembled as she sat back down on the cold tiles. She was desperately tired, but did not want to close her eyes. It may have been just a dream, but she did not want to have it again.

It had been the same dream as all of those before, but it had scared her more than any other. She and Bethany had been hiding in the pipe as usual, Ben's lifeless body lying at the entrance, but this time when the shadowy menace had come for them, he had called her Caitlin instead Alexa.

Alexa could not understand why the dream had suddenly scared her so much. She had seen Ben shot in her dreams since she was a little girl. Admittedly, until recently, she had not known that Ben was a real person, but she could not understand why she was being called Caitlin. She had never known the name Caitlin or even known anyone called Caitlin. All she knew was that she did not like the name and did not like the dream.

After sitting on the bathroom floor for almost fifteen minutes, Alexa had calmed herself enough to go back to bed. It was, after all, just a dream. Within ten minutes of laying her head on the pillow, she was fast asleep.

Bianca questioned Alexa about what happened the next morning at breakfast as she sat slowly eating her toast, but Alexa waved off Bianca's concerns. She had had too many nightmares to let them disturb her day. The dream did not even cross her mind until, at a quarter to three the next morning, it returned, again forcing her from her bed as she threw up the small contents of her stomach.

This time Alexa did not go back to bed. She did not go to bed the next night either. The prospect of another nightmare, and the consequential excursion to the bathroom, was just too daunting. It did not make any difference. Falling asleep where she sat at her desk, her peace was shattered hours later by the menacing shadowy voice calling her Caitlin as he reached out for Bethany. The effect on her body was the same as it had been the previous two nights. When her body had calmed down, Alexa showered to wake herself up and stayed in the bathroom with the light on until the sun rose, not daring to close her eyes again, irrespective of how tired she was.

However, no matter how Alexa tried to keep herself awake each night, exhaustion eventually found her, and when it did, so did her nightmare. Every single time, it tore her from her sleep and sent her scurrying to the bathroom.

"I hope you don't mind me saying so, but, Alexa, you look really bad," said Chad at dinner.

"That's because she keeps having nightmares and won't go to sleep," said Bianca.

"How often are you having the nightmares?" asked Sam, with a worried look on his face.

"Every night at the moment," replied Alexa in a tired voice. It was getting harder and harder to stay awake during the day, let alone to avoid sleeping at night.

"I don't think you should try and stop sleeping," said Sam, stroking her face gently in a way that made her instantly drowsy. "You have to remember that they're just dreams. They can't hurt you. In the end the dream comes from your own mind so you can stop them if you try hard enough.

"I used to have nightmares as a kid. That's what my dad told me and I never had a problem after that. It took a little while, but now I know when I'm about to have a nightmare and I can change the dream or wake myself up if I have to."

"I didn't know you had nightmares," Alexa replied, her eyes snapping open with amazement.

"You're not the only person who has nightmares," smiled Sam. "People have them all the time. Don't read too much into it. I get that they're probably really scary, but they are just dreams. Nothing can happen to you."

"So you don't think there's anything wrong with me?" asked Alexa hopefully.

"Well," smiled Sam, before laughingly taking her hand and continuing on more seriously. "No, you're just overreacting to it all. Dreams are dreams. If you don't want to have them, then don't. It's your mind. All you have to do is take control of it."

That night Alexa went to bed with fresh hope. She did not need to fear her dreams. She needed to control them. There was no reason to fear her nightmare now more than she ever had just because it had changed slightly. It was always changing. She would deal with whatever her mind threw at her.

So when, at one-nineteen, the nightmare returned and shook her from her sleep, Alexa fought hard against her body's natural reaction. Though her stomach rolled over sickeningly, she did not vomit. She held on to the bed and took many deep breaths until her heart started to beat at a normal pace again. Although it took many long moments for sleep to find her, she did not fight against it. She let herself sleep.

Chapter Fourteen

OVER THE NEXT week, Alexa slowly fought back against her nightmares and by the next weekend they were all but gone. However, although she was no longer troubled by them, it was one of the first things Ben mentioned when he came to see her on Saturday.

"Bethany says you're having nightmares again," said Ben, as she sat down in Mr Knight's office.

Alexa was annoyed by the topic of conversation, but it was a relief to know that Bethany was reading her letters, even if she was not replying to them, and cared enough to set Ben on her.

"I was, but they're going away. I'm not worried about them any more," replied Alexa dismissively, wanting to turn the conversation towards Bethany.

Ben looked sceptically at her, as did Mr Knight. She wondered what it would take for them to trust her word.

"You're not worried about dreams that make you throw up?" asked Ben.

"I was, but I'm not any more," Alexa replied firmly. "They're just dreams. I can make them go away and that's what I'm doing."

"So you're not having the nightmares any more?" asked Ben disbelievingly.

"No. I told you they're going away and I don't want to think more about them," she answered through gritted teeth, annoyed that Ben would not take the hint the way he usually did. "Why don't you tell me about what's happening in my sister's case?"

Ben seemed uneasy at the question and turned away from her, facing out the window to look over the grounds.

"There hasn't been much progress. The police are preparing a case against your sister and it should be in court within a few months. It's just a matter of waiting."

"How's my sister?"

The bitterness was evident in Alexa's voice as she spoke, and Ben's head dropped slightly as he answered.

"She's holding up well. At the moment she's more worried

about you," he replied with a hint of a smile.

"No one has to worry about me. I can look after myself. I want to see my sister. I don't care whether you think I can handle it or not."

"I'll see what I can do. Your holidays begin next week, don't they?" asked Ben, but Alexa had the feeling he was just saying that to appease her.

"Yes," she growled, trying to keep her frustrations under control.

"I will see what I can do," nodded Ben.

Ben left without looking at her, and Alexa did not care. She was sick of being stuck at school, knowing nothing, as Bethany sat in gaol. Mr Knight waited for a minute after Ben left before talking.

"He's just looking out for your interests," said Mr Knight, as Alexa sat in a huff. She did not answer, but shot him a scathing look. "Why are you so against people trying to help you?"

"Because they don't know how to. She's my sister. I have a right to see her. I can look after myself. I don't need anyone's help."

"So do you really have your nightmares under control?" asked Mr Knight, changing the subject, but not to one she wanted to talk about.

"Yes," she cried angrily. "I'm no longer scared of the name Caitlin and he's stopped calling me that."

"Caitlin? Who's calling you Caitlin? Why?" asked Mr Knight, looking concerned and confused.

"Doesn't matter," Alexa huffed, crossing her arms as she silently cursed herself for speaking so much. It was sometimes hard to remember what Mr Knight did not know about her.

"Glad you're handling it," Mr Knight said with a soft smile, not pursuing his previous question. He just held her gaze until her anger started to melt away and a small smile broke across her face. "That's better."

Alexa was glad he could make her smile. It would make the next conversation and the stand she was going to make that much easier. Not bothering with the preamble, she made her demands.

"You want to go to another foster family?" asked Mr Knight, sounding as concerned as he did surprised. "Why? I mean, I can look into it, but you're eighteen. This was actually always going to be a problem."

"You mean I can't leave?" asked Alexa, her voice breaking.

"Alexa, what's going on?"

"I'm not going to be stuck here – trapped here – when I don't have to be," she replied forcefully.

"Is this about being able to see your sister?" asked Mr Knight, guessing the truth.

"If I'm not here, no one can stop me seeing Bethany," Alexa answered, deciding against denying it. "I won't be stopped from seeing her. I don't care if you keep me here. I will see her."

Mr Knight did not answer immediately. He looked hard at her, speaking his words carefully.

"If being able to see your sister was not an issue, would you still want to leave these holidays? Would you still want to be placed with another family?" Alexa folded her arms, refusing to answer. She did not want to slip through some hidden loophole. "I'm on your side, Alexa. Please, just tell me if this is all about your sister or if you really want to be placed with another family for the holidays."

"I want to see Bethy," she answered in a determined voice.

"Then I will take you, every day if I have to," replied Mr Knight just as firmly. "If Ben won't, I will."

"You would do that?" asked Alexa, astounded by the offer.

Mr Knight moved around from his desk and pulled up a chair next to her. Alexa thought he was about to take her hand, but he left his hands clasped in front of him as he leaned forward.

"I will do whatever you need me to. Do you understand, Alexa? I'm here for you. I'm on your side. I don't want you putting yourself in situations like this – prepared to put yourself in with another strange family for the sole purpose of running away to see your sister. You would've been uncomfortable and distrustful."

"I don't care," Alexa cried, annoyed that he did not understand that. "You think she's not worth that? You think I couldn't put up with that? That's nothing."

"Maybe, but you shouldn't have to. It's not all or nothing. It's not all for you or all for Bethany," replied Mr Knight calmly, but she did not understand. "My point is that you need to stop feeling like you need to sacrifice everything for your sister – not when there are other options.

"Trust me. I want to help you. If the best I could have done in this situation was get you into a foster home so you could see your sister, then I would've, but I can offer you more than that. You just have to learn to come to me first."

"I did!" answered Alexa, waving her hand between them. "I did come to you. Otherwise I would've just run away. I did what you asked."

"Not quite," replied Mr Knight with a smile, which made Alexa scowl. "You came to me with an ultimatum. You weren't really looking for my help."

"I didn't want you to think I wasn't serious."

Mr Knight nodded, his lips pursed. Alexa was a little annoyed that he still thought she had not asked him for help.

"You did do what I asked," he finally conceded. "But I get the feeling you only did it because you were sure you had a back-up plan. It's fine," he added before she could argue against that truth. "I just want you to think about what I said. I'm here for you. When all this is over, when you've finished school, you're going to find a whole lot of situations that you don't know how to cope with.

"What I'm asking you to do is trust me, trust that I can help you without judging you. You get stuck somewhere in the middle of the night, I will pick you up. You get stuck with no money, I can lend you some. You need to know how to change a tyre or bake a cake, I will teach you. Understand?

"Big. Small. It doesn't matter. You're not an idiot. You're not useless, but there are lots of simple, normal things that you've never had the chance to experience. Those are the things that worry me. I don't want you to throw your future away because of bad decisions and trying to cope with everything on your own."

"I know how to bake a cake," replied Alexa with a slight smirk.

"Know how to change a tyre?"

Alexa grinned and shook her head. Mr Knight smiled as he rose and moved back to his desk. He stopped suddenly, his body tense.

"I would do all that and not expect anything in return," he said seriously, turning to face her. "When I said I would do anything you needed, I meant it. I would do anything. Even leave you alone. You're not indebted to me. Nothing's set in stone. You get to choose your future and I will do whatever I have to, to make sure you get what you want, even if it's not – even if you change your mind."

Alexa decided not to tell Mr Knight that she had not changed her mind about being with him next year or that she did not want to change her mind. No one had ever given her the freedom to make her own decisions before, and she loved him more for giving her that choice.

That conversation and the promises it entailed was what made the last week of term not just bearable, but almost exciting. The whole grade was in an exuberant mood and Alexa was able to be almost as happy. This would be their last week of classes before their exams, their last week of high school classes ever. It was an exciting transition, though Alexa's reasons for wanting school and time in general to pass were very different to her peers.

With the promise of seeing Bethany in a week, and then hopefully forever, Alexa found herself thinking more of the future and her life outside of school. However, that brought with it the one event she had been trying her hardest not to think about since it happened – their lottery win.

Alexa could not help but feel slightly anxious about claiming it now that she knew Ben. She knew that he had the right to it as much as they did, but did not want to tell him about it. Bethany might be in gaol, but she would not be there forever. If her court case was not until next year, Alexa would need all the money she had for the legal defence. Not a cent would be spared when it came to Bethany's freedom.

"Listen," Alexa said to Bianca and Ezra, as they copied Mr Pollock's notes from the board. "We need to discuss something before we get too preoccupied by study."

"The money," said Bianca excitedly, making Alexa smile slightly. If Bianca or Ezra had said the same thing to her, she doubted her mind would have flicked so quickly to this topic.

"Yeah," Alexa confirmed for Ezra's sake, who looked slightly more puzzled by the conversation. "Ezra's going to be eighteen in the middle of the finals. So either we collect it when she turns eighteen as we originally planned, or we wait until we all finish."

They all quickly looked at each other, trying to read each other's thoughts before voicing their own opinion. It was clear no one wanted to be on the outer when it came to decisions about the money. Alexa hoped Ezra would be on her side, and realised she really should have tested the waters with her first.

"I know we've waited a long time for this," Alexa said tentatively. "And there've been times when we've just wanted to try and send Bianca to get the money, but we have the rest of our lives to spend this money. If we claim it in the middle of the finals it'll only be a distraction."

"I agree," said Ezra immediately, allowing Alexa to sigh with relief.

"So do I," Bianca concurred, though none too convincingly. "I just it wish we could have though. You're right, it would be a massive distraction, but it would be a really fun one."

"We all finish with biology, right?" asked Alexa. Bianca and Ezra both nodded in agreement. "So fourth of November it is then. The first day of the rest of our lives."

They all grinned stupidly. Bianca, sitting in the middle, pulled them all into a hug, squealing excitedly and drawing Mr Pollock's condemnation.

Alexa could not feel Bianca's excitement. This was just one more piece to her puzzle. She knew she had more pieces than she ever had before, but she still had to find a way of putting them together to make a pretty picture. Right now the picture was not as bleak as it had been, but it was still a shambles – a ruined city she was not sure she really had the skills to rebuild.

Walking past Mr Knight's room on the way to the library, Alexa could not stop her feet from slowing. She really could not afford to spend a couple of peaceful hours chatting to him, but her heart still reached out to him. The door was ajar and she craned her neck to gain one tiny glimpse of him. Sometimes that little peak could get her through the whole day.

That was when she saw Ben stride across the office. His frame was so familiar that Alexa did not need more than a glance to recognise him.

"What's going on?" cried Alexa half in fear and half in fury, as she burst into the office. Ben was startled by her sudden arrival and Mr Knight looked between them with concern. "What the fuck's going on?"

Ben moved swiftly past her and shut the door. When he turned to face her, her whole body began to shake. She could not describe the look on his face, but she knew whatever news he brought was bad.

"Bethany was sentenced today," said Ben gravely.

"What? But you said –"

"She pleaded guilty to the charges and was sentenced today," continued Ben over the top of her. Alexa felt her legs weaken as she shook her head disbelievingly. "She was sentenced to four years with eighteen months non-parole period."

"No, no, no!" Alexa cried, rushing forward and pounding her fists against Ben's chest. "You were supposed to help her. You promised me! Why'd you let this happen? I would've testified. I would've defended her."

"I know," answered Ben vehemently, grabbing her by the arms

and pushing her back so he could look into her eyes. "We both knew. Bethany didn't want you to testify. She wanted to take responsibility for herself and her actions."

Alexa backed away from Ben, her face streaked with tears, until she was pressed up against the wall.

"That's why you didn't tell me what was going on?" Alexa spat accusingly. Ben nodded slowly. "Did you know?" she asked, turning her gaze to Mr Knight.

"Yes," answered Mr Knight in a soft voice, his head bowed.

"I'm sorry that I had to do this to you, Alexa," said Ben, when she just stood in silent shock. "But your sister made her up mind and I had to decide whose trust I was going to break. I thought you were in the better position to handle the betrayal."

"So Bethy trusts you?" asked Alexa, wiping the tears from her face.

"Trust is not something Bethany lacks. I told her you sent me to look after her and that was all she needed to know. She trusts you with her life."

"Then why didn't she let me help her?" cried Alexa. "You should never have let her decide that! I'm the older one. I'm the one who's responsible for her. I could've defended her. I would've stopped this. If you'd let me explain, they would've known it was not her fault."

"You wanted to stand up in court and take the blame for all of this?" asked Ben. "The break and enter, the assault and the shooting?"

"It was my fault!" cried Alexa painfully. "I came here! I left her! I went with Leo. I –"

"Alexa, don't you dare –"

"– let go of the gun. I didn't protect her."

"Damn it, Alexa," yelled Ben, grabbing her roughly to try and make her look at him, but she pushed him away angrily.

"This was not all your fault," said Mr Knight in a soothing voice.

"And it was Bethany's?" Alexa asked spitefully. "She's fifteen! I was responsible for her. I let her down. She has known no better life and it's my fault."

Ben moved towards Alexa and though she backed away he managed to grab her and pull her into an embrace. Alexa could not stop herself from curling up in his arms as she sobbed uncontrollably into his chest. Her legs weakened with the pain tearing at her heart. He held her tight to stop her from collapsing.

"You're right. This was not all Bethany's fault, but it wasn't yours either," said Ben in a thick voice as he held her tighter. "You are not responsible for the life the two of you have suffered. But it was Bethany who pulled that trigger. She was going to be punished for that. She knew you would have probably got her off, but was scared about where that would leave her – and you. Bethany made her decision because she wanted to do what was best for you."

"I don't care what's best for me," sobbed Alexa. "She's in gaol. We had to think about her. I thought you knew that. I thought you understood. You didn't do what I asked."

Ben did not reply. He sighed, but said nothing as he continued to hold her. It took almost five minutes for Alexa to compose herself. Ben sat her down in the chair and handed her fistfuls of tissues to wipe her tear-streaked face.

"Bethany wanted me to give you these," he said, handing her a stack of letters; replies to every one of hers. "She wants you to read this one first." He handed her another envelope, cupping her head gently with his hand. "I'll be back to see you on the weekend. Bethany is desperate to see you."

"You'll take me to see her?" Alexa asked disbelievingly.

"Yes, Mr Knight will organise it for you," replied Ben sincerely, though his voice was still very grave. Alexa looked up at Mr Knight, who nodded in agreement. "I'll let you read your letters. My number's there for you as well in case you need to contact me."

Alexa nodded as she watched Ben leave. She was not sad to see him go. Although she trusted him and needed him, she was disappointed in him. When he was gone, she looked down at the envelope he had given her. Her hands shook as she slowly pulled out the letter. Dried tears stained the page, smudging the child-like handwriting.

I'm so sorry Lex. I've had so much time to think in here. All I do is think. I wish I could say sorry forever for everything. I'm sorry I kept everything from you. I knew you would do everything to help me, no matter what happened to you. I couldn't let you.

All you've ever done is protect me and you always suffer so much. This time I had to protect you. I have to face the world and it's so hard without you. All I wanted was to write and see you, so you would come rescue me the way you always do. Knew you would. You always defend me, say these things aren't my fault. You think it's your fault. It's not. This time it's all my fault.

This time I wanted to do best by you. I need to pay for my sins. Not you. But I'm so scared Lex. I don't want to be here. But I have to be to keep you where you have to be. I wish you were here. I can face anything when I'm with you. You never let anything happen to me. I'm scared without you. But I want to be strong like you. I'm glad you're my sister. I'm going to make it all up to you. I need you to promise me you won't think about me. I'm OK. You need to finish school and do good on your tests.

I love you so much.
Your Angel

Alexa's tears fell silently on the letter, blending with Bethany's dried ones. She was so happy to hear from Bethany, but the pain of their separation rose quickly to the surface. Her sister was back. She was no longer the foreign drug addict who she could not reason with. Bethany was back and Alexa wanted to be with her so badly it felt as though her chest would tear apart with the pain.

"Are you all right?" asked Mr Knight, his voice soft and gentle.

Alexa wiped the tears from her face and handed him the letter. She watched his face closely as he read it, looking for any signs that he would not be able to accept Bethany in his life. It would not make her stop loving him, but it would keep them apart.

"You see," she said when Mr Knight handed her back the letter. "She's not a bad person."

"No, I know that. I never really thought she was. But she has done some very bad things."

"So have I," Alexa muttered, gathering Bethany's letters and rushing to the door. They were something she had to read in private. When she reached the door, she turned back, suddenly panicked that she could not trust anyone's word any more. "You promise I'll get to see her this weekend?"

"I promise, Alexa," nodded Mr Knight solemnly. "If Ben doesn't keep his promise, I'll keep mine."

***

It was difficult for Marcus to remember sometimes that he was the year advisor to an entire grade and not just one student. The amount of time he had dedicated to Alexa over the past eighteen months was incredible. Since Easter he felt like she was his entire workload and he could only imagine how terrible his lessons had been this year.

It would not have surprised him if his students had petitioned to have him sacked, so he could not helped but be amazed by how supportive they had been. More than once his students had randomly told him what a good year advisor he had been and how wonderful he was. It was a sad indication of just how little the school had invested into the grade, because he knew had had not done a good job. However, their incredible support did make him very proud of them; and himself, for having had the faith to take them on in the first place.

There had been plenty of issues and dramas to deal with besides Alexa, the G7 and the cheating scandal. Thankfully, next to Alexa they had all felt easily solvable. With Alexa around, there was always a good dose of perspective when it came to the other students' problems, though Marcus tried not to dismiss his students' issues too easily. It was not fair to compare people to Alexa. He never wanted anyone else to suffer the way she had.

Looking at the vacant chair in front of his desk, Marcus could not stop thinking about Alexa. He loved her, so much, but as the days counted down, he felt a better part of him emerging. He would meet her on New Years' Day, but he would no longer let himself believe that them being together was the inevitable consequence of that meeting. Alexa's life, in so many ways, was starting to get back on track. He had no right to derail that, but he also knew that she did not yet have the support she needed to make healthy decisions.

There was still a role for him in Alexa's life, and he was grateful for that fact. He could help her and he wanted to. He wanted Alexa to be happy, and knew she could be. There was only one thing that still really concerned him – where Alexa would go once she left Redgrove. He had spoken to Alexa's social worker after her demand to be placed in a foster home for the holidays. There was assistance available, but not the support he thought she really needed.

There had to be another solution and Marcus knew it could not involve him. Even if they did become involved next year, them living together was not a suitable progression. Alexa needed someone who could be a parent to her, not a lover. However, it still took three goes to complete the phone call – three attempts at trusting someone to be involved in Alexa's welfare.

"Ben, hi," said Marcus, his heart stammering as he resisted the urge to hang up. "It's Marcus Knight from Redgrove College. I need to talk to you about Alexa."

It took a few minutes for Marcus to convince Ben nothing was wrong before he could actually explain why he was calling. He was really not convinced that this was the right course of action, but he had seen Alexa with Ben. She trusted him. She let him hug her. Ben knew her. He was a police officer. If he could not trust Ben Shepard then he could not trust anyone.

"You spoken to Alexa about this?" asked Ben cautiously after Marcus had explained Alexa's impending housing predicament and that idea that Ben could take her in when she finished her exams.

"No," confessed Marcus, rubbing his face. "I don't want her worrying about it during her exams. I don't want her worried about being indebted to you. I know it's not fair to be organising her life behind her back like this, but I worry about how she'll twist it if we give her too much time to think about it."

"When does she finish?" asked Ben.

"November four – but Sam, her best friend, he finishes the next day. She'd want to be here for that."

"And if she won't come with me?"

"She will. She won't want to stay here. But if she's worried, I can make sure she can stay until she's comfortable," said Marcus, though he knew that would not be as easy as it sounded, not with Mrs Taylor determined to make Alexa's life at the school as difficult as possible. "Just make it out as if you're not doing it for her – her benefit is consequential. Make it about her sister and she'll do anything."

"Okay," agreed Ben. "I'll be in touch."

Marcus buried his head in his hands, wishing he did not know Alexa so well. It was sickening how easy she was to manipulate. Know her weaknesses and she became a puppet, forced to do your bidding. It made him glad for the knock at his door and the reminder that, this week in particular, he had a whole grade he needed to show his appreciation of.

It all culminated on the last day of term, with him organising a breakfast for the entire year twelve to celebrate their achievements. It was an elaborate feast that had been quite successfully thrown together at the last moment. He had actually spent quite a bit of time thinking about it earlier in the year, but Alexa had forced him to forget all his plans that did not revolve around her.

The response of the grade to his gesture again surprised him. Marcus had been sure they would see through it and resent him for the little he had done for them, but the level of appreciation from the grade was humbling. They really were the most amazing students and he could not help but wonder why no other teacher had devoted any time to get to know them.

"I would just like to say a few words to you all," said Marcus, standing up from the table where he was seated with a group of girls from his geography class. "I want to congratulate you all on making it this far. It's really a great achievement and you should all be very proud of yourselves, because I am very proud to have been your year advisor for these two years."

The applause from the students could have lifted the roof. They smiled giddily as they clapped and cheered. It made Marcus wonder if they had ever been praised by the school before.

"I think we need to thank you as well," said Sam, standing up on his seat. "No other year advisor has ever believed in us or even really wanted to take us on. You took us on for two years and we didn't make them the easiest. So, on behalf of all of us, I would all like to say thank you for sticking with us. We really do appreciate it."

Sam bowed dramatically to Marcus, who was glowing in the praise as the grade took to its feet in applause. Marcus remained standing as their applause died down and they resumed their seats.

"Thank you, Mr Michaels," said Marcus, smiling brightly. "These last two years have been amazing, but today is all about you guys."

"Before you get to us, I should probably say my own thank you," said Alexa, slowly rising to her feet.

Alexa's head was bowed and she would not meet Marcus's eyes. She barely looked up from the table, where her finger was scribbling anxiously. Marcus was concerned about what she would say and what people would construe, but mostly he could not believe she would publicly thank him. He had done so much to hurt her.

"You've done more for me than anyone else and I just thought that should be acknowledged, especially the part where you saved my life. So thanks."

Alexa's words ran into each other at the end with their haste to be spoken and she sat down quickly as everyone switched their gazes back and forth between her and him.

"I would have done the same for anyone," replied Marcus with a cough. "But thank you, Miss Samson. That means a lot."

It meant more than that. Marcus could not imagine what that would have cost Alexa. She was not a public speaker and he knew she had barely spoken two words in class since her return to school. Alexa did not look his way again during breakfast, and he tried to avoid looking over at her, but whenever he happened to look her way, he noticed her sitting quietly with her hand around the sapphire pendant she wore. He both hoped and feared that she knew it was from him.

***

From breakfast, the grade moved jovially to the hall. Alexa held back and slipped off to the oval. She had no intention of going back into that hall, especially not to sit through an assembly.

"What are you doing?" called Sam, standing across the oval with Ezra, Bianca, Lizzie and Chad.

Alexa did not answer, but waited as he ran over to her.

"I don't feel like going to assembly," she replied when Sam stood in front of her, his arms folded and his eyebrows raised expectantly. "I can't be bothered listening to Mrs Taylor pretend she's sad to see us go."

"I know why you don't want to go and it's got nothing to do with Mrs Taylor. Come on, Alexa, you have to face it some time."

"Actually, I don't," Alexa smiled, loving that that was true. "I don't have to go today and I've asked to do my exams in that room again. I never have to set foot in that place again."

"If you don't face it, how are you ever going to move on?" asked Bianca, as the rest of the group arrived.

"Quite easily," Alexa replied simply.

"Well, you're going to have to deal with it, because I'm not going without you," said Ezra defiantly.

"That suits me fine," replied Alexa with a genuine smile.

"I actually have to go," said Lizzie in a slightly despairing voice.

"Come on, Alexa," pleaded Chad. "Sam will hold your hand."

"How's that going to entice me?" Alexa retorted playfully.

"Fine, I will hold your hand. I know you've been waiting six long years for the offer," smiled Chad.

Alexa could not help but smile as he held out his hand to her. It was juvenile, but the way Bianca's eyes widened at Chad's offer was the only thing that allowed her to take his hand. She did not want to go into that hall, but goading Bianca just a little was kind of fun. By the way Chad pulled her closer and chuckled in her ear, she had the feeling he was enjoying riling Bianca as well.

The hall was full when they arrived. Alexa kept her head bowed as she entered, not noticing Mrs Taylor's scorn or Mr Knight's surprise. She was more focused on the panic attack that was threatening to take hold of her body. Her breath quickened with her pulse and her muscles ached, trying to control the trembling in her body. Chad glanced over to Sam with a worried look, before releasing her into his arms. Sam guided her to a seat and wrapped his arm around her shoulders, whispering soothingly in her ear.

"Welcome, everyone, to this very special day," said Mrs Taylor, trying unsuccessfully to conceal her relieved delight. "I, like the year twelves, have been waiting eagerly for this day to arrive for quite some time now. Next year will certainly be a lot quieter without you here, though I am sure there are some who will miss your antics. However, you have all made it this far and that should be congratulated. We would also like to wish you all the best of luck for the upcoming finals."

Mrs Taylor continued to praise and ridicule them in equal measure for fifteen minutes, before her biting speech was followed by farewells from each of the grades below. Then it was Mr Knight's turn. His arrival on the stage prompted a rowdy reception, which became only louder when he pronounced, once again, how proud he was to have been their year advisor.

The final speeches belonged to Nick and Lizzie, who were responsible for thanking the school on behalf of the grade. Lizzie was sweet and sincere in her thanks. Alexa could not help but be amazed at what a genuinely nice person Lizzie was and wondered if her life would have been better if she was as nice as Lizzie.

Then Nick spoke. Nick did not try to hide his lack of appreciation for how their grade had been perceived and treated by the school. It was much more in line with Alexa's sentiments, and made her feel a little more normal than Lizzie's speech had.

"We've got a few more year advisors than the average grade to thank," said Nick, with a large smile on his face as he went on and listed the mediocre achievements of their first four year advisors. "To all of you, our grade would like to thank you for not bothering to invest any faith in us as students or people. I can tell you, it did the world of good for our self-esteems.

"This leads us to Mr Knight who, despite all the trials and tribulations of this year and last, has stood by us. He has stood up for us and supported us. He has been there for us whenever we've had a problem – big or small, day or night. For all of that, and everything else you have done, we would like to thank you. Thank you for showing faith in us. Thank you for believing in us when the rest of the school had turned its back on us. Thank you."

The back of the hall stood in rapturous applause for well over a minute, cheering not only Mr Knight, but also Nick's brave speech. When the applause died down, Lizzie headed off the stage followed by Nick, but halfway across the stage he turned around and headed back to the microphone.

"Sorry, I forgot. Just one last thank you," said Nick with a sly smile. "To Mrs Taylor, thank you for all the support you've shown our grade, especially the G7, as you liked to call us. I just hope that you have new scapegoats ready to go, because we won't be here next year and you may finally realise that we were never responsible for half the things you wanted to blame us for."

The hall gasped in horror. No one had ever been so up front or insulting to Mrs Taylor, except possibly Alexa, but never in public. Even Alexa was surprised by Nick's gall. Nick smiled and left the stage to a rousing reception from the other G7 members, who all stood up on their chairs to show their support. As Alexa cheered from the top of her chair, she saw Mr Knight's worried face follow Nick back to his seat. It was clear he was not happy that he might have to again save one of his students from expulsion.

"That was awesome," said Chad, as they made their way over to Nick after assembly.

"Thanks," said Nick, with a broad smile. "I thought it was time someone set the record straight."

"Too right," said Alexa.

"I just can't believe Mrs Taylor didn't say anything," said Sam.

"I think she was just too stunned," smiled Alan.

"I think she's saving it all up for later," said Mr Knight, breaking into the little circle they had formed. "That was not the smartest thing you could have done, Mr Poulos."

"Yeah, but it was all the truth," replied Nick with an unapologetic shrug of his shoulders.

"One version of it. You failed to mention all the trouble you lot *have* caused throughout those years," countered Mr Knight.

"We wouldn't have caused any of that trouble if they didn't blame us for everything anyway," said Sam.

"Come on, Sir, you know we'd never have been like that if we'd had you from the start," said Chad. "Troubled students are different to troublesome students."

Alexa felt everyone's eyes involuntarily turn her way. Her eyes flicked down to avoid their gaze. She was not really sure how any of the other four would be classified as troubled, or troublesome for that matter. Compared to her, everyone else was an angel.

"I still think it was a stupid thing to do, especially because I now have to listen to Mrs Taylor rant and rave at me for the next hour," smiled Mr Knight, clapping Nick on the back before walking off towards Mrs Taylor's office. "Think of me next time if I'm such a great year advisor," he called over his shoulder.

They all laughed, though Alexa could not help but sigh. That was the first time she had viewed Mr Knight as wholly teacher-like in a long time and it sat strangely with her. She did not want to be involved with a teacher. Grasping her pendant, she thought about Marcus – just a guy who had the remarkable ability of being able to love her.

That afternoon was one of celebration and relaxation for the year twelves as they tried to shut out the knowledge that this was their last moment of freedom for almost two months. As Alexa lay on the oval with Sam, Chad, Bianca and Lizzie, she tried to properly contemplate her life after school.

Things had been turned upside down with Bethany's arrest and conviction. There was no more rush to save Bethany from the streets. There was no one for her to take care of. For the first time, Alexa was free to think of herself; and she had not the first clue what to do.

It was a very different world to the one she had been expecting. Despite knowing of the financial windfall that was waiting for her, Alexa had never been able to give it much thought, because she knew she would have spent every single cent of it getting Bethany off the streets and off heroin. There had been no reason to plan. Plans never worked out when it came to Bethany.

Alexa was suddenly faced with the opportunity to decide what she wanted to do, but it was a useless proposition. All she had ever wanted was to be free, have a clean Bethany in her life and be happy. Even Marcus was an afterthought to all that.

That was when Alexa realised just how much eight million dollars was and that, for now, with just herself to look after, it seemed like an excessive amount of money. To truly secure her and Bethany's future, she had to know how to manage all that money so that, no matter what happened, they would always be provided for.

A new plan started forming in Alexa's mind. It was not grand by anyone else's standards, but it gave her direction and purpose for the first time in many, many months.

***

Alexa woke early on Sunday, unable to sleep with the anticipation of seeing Bethany. Trying not to wake the others, who had been up late the night before studying, she showered and dressed quietly before leaving for breakfast. There was no one in the dining hall when she arrived so she sat down and made herself some toast. By seven she could sit still no longer, so she walked around the oval and paced the quadrangle.

"Nervous?" asked Mr Knight, as he leant against one of the walls surrounding the quad.

"I just can't wait. I can't sit still and no one else is awake yet."

"Why don't you come and wait in my office. I'll make you some tea. It might help to calm you down."

Once inside Mr Knight's office, Alexa felt a small wave of calmness flow over her. It was not enough to allow her to sit and stop pacing, but she at least knew that Ben would arrive in just under three hours.

"Are you worried about today?" asked Mr Knight, handing her a cup of tea.

"Why would I be worried?" asked Alexa, genuinely confused by the question.

"You were about to wear a ditch into the concrete with the way you were pacing."

"I just want to go. I don't want to wait. Why would I ever be worried about seeing my sister?"

Mr Knight raised a bemused eyebrow as he sat down.

"I think I'd be a bit nervous about seeing my sister if the last time we met she held a gun to my head."

"That wasn't the same person. She's so different when she's clean. She's amazing."

"I think you're the amazing one."

Crimson filled Mr Knight's cheeks and Alexa gave him an embarrassed smile.

"You don't know how drugs change people. They're still there, but it's like they can't break through the façade that the drugs build up in front of them," explained Alexa, hoping Mr Knight understood.

"Bethany's lucky to have a sister like you. There aren't many people who'd be so understanding."

"It's amazing how understanding you can be when you love someone."

Mr Knight looked down and nodded solemnly. It made Alexa wonder what he was thinking, if it was about her and if he perhaps regretted liking someone like her. She did not know what would happen between them next year, and was not naïve enough to believe in happily ever afters, but she knew she would always love him for being the first person to like her in the face of every imaginable obstacle.

By the time Ben arrived, Alexa was sitting down calmly in the chair drinking her second cup of tea. Being with Mr Knight was so natural and easy that she had not even noticed the time go by.

"Are you good to go?" asked Ben as he entered.

"Yeah," replied Alexa. Pushing her half-drunken tea on to Mr Knight's desk, she was at the door in a flash. "Let's go."

"Do you want to clean that up first?"

Alexa turned around to see her cup on the floor and the tea quickly soaking into the carpet.

"Oh shit, I'm sorry."

"Don't worry, I'll clean it up. You two go," said Mr Knight, walking out from his bedroom with a towel.

"Are you sure?"

"Go."

Alexa smiled up at Mr Knight, catching his gaze and wondering if she could really be this lucky. The desire to kiss him was building in her body and she could see his eyes glowing with the same yearning. At that moment the world could have collapsed around them and they would not have noticed. Indeed, for that moment, they completely forgot that Ben was even in the room.

"We should get going," said Ben, taking her by the hand.

Alexa felt her heart stop. Mr Knight's face looked horrified as he quickly crouched down to clean up the tea.

Ben did not say anything as they walked to the car, and by the time they had driven out of the school Alexa's thoughts had turned completely to Bethany. Ben, however, was less able to forget what he had seen.

"Alexa, I think you need to be careful. I know that you get along with Mr Knight, but he is your teacher and that's all he should be."

"That's all he is," replied Alexa forcefully.

"Alexa, I was there. I saw the way he looked at you. If I hadn't been there –"

"Nothing would've happened. We would never let anything happen."

"We? What do you mean 'we'?" Ben kept turning with horrified eyes between her and the traffic ahead of them.

"Look, this isn't your concern. I can take –"

"I'm well aware of the fact that you think you can take care of yourself," snapped Ben. "This is serious, Alexa. I would've thought you'd learnt your lesson about getting involved with teachers. My God, they're only after one thing. They're just using you. Don't you understand that?"

"This is none of your business," sighed Alexa. "Who the hell are you anyway? What do you care what I do? My life is none of your business. I don't even know you. I only used you to make sure Bethy was taken care of."

Ben turned off the main road and into a quiet side street, stopping the car and turning off the engine. Alexa's heart began to race. She really did not know Ben at all and now she was alone with him in the car and she had made him angry. This was possibly the biggest mistake she had ever made.

Chapter Fifteen

"I'M NOT ANGRY, Alexa. I'm not going to hurt you," said Ben immediately, as she tried to move inconspicuously away from him. "You don't remember me at all?"

"I told you, I've seen you in my dreams. I never even knew you were real until … until we met."

"And you don't remember what those dreams are about?" asked Ben in a pained voice.

"They're just dreams. They're not real," sighed Alexa, wishing everyone could forget about her nightmares. "Besides, this is not about my dreams. This is about you. Marcus has a reason to care for my welfare. Why do you care what happens to me? What's in it for you?"

"An easing of my conscience, I guess," replied Ben as he slouched over the steering wheel and stared out into the street, watching a past only he remembered.

"I don't remember you. I don't remember what happened and I don't want to. I can't ease your conscience and I can't forgive you. I don't know what you did."

"I never looked out for you the way I should've."

"Why should you have?" asked Alexa, suddenly very scared and curious. "I mean, you're not my father or anything like that, are you?"

"No," replied Ben forlornly, as though he actually regretted that fact. "I'm a police officer. I had a duty to protect you."

"I don't need protection from Marcus."

"You're calling your teacher by his first name. Can't you see the danger you're putting yourself in? He's just using you."

"He's not getting anything from me," Alexa replied firmly.

"I know what I saw!" cried Ben in a frustrated tone.

"He's in love with me. I'm in love with him. That's what you saw," Alexa spat angrily. "It's been that way for a long time, but that's all. He's never touched me and I've never touched him, and as long as I'm his student that's the way it'll stay. I'm not stupid."

"Alexa, this is –"

"Ben, I want to see my sister."

Ben opened his mouth to argue, but just sighed heavily before pulling back on to the main road. Alexa was glad, but feared she had not heard the last of Ben's anger. It made her anxious, something she did not need to be as she continued to scour the skyline for Bethany's prison home.

When it finally came into view, Alexa was surprised that the walls of the juvenile detention centre that kept Bethany from the rest of the world felt somehow less imposing than the ones that kept her in school. The detention centre was more welcoming than she had dared expect. There were bars and barbed wire, but it was not dissimilar to the bars and high fences that surrounded Redgrove College. All in all, Alexa had to reluctantly admit that it was not the worst place Bethany could have been sent. It made her glad Bethany was still a minor. She was sure no adult prison would be even moderately comfortable.

Ben led Alexa through to a large room with many tables and chairs bolted to the floor. Broken families sat around the tables trying hard to cover the pain that burned in all their eyes. Some smiled, some frowned, some shed tears of heartache and desperation. Ben guided Alexa to an empty table next to the wall. He did not sit with her, instead stood leaning against the nearby wall. Within a minute of their arrival, Bethany rushed through a door towards them.

Bethany's embrace was the sweetest thing Alexa had felt in the longest time. She grasped Bethany tight, squeezing her hard, wishing their bodies would fuse together so that they could never be torn apart again. It was not to be. Ben pulled them apart as a guard walked towards them.

"Just keep the physical contact to a minimum," whispered Ben, before stepping away.

Alexa and Bethany sat down at the table, their eyes never breaking contact. Bethany smiled at her as though she had not seen her in years and Alexa knew how Bethany felt. It had been a long time since Bethany's eyes had looked out on the world without drugs tainting her view. Alexa felt her insides burn with more emotion than she had felt in her life. Joy tingled through her heart at the sight of Bethany, while fear and sadness pulled at the strings that held the broken pieces together. This was not the way their lives were supposed to turn out.

"I'm sorry, Lex," said Bethany, wiping away the tears slipping down Alexa's cheeks. "Please don't cry. Please don't cry because of me."

"I'm okay," said Alexa, trying hard to smile, but one look into Bethany's eyes sent a spike of pain through her chest and she lunged forward, pulling Bethany tight into her arms. "Oh, Angel, I thought I lost you. I don't know what I would've done without you. I can't live without you."

Bethany held Alexa as long as the guards let them, before pushing her away and wiping the tears from her face.

"You haven't called me that for a long time," said Bethany sweetly, a hint of nostalgia in her voice.

"That's who you are. My Angel," replied Alexa, trying hard not to break down completely. "You've just been missing for a while."

"I know, but I'm back now and I'm not going anywhere."

The double meaning of that statement struck like a knife, but Alexa tried not to focus on that. There was good to be salvaged from this situation, and while they both lived, they would live for only the good.

They talked for an hour before they went for lunch. It was the one day in the month where visitors were allowed to eat with the inmates. Alexa paid little attention to the food, unable to keep her eyes off Bethany. After lunch, Bethany showed her around parts of the detention centre that had been opened for the day.

"It's not the worst place in the world, I guess," said Bethany, as they sat on a bench in the warm afternoon sunlight. "I was surprised how much it looked like your school. I didn't feel so bad about being here after that. I mean, if you can go to school in a place like that I can survive here for a few years."

"I'll make sure you survive. I'll make sure you have everything you ever need, okay?" replied Alexa immediately.

"I don't want you looking after me, Lex. I need to learn how to stand on my own two feet," countered Bethany just as quickly. "I know you've spent your life protecting me and I'm so grateful. I'm not sure that I could've ever survived everything you've been through, but it's time I faced the world myself."

"Don't shut me out, Bethy, please."

"I'm not shutting you out. I just don't want you standing in front of me, taking all the hits for me, but that doesn't mean that I don't need you by my side. I'm scared as all hell, Lex."

"I will never leave your side. Never," Alexa reassured Bethany firmly.

There was not a chance in the world she would abandon Bethany now. It did not matter what she had to do to be there for her, she would do it. She would sacrifice everything she had for Bethany, but did not say so. Alexa did not care what Bethany or Ben or anyone said. Bethany was her life and no one was going to keep them apart more than the law necessitated.

"So what do they make you do here?" Alexa asked Bethany, turning her gaze away from Ben, who was standing nearby, watching everything they did.

"We have different duties; cleaning, cooking, that sort of thing, but they also educate us as well. I'm finishing year ten and learning a trade as well. They're teaching me woodwork and carpentry," answered Bethany with a small smile. "I'm going to be able to make and build things by the time I get out of here and they said they'd help me get work when I leave, so I can finish my apprenticeship. I'm going to make you proud of me, Lex. I'm going to make me proud of me as well."

Alexa smiled and kissed Bethany on the side of her head.

"I know you will. You'll be the best carpenter in the world," said Alexa, sure that it was true. Bethany had an amazing ability to do whatever she set her sights on – good and bad.

"But what about you? I'm here and I'm making the most of it. What are you going to do?" asked Bethany in a concerned voice. "Are you studying much?"

"I've been too worried about you and then I was too excited about coming to see you," replied Alexa with a dismissive smile.

"Like I said, Lex, I'm really grateful that you care so much, but it's time you cared that much about yourself. I'm okay. What are you going to do at uni?"

"I don't know for sure yet. I was thinking economics or something similar so I knew how to look after us financially – make sure that we'll always have enough money. I just have to find the right course to do that."

"But what do you really want to do?" asked Bethany in a slightly frustrated tone. "Lex, you can't even pick a degree without thinking about me. What about you?"

"I don't know, Bethy. I don't know," cried Alexa, finally telling the truth. "I wouldn't have a clue what I want to do. I don't even belong to the outside world. When was the last time I was really in it? I just want to be able to look after us. That's what will make me happy. I just want to live. I don't care what I do. I want to live. I want to be happy. I want us to be a family again. I don't have any wants or needs beyond that."

"Okay," said Bethany tenderly, placing a calming hand on Alexa's. "But for that you still need to study. I'm not going anywhere. I don't want you to worry about me until you finish. Then you can spend every free moment coming to visit me and I will expect no less," she added, seeing that Alexa was about to protest.

Alexa smiled and brushed Bethany's cheek. It was amazing by how quickly Bethany had grown up, but Alexa supposed gaol would do that. There really was no escape from reality for Bethany now.

"I can't leave you here all alone. You need to see a friendly face occasionally," said Alexa, still determined to have her way.

"You sent me a friendly face," replied Bethany, tilting her head.

"Ben?" asked Alexa, looking over at him and feeling her stomach churn uncomfortably. Ben had kept his distance during the visit and Alexa was glad, though she was now worried that she had trusted him with too much too quickly. "Look, I just wanted someone to make sure you were taken care of after you were arrested. He seemed to know us and I thought I could use him. I don't know that you should rely on him."

"How can you say that?" cried Bethany "You've dreamt about him since we were kids."

"I've see him die. I don't remember him. I don't know him or what that dream's even about."

"But yet you trusted him anyway. You know you did. You would never have sent someone you didn't trust to look after me – even if you were just using them. Has he told you anything about him? About the dreams?"

"No, and I haven't asked," replied Alexa forcefully.

"But he can help you. You can't keep having nightmares, especially ones that make you vomit. Don't you want answers?" urged Bethany.

"No. I don't need any more bad memories," replied Alexa emphatically. "He told you about us, didn't he? It wasn't a happy story, was it?"

"No, it's not," replied Bethany hesitantly. "But it might help you."

"Does it help you to know about our past? To know the things you don't remember?" asked Alexa forcefully.

"Yeah, it does," replied Bethany just as determinedly.

"That's good, Bethy, it really is and I'm glad Ben helps you, but he can't help me."

"You don't know that."

"Yeah, I do. Knowing more about our past is the last thing I want. What I do remember is more than enough."

"Okay, but you sent him to me because you trust him. I trust him because you trust him and he is helping me. I know why you trust him. I won't tell you, but you trust him for a reason, Lex, and I will always trust you."

It was a convoluted explanation, but Alexa understood it, and she was reassured by Bethany's assurances. If Bethany knew why she trusted Ben and believed Ben was worth trusting, she would accept that. It was the best she could do in the determined absence of that knowledge herself.

When the late afternoon arrived, Ben finally walked over to them. They knew what his arrival signalled and they grabbed each other tight. Despite Ben's warnings and urgings, they continued to hold on to one another until they were forced apart by the guards, who started leading Bethany away. Tears streamed down their faces, but they did not brush them away.

"I will write every day, no matter how much study I have. I will write every day, I promise," choked Alexa, having lost the battle over visiting while she was completing her exams.

"I know you will. I'll reply every day," called Bethany, as she walked backwards away from her.

"I love you, Angel," cried Alexa, so glad that Bethany had not tried to talk her out of writing as well.

A smile spread across Bethany's tear-stained face.

"I love you too, Lex."

And then she was gone.

Ben placed a gentle, guiding hand on Alexa's shoulder, but did not speak as he led her to the car. He retrieved a crushed box of tissues from the boot and placed them next to her in the car. She said nothing.

It was a little after six when Ben pulled into the school car park. Alexa's heart deflated slightly at their arrival, but she knew she could withstand the next six weeks. She had a purpose now. She was doing this for Bethany as much as for herself, perhaps even more so, but she was sure she would reap the benefits later.

"I'll walk you back," said Ben, unbuckling his seat belt.

"No, I'll be fine, but thanks," Alexa replied softly, keeping her gaze averted. Back at school, she remembered why she had been so worried about Ben's interference in her life.

"Then take this." Alexa took a small card from Ben's hand and examined it. "You can contact me anytime. No matter what the problem is, big or small, just give me a call and I'll be here in an instant."

"Thanks, but I'll be fine. You just worry about Bethy. You help her. She's the one that needs you more."

Alexa put the card in her pocket and hopped out of the car.

"Alexa," called Ben, turning her around. He was about to speak, but hesitated.

"What, Ben?" she asked, her voice defiant and defensive, hoping to ward off any attacks.

"Good luck – with your exams. I'll come see you when you finish. Take you to see Bethany."

"Thank you," replied Alexa softly, her heart beating again.

Though Alexa was still unsure she could trust Ben, she needed him and she would use him to her own end until she had the means to take care of herself and Bethany without anyone's interference.

Five minutes later she walked into Mr Knight's office. He was at the window looking out over the school grounds. Alexa thought he looked tired, but he smiled warmly when he turned and saw her standing in front of his desk.

"How was your day?" he asked, sitting down.

"It was good, really good. We talked a lot. I'm going to miss her, being here, but it's only for a few more weeks."

"You're not going to see her again?" asked Mr Knight in a surprised voice.

"Not before the end of the finals. She made me promise I'd study and do well," said Alexa, rolling her eyes.

"That sounds wise," replied Mr Knight with a soft smile.

"Maybe, but to do that I need a favour from you as well."

"Anything."

"I don't want to see you before then either. I mean, nothing has changed," Alexa added quickly. "I just can't … I need to block everything out and just concentrate on studying."

"I can do that," nodded Mr Knight with a smile, and Alexa was sure he was even a little relieved. It could not be easy for him doing the wrong thing. "I won't be here again until term begins and after that I'll make sure I avoid you as much as possible."

"Thank you. We also can't risk anyone else finding out. Ben knows and he's not happy."

A worried look spread across Mr Knight's face and he turned ghostly white. He stood from his chair, running both hands agitatedly through his hair.

"Did he cause you too much trouble?" he asked in a shaky voice.

"No, it's okay. I don't think he'll say anything."

"I'm sorry. The last thing I want is to cause more trouble for you."

"And you don't want to lose your job either."

"I love – I'm not worried about my job. I'm not sure it's not what I deserve anyway."

"You haven't done anything wrong," replied Alexa forcefully. "Neither of us have. Nothing will happen. I can assure you of that."

Mr Knight tried to smile, but he seemed not to have the strength. His face was still pale and Alexa could see his arms shaking on top of his head.

"I'm hungry so I'm going to grab some dinner. Have a good holiday, okay. There's no problem, but you needed to know. I'll take care of everything," Alexa smiled, looking deep into Mr Knight's eyes to try and alleviate his panic. He smiled back weakly as she left.

***

The days were long, monotonous and tedious, but Alexa was surprised by how quickly they began to pass by. The first thing she had done on Monday morning was write up a study schedule right up until her last exam. Her time was marked out in three-hour blocks, with slots dedicated to each subject.

Her selection of subjects for her senior years now seemed completely mismatched to her future. She had picked them based on Sam and Ezra's subject choices and the teachers who had given her the least amount of grief. There had never been any thought for her future.

Marking each study block off as she went, Alexa found some satisfaction in the continued progression of time, though the days themselves were still too long. The final hours in each day seemed to drag by until the clock finally ticked over to nine o'clock. That was the time she allowed herself to close her books and write to Bethany.

True to her word, Bethany replied every day. It was the only thing that made the entire process possible. The weekends, and their lack of post, were the longest and most unrewarding. Alexa kept Bethany's letters on her desk in a pile. She did not let herself read them while she was studying, but just being able to look at them and touch them was enough to put her head back down and continue her study. Bethany's letters negated the distance that separated them and made it feel as though they were right by each other's side.

Bethany was always encouraging and supportive. Every letter brought more praise – until the following Monday – when Bethany suddenly wanted a lot more information about her relationship with Mr Knight. Ben and Peter had spent two hours grilling her over what she knew. Bethany had told them everything she had known, but that had apparently not been enough. Alexa was sure Ben had all but written Bethany's letter, so her reply was to him as much as Bethany. Alexa was not sure what Peter would think about the situation.

She was grateful that Bethany had stood up for her and defended her feelings for Mr Knight. She was also relieved that she had told Mr Knight to keep his distance. The resulting letter was thus a truthful recollection of all that had not happened in the past, a mostly truthful summary of the present situation and a somewhat dishonest representation of their planned future interactions.

Hoping her letter would be enough to stave off any problems with Ben over Mr Knight, Alexa slipped between her sheets and closed her eyes, her hand tightly clasped around the pendant hanging loosely from her neck. She tried to imagine where Mr Knight was and hoped he was thinking of her. With his face floating lightly on her pillow and his hand gently stroking her hair, she fell asleep to the warmth of his embrace.

The rest of the holidays passed in a blurry haze. Mr Knight did not quite keep his promise to be away all of the holidays. He returned on the last Thursday to run additional revision classes for his geography students. Alexa knew from Lizzie's comments that he had already spent most of the holidays answering questions on a study page he had set up for them online and would be available during all their regular class times for extra tuition when school resumed.

Mr Knight was not the only teacher going the extra mile for their students. Alexa was surprised by how willing her teachers were to work with her on the things she had missed. They were even friendly and supportive, and it made Alexa question how much of what Mr Knight had done for her had been because he liked her. Part of her was starting to consider it was just because he was a dedicated teacher and would have done the same had he not cared for her at all.

With day after day being marked off her calendar, Alexa was surprised when her first exam was just two days away. Everyone started with English. It was not her favourite subject. She had barely managed to read all the books they were supposed to study, let alone memorise quotes from them, and she had very little faith in her ability to write anything insightful about the poems she was still trying to learn.

Despite this, Alexa found herself less nervous than everyone else as the first exam drew closer. She knew it was partly because she had less to lose. Just passing would be an achievement, though that made her question what she would do if she failed to get the marks required to get into university. She wondered if she could buy a spot with her money.

When the day of her first exam finally came, Alexa dumped her half-eaten breakfast in the bin. The amount of discarded food had suddenly tripled as butterflies filled stomachs instead of toast and cereal.

Alexa gathered with everyone outside the hall. Sam was unusually quiet and stony-faced, while Lizzie bounced around frenetically, speaking at a hundred miles an hour. Bianca fidgeted nervously, as Ezra sat calmly, if a little more quietly than usual. Everyone started to wish each other luck as the start time drew near. Mr Knight walked among them, calming nerves and speaking words of encouragement. Alexa watched him, and though he never seemed to look her way, he still managed to avoid being too close.

With a final wave of good luck, Alexa started moving towards her examination room. She may have survived one assembly in the hall, but did not believe her concentration would survive sitting an examination in that place.

Deep breaths helped to calm her nerves, but it was not until she looked up and saw Mr Knight smiling softly at her that she realised that she was clasping his pendant. He walked towards her and her heart began to pound once more. She wished he could hug her and tell her she would be all right.

"Good luck, Miss Samson," said Mr Knight as he placed his hand on her shoulder and tapped it lightly. "Just take your time and you'll be fine."

With a supportive smile, Mr Knight continued on, his words to Sam and Chad almost identical.

The warmth of Mr Knight's touch helped to propel Alexa forward and into her examination room. Although it was daunting to be alone with just her examiner, Alexa was glad that the examiner was an elderly lady, and she was sure that Mr Knight had arranged for it to be that way. The thought warmed her heart, knowing how much he had done to help her through this.

"You may begin," said the lady formally.

Alexa felt her heart race, making it hard to read the first question properly. With several deep, steadying breaths, her mind started to calm and she began writing.

Time moved in strange ways over the next three hours, crawling and speeding along in unequal measures, but before her time was up, Alexa had managed to complete an answer for all the questions. With ten minutes to spare, she tried to make them better answers, but was relieved when the examiner called for pens down.

"Well done," said the lady kindly.

"Are you going to be here for all my exams?" asked Alexa.

The lady quickly answered in the affirmative. Alexa was not sure why that made her smile or put her at ease, but it was nice to know that she would be met by a familiar face for her next exam.

Ignoring most of the exam chatter at lunch, Alexa headed straight back to her desk when she had finished eating and marked the morning off her calendar. There were now only two and a half weeks to go.

For the first time, Alexa felt like studying had a purpose. She could see the silver lining starting to shimmer around all the clouds and she could not wait to be out amongst them – free.

Every day was now a countdown. A countdown to the next exam, a countdown to the next week, a countdown to the end. There was so much to look forward to. Alexa could not wait for the day that she packed her bags and walked through those large steel gates for the last time.

That exit would lead her to a new world, her own world, where she could see Bethany, live in her own house and even date Marcus. It was the first time she had felt optimistic about anything, and suddenly she was feeling optimistic about everything.

That optimism was dented after her second English exam, but when Alexa crossed it off her calendar she was determined not to think about it again. The focus was now on maths.

There was at least a pleasant rhythm to her maths study. Alexa found some comfort in the consistency and certainty of numbers. It was so different to the vagaries of English. Although the maths exam was hard and there had been two questions she had struggled to answer at all, Alexa was almost buoyant when she finished it. There were now just three more to go.

Alexa had taken up German on a whim. It had been the one daring subject selection in her entire school career. Stacey had been the only person she had known in the class. Lizzie had done it in earlier years, but they had not been friends then and she had dropped it for her senior years.

Having already completed the oral and aural examinations, Alexa was now concentrating on her writing and reading skills. She was not confident. Never able to dedicate the time and effort required to her study, she had always been at the bottom of the class.

When she had mentioned that in the extra tutorials Mr Merkel had given her, he had just told her straight out that someone had to come last.

"May as well be you," said Mr Merkel matter-of-factly. "You never study. But you are also disadvantaged because you never learnt English properly. How can you learn this language when you barely know what a verb is or a conjunction?"

It had not been the most inspirational speech Alexa had ever received, but she could hardly disagree. She had no idea what a conjunction was.

"You want to learn this language?" Mr Merkel had asked seriously. "Then go to Germany. That is how you will learn it. Here you have too many things to worry about. Go there and you will have no choice but to speak it. You will hear it and read it and all you have learned from me will finally make sense."

It was a nice thought, but not one Alexa could indulge in. She could not leave Bethany. She could not run away from her responsibilities and she did not want to walk away from her chance to be with Marcus. Pushing those thoughts to the side, Alexa pulled her textbook towards her and started to translate the passage in front of her.

With expectations fairly low, Alexa was not disappointed with herself when she walked out of the exam. It had been tough, but the things she had not known were the things she had always struggled with and there was never going to have been enough time to build those skills.

It was finally all drawing to a close. Alexa's heart skipped a beat when she crossed off another day and sat to write her letter to Bethany. One week, two exams. The prospect of the end was so exciting at times that Alexa struggled to focus. In a week she would be able to see Bethany. They will have claimed their money and she would be able to start setting up her own life, with her own rules and no one dictating what she should do, when or how.

So close she could almost taste it, Alexa had to almost pretend it would never end just to open her chemistry book. Banishing all other thoughts, she focused solely on chemistry for two days straight, waking on Friday morning with a dampened sense of dread. There was still so much she did not know or understand and it was too late to learn it.

Thankfully, the exam was not as bad as Alexa expected. The big questions had focused on the topics she knew well, helping her to believe that she could make up for all the little questions she could only guess an answer for.

"I can't believe it's almost over," said Bianca, as they walked to dinner on Sunday night. Their final biology exam was on Tuesday morning.

"I know. When are you leaving?" asked Alexa.

"I have to wait until next weekend. Can you believe that? Three whole extra days here!" moaned Bianca. "What about you?"

"I don't know," replied Alexa truthfully. She had been blocking out all thoughts of what would happen after her last exam – good and bad. "I don't actually have anywhere to go. I don't know what I'm going to do."

"Surely there's someone you can stay with," said Bianca a little dismissively.

"Nope. That's the thing about being homeless. Really does mean you have nowhere to live."

"That won't matter for too long, though," smiled Bianca enthusiastically. "We're going to be very rich on Tuesday afternoon."

"I doubt they give you the money that day and even so, I can't go out and buy a place to live in a day either. I want something nice, some place I'll be really happy to stay," said Alexa, choosing her words carefully.

"Still, it's so exciting," continued Bianca happily. "I've been struggling to keep my mind on the exams. All I can think about is the money. I just can't believe that after all this time it's finally going to happen. We're going to be rich."

Alexa was thankful she had become so good at suppressing her feelings lately, making her able to smile and nod in response to Bianca's excited raving. They really did inhabit two very different worlds and she realised that she and Bianca were simply never going to be on the same wavelength.

However, tuning out Bianca's excitement was harder than Alexa thought. The money, despite now being so close, was still such an abstract concept that it was hardly real. Homelessness was a far less foreign experience. Alexa could not believe that she had thought so little about where she was going to live once she finished her exams. She knew that Mr Knight was unlikely to let her leave without somewhere to go. The real problem was that she had nowhere to go.

It was a scenario that made Alexa feel much more anxious than she thought she ever would be. She had spent the last couple of months going to sleep to the image of Mr Knight's arms around her, yet the idea of him offering to solve her housing crisis by letting her live with him terrified her. Although she had been able to trust him at school, outside it was a very different matter. Without her own independence, she felt as though she would be at his mercy and would not have the strength to deny him what she felt she still owed him.

Alexa did not put those concerns in her letters to Bethany. Locked away in gaol, Bethany did not need to know that she had nowhere to go. Instead, Alexa focused on her excitement at being able to see Bethany again.

When Tuesday morning broke, Alexa woke with a stomach full of nerves. This was the end. She had officially reached the end of the tunnel, but the light was so bright she felt blinded and was almost terrified of the prospect of stepping out into the unknown. She did not touch her breakfast and was silent as she walked with Lizzie and Bianca towards the hall.

"Miss Samson, can you come in here for a couple of minutes?" asked Mr Knight, walking out from his office as they walked by.

Alexa waved the others on, her nerves turning to nausea as she closed the door behind her and sat down in front of Mr Knight's desk.

"You ready? Last exam," asked Mr Knight. He was smiling, but Alexa could only grimace. "I've been meaning to talk to you, but I didn't want to disrupt your study." Alexa's heart skipped a beat. She saw Mr Knight hold out a hand as he quickly spoke again. "No, no, nothing bad has happened. I just thought you might have been worrying about where you would go once your exams were finished."

"Only recently," Alexa admitted. "Feel like an idiot forgetting that I'm homeless."

"You won't be," nodded Mr Knight solemnly. "I promise. I've talked Mrs Taylor into allowing you to stay here as long as you need, though I know you won't want that to be very long." He smiled slightly at that comment. "You have a couple of options. Why don't you come round after school tomorrow and we can chat about them. You won't have to go anywhere you're not comfortable."

"What if I need to leave the school between now and when I find a place to live? Can I come and go? Can I see my sister?"

"No," replied Mr Knight with an unhappy shake of his head. "You know what Mrs Taylor's like. Her specific conditions – which all teachers have been made aware of – are that *any* students remaining at Redgrove beyond the date of their last exams can do so, but under the conditions they would be subject to as normal students."

"What does that mean?" asked Alexa with slight trepidation.

"It means you would have to wear school uniform, attend assembly and will be supervised in a classroom during school times."

"Wow, she really does hate us."

"I know you think you have nothing to lose, but don't push this, Alexa. If you need to leave, for any reason, tell me. I will do everything I can to make it happen. Don't let them cause trouble for you, not now you're almost free."

Mr Knight looked over at his clock and ushered Alexa towards the door. It only made her sick again. She knew she had to tell him about their plans for that afternoon, but her exam was starting in fifteen minutes.

"Don't worry," said Mr Knight with a smile. "It's just one more day. We'll work it all out tomorrow. Focus on your exam. You deserve to do well."

Alexa quickly found Ezra, who was waiting with Bianca and Lizzie outside to hall, to wish them good luck before rushing down to her examination room.

"Last one?" asked Alexa's examiner as she sat down.

"Yeah," replied Alexa anxiously.

"You'll be fine," smiled the lady encouragingly.

Alexa struggled to believe her. The entire reading time was spent worrying about how hurt Mr Knight would be if she snuck out of school this afternoon, and how she could explain to him why she needed to go. It took all her energy to force herself to forget absolutely everything but the biology exam, and she was relieved that the first three questions were easy to answer. The next two required more concentration and focus, which slowly developed as the time wore on, but Alexa was horrified by how quickly it was passing. She managed to finish all the questions with less than five minutes before the end of the exam, giving her time to fix one mistake, but she was stopped from fixing another by the examiner.

"Pens down," said the lady formally.

"Urgh!" sighed Alexa, dropping her pen and covering her face with her hands. "Didn't get to fix that answer," she said, pointing to her paper.

"Don't let yourself worry about it," smiled the lady, gathering her paper. "I'm sure you did well anyway."

"Thank you. I can't believe it's finished."

"Congratulations," smiled her examiner as Alexa gathered her belongings.

After six long years, it was really all over. She was free.

Chapter Sixteen

ALEXA RAN TOWARDS the front of the hall, where everyone was already milling in the courtyard. Bianca and Ezra were bouncing in each other's arms, Bianca squealing wildly. Ezra immediately opened her arms to include Alexa in the emphatic embrace as she approached them.

"We're finished! It's all over!" rejoiced Ezra.

Lizzie patted them quickly on the shoulder before departing. Her last exam was not until tomorrow and she was not yet ready to celebrate. Alexa waved goodbye, catching Mr Knight's eye as she did. He smiled warmly at her, making his way towards them as he congratulated all the other students who had finished with them.

"Congratulations, ladies," Mr Knight smiled as he reached them. "I hope you finished on a high."

"Thanks, Sir," replied Bianca and Ezra excitedly.

Alexa could not speak and she hoped that Mr Knight could not see the discomfort in her eyes as her stomach squirmed. He smiled again before moving on to the next group of students.

"I can't go," Alexa spluttered, watching Mr Knight leave. "I don't care about the money. I can't go."

"What?" gasped Bianca and Ezra simultaneously.

"We're not allowed to leave. I asked. I can't do it. Me and Bianca should be out of here by the weekend. Can't we just wait until then?"

"If there's one time you should sneak out of school, this is it," said Bianca. "We've waited so long."

"Then what's a few more days?" pleaded Alexa, her eyes following Mr Knight.

"No!" cried Bianca. "I'm going home this weekend – as in Europe. We have to go today. You'll have to sneak out sometime."

"I can't. Don't you get it? I can't do it. We need to think of another way to get the money."

"Mr Knight's never going to get you into trouble," said Ezra, trying to be encouraging.

"That's not the point," Alexa cried softly.

"That is the point!" argued Bianca. "He likes you. Take advantage of it."

"I can get us out of here, just not today. I just need to talk to him – to work it out."

"If you don't want to come, then don't," replied Bianca angrily. "But we're going. You've held us back from this for ages. You should've just given me the tickets when I turned eighteen."

"You could never get out of here either. And I have to go. The tickets are with my lawyer," replied Alexa timidly. She did not want to fight with Bianca.

"So you're going to continue to hold us to ransom over this?" spat Bianca

"No! I just don't – what time's your flight? Can't your parents get you out of here a day early? Do that and we can collect it on Friday."

"No," answered Bianca simply. "I want the money today. I don't want to wait. We've waited long enough."

"Come on," urged Ezra gently. "You deserve this more than we do. It's just a few hours."

"I'm not going without talking to him first," said Alexa, turning to follow Mr Knight back to his office.

"And tell him what?" questioned Bianca fiercely, grabbing Alexa's hand and pulling her back. "You going to tell him about the money? This is our money. It has nothing to do with him. You get that? I'm not splitting this another way just because you don't want your boyfriend to feel left out. Remember, to the rest of us, he's just a teacher."

Alexa pulled her hand out of Bianca's grasp and stormed off. She had only gone a few metres when Ezra rushed in front of her and blocked her path.

"You can't tell him," said Ezra earnestly. "You don't know that you can trust him, not with this. You can come straight back. With everyone celebrating and moving around, no one will even know you're gone. You deserve this – and you need it. You need this more than either of us. It'll be fine. If we go now, you'll be back before dinner."

"Promise?" asked Alexa gravely. If they could get back before dinner then Ezra was right, they probably would not be missed, and they could easily claim to have been somewhere in the grounds.

"Yes," said Ezra.

"Yes," sighed Bianca, rolling her eyes. "We'll go, we'll come straight back."

"Okay," sighed Alexa, reluctantly agreeing.

Walking casually out on to the field, they were able to slip slowly out of sight and down to the fence. Alexa showed them to one of the few gaps they could get through. To avoid being seen by any exiting day students, they walked to the next station and boarded a train to the city from there.

Finally on their way, Bianca's mood rose instantly, although she could not help but continually lament the fact that they had never known where the tickets had been kept.

"I mean, it would've just sat there forever if you'd died this year. How could we have ever proven we'd won?" mused Bianca, as Alexa bit down on her response.

It was clear that Bianca had never really learned to trust her, and Alexa decided not to tell her the lengths she had gone to secure their shares in the windfall. In truth, she had done it for Bethany, but that was beside the point.

Ezra stayed silent and Alexa was not sure if that was to help pacify her or because she agreed with Bianca. Either way, Alexa was glad this would be one of the last days she would have to deal with this life. Ezra had been a great friend for the past six years, but Alexa was not sure what role she would play in her new life. She was positive Bianca would play almost no role.

However, when Bianca was not lamenting what could have been, Alexa had to admit that she found her enthusiasm contagious. This was really happening.

Their first stop was to pick up the tickets. Alexa hoped that Peter was not in court, making her realise that she really had not thought this plan through.

"Hi, I'm here to see Peter Lam," said Alexa to the bored receptionist at Peter's legal firm, while Bianca and Ezra sat uneasily in the leather chairs.

"Is he expecting you?"

"Um, no, not really," replied Alexa, biting her lip.

"What is your name?"

"Alexa Samson."

"Wait over there, please," said the receptionist, waving her away. Alexa moved a few feet away as the receptionist called Peter, but did not sit down with Bianca and Ezra. "I have an Alexa Samson here to see you. She doesn't have an appointment. I can get ri – okay." The receptionist hung up the phone, looking slightly

284

disgruntled. "He will be out in a minute," she sneered.

Alexa smiled broadly.

It was five minutes before Peter emerged from a door on the other side of the reception.

"Alexa, come through," said Peter warmly. "Just Alexa, if you don't mind," he said when he saw Bianca and Ezra stand up and start to follow. "So, what can I do for you?" Peter asked kindly as he sat down in the large chair that stood behind his huge oak desk. "You're not in any trouble, are you?" he added as an anxious afterthought.

Alexa smiled as she shook her head and realised that Peter really must dread hearing from her.

"Wow! This is a much better view than your last office," marvelled Alexa, walking over to the window.

"It's not bad. I manage to find myself the odd client that pays."

"I told you I'd give you money for defending Bethy," replied Alexa angrily.

"I was joking, Alexa. I made a promise to the two of you years ago that I would be your lawyer whenever you needed one."

"I don't remember that," Alexa admitted tentatively.

"I suppose it was more a promise to myself, then," shrugged Peter. "But I still intend to keep it. I'm here for the two of you whenever you need me – free of charge."

"Well, I'm here for the tickets. We're going to collect the money today. You still don't think we should have any problems?" Alexa asked hesitantly. It really did not feel right to be trying to claim so much and still not pay her way.

"I can't see why you should and if you do, you have my number," replied Peter confidently.

Peter left Alexa in his office while he collected the tickets from the safe. She looked out from the floor to ceiling windows on to the city below. She had so many memories of days and nights spent on those streets and wondered if that was where she would be spending the next few nights when she left Redgrove.

"Here you go," smiled Peter, handing her a large envelope as he sat down in his chair next to where she was standing. "Do you know what you're going to do with the money?"

"Get a place to stay. Take care of Bethy. Give some to the Whites. They're the only things I know for sure."

"You miss them?" asked Peter sincerely.

"I try not to."

"Is it that easy?"

"Sometimes," Alexa shrugged, trying not to think too much about the answer. "Maybe after I give them the money it'll make it easier – I won't feel so guilty every time I think about them. It's just money, but maybe it'll help repair some of the damage."

"I don't think you have much to feel guilty about," said Peter genuinely. "You saved Hayley's life. They know that."

"I'll need your help tracking them down. I just want to give them the money anonymously," Alexa replied, refusing to engage in that conversation. She could not afford to think about the Whites and her former life with them.

"They will want to see you," said Peter firmly.

"They'll never know the money was from me and I'm not about to risk their safety. I'm not worth that."

"I'm not sure – have you got permission to be here?" asked Peter, thankfully giving up the argument about the Whites.

"No, so I should go. We need to get back before dinner."

"So you've finished your exams, then?" asked Peter in an upbeat voice.

"This morning," Alexa replied with a half-smile.

"Congratulations."

Alexa smiled and walked backwards towards the door.

"Thanks for all this," she said holding up the envelope. She felt guilty for all Peter had done for her and Bethany, knowing the only thing she could give him in return was money and he was determined not to accept it.

"Listen, Alexa," said Peter solemnly, halting her departure. "Bethany will have to serve at least eighteen months. You should take this time to really do something for yourself. Ben and I are looking after Bethany. She'll be fine, but she'll need you when she's released. Don't wait to make your own life. You can't help her if you don't have your own life sorted out."

"I know. I'm working on it," Alexa replied solemnly. "I'm just not sure how I'm going to do it yet."

"Well I'm always here. It would be nice to hear from you occasionally when you're not in trouble."

"Okay. Thanks again, Peter, and thank you for helping Bethany. It means a lot to me."

"I know," nodded Peter earnestly, and Alexa supposed he really might.

Tickets in hand, the trio ran through the crowded city streets towards the lottery office. It was just after two when they reached their destination. They stopped at the front door and looked at each other.

"Are we ready for this?" asked Alexa.

"Hell yeah," answered Ezra emphatically.

"I've been ready since last Easter," added Bianca.

Alexa tried not to roll her eyes as she reached for the door. The reception was bright and filled with photos of happy people holding oversized cheques. Alexa and Ezra both looked at Bianca as they edged towards the receptionist, indicating that she was going to be the one doing the talking.

"Hi," said Bianca nervously. "Um, we were – we wanted to, err, claim a lottery win."

"Do you know which draw it was?" asked the receptionist in an even voice, as if this was an everyday occurrence.

Bianca and Ezra turned to Alexa, who shrugged before opening the envelope and rifling through its contents.

"It was the big one from Easter last year," said Bianca, as Alexa continued to flick through the numerous tickets.

"The twenty-five million dollar draw that they've been searching for the winners for over a year?" asked the receptionist, who was suddenly much more animated.

"Yeah, that one," replied Ezra sheepishly.

"Just hold on a minute," said the receptionist, picking up the phone and dialling frantically.

"You have the tickets, right?" asked Bianca anxiously.

"Yeah, but I have all the non-winning tickets as well. I didn't want to say the wrong draw."

"Yes, yes they claim to have the winning tickets," said the receptionist in a hurried voice. "I'm not sure. They look very young."

It took less than a minute for someone to come rushing into reception to greet them.

"Hi, my name is Grant Haddon. How are the three of you today?" asked Grant pleasantly. The trio smiled and shrugged, unsure who was supposed to answer. "I hear you think you have the winning tickets from last Easter's twenty-five million dollar draw."

"Yes," said Bianca, again taking up the role of spokesperson.

"Why don't the three of you come through to my office and we'll check those tickets."

The bright reception gave way to a much less vibrant office space with partitioned desks and several glassed-in offices. Eyes trailed their progress as they followed Grant through to a large office in the corner.

"Sit down, please," said Grant as he moved behind his desk. "I guess the first thing to do would be to check the tickets."

Alexa handed him two pages of entries. Grant looked down the list and started smiling and nodding. He was about to start talking when Alexa's heart gave a sick jolt.

"Oh wait, those are the wrong tickets," she said, holding her hand out to take them back.

"No, I remember the numbers –"

"No, it's the wrong day. They are from the first Saturday, I think – these are the winning tickets."

A bewildered look crossed Grant's face as he looked between the near-identical tickets.

"Why don't I check all the tickets for you?" said Grant with cautious bemusement.

Alexa shrugged and handed over all the tickets to Grant, who rushed back out of the office. Through the glass walls, Alexa, Bianca and Ezra watched Grant move through the main office. The people in the office watched them just as closely. It took over ten minutes for Grant to reappear and when he did he was accompanied by a short, balding man in his fifties.

"I'm Mr McCarthy," said the second man, introducing himself to the trio. Each shook his hand in turn and watched anxiously as he sat down behind Grant's desk. "The three of you look very young. I hope you can all prove that you're over eighteen."

They all quickly rummaged in their bags for identification and handed them over, looking nervously between Mr McCarthy and each other.

"So does mean that we won?" asked Bianca in a shaky voice when Mr McCarthy looked up at Grant, who started nodding and smiling again.

"That's exactly what it means," replied Mr McCarthy.

Alexa sat glued to the chair until Bianca pulled her up into an excited embrace. Ezra quickly joined in, wrapping her arms around the both of them. Bianca's screams were almost deafening, while Ezra laughed and smiled as tears trickled down her cheeks. All Alexa could feel was relief, a numb abstract relief, and then sadness.

This was the money that was supposed to help her protect

Bethany and her child. Bethany was now in gaol and her baby never made it to birth. Heavy guilt weighed down on Alexa as she hugged and jumped in time with her two friends.

Bianca's screaming did not cease for almost five minutes. Mr McCarthy's serious face gave way to a broad smile as he watched the three of them bounce around the room. Grant stood in the corner with an equally broad grin. Alexa was the first to sit back down, guilt still gnawing hungrily at her insides.

"There are a few things we'd be interested to know," said Mr McCarthy, directing Bianca and Ezra back to their seats, their smiles reaching right across their faces.

"Like what?" asked Alexa hesitantly.

"First of all, you're all only just on eighteen and this draw was well over a year ago. How did that come about?"

"We had Ezra's cousin enter for us," replied Alexa, her voice measured and calm. She had prepared herself for these sorts of questions. "We gave her the money and the numbers and she bought the tickets for us."

"What about the numbers?" asked Grant, still bewildered by that part. "Four draws, and you entered the same numbers in each of them – and you seemed certain about five of them the whole way through."

Bianca and Ezra turned to Alexa, waiting to see if she would answer.

"I had a dream," said Alexa, after almost a minute of silence. She did not want to explain this, but knew a little truth was better than more lies – no matter how hard it was to tell. "I had a dream and I had five numbers, but my sister had the sixth. I didn't know what it was. Ezra said that they might be winning lottery numbers. We thought it was worth a shot, but we didn't know when they'd be drawn. That's why we entered so many draws. That was our last shot. We ran out of money after entering those."

"You're kidding?" asked Mr McCarthy.

"No," replied Alexa simply.

"That's quite a story," nodded Mr McCarthy. "But why did you wait this long to claim the money?"

"We wanted to wait until we were all eighteen," said Alexa quickly, wanting the official story told, not Bianca's petulant sob story. "Ezra, who's the youngest, she turned eighteen in the middle of our final exams, so we waited until we all finished our last exam. That was this morning, so here we are."

"You all finished your finals today? Wow, this is an amazing story. The press will go wild for this."

"Do you have to tell them?" asked Alexa nervously.

"We'll release a statement. We always do when a large prize is won," explained Grant.

"I don't want to be named. You can tell them about the other stuff if you have to, but I don't want to be named," Alexa replied anxiously.

"Yeah, actually, either do I," said Ezra.

"Me either," said Bianca.

"That's fine. None of you will be identified, but the press will want to speak to you," said Mr McCarthy. It was clear they liked the good news stories.

"No interviews," said Alexa firmly, and she was glad that neither Grant nor Mr McCarthy pushed the issue.

"So how much money did we win exactly?" asked Ezra, as they started filling out all the paperwork.

"There was the first division prize of twenty-five million dollars, of course, but you also won multiple second division prizes with the other games, which totalled over four hundred thousand," smiled Mr McCarthy.

"Wow," gasped Bianca.

"So between the three of you that would make around eight-point-four million dollars each."

"Wow," said Ezra and Bianca.

"Holy shit," gasped Alexa, still unable to truly comprehend such a truth. It felt so unreal and none of the formalities that followed made it feel any more believable.

It was nearing four o'clock when the trio left the lottery's office. There had been much more paperwork than any of them had envisaged. Alexa looked at a nearby clock with concern.

"We need to go," she said, stopping the others who had started bounding down the street. "I want to get back to school before we're missed."

"What!" exclaimed Bianca. "Come on, we have to celebrate. This is the greatest day of our lives and you want to go back to school."

"Yeah, Alexa, it only takes half an hour to get back," said Ezra, looking at her watch. "It's nowhere near dinnertime and I'm starving. We haven't even had lunch yet."

"Fine, but we're leaving by five-thirty," replied Alexa grudgingly.

Alexa followed Bianca and Ezra as they made their way to the nearest pub. Ezra ordered the food, while Bianca ordered the drinks. Alexa picked at the food unhappily, constantly checking Ezra's watch as the minutes ticked slowly by.

"Your round," said Bianca, throwing back the last of her drink. She had downed three bottles of some vodka-based drink in just twenty minutes.

"I don't have any money," replied Alexa.

"Why didn't you get some when we all went to the ATM?" sulked Bianca, storming off towards the bar.

Alexa tried not to think about the last time she had withdrawn money from an ATM.

"It's okay, just relax. You won't get in any trouble, even if you miss dinner," said Ezra, squeezing her hand. "They're not going to do a head count. You skip meals all the time."

Alexa decided not to argue. They had no idea just how many times she had seen teachers watching her the times she did skip meals. She decided to just go back by herself, but when she tried to leave, Ezra and Bianca both argued with her, forcing her to order food and demanding that she relax. It was an impossible request.

Bianca and Ezra kept drinking and celebrating merrily. Ezra was fairly restrained in her alcohol consumption, but Bianca cut loose, decrying any attempts at moderation as trying to stop her from having fun.

Eating only because of the tearing hunger in her stomach, Alexa finished half her meal before standing up and demanding they go. She pointed at Ezra's watch and was horrified to see that it was somehow seven-thirty. The early minutes, when she had been watching the clock so closely, had dragged by so slowly, and now somehow almost two hours had rushed by. Alexa's heart sank, knowing there was little chance her absence would be missed.

"We really have to go now," Alexa said, trying to pull Bianca up from her seat. "You have any money? It'll be a lot quicker to catch a cab."

Bianca had stopped arguing against going back to school, but she was so drunk that her body would also no longer comply with her brain's commands.

"No, I spent all mine," replied Ezra apologetically.

"Shit! Check Bianca's wallet."

"No, she's dry as well."

"Shit!" cried Alexa, feeling her stomach turn to lead.

With one of them on either side of Bianca, Alexa and Ezra walked Bianca to the train station. They got Bianca to their platform, laying her down on an empty bench as Alexa checked the indicator board.

"Fuck! The next train doesn't come for fifteen minutes," she moaned, her heart sinking.

"Do you want me to wait with you?" asked Ezra.

"No. You go. I'll be fine," Alexa muttered in response, not really caring for Ezra's assistance now. "Dead, but fine."

"He won't get you into trouble," said Ezra, looking at Alexa as though she was blowing the situation out of proportion.

"That was never the point. I shouldn't have put him in that position. Besides, if it's someone else who notices that we're gone, there's nothing he can do."

"It'll be all right. I'll talk to you soon. Let me know if you need a place to stay. My parents are fine with you staying with us."

"Yeah, thanks."

Alexa was touched by the offer, but what she had really wanted was to leave two hours ago. To make matters worse, the train was five minutes late and they almost missed it as Alexa tried to haul Bianca on it. Bianca flopped down on the seat, her head lolling on to Alexa's shoulder.

"Aren't you glad we stayed out, Alexa? See how much fun you would've missed out on if we'd gone back to school," smiled Bianca drunkenly.

Alexa did not answer. She got Bianca to her feet the stop before theirs to make sure they made it off the train. The motion of the ride had begun to make Bianca nauseous and Alexa hoped she could get her off the train before the night's drinks made the return journey from Bianca's stomach.

They made it off the train, but not off the platform. Bianca pulled away from Alexa at the base of the stairs and starting vomiting over the side of the platform. Alexa quickly pulled her back from the edge and tried to guide her towards the bin in the middle of the platform.

The stairs took ten minutes to negotiate. Bianca swayed heavily and Alexa, being much smaller, struggled to keep her upright. The ten minute walk uphill from the station took them over twenty and when Alexa finally dragged Bianca through the fence it was nine o'clock.

Alexa looked longingly up at Sam's window. It was tempting to just leave Bianca where she was and climb up the downpipe to safety. It went against her basic morals, but it was also useless. If Bianca was caught, she was not going to take the blame herself.

Knowing there was no way in except the front door, Alexa walked Bianca around, hoping they were running late locking up for the night.

"We're millionaires, Alexa, multimillionaires!" shouted Bianca, throwing her hands up in the air and twirling drunkenly. "This is the absolute best day of our lives."

"Quiet down. I'm trying to get us in unnoticed," snapped Alexa in a low voice as she gently pulled on the door. It was locked. "Shit. Get off me, Bianca. I have to find a way in."

"Just knock. We're finished. Can't do anything to us now," said Bianca dismissively, leaning over Alexa and banging loudly on the door.

"Shut up!"

Alexa turned and grabbed Bianca by the wrists, before pushing her roughly against the wall. She shoved her once more before turning back to the door.

"Just give me a minute. If anyone but Mr Knight finds us, we're dead," sighed Alexa, feeling like Bianca was trying to ensure that everyone but Mr Knight found them.

Bianca slumped to the ground, glaring angrily at her. Alexa did not care for Bianca's disapproval. Whether they got into the dorms undetected or not, the first person Alexa wanted to see was Mr Knight. She would fall at his feet and apologise, and beg him to understand. It would be horrible to see his disappointment, but he had to appreciate that this would not be the last time she let him down. Her life was just like that.

Alexa opened her wallet and pulled out two large paper clips that had been twisted out of their original shape. She inserted one after the other into the lock and swivelled them around until the she heard the lock click.

Breathing a sigh of relief that they would not have to spend the night outside, Alexa got Bianca back on her feet. Bianca was thankfully more subdued as Alexa struggled up the stairs with her. They made it to the fourth floor without encountering anyone. With their landing in sight, Alexa breathed another sigh of relief. They had not been caught, and she could go and throw herself at Mr Knight's mercy.

"Looks like you still consider this school to be your personal hotel."

Alexa's breath caught in her throat as her heart started thumping painfully. Ms Carter was standing outside their bedroom door with a vicious smile on her face.

"We were just celebrating," slurred Bianca belligerently.

"And still being a negative influence on your friends, I see," noted Ms Carter with raised eyebrows. "Do you really think you were going to sneak in here without me knowing?"

Alexa stared back at Ms Carter, her body paralysed by fear. She clung to her pendant hoping it would draw Mr Knight to them. Ms Carter moved closer, stopping when she was just inches from Alexa.

"I've been waiting a long time for this day and you walked straight to me. I'm going to take your friend here to the sick bay. You'll be waiting for me when I return."

"What's going on?" called Mr Knight, walking up the corridor.

Alexa exhaled with unimaginable relief. Mr Knight would be mad, but she could explain – and beg for his forgiveness. She hated the thought of his disappointment, but knew she would endure a lifetime of that to avoid another moment with Ms Carter.

"I found these two sneaking into the dormitory. Out celebrating, apparently," said Ms Carter viciously.

"Hey, Sir," waved Bianca drunkenly. "We're finished!"

Mr Knight looked between Alexa and Bianca, his disappointment written all over his face. Alexa tried to express an apology, but he would not look directly at her. She felt sick with the pain she had caused him.

"I will take it from here," said Mr Knight in a low voice, turning away from Alexa.

"I think it would be best to punish them together, when both of them are in a healthier state," said Ms Carter, tilting her head towards the swaying Bianca. "Why don't you take Miss Ross to the sick bay and I will make sure Miss Samson gets to bed. You can deal with the two of them tomorrow."

Panic shot through Alexa at Ms Carter's suggestion, and Alexa looked desperately at Mr Knight. He did not answer as he urged Bianca to follow him. Bianca took one step and stumbled. Alexa grabbed Bianca and held her up, hoping she could walk with her to the sick bay and avoid Ms Carter that way.

"Where we going? Wanna go sleep. Don't wanna go with you. You should be taking Lexa to bed. She's your girlfriend. Oooooh," giggled Bianca.

Alexa and Mr Knight both stopped dead. He looked her hard in the eyes before taking Bianca from her shoulder. He slung Bianca's arm around his neck. Bianca continued to protest, making more snide comments about him and Alexa. From the corner of her eye, Alexa could see Ms Carter smirking. It was as if everything was going exactly as she had planned.

Mr Knight turned away from them. His voice was controlled and measured, but Alexa had not heard him so angry for such a long time that it sounded almost foreign.

"Miss Samson, go to bed. I expect you at my office the minute school finishes tomorrow. You will be in uniform and in class tomorrow with the other boarders. You will not be a second late and you will not put a toe out of line."

Alexa watched Mr Knight walk away. She willed him to turn around, needing him to know what would happen as soon as he was out of sight, but he disappeared without a backwards glance.

It took a moment of indecision before Alexa realised she had to run after him. She had to protect herself and make things up to him, but she did not get two steps before Ms Carter seized her arm. She wrestled, but Ms Carter was stronger.

"Scream and your life won't be worth living," snarled Ms Carter.

Chapter Seventeen

THE DOOR TO Ms Carter's room closed behind Alexa, the lock clicking as though it was a gaol door. Ms Carter released Alexa in the middle of the room and picked up her cane. It was her nightmare that kept coming back. Only this time Alexa had spent a year lulling herself into a false sense of security, believing she had beaten it forever. Neither Ms Carter nor Mrs Taylor had given her too much grief this year and she had never known if it was because of Clinton's absence or Mr Knight's support. All she knew was that right then she had no protection at all.

"Do you really think I'm going to stand here and let you hit me?" asked Alexa defiantly, hoping she had another option.

Ms Carter said nothing as she advanced and swung the cane at Alexa's head. Alexa managed to raise her arm in front of her face in time to protect it, only to feel a crippling pain spike through her wrist. The second blow struck her wrist again, the pain sending her to her knees. The third strike hit her unguarded back.

"I've been waiting for this moment for a long time," said Ms Carter in a viciously triumphant voice. "Did you really think I was going to let you get away with sending your trash sister here to attack me?"

"You're never going to get away with this. I'm finished here. I don't have anything to lose," said Alexa through gritted teeth.

"When has anyone believed you before?"

"Mr Knight will believe me."

"We'll see about that," sneered Ms Carter. "After tonight, you may find you don't have the support you thought you did."

Alexa looked up in horror only to see Ms Carter smile and swing the cane again. Once more, Alexa raised her arm to protect her head and the cane slammed into her forearm. Pain pulsed through her arm and wrist. Determined to escape this, Alexa turned and raced for the door. Ms Carter's cane slammed down over and over against her back and head, and across the side of her face, as she fumbled with the lock.

When the door finally opened, Alexa almost fell through it. The final jab from Ms Carter's cane stabbed Alexa's left kidney, bringing her to her knees, but she was in the corridor now. Scrambling on hands and knees, Alexa made it to the door to her room. She wanted to make it to Mr Knight's office, but the corridor spun sickeningly as she got to her feet.

The pain in her wrist was almost blinding, and her head and back throbbed out of time. Alexa could barely see in front of her as she opened the door. Lizzie was sitting at her desk studying, while Martha and Natalie were sitting on Martha's bed behind closed curtains. Lizzie did not turn around until Alexa was out of sight.

"Where've you been? Where's Bianca?" asked Lizzie frantically. "You guys are in lots of trouble."

"I'll talk to you tomorrow," replied Alexa, breathing deeply to keep her voice calm. "You study. I'll see you after your exam tomorrow."

"Are you okay?" asked Lizzie, concern filling her voice.

"Yeah, I'm fine. I'm just going to sleep."

Alexa was not sure if Lizzie believed her, but she did not ask her any more questions.

Trying to change out of her clothes proved to be too agonising so Alexa had to settle for kicking off her shoes and trying to find a pain-free way to lie on her bed. It was almost impossible. Her wrist was screaming in agony and her back was too painful to lie on. Resting on her stomach, with pillows under her chest, she was still wide awake when Lizzie turned out the lights just before midnight.

At some point pure exhaustion took over and sleep took hold, but it was punctuated by painful awakenings when the throbbing in her wrist became too great. It only got worse as the night wore on and it became harder for Alexa to cope in silence. In the end it was impossible.

"Alexa, are you okay?" asked Martha, pulling back the curtain around Alexa's bed after she had cried out in pain. "What happened to you?"

"What time is it?" asked Alexa, trying to speak through the pain as she sat up.

"It's almost nine. We're supposed to go sit in a classroom if we don't have exams."

"Can you get Mr Knight for me? Please."

Alexa kept herself up in bed, her back too sore to even lean on. Warmth burnt in her heart knowing that Marcus – now school was over, he could be Marcus – would soon be by her side and that he would scoop her up in his arms and make all her pain disappear.

The door clicked and Alexa knew she was going to be okay. She closed her eyes, not wanting to see his reaction to yet another of her disasters. She knew he would feel guilty about what had happened, but she did not want him to. If she had not betrayed him, he would never have been so hurt.

"Um, Alexa, he won't come. I don't know what's wrong," said Martha hesitantly. "We told him you looked really sick, but he said that he had to get to class and that we should take you to the sick bay if you weren't well enough to go to class."

Alexa's insides turned to lead and pain ripped through her heart. She forced her eyes open to make sure Martha was not telling some sick joke.

"Do you want us to take you to the sick bay?" asked Martha tentatively.

Alexa could only shake her head. Maybe Mr Knight had known what would happen to her. Maybe he had always known – just like Clinton. She had broken their deal and he had shown her that it was his way or no way – just like Clinton.

Tears began to slip down Alexa's cheeks as she realised just how alone in the world she was. She had just lost the very last person who had cared about her. Then she remembered that she had not lost the last person who could protect her, who was bound – not by her, but by duty – to protect her.

Not caring that she was still dressed in yesterday's clothes, Alexa climbed gingerly out of bed under the worried gazes of Martha and Natalie. Ignoring their concerns, she walked slowly down to the common room where they had a phone they could use.

The first call went through to message bank. Alexa dialled again, then again. On the fifth attempt the phone was finally answered.

"Senior Detective Shepard speaking."

"Ben," choked Alexa, trying hard not to cry.

"Alexa, is that you? What's wrong?" asked Ben anxiously, repeating the question when she failed to immediately answer.

"Can you come here?" Alexa asked, not offering any explanation.

"I'm on my way."

It took Ben barely more than twenty minutes to pull into the car park. Alexa heard the siren, but did not move. She waited inside the school grounds, sitting hunched on the low fence with her wrist held up against her shoulder, as Ben and Detective Parker ran through the car park to her.

"Oh shit," said Ben, looking at her swollen wrist and bruised face. "Come on, I'm taking you to the hospital."

"We can't just take her off school grounds," said Detective Parker in a low voice.

"I don't care," growled Ben. "Look at her!"

"Who did this to you?" asked Detective Parker, but Alexa did not answer.

"Who did this to you, Alexa?" asked Ben, crouching down and cupping her cheek to force her eyes to meet his.

"Ms Carter," breathed Alexa.

"Does Mr Knight know? Why didn't you go to him?" asked Ben frantically.

"He knows. He doesn't care," replied Alexa, the words tearing at her heart as she spoke them.

Ben rose to his feet looking mutinous.

"Can you manage for a little while longer?" he asked, barely waiting for her to nod her head before pulling her to her feet.

"What are you doing?" asked Detective Parker.

"We're going to arrest the bitch that did this to her and then we're going to deal with Marcus Knight."

Ben stayed with Alexa until uniformed officers arrived. Alexa directed them to the places they were likely to find Ms Carter during the day and where she kept her cane. Ben then helped her to her feet, this time much more gently, and walked her to Mr Knight's office.

"Come in," called Mr Knight in response to Ben's knock. Alexa's stomach churned uncomfortably with anger and fear as Ben entered ahead of her. "Ben, what are you – oh my God, what happened?"

"That's exactly what I would like to know," snarled Ben, his voice low and dangerous.

Alexa did not look up as she slumped into the seat in front of her, keeping her badly swollen wrist up against her shoulder.

"I didn't – I took – I don't know what happened. She didn't look like this when she arrived back at school last night," stammered Mr Knight.

"But when you were told that she was ill this morning you didn't want to know about it," retorted Ben angrily.

"I thought she was hung over. Miss Ross –"

"Did she appear at all drunk last night?" cried Ben.

"I didn't think so. Miss Ross – Bianca – was, so I took her to the sick bay. Ms Carter took Alexa to her room. When would this have – no – you can't be suggesting that Ms Carter –"

"She's being arrested as we speak. Did you know what was going to happen when you left Alexa in her care?"

"What? No! God, do you honestly think I would ever let anything like this happen to her?" cried Mr Knight.

"You had very little concern for her this morning."

"I told you, I thought she was hung over," cried Mr Knight, trying to justify his actions.

"But you didn't think she was drunk last night!" Ben yelled over the top of him.

Alexa could see Mr Knight struggling to put his thoughts together. In the back of her mind she already knew that he had not known what would happen to her, but she was not ready to believe that.

"I was angry and disappointed. I thought she was trying to take advantage of the fact that I wouldn't get her into trouble if I didn't have to. I thought if someone else disciplined her –"

"So you did let her go with Ms Carter? Let Ms Carter discipline her?" asked Ben in an interrogatory manner.

"I didn't know she was going to get hurt. How could I have possibly known that?" cried Mr Knight defensively. "I was going to deal with her and Miss Ross this afternoon."

"You knew," said Alexa, her voice shaking with pain.

"What – no – Alexa, I didn't know," replied Mr Knight immediately. He moved towards her, his face full of sorrow, but Ben moved between him and her, forcing him to retreat. "I would never let anything bad happen to you. Please, Alexa, you have to believe that."

"You knew, just like Clinton knew," replied Alexa softly. "It was a ploy, rescue the damsel in distress and you get to keep the girl."

"No," gasped Mr Knight, shaking his head.

"What do you mean Clinton knew?" asked Ben. "You never mentioned this before. Has this happened before?" Alexa sat in silence. She did not want to relive that past. "Oh heaven, Bethany. That's why she assaulted Ms Carter, because you told her what she'd done to you. You smiled just slightly when you were told about it."

Shocked silence hung in the room for over a minute. Alexa did not care. The pain in her wrist was so great she barely even noticed her surroundings, though she could see the pained expression on

Mr Knight's face. It was further confirmation of his innocence, but she still blamed him for not coming back for her.

"Who else knew?" asked Ben, kneeling in front of Alexa.

"Mrs Taylor," Alexa answered softly. "She didn't believe me. Clinton did, but said no one else would. He said he would stop her for me, because he knew her, and he did. That's when we started seeing each other. I always knew it was payback for his help."

Alexa saw Mr Knight pull his hair back off his face, pained disbelief in his eyes.

"Why didn't you say anything to me? Why didn't you say this when you told the police about Mr Marsh?" asked Mr Knight desperately.

"I wanted to be believed about Clinton," Alexa explained, but to Ben, not to Mr Knight. "I thought if I said anything about Ms Carter people wouldn't believe me about Clinton. I was sure I could handle her if Clinton wasn't around."

"But you couldn't," surmised Ben sadly.

"No, I could. She didn't do anything again until *he* gave me to her," said Alexa, tilting her head towards Mr Knight. "I even kept her away from Mel."

"Mel? Who's Mel? This was happening to someone else?" asked Ben angrily.

"Melissa Michaels, Sam's sister," said Alexa closing her eyes. There was no point keeping secrets any longer, and she wondered if she would lose Sam's friendship to this horrible day as well. "She was Clinton's next in line, but he was gone before anything really happened between them."

"Would she give a statement?" asked Ben, sounding somewhat hopeful.

"I don't know," Alexa shrugged, struggling to even care. "She still likes Clinton so she would never admit anything to me, but I knew and Ms Carter all but admitted it."

***

Marcus was almost shaking when he left to find Melissa. He could not believe what was happening. He could not believe it was his fault. He had turned his back on Alexa in a moment of anger and sent her straight into the arms of a maniac. It was like a sick joke, a movie that was too awful to possibly be true.

"Miss Michaels, I need to see you in my office immediately," he said, as Melissa sat eating her lunch in the dining hall.

"Why?" retorted Melissa defiantly.

"Just come with me, please."

"I have the right to know what I've done," continued Melissa, showing no sign of complying.

"You haven't done anything. You're not in trouble. I just need to ask you a few questions," replied Marcus, trying to be compassionate. Melissa's distrust could have as sinister origins as Alexa's had.

"What's going on?" asked Sam, arriving at Melissa's table wearing a triumphant grin after finishing his last exam moments earlier.

"I just need to talk to your sister about a few things," sighed Marcus.

"Like what?" queried Sam sceptically. It really was not usual for another year advisor to ask a student they did not teach into their office.

"Just let me do my job," snapped Marcus. "Miss Michaels, come with me now."

Sam drew back, stunned by his frustrated tone. Marcus had never spoken to Sam that way before. He had rarely spoken to anyone that way.

"What's going on?" asked Sam, suddenly serious.

"I just need to talk to Miss Michaels," sighed Marcus angrily.

"Then I'm coming as well," replied Sam seriously. "Come on, get up."

Sam pulled Melissa to her feet and started walking her towards the door.

"You don't need to come, Mr Michaels. I only need to speak with Miss Michaels," said Marcus, not wanting Sam to see Alexa in such a state.

"If you want to talk to her, then I'm coming as well," snapped Sam in response.

It was an angrily silent walk to back to his office. Marcus knew that if he explained anything to Sam now that Sam would not wait until they reached the privacy of his office to explode.

"Now, you tell me what's going on," said Sam furiously as he burst into the office. A second later he saw Alexa and instantly dropped to his knees in front of her. "What happened? What happened to you?" Alexa did not answer as tears welled in her eyes. "This isn't why Ms Carter was arrested, was it?"

"I'm afraid so," said Marcus, unable to look at Alexa.

"Then what has this got to do with Mel?"

"She hit Mel as well," confessed Alexa. "That's how Clinton found us. He used Ms Carter."

Sam kept looking between Alexa and Melissa, as if waiting to be told it was all a sick joke, but the tears in Alexa's eyes confirmed that it was all true. Melissa looked out the window, avoiding his stare.

"You knew and you didn't tell me. My sister and you didn't tell me!" Sam yelled, jumping to his feet.

"I didn't know until after Clinton left," cried Alexa in a defeated voice, piercing Marcus's heart. "I confronted Ms Carter and I was sure she wouldn't dare touch Mel, and with Clinton gone I thought she'd be safe."

Marcus watched Sam move across the room to Melissa, who was still looking out the window, staggered by what Alexa had faced on her own. She had been beaten and tortured by Ms Carter for who knew how long, yet had had the courage to face her again to try and protect Melissa. It sat in sickening contrast to his actions last night.

"Why didn't you tell me? I would've protected you. I would've made sure they stayed away from you," Sam asked Melissa tenderly, reaching out to put his arm around her shoulders.

"I didn't need your protection," replied Melissa callously, throwing off Sam's comforting hand. "She never laid a hand on me. She wouldn't have dared."

"But –"

"I don't know why you always clung on to the idea that you somehow protected me," Melissa hissed at Alexa. "Like I said to you before, Ms Carter hassled all the scholarship students, but do you think Clinton would've ever let her hurt me?"

"What do you mean 'Clinton'?" asked Sam in a shocked voice. "Please don't tell me that you and him –"

"You were a game, a project, nothing more," replied Melissa, ignoring Sam and continuing at Alexa. "Didn't you ever realise that? You and Sam together, it made me sick. You, when did you ever think you were good enough for my brother? But he was so taken by you. There didn't seem any way of breaking the two of you up."

Silence fell across the room as Melissa spoke. Sam backed away from her, his hand atop his distressed face. Marcus slumped in his chair in shock, staring at Alexa, who just sat there, wide-eyed, while Melissa attacked her.

"So you set the whole thing up?" asked Ben, placing his hand on Alexa's shoulder.

"I told Clinton how much I despised her, but that no one would be able to break them up. He offered to try so we came up with a plan," answered Melissa, in a voice that almost sounded proud. "Clinton tried to attract Alexa's attention, but she took no notice. So we had to change tact. Ms Carter already hated Alexa so it wasn't hard to convince her to harass her a bit more. We knew she would never tell Sam. He would've gone crazy.

"In the end she cracked. The two of you broke up, but Sam was intent on getting you back so we had to keep going. You were just so easy to manipulate. God, it was so easy, but then you had to get pregnant. Clinton was going to let you have it and just pay you off, but I knew we couldn't let you hold something like that over us forever. So I told him to make sure you lost the baby," continued Melissa, becoming more agitated with every word. "But Sam still wouldn't leave you alone. I wanted Clinton to give up on you. I wanted both of them to give up on you."

Marcus could not comprehend what he was hearing. A schoolgirl crush and a sense of superiority had connived to turn Alexa's life into a living nightmare. There had to be another explanation. This could not all be true.

"Please tell me this is all a sick joke," begged Sam, his voice shaking.

"You deserved more than that trash," cried Melissa, throwing her arms out to Sam. "We only gave her as much as she deserved. You'll thank me in time. You'll see what Clinton and I did was for the best."

"He raped her and tried to kill her. You have to be kidding me," gasped Sam, his voice nearly failing him.

"That's a lie! He never did any of that," cried Melissa hatefully. "That was just her trying to keep her horrid secret. He would never hurt me. He loves me. She was nothing. She is nothing!"

"I don't know you," gasped Sam, his eyes wide with shock. "How could you do this to Alexa? How could you do this to me? She was my whole world!"

Marcus's head fell into his hands. He had never felt sorrier for Sam in his life. Sam and Alexa should have still been together – happy – and he would never have had feelings for her. It was difficult to believe that a student such as Melissa Michaels, who had never once been in trouble, could possibly have wrecked so much havoc on so many lives.

A loud click brought Marcus's attention back to the room and he noticed immediately that Alexa was gone. Rising from his desk, he tried to deal with Melissa as quickly as he could. In reality, he had no idea what he was supposed to do with her. It was not as though she had exactly broken school rules and he did not care about Melissa's fate. He cared about Alexa.

He could not help but think of all the things he could have done – should have done – that could have averted this whole situation. It seemed so easy now to stop it, but there was just no way of going back and undoing Ms Carter's terrible actions.

Looking out the window, Marcus saw Alexa walking with Ben across the field. Leaving Sam and Melissa in his office, he sprinted after her. He had to make this right somehow.

"Alexa, wait, please," puffed Marcus, as he ran across the empty oval towards them. "Alexa, oh, Alexa, I'm so sorry. You have to know that I had no idea about Ms Carter. I never would've let this happen to you if I knew. Please believe me."

"You have some nerve," growled Ben, grabbing Marcus by the collar. "I should've arrested you when I found out about the two of you. I should've made sure that you were out of her life. You let this happen to her. How could you ever profess to loving her? You make me sick."

Marcus did not care what Ben thought. His eyes never left Alexa's and hers never left his, but it was not the loving look he had come to know. Her eyes were cold and hollow.

"You didn't come. I was hurt and you didn't care," she said.

Marcus wished that Alexa sounded angry or hurt, but her voice was emotionless and hollow and it tore a guilty knife through his chest. He looked down at her naked neck and knew it was over. It had been the plan right from the start and he had even hoped sometimes that Alexa would simply tell him that her infatuation was over. She was always supposed to have walked away from Redgrove without him, but not like this. Never like this.

"I'm sorry," Marcus whispered.

Nothing registered in Alexa's cold eyes and the pain it caused Marcus completely blocked out Ben grabbing him tighter around the collar.

"You stay away from her," growled Ben, shaking him hard with every word. "Don't try and find her. Don't try and contact her."

"Ben!" Detective Parker ran between Ben and Marcus and tried to pull them apart. "What the hell are you thinking? Let go of him."

Ben released Marcus and placed a guiding hand on Alexa's shoulder. Alexa never looked back as she walked away and out of his life.

Chapter Eighteen

AFTER GOING THROUGH the now sickeningly familiar routine of trekking to the hospital followed by the police station, Alexa could only sit in the interview room and wonder what would happen next. Now she really did have absolutely nowhere to go.

Peter had met her at the police station and sat with her while she made her statement. She had been surprised when Ben had not been one of the officers to interview her.

"Peter, you know I can pay you back, but can you lend me some money for somewhere to stay until my money comes through?" Alexa asked softly.

"Of course I will," replied Peter, squeezing her good hand. "But I think Ben has made other arrangements for you."

"What arrangements?" asked Alexa fearfully.

"He was going to see if you wanted to stay with him," said Peter tenderly.

"You think that's okay?" Alexa asked, feeling her body shake. She no longer trusted her judgement about anyone. "You think I can trust him?"

"Yes, I do," replied Peter, wiping her tears from her cheeks. "And if that doesn't work out, you will come and stay with me and my family. I will help you buy a place and help you set yourself up. Free of charge," he added with a smile.

Alexa was surprised when she smiled back, choking on a laugh. Peter hugged her tenderly and she was amazed how fatherly his touch was.

"It's okay. It'll be fine now. You're out of that place. We're going to get your life sorted out. We're going to get Beth sorted out and you two are going to live wonderful lives. I promise."

The warmth of Peter's promise was more soothing than Alexa expected. She did not believe he could possible keep it, but she was glad he wanted to try.

When Ben came in five minutes later and asked if she would consider staying at his place for a while, it only took another reassuring nod from Peter to allow Alexa to agree.

There was dinner waiting for them when they arrived at Ben's house. It was a nice, modest house, but Alexa felt strangely uncomfortable there. It was not helped by the somewhat frosty reception she received from his wife.

"How long are you planning on staying?" asked Penny as soon as they sat down to dinner.

"Not long, I –"

"As long as she needs to," answered Ben over the top of Alexa with a firmness that made her understand that she was not really welcome.

Retreating from the dining room as quickly as possible, Alexa was shocked to see that the room Ben had prepared for her looked as though he had been expecting her for weeks.

"I knew you didn't have a lot of options," Ben confessed as she looked around with a stunned expression. "I wanted you to have the option. I hoped you'd want to stay."

"I want to see Bethy," said Alexa, trying not to wish her life would simply dissolve.

"I know. Let's wait til the weekend. Then you can spend all day with her," replied Ben. "I promise, I will take you there as soon as they open."

It was not the answer Alexa really wanted to hear, but she accepted it without complaint. She no longer had the strength to fight the world. The battle against her will to live was hard enough.

For the next three days Alexa did almost nothing. She barely ate, never spoke and hardly left her room. During the day she poured over the photo album the Whites had given her less than a year ago. It seemed like another lifetime ago that she had been a part of their family. At night she wrapped herself in Marcus's shirt, which she had kept since their day at the beach the year before, and ringed her fingers through the necklace he had given her.

Her attempts to stay angry with Marcus came to no avail. Deep down Alexa knew that he had not known about Ms Carter or what Ms Carter would do, and she knew how badly she had hurt him by sneaking out. Despite this, the pain would not subside and she could not forgive him.

On Sunday, Alexa made the effort of setting an alarm, but even the prospect of seeing Bethany could not cheer her. Ben walked her through to the meeting room at the detention centre and stayed with her until Bethany arrived. Alexa watched Bethany race towards her and stood in readiness, but collapsed in tears before

Bethany even reached her.

Bethany held on to her until guards pulled them apart. Alexa could see the horror in Bethany's eyes. She had never broken down in front of her this way. Bethany stroked her bruised face and traced her fingers over her cast, but they said nothing. They did not need to speak. Bethany did not need to ask what had happened. Alexa's letters had explained everything.

All they could do was draw pictures on her cast, Bethany writing motivational messages in between them. Alexa knew she would need more than that to get her through this, but loved that Bethany cared. She loved that she had her little sister back.

Away from Bethany, Alexa found it hard to see any points of light as she stumbled along in her very dark tunnel. There seemed no reason to dare hope for something better. Sitting on her bed, looking out the window at the paling fence as the night grew dark around her, tears started to slip down her face. They dried almost instantly in the warm breeze, but new ones came, tracking their way down the well-worn paths. Suddenly, everything was lost again.

"Can I come in?" asked Ben, as he knocked on the door. Alexa nodded and he sat down on the bed next to her. She liked that he did not turn on the light. "We interviewed Mr Knight again today." Alexa just nodded. "I really don't think he knew about Ms Carter and what she planned to do to you."

"I know," Alexa replied in a whispered voice.

"He's very upset about what happened and is very concerned about you."

"You didn't tell him I was here, did you?" she whispered fearfully.

"No, and he didn't ask," said Ben firmly, before softening his tone. "He just wanted to know how you were."

"What did you tell him?"

"The truth – that you've barely spoken or eaten since you left school."

"It wasn't supposed to work out like this," Alexa cried softly. "It was supposed to be the best day of our lives."

Ben moved closer and rested her head on his shoulder as she sobbed.

"Can I ask you about that day?" questioned Ben tenderly. "There've been some interesting reports in the media about three girls who'd just finished their finals and picked themselves up over twenty-five million dollars."

"We were celebrating," answered Alexa, knowing there was no point denying it. "I wanted to go back to school, but they wanted to stay out. Bianca was so drunk. I could've gotten back in, but there was no way she could have."

Alexa made herself stop speaking. She had promised herself she would not blame anyone else for her life, but it was hard not to be angry at Bianca, and even Ezra. However, she was determined not to start her new life full of anger and bitterness. That was not the life she wanted to set up for her and Bethany. As hard as it was, she needed to let it go. She would probably never see them again anyway.

"Were you the one who had the dream?" asked Ben, stroking her hair.

Alexa nodded as she sat up and away from Ben.

"I had it while I was pregnant," she said, knowing she needed Ben to find out about his involvement now. "You sat at the end of a large pipe. Bethy and me were sitting in the pipe. You told me you could help me protect Bethy and my baby and you rolled down six marbles. Had numbers in them. I picked up five. Bethy had the last one. So we entered the five numbers and guessed the sixth."

"I helped you win?" asked Ben in a bright voice, a hopeful smile on his face.

"I can give you some of the money," Alexa nodded. "It's half yours anyway. I don't even know if it's come through yet, but when it does I'll give you it."

"Oh, Alexa, I don't want your money," said Ben, gently squeezing her hand. "I don't need it and I won't take it from you. You deserve that and so much more. I'm just glad that I could help you, but it should never have been this way. I should've protected you and Bethany. None of this should have ever happened."

"There was nothing that you could've done," Alexa replied flatly.

"Yes there was," sighed Ben heavily. "I planned to take you and Bethany in when you were five," he said before she could stop him.

Alexa had insisted that Ben reveal nothing about his previous involvement in their lives. However, now that he had said that, she could not help but want to hear more. Ben had wanted them. Someone had wanted them. Images of what could have been suddenly flickered through her mind, though Ben and Penny were often replaced by Pam and Karl. Alexa closed her eyes and willed those thoughts away.

"What happened?" she asked tentatively. Perhaps it had been her fault. "Did I do something wrong?"

"No. God, Alexa, no," replied Ben, stroking her face. "You and Bethany, you were perfect. I had everything set up, but then your mother said she wanted the two of you back and everyone else was busy trying to change my mind. In the end they did. I let you go.

"I tried to keep track of you, but people thought I was obsessed and they kept information from me. I didn't know about your mother until after you started high school and Bethany started getting into trouble. If I had known about your mum, I would've made sure you both came here."

"I don't care for what could've been," replied Alexa flatly, refusing to think of the possibilities. She did not need more reasons to be bitter. "It makes no difference, not any more. It doesn't matter where we were, all these bad things would've found us somehow. I just wish I knew how so I could've gotten out of the way."

"Oh, Alexa."

Ben pulled her back into his shoulder and hugged her tight as her tears soaked into his shirt.

"I just don't understand why all these things happened to us," she sobbed, unable to restrain the pain. "I tried to be a good person, I really did."

"You're not a bad person, Alexa. I don't know why these things have happened to you either, but I know it's not because you're a bad person. I don't ever want you to think that."

Alexa shook her head and Ben held her tighter, sighing as he squeezed her.

"I do know why these things happened to you," he said with another heavy sigh. "And I promise it's not because you're a bad person."

Alexa looked up, desperate for any kind of explanation.

"It's just damn bad luck," said Ben, shrugging his shoulders slightly. "It's horrible to think that's all it is. You had the bad luck of being born into the family you were. I don't know what things were like when you were born, but I know what they were like when I first met you. You practically lived in poverty.

"You lived in a bad neighbourhood. Your parents didn't work. Your mother was taking drugs. You were amazingly self-sufficient, but the first skills you learned were the same ones that were predisposing you to a life not dissimilar to your parents.

"I don't know much about your life in those middle years, but I know that scholarship to Redgrove was possibly the worst thing they could have given you. A token gesture to make them feel like they were making a difference. All it did was put you in the middle of other people's privilege.

"Clinton Marsh found you, was able to do those things to you because you were vulnerable – more vulnerable there than you would've been in a normal school. Isolated and alone, never given the chance to find a family, you were just ripe for the picking of any man who wanted to manipulate you for his own selfish desires."

Alexa was glad that Ben did not mention Marcus specifically in his tirade. She knew how tortured Marcus had been by his feelings for her.

"I know everything you have suffered, but I worked in your area for many years and I don't know that I can say that what you and Bethany went through was even the worst I saw," said Ben sadly. "You survived. So many children from homes like yours, they just never made it this far. In my years as a police officer I've seen children who have been beaten to death, starved. I've seen the kids who society has never given a chance end up dead on the streets with a needle in their arm.

"You, even when you were very young, had this amazing sense of right and wrong. You had a strength I don't know how to describe. You are the reason Bethany survived. You have struggled through and overcome all the odds. Alexa, you don't know how rare that is. Society stacks everything against you.

"Born into the some of the lowest levels of our society, you were denied access to the opportunities that would've helped you make something better of your life. The presumption always is that there must be something innately wrong with people like you – people born into those situations. It makes society feel better for never giving children like you a chance, for condemning you from the start so that by the time you have the capability to do something for yourself and escape the origins of your birth, the gap is so great few can overcome it.

"That is the social injustice that left you associating with drug dealers and paedophiles. That was what put you in the circumstances that left you choosing between leaving your sister to die on the streets or selling your body to try and save her. And even when you were doing an amazing job at scraping out a good life for yourself, those were the circumstances that saw all those early acquaintances come back and tear your life to shreds.

"What happened to you was not your fault. It was our fault – society's fault – but society will always shun its responsibility. It will turn it back on you and that's why you believe that it's some failing of yours, but it's not. I know it's not."

Alexa had never heard Ben speak so passionately about anything. She had seen him angry and determinedly calm, but never fervent like this. It was clear he believed everything he said. She was just not sure she did.

"The good thing," continued Ben, his voice a little lighter. "Is that you can break free of your origins. I'm going to be here for you and I will give you all the support you and Bethany need to set up amazing lives. You have money now. You will have the means to buy the things you need, buy the opportunities you have always been denied. You have time. You and Bethany are still so young.

"Bethany will be out in a little over a year and you'll have your sister back. Her crimes were committed as a juvenile, so she gets to start with a clean slate when she's an adult. These things won't be bricks around your neck, drowning you when you try to swim. You will both be free of your past.

"I know this is not the life you had planned a few months ago, or even a few weeks ago, but you still have the world at your feet. Don't forget that. Your life hasn't ended. It's just beginning."

Alexa thought about the life she had planned and the one she now faced. Fantasy and reality. She had been a fool to believe in the first place, but there was one part of her fantasy she missed the most.

"I still love him. I know I shouldn't, but I do," she confessed mournfully, hoping it would somehow ease her pain.

"I know … and I think he loved you too," sighed Ben, hugging her tighter. "You know I'm not Marcus Knight's biggest fan, but I do believe he loved you – that he still loves you – so much that he's prepared to do the right thing and let you go."

"You don't know that it's the right thing," Alexa murmured in reply.

"Yes, I do – and so do you. He's your teacher. I'm not saying what you felt wasn't real, just that a relationship with him isn't right," said Ben in a firm voice. "Alexa, you are just eighteen. This is not the last time you're going to have your heart broken. I know you don't want to hear that, but that's what life and love are all about. You'll move on and find someone new and they will love you the way you deserve. I promise."

Alexa was glad that Ben did not dismiss her feelings for Marcus as nothing. She was not always sure of exactly what they were, but they were real. However, she knew she could not accept the way Ben dismissed Marcus from her life.

Hating Marcus sat so uncomfortably with her, and Alexa did not want to be angry with him any more. She wanted to forgive him. She wanted to be able to love him again as she once had. It was the one motivation she needed to get up in the morning, shower, dress, and finally leave the house.

Chapter Nineteen

THE AFTERNOON SUN blazed as Alexa carried food and drink out on the balcony. Hordes of picnickers had started to gather in the park below. She searched the crowd, looking for that familiar face, but there were already so many people crammed into the small space that she began to question the sanity of her original plan.

"This is an amazing view you have, Maria," Alexa said to the small lady in her sixties sitting across the table. "It must be so peaceful – when it's not New Year's Eve."

"It's nice to be able to share it with somebody," said Maria with a kind, but wistful smile.

"Don't your children ever want to celebrate with you?"

"No, not really," shrugged Maria. "They want to be able to celebrate here, but I'm not so sure they care if I'm around or not."

"Oh," was all Alexa could say. It was not the right response by far, but she had still not learned how to comfort people very well.

The conversation went silent and Alexa looked back out over the harbour. It still shocked her that she was even here. She had been coming down to the Rushcutters Bay park day after day, looking for a safe vantage point from which to experience the New Year festivities. Although she wanted to see Marcus again, wanted to know if he truly was sorry for what had happened with Ms Carter, she was not sure she could handle meeting him. She had nothing to offer him, but she needed to see him all the same.

Marcus had always been so appropriate, always pushing her towards what was right, not what he wanted. It made Alexa think that he would be proud of the decisions she had made recently, and had they stayed in contact that he would have actively helped her make them, never allowing her to hold herself back. She missed him, missed their talks and the calmness she felt in his presence. Without her noticing, they had become friends and she missed their friendship.

Leaving her post on the balcony, Alexa went inside to help Maria with dinner. In the last couple of weeks, Maria had helped her quadruple the number of dishes she knew how to cook. Maria seemed to enjoy introducing her to new foods and flavours, and Alexa had never eaten as well as she had in the past month.

They had met the week after Alexa had left Redgrove. Alexa had been sitting in the park opposite Maria's apartment block when she noticed one of the apartments was open for inspection. Her money had come through into her bank account and she had been determined to buy somewhere to live sooner rather than later. She did not enjoying living with Penny, who did little to disguise just how unwelcome she was – at least when Ben was not at home.

Maria had been in the elevator with her bags of shopping at the same time as Alexa had made her way up to the apartment for sale. Alexa must have put her foot on the edge of one of the plastic bags, because when Maria had picked them up, a bag had torn, spilling its contents all over the elevator floor.

Alexa had been mortified. She gathered all the food she could carry in her arms as she apologised profusely. Maria had been much less concerned as they carted the groceries into her apartment. Alexa could not apologise enough and was completely thrown when Maria offered her a drink.

"Oh, no, I was – I am – I was just going up to check out the apartment for sale," replied Alexa pointing to the ceiling.

"Ooh, I wouldn't mind seeing that. I'll come with you."

Maria did not wait for Alexa to reply and started back towards the lift. Alexa could only follow the stout, old lady up to the apartment and walk with her as Maria critiqued everything she saw.

"What do you think? You interested?" Maria had asked inquisitively. "You seem like a lovely young girl. It would be good to have you as a neighbour."

"Really?" replied Alexa automatically.

Maria had only laughed as her response.

"Actually, I still think I'd prefer to live near the beach," replied Alexa, refusing to meet Maria's eye. She did not know what to make of her.

Alexa had been thinking about her future housing options for a long time. One of the best days of her recent life had been that day with Marcus at the ocean bay he had taken her to. She had no idea where that was, but the smell of the ocean was only ever associated with good things in her mind. If she was going to live somewhere she loved, that seemed like a good place to start.

Maria nodded thoughtfully, but said nothing. Alexa felt

awkward and ended up declining Maria's second offer of a drink, lying that there was somewhere else she had to be.

Although Alexa did not return to that apartment again, she made regular reconnaissance visits to the park over the next couple of weeks, while continuing her quest for the perfect beachside apartment. Neither was proving to be as fruitful as Alexa had planned. Ben came house hunting with her when he could. Alexa had resisted his presence at first, but then realised there was so much she did not understand about buying property. She just hated the idea of owing Ben more than she already did, so chatted about her plans with him while they were at home and carefully tried to schedule inspections for when he was at work.

It was before one of those planned inspections that Alexa had detoured back to the Rushcutters Bay park. She had still not managed to find a safe vantage point from which she could spy Marcus without being seen herself. Sometimes that thought terrified her, but more often, lulled into a more content state of mind by the gentle bobbing of the boats on the harbour, she found herself looking forward to the opportunity to talk to him again.

Sitting on the seawall, contemplating how any future meeting with Marcus might play out, Alexa had had to catch herself to stop her falling forward when Maria had suddenly approached her from behind.

"Are you still looking for that beachside apartment?"

Alexa had barely been able to nod her head in response as her heart pounded frantically, wondering how this strange woman had known who she was and what she was doing. It was only when Maria had smiled and pointed up to her apartment block that Alexa had managed to squeeze out a verbal answer in the affirmative.

"Good. Why don't you come up to my apartment for that drink. I think I have an offer for you," Maria had smiled, waving for Alexa to follow her.

Looking back, Alexa could still not remember how she had declined Maria's offer, but she did recall seriously contemplating jumping into the harbour to escape. Although clearly concerned by the level of fear she had elicited, Maria had been patient and understanding enough to suggest a more neutral venue for their conversation.

Sitting down to dinner with Maria, Alexa found it hard to believe that she had ever been scared of her. Maria's offer ended up being an apartment just a ten minute walk from the beach her son was planning to sell. It was not yet on the market, which left Alexa with first option on buying.

It was hardly even an option. Alexa fell in love at first sight. There had been almost no thought of rejecting the offer. As Maria's son had avoided the expense of advertising and selling through an agent, the price had also worked in everyone's favour. When all of the checks Peter insisted on making came back favourably, the purchase was made.

It still felt very surreal, perhaps because despite having made the purchase, the apartment was still not actually hers. The contract would be finalised in the second week of January, and until Alexa moved in she was sure she would never really believe it was hers.

The turn of events that had happened in such a short period of time was unsettling. Alexa could not convince herself that it was not the world setting her up for yet another disaster. If not for Maria's influence over that time, Alexa was sure she would have retreated back into her shell and stayed there until she could escape to the sanctuary of her new home.

Almost every day since Maria made that offer of her son's apartment, she and Alexa had been in contact. Maria had a strange ability to bring her out of herself, and Alexa was surprised by just how much she had told Maria in that time. She had never had a strong relationship with an older woman and never realised how deeply she craved a maternal figure in her life. Pam had been amazing, but she was too close to a mother that Alexa had had to keep her at a distance. Maria had never felt like a mother, perhaps she was grandmotherly, but Alexa had never had one of them either, so did not know.

"I think we may have over-catered," said Alexa, looking at all the food piled on the table.

Although Alexa loved the food Maria had recently introduced her to, her appetite had never returned to its famished state. Her weight had stabilised somewhat, but it still left her much slighter than she had been eight months earlier.

"Don't worry about that," replied Maria dismissively. "What time is it?"

"It's quarter past eleven."

"Oh good. When you said you didn't drink I went out and found some non-alcoholic wine for us. I mean, I shouldn't be drinking either with all the tablets I'm taking, so it worked out well. I had to search around a bit, but I'm sure it'll be worth it."

Maria shuffled back into the house and came back with two wine glasses and the bottle of non-alcoholic wine.

"And don't worry. I bought six bottles of the stuff. We'll be right for the night," said Maria cheerfully.

A smile crept unintentionally across Alexa's face. Maria really was amazing. There was just no other way to describe the way Maria had treated her. It was strange, because few people who had not known her had been so open and trusting of her. Maria had already found out many things about her life that would have sent most people screaming, yet here Maria was, allowing her into her apartment without the slightest hint that she was concerned about the consequences.

They drank merrily as the minutes ticked by and the year faded to a close. Alexa was certainly not sad to see it go. More recent events had seen her inadvertently hoping for better next year – a new start and a new life – though she could not help but wonder if that was being ridiculously naïve. Nothing in her life ever went that smoothly.

"Have you seen him yet?" asked Maria, as they drank their wine. It had to be about the tenth time she had asked that day.

"No, but I said New Year's Day, so I don't expect to see him yet. I'm not sure I expect to see him at all," Alexa replied, trying not to get her hopes up. There was a good chance Marcus had completely forgotten her by now.

"What are you going to do if he does show?" asked Maria. It was another question she had asked a number of times today. It did not escape Alexa's notice that Maria did not appear concerned that Marcus would not show up.

"I haven't decided yet," replied Alexa, repeating the answer she had been giving Maria since she had first confessed her plan. "I was hoping the decision would be made for me when I saw him."

"Ooh, what time is it? I think it's almost time," said Maria suddenly and it took Alexa a moment to realise she was not talking about Marcus.

Maria jumped from her seat, pulling Alexa up at the same time. Grabbing the bottle of wine, Maria filled their glasses as the crowd below became rowdier.

"Ten, nine, eight," called the crowd. Alexa and Maria joined in boisterously. "Seven, six, five, four, three, two, one, Happy New Year!"

Alexa and Maria charged their glasses and poured the contents down their throats, before Maria suddenly grabbed Alexa and pulled her into a warm embrace.

"Happy New Year, Alexa."

"Happy New Year, Maria," replied Alexa, pushing hesitantly out of Maria's hug with the silent excuse of wanting to watch the fireworks. Being touched by people was something she still struggled with, even by people as wonderful as Maria.

Explosions of colour lit up the night sky for the next twenty minutes, wowing the thousands gathered below. From the balcony, they had an uninterrupted view of the harbour and the fireworks that cracked above them. Alexa watched dumbfounded, unable to remember the last time she had seen fireworks so close.

"This is so cool," she said, her neck starting to ache from the constant craning.

"When you see them every year they begin to lose their novelty," replied Maria with a slight sigh.

"I hope I can say that one day," said Alexa, trying to keep her bitterness at bay. "I feel like I've missed out on so many normal things."

"Get to my age and you won't find much left in life that's novel."

"Surely I am," smiled Alexa, as she sat back down next to Maria. "How often do you sell your child's apartments to the kid that stomps all over your groceries?"

"Yes, indeed," laughed Maria, before her smile faded. "It will be strange not having you around. I've become used to you."

"You know I'm going to stay in touch. I'll still visit you when I can," said Alexa sincerely. "It's nice to have a friend."

"I know what you mean."

The sadness in Maria's voice picked at Alexa's heart. Maria was such a wonderful person and it seemed unfair that all she had to offer in exchange was her company. It was a very uneven swap.

The post-midnight exodus was rapid, and Maria was just as keen to retire from the balcony and to her bed as the other revellers. Alexa could still not quite believe that Maria would trust her to stay unaccompanied in the apartment, and checked several times just to be sure.

"Of course I'm sure," laughed Maria. "What do you think you would possibly do?"

"You're not worried I might rob you or hurt you?" asked Alexa tentatively.

The smile fell from Maria's face. "I've lived long enough to know that anyone can betray your trust, but no one can be proven trustworthy until they're given the chance to let you down. I choose to give you a chance. What you do with it is up to you."

Maria went to bed with a slight half-smile. Alexa immediately started tidying the balcony, while keeping a continuous eye on the park below. It did not take long for her to notice one man sitting alone on a bench who had seemingly little interest in dispersing with the rest of the crowd.

It was difficult for Alexa to make out the man's features in the low light, but as the moon began to crack through the clouds her heart gave a frightening lurch. It was Marcus and he showed no sign of leaving. He had not just come to see if she was waiting for him. He was waiting for her.

"Is that him?" asked Maria as she yawned herself out on to the balcony at daybreak.

"Yeah," nodded Alexa, not able to say anything else as her throat constricted.

"How long's he been there?"

"I first saw him at one."

"And you haven't gone down?" asked Maria with a hint of incredulity.

"No, I can't."

Alexa was glad her resolve was holding. The very sight of Marcus made her heart ache so intensely she was not sure if it was breaking or swelling to twice its normal size. However, as daybreak gave way to a bright, hot morning, and Marcus did not move from the bench, her resolve began to waver.

Marcus sat with his head in his hands, occasionally looking up and scanning the park, before returning his eyes to the ground. Alexa sat in a similar posture, scared to look up and see that he was still there, but terrified that when she next glanced that way he would be gone.

"He's definitely keen," said Maria, after rising properly from her sleep at half-past ten. "Why don't you just go down and talk to him. At least put him out of his misery, if you don't want to be with him."

"I do want to be with him. That's the problem," replied Alexa, trying not to cry out with the pain of that truth. "If I go down there, I don't think I'll have the strength to walk away."

"Then why walk away? If you two feel so strongly about each

other," questioned Maria, as though she were also questioning Alexa's sanity.

"Because I want it to be right. We waited all this time because it was wrong that we be together back then."

"And what's making it wrong now?"

Alexa loved that Maria's sense of romance had always been able to see more good than bad in her relationship with Marcus. Now that she had left school and Marcus had ceased to be her teacher, Maria failed to see much bad at all.

"Me," answered Alexa. "I make it wrong. He once told me that he thought I was an amazing woman, but I still feel like a little, helpless girl. While I'm still a child, we'll never be right."

"So you think you're going to grow up by going overseas?" asked Maria sceptically.

"It'll be a start," Alexa replied with a sigh.

The need to escape living with Ben and Penny had pushed Alexa to find a more immediate solution than buying her apartment could provide. She was also far too restless to settle down just yet, and did not have the courage to face another classroom. Eventually, it had been a combination of all the advice she had been showered with in the previous few months about what she should do with her future that had convinced her.

With little regard for cost or criticism, Alexa had booked her plane ticket to Europe. The options were endless and beyond her accommodation for the first few nights in London, she refused to have a plan. She had a guide book and she would take it as it came. It was something so far out of her comfort zone that even now she refused to think about it, fearful that she would cancel the whole thing.

"Love is not something you can just put on hold. How do you know he'll still be waiting for you when you return?" asked Maria tenderly. It was the way she gave all her advice.

"I don't, but we deserve a proper chance and I can only hope that in time we'll get it."

Maria only shrugged, clearly unconvinced by Alexa's reasoning. Alexa was glad Maria and Ben had never been able to spend too much time together. Although Maria had assured her that she was good at keeping secrets, this potential meeting with Marcus was something Alexa had wanted Ben to remain completely ignorant about. Ben had already expressed his concerns about her friendship with Maria, and Alexa was sure that if he had any clue that Marcus was so close to her now he would have Marcus arrested and her locked in his house until he could talk his version of sense into her.

It was nice having someone like Maria around who was prepared to trust her judgement, even when they did disagree. It made Maria a nice companion on the balcony as the morning rose to the afternoon and the afternoon faded to dusk. Marcus had not once moved from the bench – not to eat, drink or use the bathroom. Alexa had been just as stationary, though Maria had been kind enough to supply refreshments.

Alexa did not know how long the impasse could last, but she did know that all the lingering resentment and anger she had held towards Marcus had now disappeared. This was not a man waiting for a conquest. She knew if she went down to him, he would want to do nothing more than apologise. What Alexa did not know was if she was strong enough to walk away from him, and not fall at his feet and promise to give him all she believed he deserved.

At times, it took all of Alexa's strength to stop herself from running down to Marcus and telling him his waiting was not in vain, but that was not entirely true. This coming separation would be a test of him as much as her. She wanted – she needed – to know that what he felt for her would last, and that what she felt for him would not fade outside his presence and the confines of her school-like prison.

When the sun finally faded out of sight, Marcus drew his head out of his hands and took one last look around the park. Alexa felt her heart strain as he stood up and walked away from the bench. Part of her was urging him to turn around and look up at her. Marcus hesitated and her heart stopped as he turned back towards the bench. Circling, Marcus looked around the park, hoping for the miracle she would not deliver. The longer he lingered the weaker she became, until finally, on his fifth circle, he walked away, as she stood, holding herself back, at the balcony door.

"Is he gone?" asked Maria.

"Yes."

Alexa wiped a tear from her eye before joining Maria inside.

"And when do you go?" asked Maria a little mournfully.

"Tomorrow afternoon, as soon as I've said goodbye to Bethy."

"I still think you're just running away from this," said Maria. Alexa stared back out the window as the stars started to fill the night sky. "When do you come back?"

"When I don't feel the need to run any more," Alexa answered, hoping that such a time would one day exist.

Taking one last look out the window, Alexa watched as the moon rose brilliantly in the sky, coating the clouds in the most beautiful silver she had ever witnessed. It was what she had spent the last two years waiting for, that silver living their miracle lottery win had represented, but now that it shone before her it was still out of her grasp.

Alexa hoped that she had not been right when she had told Bianca last year that the only way to touch the clouds – to reach a silver lining – was to die. There was so much more from life that she wanted now, that she felt she deserved, and hoped that it was just a matter of waiting.

www.ingramcontent.com/pod-product-compliance
Lightning Source LLC
Chambersburg PA
CBHW031152120726

47905CB00006B/1910